Praise for Susan Wiggs and The Bella Vista Chronicles

The Apple Orchard

"Wiggs tells a layered, powerful story of love, loss, hope and redemption."

—*Kirkus Reviews*, starred review

"This brilliant and epic family drama…fills the senses…courtesy of Wiggs's amazing narrative and supreme skill as a writer."

—*RT Book Reviews*, Top Pick!

"A tale with universal appeal."

—*Booklist*

"This is classic Wiggs, with its emphasis on the strength of family and friends, and a landscape integral to the plot."

—*Publishers Weekly*

The Beekeeper's Ball

"Wiggs' carefully detailed plotlines, one contemporary and one historical, with their candid look at relationships and their long-term effects, are sure to captivate readers."

—*Booklist*, starred review

"A dazzling intergenerational tale."

—*Publishers Weekly*

"A satisfying, engaging read."

—*Kirkus Reviews*

"Highly recommended."

—*Library Journal*

SUSAN WIGGS

The Beekeeper's Ball

mira

ISBN-13: 978-0-7783-3172-8

The Beekeeper's Ball

First published in 2014. This edition published in 2021.

This edition published by arrangement with Harlequin Books S.A.

For questions and comments about the quality of this book, please contact us at CustomerService@Harlequin.com.

Mira
22 Adelaide St. West, 40th Floor
Toronto, Ontario M5H 4E3, Canada
BookClubbish.com

Printed in Italy by Grafica Veneta

Recycling programs for this product may not exist in your area.

For two beautiful ladies named Clara Louise—
my mother and my granddaughter.

The Beekeeper's Ball

PART I

A honeybee that is engaged in foraging for nectar will rarely sting, except when startled or stepped on. If a bee senses a threat or is alerted by attack pheromones, it will aggressively seek out and sting. The worker bee's stinger is barbed, and when it lodges in the victim's skin, it tears loose from the bee's abdomen, causing its death within moments.

However, the queen's stinger is not barbed.

The queen can sting repeatedly without dying.

BEE STING CAKE

The traditional *Bienenstich* (Bee Sting Cake) is a complicated production of brioche dough and pastry cream, topped with a crunchy caramel made of almonds, honey and butter. This simplified version is every bit as delicious, particularly with your morning coffee.

DOUGH

2½	cups flour	¾	teaspoon salt
4	tablespoons butter		
2	tablespoons honey	2	eggs
1½	teaspoons instant yeast	¼	cup warm water or milk

Combine all of the dough ingredients in a mixing bowl and stir to create a sticky, elastic ball. Transfer the dough to a lightly oiled board and knead for 5 to 7 minutes until smooth. If your mixer has a dough hook, use that for 4 to 7 minutes at medium speed. Place the dough in a bowl oiled with melted butter, turn to grease all sides, cover the bowl with a damp tea towel or plastic wrap and let it rise for about an hour, until it looks soft and puffy.

Transfer the dough to a lightly oiled board, fold it over (you might hear a sigh of escaping gas), then roll into a ball. Place the dough in a buttered 10-inch springform pan. You can also use a 13 by 9-inch cake pan. Don't worry if the dough shrinks away from the edge of the pan. Allow it to rest so the gluten will relax, making the dough easier to work with. After about 30 minutes, gently stretch and pat the dough out to the edges of the pan.

While the dough is resting, make the topping.

HONEY-ALMOND-CARAMEL TOPPING

6	tablespoons butter	2	tablespoons heavy cream
⅓	cup sugar	1½	cups sliced almonds
3	tablespoons honey		a pinch of salt

Melt the butter in a pan over medium heat. Add the sugar, honey and cream. Bring the mixture to a boil, and cook for 3 to 5 minutes to achieve a golden syrup. Stir in the almonds, let the mixture cool slightly, then spread gently over the cake dough.

Bake the cake in a 350 degree oven for about 25 minutes, until the almond crust has a deep golden color and the cake tests done with a toothpick. Set on a rack to cool completely.

While the cake is cooling, prepare the pastry cream.

PASTRY CREAM

1   cup minus 2 tablespoons heavy cream, whipped to soft peaks
2   cups vanilla custard or vanilla pudding. Use homemade, store-bought, or pudding from a mix, depending on your level of skill and commitment.
1   tablespoon honey
1   tablespoon Bärenjäger or other honey liqueur

Serve the cake in wedges or squares, with a side of pastry cream and a dram of Medovina, coffee or tea. Medovina is mead, a sweet wine made from honey. It's the oldest known alcoholic beverage.

[Source: Adapted from a traditional recipe]

CHAPTER ONE

The first rule of beekeeping, and the one Isabel swore she would never break, was to remain calm. As she regarded the massive swarm of honeybees clinging to a Ligustrum branch, she feared she might go back on her word.

She was new to beekeeping, but that was no excuse. She thought she was ready to capture her first swarm. She'd read all the beekeeping books in the Archangel town library. She'd watched a dozen online videos. But none of the books and videos had mentioned that the humming of ten thousand bees would be the creepiest sound she'd ever heard. It reminded her of the flying monkey music in *The Wizard of Oz*.

"Don't think about flying monkeys," she muttered under her breath. And that, of course, guaranteed she would think of nothing else.

It took every fiber of power and control in her body to keep from fleeing to the nearest irrigation ditch, screaming at the top of her lungs.

The morning had started out with such promise. She'd

leaped out of bed at daybreak to greet yet another perfect Sonoma day. A few subtle threads of coastal mist slipped through the inland valleys and highlands, softening the green and gold hills like a bridal veil. Isabel had hurriedly donned shorts and a T-shirt, then taken Charlie for his morning walk past the apple and walnut trees, inhaling the air scented with lavender and sun-warmed grass. Paradise on earth.

Lately, she'd been waking up early every day, too excited to sleep. She was working on the biggest project she'd ever dared to undertake—transforming her family home into a destination cooking school. The work was nearing completion, and if everything went according to schedule, she would welcome the first guests of the Bella Vista Cooking School at harvest time.

The big rambling mission-style hacienda, with its working apple orchard and kitchen gardens, was the perfect venue for the project. The place had long been too much for just her and her grandfather, and Isabel's dreams had always been too big for her budget. She was passionate about cooking and in love with the idea of creating a place for other dreamers to come and learn the culinary arts. At long last, she'd found a way to grow into the house that had always felt too large.

Isabel was determined to revive the house in every possible way, filling it with the vibrant energy of the living. These days, she felt grateful that she finally had the resources to restore the place to its former glory.

That meant opening the hacienda back up to the world. She wanted it to be more than just the place where she and her elderly grandfather spent their days. She'd been a hermit for far too long. This summer would bring a wedding filled with well-wishers. In the autumn, she would host guests of the cooking school.

Her head full of plans for the day, she'd gone to check the

bees with Charlie, her rangy German shepherd mutt. When she'd reached the hives, located on a slope by a rutted track at the end of the main orchard, she'd heard the flying monkeys and realized what was happening—a swarm.

It was a natural occurrence. Like a dowager making way for her successor, the old queen left the hive in search of new digs, taking along more than half the workers. It was rare for a swarm to occur so early in the day, but the morning sun was already intense. Scout bees were out searching for the ideal spot for a new hive while the rest clung en masse to the branch and waited. Isabel had to capture the swarm and get them into an empty hive before the scouts returned and led the whole mass of them away, to parts unknown.

She had quickly sent a text message to Jamie Westfall, a local bee expert. Only last week, he had left a flyer in her mailbox—*Will trade beekeeping services for honey harvest.* She'd never met him, but kept his number in her phone contacts, just in case. Unfortunately, a swarm in this intermediate stage was ephemeral, and if the guy didn't get here quickly, Isabel would be on her own. She'd thrown on her jumpsuit, hat and veil, grabbed a pair of loppers and a cardboard box with a lid, and approached the hanging swarm.

This should be simple, she thought. Except that the thing draped from the bush looked like a horrible, reddish, living beard. The humming sound filled her head and then flowed through her like the blood in her veins. She kept reminding herself that there was nothing to fear despite the fearsome appearance and furious sound of the swarm. They were looking for a home, that was all. Anyone in the world could understand that need. And if there was anything Isabel craved, it was to feel at home in the world.

"Okay, then," she murmured, her gaze never leaving the dense cluster of honeybees, her heart pounding. Capturing a swarm was supposed to be exciting work. It was the ideal way to fill more hives, and it prevented the bees from nesting in places where they'd be a nuisance, like in Grandfather's prize apple trees.

The bees were docile at this stage of swarming. They weren't defensive because they were engorged with honey and had no home to defend.

Charlie reclined laconically in the high grass at the side of the hill, sunning himself.

"I've got this," she said. "It's the perfect swarm. Ha-ha, get it, Charlie?" She looked over at the skinny dog. "The perfect swarm. I crack myself up."

Isabel didn't feel strange, talking to a dog. She'd always done it, an only child growing up at Bella Vista, secluded by the surrounding orchards and vineyards and overprotected by doting grandparents. As a child, she had learned to be happy in her own company. As an adult, she guarded herself, because that was what life had taught her to do.

"Here goes, Charlie," she said. "I'm going in. No loud noises, no sudden movements."

She set her cardboard box on the ground under the branch, which was sagging now under the weight of the bees. Yikes, this was a big swarm. The sun beat down on her back, reminding her that time was running out.

Her hands trembled as she scissored the loppers. "Now," she said, steeling herself. "I'd better not wait any longer." She was tired of missed chances. It was time to seize the moment. Heart thumping, she opened the jaws of the loppers and chopped off the branch. The swarm landed in the waiting box—most of it, anyway.

The humming intensified, and individual bees broke away from the cluster. It took all her control not to flee. She was just inches from breaking the unbreakable rule by freaking out. So what if the swarm disappeared? It was hardly a matter of life or death.

But it was a matter of pride and will. She wanted to keep bees. Bella Vista had always been a working farm, its orchards and gardens sustaining the Johansen family since the end of World War II.

"All right, guys," she said through gritted teeth. "Here we go." She bent down and gently adjusted the branch so it would fit in the box. The bees that dropped free of the box crawled back again, joining the cluster. They would stay with the queen. It was the only way to survive.

Shaking from head to toe, Isabel lifted the box. It was heavy. Heavier than she had imagined. And the bees seemed agitated. They were moving faster, or maybe that was just her imagination. She wondered if that meant the scouts were returning.

A fiery pinching sensation on her shoulder nearly made her lose control. "Ow," she said, "ow, ow, ow. You're supposed to be docile. What's wrong with you?" She had probably trapped the poor thing under her jumpsuit. To herself, she added, "Slow and careful. I'm supposed to be good at being slow and careful. Too good, if you ask Tess."

Tess was by far the more impulsive sister. Sometimes she got exasperated by Isabel's deliberation and caution.

The crucial moment was upon her. The next task was to get the swarm into the waiting hive.

Just then, Charlie gave a *woof,* stood up and trotted toward the road. Isabel heard the sound of a motor, its pitch different from the humming of the bees. An orchard worker?

She turned as a banana-yellow Jeep with a roll bar and its top down crested the hill, jolting over the rutted track and spitting gravel out the sides of the tires. A flurry of bees erupted from the box. Several landed ominously on the veil covering her face.

Slow down, she wanted to yell. *You're disturbing them.*

The Jeep scrabbled to a halt in a cloud of dust, and a long-bodied stranger jumped out, levering himself with the roll bar. He had long hair and big shoulders, and he was wearing army-green cargo pants, a black T-shirt and aviator shades. There was a hinged brace on his knee, and he walked with a pronounced limp.

Jamie Westfall? Isabel wondered. She wouldn't mind a little help at the moment.

"This the Johansen place?" asked the deep-voiced stranger.

Charlie made a chuffing sound and sat back in the grass.

"Oh, good, you got my text," she said, keeping her eyes on the heavy, moving cluster in the box. "Great timing. You're just in time to give me a hand."

"What, are you high?" he demanded, peering suspiciously as though trying to see her through the veil. "That's a swarm of frickin' bees."

"Yes, so if you don't mind—"

"Shit, I got stung." He slapped at the side of his neck. "What the hell—? Christ, there's a dozen of the little f—*Jesus Christ.*" In the next few moments, he swore some more as he swatted violently at a few stragglers. He swore a lot. He used swear words to modify his swear words. His swatting motions agitated the bees further. Isabel felt another fiery pinch, this one on her ankle, where the fabric of her suit ended in a cuff.

"Be still. You're making them defensive." *Some beekeeper,* she thought.

"Oh, you think? Lady, I'm out of here. I am—"

"I thought you came to help." The humming crescendoed, and the swarm in the box moved faster, undulating like a living storm cloud. "Oh, no…." She waved her hand at a flurry of bees. The scouts had returned. She felt another sting—her wrist this time—and set the box on the ground.

"Shit, look out!" The strange man grabbed her and threw her to the ground, covering her with his body. Charlie gave a sharp bark of warning.

Panic knifed through Isabel, and the fear had nothing to do with bees. It felt like a cold blade of steel, and suddenly she was lost, hurled back to the past somewhere, to a dark place she never thought she'd escape. *"No,"* she said in a harsh whisper. She bucked, arching her back like a bow, bringing up one knee and connecting with…something.

"Oof, holy shit, what the hell's the matter with you?" The guy rolled to one side, drawing his knees up to his chest and holding his crotch. The shades flew from his face as a groan slipped from him.

Isabel crab walked away, not taking her eyes off him. He was big, he smelled of sweat and road dust, and his eyes reflected a fury of pain. But he hadn't hurt *her.*

She was as startled as he by her overreaction. *Easy,* she told herself. *Take it easy.* Her pulse slowed down by degrees, dulled by mortification. Then she tore her gaze from the stranger in time to see the swarm lift up en masse, a thick, spreading veil of heavy silk, the entire colony sailing off into the wilderness. The dark cloud of insects grew smaller and smaller, drifting away like an untethered balloon.

"You're too late. They've gone," she said, rubbing her shoulder. Glowering, she stood up, kicking the cardboard box in defeat. A few dead bees tumbled from the now empty branch.

"You can thank me later," the guy said. He was sitting now, too, regarding her with narrowed eyes.

"Thank you?" she demanded, incredulous.

"You're welcome?" he returned.

"What kind of beekeeper are you?"

"Um, do I *look* like a beekeeper? You're the one who looks

like a beekeeper, unless that headgear is some new style of burka."

She peeled off the hat and dropped it on the ground. Her hair was plastered to her head and neck by the sweat of her fruitless hard work. "You're not Jamie Westfall?"

"I don't know who the hell that is. Like I said, I came looking for the Johansen place." He regarded her with probing eyes. She couldn't help but notice the color, deep green, like leaves in the shade. He was ridiculously good-looking, even with his face pockmarked by beestings.

"Oh, my gosh," she said, "you must be one of the workmen." The tile guy was on the schedule today to finish the majolica tile in the teaching kitchen.

"If that's how you treat a worker, remind me not to get on your bad side. But no, let's start over." With a groan of discomfort, he got up. "I'm Cormac O'Neill," he said. "I'd shake hands, but you're scary."

The name meant nothing to her. O'Neill was not on the list of contractors she had been working with over the past year.

"And you're here because…?"

"Because, oh, Christ… I think I'm dying." He slapped at his beefy bare arms, his face and neck.

"What? Come on, I didn't kick you *that* hard." She turned just in time to see him hit the ground like a dropped sack of potatoes. "Really?" she asked him. *"Really?"*

"I got stung."

"I can see that." In addition to the bites on his face, welts had appeared all over his neck and arms and hands. "I'm sorry. But they're honeybees," she said. "It's not as if their stings are lethal."

"Only to people who are highly allergic," he said, trying to sit up and speaking as though his tongue was suddenly thick. A whistling sound came from his throat.

She knelt down beside him. "You're allergic? Highly allergic?"

"Anaphylaxis," he said, yanking at the neckline of his T-shirt.

"If you're so allergic, why did you come running?"

"You said I was just in time. You said you needed a hand." His throat was bulging, his eyes glazing over. He looked as if he was just inches from dying.

I shouldn't be surprised, thought Isabel. *I've never had much luck with men.*

CHAPTER TWO

"What can I do?" Isabel unzipped her jumpsuit and started digging in her pocket for her phone. Then she remembered she hadn't brought it with her.

He grabbed her wrist, the sudden touch startling her again. This time, she didn't lash out but stiffened at the unaccustomed strength of his grip. "Hey," he said, then coughed and wheezed some more. His face turned bright red as he struggled for breath. "Duffel bag," he said. "There's an EpiPen. Hurry."

Shoot. This was turning into something very bad. His breathing was labored, the veins standing out in his neck. She dove for the back of the Jeep and yanked out a disreputable-looking army-green duffel. Massively heavy, it landed in the dust with a dull thud, kicking up a cloud. She unzipped it. A smell of dirty socks and sunscreen lotion hit her. She pawed through wadded up T-shirts and jeans, shorts and swim trunks.

"Are you sure it's in here?" she demanded. With growing urgency, she began throwing things backward over her head. Pieces of mail. A tangle of cords. Books. Who traveled with so many books? Not just travel books, like *Hidden Bali*. But *Selected Works of Ezra Pound*. *Infinite Jest*. Seriously?

"Purple canvas bag," he said.

"Aha." She found the oblong bag and unzipped it. "What am I looking for?"

"EpiPen," he said. "Clear tube with a yellow cap."

The kit was crammed with a traveler's flotsam and jetsam. She turned it upside down and shook out the contents. Everything rained down—toothbrush, toothpaste, Q-tips, jars and tubes, packets of airline snacks, disposable razors.

She found a plastic tube with a prescription label and scanned the instructions on the side.

"Inject it, quick," he said. The welts were causing his hands and face to swell, and his lips were blue now. "Christ, just jab the sucker into me." He gestured vaguely at his thigh.

She popped the top off the tube and slid the injector out. She had an imprecise knowledge of the procedure, having learned a little about it in culinary school, during a seminar on food allergies. "I've never done this before."

"Not...rocket science."

With a firm nod, she moved over next to him and pushed the injector at his thigh. She must have angled it wrong, because a short needle poked out and caught in the fabric of his pants, spraying a small amount of liquid.

"Oh, my gosh," she said, "I broke it."

"Grab the other one. Should be...one more."

Trying not to panic, she fumbled around and located the second injection kit. She turned to him to try again, and was shocked to see that he'd yanked his pants down on one side to bear a very male, muscular thigh. And she couldn't help but notice that he went commando.

"Hand it over," he gasped, taking the tube in his fist. Then, with an aggressive stabbing motion, he jammed the injector at his bare thigh. An audible click sounded as the spring-loaded needle released.

Isabel sat back on her heels and stared at him while the panic subsided. She felt as if she'd been hit by a truck. He *looked* as if he'd been hit by a truck. He sat propped on one arm, his trousers around his knees, one leg caught on the knee brace. Rashy blotches bloomed on his cheeks, the backs of his hands, his bare ass. "Are you going to be all right?" she dared to ask. "What do we do next?"

He didn't say anything. He was wheezing, staring at the dusty ground. Yet very slowly, color crept back into his face. His breathing began to even out.

She stared at him, unable to move. He had a small gold hoop earring in one ear. Longish dirty blond hair. The black T-shirt sleeves taut around his biceps.

How had this day gone so wrong? Only a short time ago, she had jumped out of bed in excitement, filled with plans for the transformation of the hacienda into the Bella Vista Cooking School. Now she was seated in the middle of a field with a half-naked man who looked like a reject from a Marvel Comics movie.

He grabbed his cane and pulled himself to a standing position, then very casually hiked his pants back up. "I don't feel so hot," he said, just as she was thinking how hot he was.

She noticed three stingers in the back of his hand, which was now so swollen the knuckles had disappeared. "Do you have some tweezers? I could pull out the stingers."

"No tweezers," he muttered. "That causes more venom to be released."

"Get in the Jeep," she said. "I'll drive." She spent a few minutes throwing his things back into the duffel bag. There were a couple of hard-shell cases, probably containing a camera and laptop. More books. Shaving soap and toothpaste in a tube with Middle Eastern characters on the label. Condoms—lots of condoms. A travel alarm with a photo frame on one side, displaying a photo of a dark-haired woman, unsmiling, with large haunted eyes.

His personal stuff is none of your business, she told herself, hoisting the bag into the back of the Jeep. Then she retrieved his sunglasses and tossed the now-empty cardboard box into the backseat. "Go on, Charlie," she said, shooing the dog. "Go back to the house." Charlie trotted down the hill. She turned to the stranger. Cormac, he'd said his name was. Cormac Something. "There's a clinic in town, about ten minutes away."

"I don't need a doctor." He already looked better, his breathing and coloring normal.

"The instructions on the EpiPen say to seek medical help as soon as possible." The last thing she needed at this point was for him to relapse. She adjusted the seat and took off. The Jeep was an older-model Wrangler with a gearbox. She'd grown up driving tractors and work trucks, so the clutch was not a problem for her. "I thought you were Jamie," she said as the Jeep rattled over the gravel track. "The beekeeper."

"Cormac O'Neill, like I said," he said. "And hell, no, I'm not a damn beekeeper."

"O'Neill," she said. "You're not on the list of workmen."

"There's a list? Who knew?" He braced his hands on the sides of the seat, looking queasy and pale now. "Did I take a wrong turn somewhere?"

"This is the Johansen place." The Jeep jolted over the rutted track as she headed down toward the main road into town. "I thought you might be a workman because we're remodeling."

"Oh, yeah, Tess mentioned something about that."

"You're a friend of Tess?" Isabel whipped a sideways glance at him. He was pale and sweating now, probably from the rush of Adrenalin delivered by the shot. "My sister invited you? Oh, my gosh, are you the wedding expert?"

He gave a wheezing laugh that ended in a cough. "That's the last thing I'd be an expert at. I'm here for Magnus Johansen. You know him?"

"What do you want with my grandfather?" she asked, instantly suspicious. In recent months, Tess, an antiquities expert, had unearthed a family treasure worth a fortune. Ever since, their grandfather had been hounded by everyone from insurance actuaries to tabloid journalists.

"I'm working on his biography."

She glared at the road ahead. Lately, the whole world wanted to know about Magnus Johansen. "Since when?"

"Since I made the deal. So he's your grandfather. And you are?"

"Isabel Johansen." She had a million questions about this so-called biography. Glancing to the side, she saw that he was leaning back, eyes shut, face gray. "Hey, are you all right?"

He answered with a vague wave of his hand.

She kept sneaking looks at him. He had strong, chiseled features, his jaw softened by a day or two's growth of beard. And those shoulders. She'd always been a sucker for a guy's strong shoulders. Big square hands that looked as if they did harder work than writing biographies.

No wedding band. At thirty, Isabel couldn't help noticing a detail like that.

She paused at the end of the lane where it intersected with the paved road. On the corner was a pretty whitewashed building with a wraparound porch and flowers blooming from window boxes. A sign hung from the eaves—Things Remembered.

"That's Tess's shop," she pointed out. "How do you know my sister?"

He made a vague wheezing sound.

"Never mind," she said, "we can talk later."

An easel sign at the roadside invited passersby to browse the antiques, local gourmet products, vintage items and ephemera. Before long, there would be another sign, one directing guests to the Bella Vista Cooking School. Isabel didn't mention it to the stranger, though. He didn't seem very interested in anything as he leaned back against the headrest with beads of sweat forming on his upper lip.

She gripped the steering wheel harder and sped along the paved farm-to-market road. Over the top of a rise, the town of Archangel came into view, its stone and timber buildings, parks and gardens as familiar and pretty as a framed picture, surrounded by the blooming Sonoma landscape. Isabel had lived here all her life. It was home. Safety and security. But next to this wheezing, blotchy stranger, she didn't feel so safe.

She pulled into a parking spot next to a shiny red BMW. The clinic was situated in a mission-style plaza that also housed the Archangel city hall and chamber of commerce.

"Can you walk?" she asked her passenger.

"Yeah. I think I left my cane in the back."

"Sit tight. I'll get it for you." She went around to the back of the Jeep and nearly ran into a man on a mobile phone who was headed to the car parked next to her.

He stepped out of her way with a gruff, "Whoa, watch where you're—" And then the hand holding the phone dropped to his side. *"Isabel."*

Her heart lurched into panic mode. "What are you doing here?"

She hadn't seen Calvin Sharpe in years, not since she'd fled from culinary school in a fog of shame and hurt. Seeing him now didn't hurt anymore, but the shame was still there like a nightmare she couldn't shake. She'd heard rumors that he was looking for a new restaurant venue, but she'd refused to believe he would have the nerve to come to Archangel. "Never mind," she said, her voice tight. "I don't care. Excuse me."

He didn't. He took a step closer, his gaze coasting down over her, then upward. "Archangel is everything you said it was."

She couldn't believe there had been a time when she'd imagined them together, here in her hometown. "I'm busy," she said.

"You look good, Isabel."

So did he, she noticed, his dark hair and chiseled features refined by the patina of success. His teeth were too white and too perfectly aligned, like a row of chewing gum tablets. She grabbed the cane from the back of the Jeep. "I don't have time for this," she stated quietly.

"We should catch up."

Her stomach churned. She hated that, after all this time, he still wielded some kind of power over her. Why? Why did she let him?

A large shadow fell over Calvin. "Is there a problem here?" asked Cormac O'Neill. The red welts and swelling on his face made him look bigger and meaner than ever.

Calvin's eyes narrowed, then he offered the signature smile that had endeared him to a huge TV audience. "Just catching up with an old...friend." He made sure to say it in a way that implied they'd been more than friends, or so it sounded to Isabel.

"Uh-huh," said Cormac, somehow managing to inject a world of meaning into two meaningless syllables. With his worn clothes, his hands and face swollen like a prizefighter's, he looked like a guy no one in his right mind would want to tangle with. "The lady said she's busy," he added.

"Yes, we have to be going," Isabel said with crisp decisiveness, hating the fact that her heart was still pounding crazily.

"Sure," Calvin said smoothly, his delivery as polished as the TV chef that he was. "See you around."

O'Neill stood unmoving while Calvin got into his cherry-red BMW and backed out with an angry stomp on the accelerator.

Cormac staggered and grabbed the Jeep. Under the red blotches, his face was ghostly pale. She quickly handed him the cane.

"Sorry about that," she muttered. "Here, let me help you."

"Sorry about what?" he asked. "That some douche bag was bothering you?"

"Was it that obvious?"

"That he's a douche, or that he was bothering you? Yes, and yes. Who the hell is he?"

"He's just some guy I used to know," she said, trying to sound dismissive. "Come on. You need to get to the doctor." She hurried to help him as he leaned on his cane, swaying slightly. Fearing he might topple over, she fitted herself against him. God, those shoulders. Dead weight against her. He smelled like a man. Uncomfortably aware of his muscular frame, she brought him into the clinic and waved to the guy at the reception desk.

"He's allergic to beestings," she said. "He got stung all over. We gave him an EpiPen shot but he needs to be seen."

The receptionist hit a buzzer. A nurse in marigold-colored scrubs appeared. "Sign this form, and you can finish filling it out later. Let's get you into an exam room," she said, her gaze flicking expertly over the guy's face. "Hey, Isabel."

It was Kimmy Shriver, a friend from way back. They'd been in the 4-H club together in their school days. "I thought he was the beekeeper," Isabel explained.

Kimmy grabbed a clipboard and motioned the guy through

a doorway and into a curtained area. "Is he going to be okay?" Isabel asked.

"We'll fix him right up."

"Thank you. I'll wait out here."

"Sorry about your bees," said Cormac O'Neill.

"Hey, just do me a favor and don't die, okay?" After he'd gone to an exam room, she sat down and paged through a magazine, trying to forget the encounter with Calvin Sharpe. The magazine's pages, nervously thumbed and dog-eared, displayed articles about couples breaking up, makeovers for mudrooms, recipes calling for canned mushroom soup, how to make a skirt out of four scarves, "What To Do When He Doesn't Notice You." She set the magazine aside and looked around, wondering how long it took to keep a giant stranger from dying.

She peeked at the "What To Do" article: *Play up your air of mystery. Good one,* she thought. There was nothing mysterious about her. She lived in the house where she'd grown up, she had a singular passion for culinary arts and teaching cookery with food from local sources, and she was following her dream. Some people claimed to be mystified by the reason she was single— "So pretty, at your age, I'll bet the guys are flocking to you…" but there was no mystery about it. Isabel knew exactly why she was single and why she intended to stay that way.

On one side of the waiting room was a young mother and a toddler in a food-stained onesie. The harried-looking woman was wrestling with the kid to wipe the greenish sludge from his nose. In another corner was an older woman placidly reading a library book. Isabel had spent her share of time in the clinic. When she was little, she'd come for the usual immunizations. She'd also suffered the usual childhood ordeals of bumps and bruises. A dislocated shoulder from falling out of an apple tree. A gash on her arm, sustained while climbing a barbed wire fence. A raging fever in the night from an ear infection. And through it all, one of her grandparents had always been present, soothing her with calming words.

Later, when Bubbie fell ill, Isabel had been the one to worry and soothe, her heart breaking as she watched her grandmother getting sicker and sicker.

Restless, she gave the article another glance. *Break out of your routine. Do something unexpected.* Beekeeping. That wasn't routine, was it?

Setting the article aside, she wandered over to a display of brochures on a variety of topics—immunization, food-borne illnesses, STDs, domestic abuse—*Love isn't supposed to hurt.* She turned away, flinching at darker memories from nine years back, stirred up by the encounter with Calvin. She still remembered the night she'd driven at breakneck speed all the way from Napa, where she'd been attending cooking school. She had walked into the clinic, shaken beyond reason, unable to speak the words to explain what had happened to her.

There'd been nothing broken, only bruised, though she was bleeding. A miscarriage, the doctor concluded. It happens, he and the nurse told her. Many early pregnancies were not viable.

They asked her about the fear they must have seen in her eyes. They asked her if she was safe, if there was someone she could call.

I'm safe now, Isabel had told them.

They urged her to file a report. Isabel—to her eternal regret—had refused. She filed the incident away in the journal she'd always kept, closed the book on the past and went home. At Bella Vista, she'd buried the memory along with her dream of becoming a famous chef.

She'd spent the next several years trying to forget that dream and trying to ignore Calvin Sharpe's rise in the culinary world, his smarmy television show, his chain of signature restaurants, making the most of his fame as a TV personality.

Why here? Sonoma was dotted with charming small towns frequented by tourists. Why Archangel, of all places? And why now, just as she was creating the life she'd always wanted?

She grabbed the magazine, determined to distract herself, and caught a glimpse of another tidbit of advice: *Take down your walls. He can't see you if you're hiding something.* Oh, boy. When it came to putting up walls, she was a master bricklayer. But how would a guy notice if she quit doing that?

Wear something sexy was next on the list. Clearly, this article was not meant for her. She brushed at a grass stain on her bee-keeping coveralls and impatiently turned the page.

A piece called "Wedding Wonders" jumped out at her. Perfect. As Tess's maid of honor, Isabel was knee-deep in wedding plans. The article admonished her to keep things simple. *Right,* she thought. With Tess and Dominic, nothing was ever simple. Dominic had two kids from his previous marriage, and multiple relatives, some of them coming all the way from Italy. Keeping track of everyone was a major juggling act. Yet Tess was blissful; that was clear to anyone seeing the light in her eyes.

As a girl, Isabel used to dream of her own wedding, but she'd put that aside at the same time she'd set aside her plans to study the culinary arts and earn her chef's credentials. She had found other things to focus on—Bubbie, whose cancer diagnosis and subsequent treatment had thrown darkness over everyone at Bella Vista as she became sicker and eventually passed away. Then the estate itself, sinking deeper and deeper into debt as they battled the insurance company that had rejected the claim for Bubbie's treatment. On the heels of that, Grandfather had fallen from a ladder in the orchard and was in a coma for weeks. Tess, whom Isabel had not met until that incident, had appeared out of nowhere, a redheaded reminder of the fact that their mutual father, Erik, had been a scoundrel right up until the moment of his death in a fiery car crash.

But as Bubbie used to say—out of the worst winter will always come a brilliant springtime. Tess and Isabel had turned into the best of friends, and thanks to Tess's relentless research, they'd recovered from the brink of disaster, and had turned the fortunes of Bella Vista around.

Life could be very distracting, thought Isabel. And that was a good thing. It kept her from focusing on things that couldn't be changed, such as the fact that she'd never finished culinary school, or that she'd allowed one failed relationship to keep her closed up tight inside a hard, protective shell. Now she had a new project that consumed her every waking moment—the cooking school. It was true that she didn't have the official certification from a prestigious institute, but she had something that couldn't be taught—a God-given talent in the kitchen.

She clung to that gift, grateful to let the passion consume her and fill her days with a joyous pursuit. She believed living and feeling well came from eating well, appreciating the simple things in life and spending time in the company of family and friends, and that was the mission of the Bella Vista Cooking School. The last thing in the world she needed was something to divert her attention from creating the world she had always dreamed of.

Cormac O'Neill returned to the waiting room, wearing a cotton print hospital smock that was open in the front from neck to navel, revealing his chest and abs. His abs had ridges. *Ridges.*

He didn't seem to notice the way she was staring. "The patient will live to fight the swarm another day," he said. "I need to grab a clean shirt and my wallet from the car." Leaning on his cane, he ducked out briefly, then returned. Now he wore a clean black T-shirt with an Illuminati logo, the fabric stretched taut across his chest, defining its muscled shape.

"I'm glad you're feeling better," said Isabel, pretending not to notice the muscles.

He gave a clipboard and insurance card to the receptionist. "I'm okay to drive," he said to Isabel. "I'll give you a lift back to your place."

"All right." She quit trying to be sneaky about checking him out. He was probably onto her, anyway. He had to be used to it, surely. A guy couldn't just walk around looking like that—flamboyant hair, big shoulders, piercing green eyes—and attract no notice.

She tucked the magazine under her arm. It was an outdated issue, anyway. No one would care if she borrowed it to finish a couple of articles.

"…if you don't mind," he said.

"Uh…mind? Mind what?" She made herself focus on his words.

"I need to stop at the pharmacy. The doc phoned in a couple of prescriptions. She said it's just a few doors down."

"Vern's, with the striped awning," she said as they left the clinic. "I'll wait for you."

She watched him make his way to the drugstore. Even with a limp and a cane, he seemed to walk with a swagger.

Tara Wilson, a teller at the bank, walked past with a cardboard tray of steaming coffee cups from Brew Ha Ha, a busy local café. She spied Cormac and nearly dumped the tray as she did a double take.

So it's not just me, thought Isabel, getting into the Jeep. For the first time in ages, she tried to recall the last time she'd gone out with a guy, or even stayed home and made out with one. Ah, she was so bad at dating. It simply had not been a priority of hers. She didn't like that vulnerable feeling that took over when she was drawn to someone—and so she didn't allow herself to be drawn to anyone. Sometimes, though, it couldn't be helped.

While she waited, she paged through the purloined magazine and tried not to snoop around the Jeep, but it was hard to resist. The contents of a person's car said so much about him. This one was cluttered, though not dirty. The dashboard was littered with receipts and a couple of maps with frayed edges. Who used a paper map anymore, in the age of smartphones and navigation devices? The stereo was old, too, the dial set to Pacifica Radio. There were CDs in the console—The Smiths, David Bowie, Led Zeppelin. Who played CDs anymore? She noticed some cards tucked in the visor—a parking pass of some sort, a driver's license from out of state. She craned her neck and tilted her head to see. There were foreign characters on it, and from what she could see of the picture, he had a beard and mustache.

"Saudi Arabia," he said, opening the door.

She cleared her throat. "I beg your pardon?"

"The license. It's from Saudi Arabia."

"Do you live there?"

He tossed the pharmacy bag in the back and started the engine. "I don't live anywhere."

CHAPTER THREE

Isabel stood in the shower with the hot water pounding down on her. It was not yet noon, and her day had already been derailed. She tried to shake off the trouble—the lost swarm, the stranger showing up unexpectedly, the hasty trip to the clinic and then running into Calvin Sharpe, of all people.

She wanted to believe she'd moved on, that she was immune to him now, but she still remembered the naive trust she'd put in him, a chef instructor at the culinary institute, her mentor, her lover.

On the day all those illusions had been shattered, she had gone with him to one of the teaching kitchens to set up a laptop webcam so they could film a presentation. She had felt a special air of privilege at being his anointed favorite. It was then that she chose to confide in him that she'd missed her period; the home pregnancy test had registered positive.

She had not imagined he'd be pleased. But she never could have anticipated his reaction. Fury flashed like a lightning bolt. He'd slammed her against a stainless steel counter, pinning her there while he called her names that sliced her to ribbons and accused her of conniving to trap him. He'd slapped her across the face, and thrown her to the floor, her head striking the tiles with enough force to cause her to see stars. The attack was like being hit by a speeding car. It was that quick, that violent.

Long afterward, when she looked back on the incident that had broken her apart, she realized the signs had been there, if only she'd known how to read them. Calvin had been the classic and incredibly convincing charmer, drawing her into his exciting world.

What she'd failed to notice was his subtle exertion of power and control over her. He'd drawn her focus away from other instructors at culinary school. His way of playing the mentor had included subtle put-downs, eroding her confidence in ways she didn't recognize until it was too late. He'd had answers for everything—what she should wear, how she should style her hair, the way she should angle the knife for julienne or *brunoise*. He expected her to be available every moment. Initially, she'd reveled in the attention, but as time went on, she came to realize he'd eclipsed everything else, even her long-held goals.

Her accidental pregnancy had taken the power and control away from him, and that was probably what had made him snap, his roiling anger erupting into pure violence.

Somehow she'd managed to drag herself up off the floor. With Calvin's threats ringing in her ears, she had grabbed her things and left culinary school forever. He had overlooked one detail, however. The webcam on her laptop had recorded the incident. But she'd been too scared to take action by filing a complaint with the school, let alone the police. Instead, she'd buried her shame and kept herself hidden in the only safe place she knew—Bella Vista.

Today she was dealing with another unexpected arrival—a man with whom she had no past at all. Cormac O'Neill didn't appear to have a cruel streak, but he was distracting in an entirely different way. He made her think about things like how lonely she sometimes felt, even when she was keeping herself busy with other things.

Wash away, she told herself. *Let's just wash the day away and hit the reset button.* She used soap made from Bella Vista honey and lavender, inhaling the scent of the luxurious foam and wishing she could just stand here all day. Not possible. There was too much to do. She was not going to let a stranger named Cormac O'Neill rearrange the day's plans for her, even though he'd already set back her schedule by two hours.

She dressed in a softly gathered skirt, sandals and a gauzy, loose-fitting blouse, light and comfortable in the warm weather. Her dark heavy curls—a legacy from the mother she'd never known—would dry in the sunshine today. Spring was in full bloom, and she had tons to do, starting with supervising the workers who were fixing a pergola over the new section of the patio, which had been expanded to make way for guests.

With its central fountain, wrought iron chairs and café tables with cobalt-blue majolica tile, the open-air space would be a gathering place—first for Tess and Dominic's wedding guests, and later, starting in the fall, for people who came to attend the cooking school. Isabel wanted it to be as beautiful and inviting as a vintage California hacienda, and she'd planned the project down to the last golden limestone paver.

This had always been a private home, but this summer, it would be opened to the world. The estate had lain in slumber like an enchanted kingdom, and now it was finally waking up, opening its embrace to new energy. New life.

Yet despite all the details that needed attending to, her mind kept flitting to Cormac O'Neill. She reminded herself that his business was with her grandfather, not her. A biography. Why hadn't Grandfather told her about this?

On her way down to the kitchen, she paused on the landing, which featured a wall-sized mirror. For some reason, she flashed on a bit from the article she'd seen in the waiting room—*Wear something sexy.* It just wasn't her style. She favored clothes that were long, loose and drapey. *Concealing.* The most formfitting garment she owned was her chef's apron. Sometimes she wished she had her sister's natural eye for fashion, but when Isabel tried for that, she felt self-conscious, like a kid playing at dress up. She hadn't even settled on her maid of honor dress.

Tess was at the kitchen counter, gazing out the window and eating a wedge of bee sting cake, cream filled and glossy with a crust of honeyed almonds. "If you don't quit feeding me like this," Tess scolded, "I'm never going to fit into my wedding dress."

"That was for the workmen," Isabel said. She'd quickly learned that construction guys needed baked goods to keep them at peak performance.

Tess shook back her glossy red hair. She had been growing it long in order to wear it up on her wedding day. "Couldn't resist. Sorry. So where have you been all morning?"

"Dealing with your friend, Cormac O'Neill."

Tess brightened. "Oh! He's here?"

All glorious six-foot-something of him. "He got stung by bees and had an allergic reaction, so I took him to the clinic in town."

"Oh, my gosh. Is he—"

"He'll be fine. He says he's here to work on Grandfather's biography. Do you know anything about that?"

"Sure." Tess paged through her wedding notebook, which was stuffed with lists and clippings of flowers, food and decor.

"Why didn't you tell me about this project?" With a twinge of irritation, Isabel studied her sister. In one short year, they'd grown close, though at times there were moments of tension. Like now. In some areas, they were still finding their way.

"We just got word yesterday that Mac's available."

Mac. Like the truck.

"I would have told you, but it's been a whirlwind around here, and you've had enough on your plate, helping me with the wedding and getting the place ready for the cooking school. The plan came together really fast. Mac wasn't available, and suddenly he was, so I jumped at the chance. Magnus's story begs to be written, and Cormac O'Neill is the perfect one to do it."

"You should have checked with me."

"You're right. Look, if having him here is going to be a problem, we can find someplace else for him. He could stay at Dominic's."

"Your fiancé doesn't need a houseguest. He's already got half of Southern Italy coming for the wedding. It's fine for this guy to stay for a while. Lord knows, we've got nothing but room." She looked around the kitchen, a big bright space where she'd grown up learning to cook at her grandmother's side. "That's not what I'm worried about. Does Grandfather want his life story out there for all the world to know?"

"That's the point, isn't it? But he wants it done right, and that's where Mac comes in." Tess unceremoniously licked the crumbs from her plate. "Holy cow, that's delicious. The workmen are never going to leave. You keep feeding them like this, and they'll perform miracles. Can we have this for the wedding breakfast? God, I'm obsessed, aren't I?"

"You're the bride. You are supposed to be obsessed with your wedding."

"Okay, but you get to tell me if I'm unbearable."

Isabel was excited for Tess and Dominic and his kids, but sometimes, when she lay awake at night, she felt an unbidden curl of envy. Tess made love look easy, while Isabel hadn't had a date in years. She knew she needed to take down her walls, but how did someone do that?

She batted away the thought. "Don't try to change the subject. Cormac O'Neill."

"You're going to be glad he's the one to document Magnus's life. Our grandfather has a unique story. An important one. It's not just family pride, Iz. He was a key player in the Danish Resistance. There were eight thousand Jews in Denmark during the German occupation, and Magnus's group helped rescue seventy-five hundred of them. It's a rare bright spot in the middle of the darkest of times. Most of all, it's something Magnus wants."

Isabel tucked a damp stray curl behind her ear and looked out the window. From one side of the kitchen, she could see the rows of trees, some of the stock decades old. The blossoms of springtime were flurrying down as the new fruit emerged, a tangible sign of renewal. She loved Bella Vista, loved the rhythm of the seasons. She was lucky to be a part of it.

"Yes," she said quietly. "Grandfather did say that." Neither sister stated the obvious—that their grandfather wasn't getting any younger. "So tell me about this guy."

"He's written award-winning nonfiction," Tess said. "He's won all kinds of literary prizes. He already has a publisher on board—assuming the project gets done. Anyway, the important thing is, he's here with us now, and I think he'll be perfect for Magnus."

"Where is he going to stay?" Isabel asked.

"I thought we'd put him in Erik's room."

Erik—their father. He had died before either of them was born, leaving their separate mothers both pregnant and alone, unaware of each other. Over the past year, Isabel and Tess had spent hours speculating about the situation, but frustratingly, had never been able to figure out what had driven Erik to do the things he'd done.

"Why Erik's room?" asked Isabel.

"Because it's available, and he doesn't need anything fancy. I thought Erik's room would be a good choice. The history, you know? If he's going to do a thorough job, Mac needs to be wrapped into the family."

The idea made Isabel distinctly uncomfortable. "Suppose we don't want to wrap him into the family?"

"Our grandfather wants it. I swear, it'll be fine. Just fine." Tess put her dishes in the sink, then poured herself a cup of coffee and took a sip. She never seemed to be completely still, physically or mentally. She was always thinking, planning, doing. She had the kind of energy that made caffeine jumpy. "I'm really sorry, Iz. Don't be mad, okay?"

"I never get mad," said Isabel.

"I know. It's freaky. I'm about to become a stepmom to two school-age kids, so I need to take lessons from you on how to be mellow about things."

Isabel flashed on Calvin Sharpe, and she felt anything but mellow. "Hey, off the subject, but did you attend the last Chamber of Commerce meeting?"

"Yep. I'm a card-carrying member. They're going to feature Things Remembered on the Chamber website in December. Cool, huh?"

"Very cool. And, um, was there any talk of that new restaurant coming in? It was in the newsletter…"

"Yeah, I think it's kind of a big deal. Some famous chef…
Cleavon or Calvin…?"

"Calvin Sharpe. A TV chef." Isabel kept her face neutral.
You never get mad. Great, just great.

"Yeah, that's the one. Super good-looking, and he had an
entourage with him. I remember now—he's calling the new
place CalSharpe's. So, you know this guy?"

"He was an instructor at the culinary institute when I went
there, years ago."

"And? What's he like?"

"Like a guy who thinks the sun rises every morning just to
hear him crow," Isabel said. "But he can cook. And it appears
he's got a restaurant empire going." She didn't want to talk
about it anymore. She'd already given him too much space in
her head. "Anyway. Back to the other guy—Cormac O'Neill.
You call him Mac."

Tess grabbed her arm and pulled her toward the lounge
room. "Come here," she said. "Let me show you something."

She led the way to the big room, which had already been
refurbished for the cooking school. It was light and airy with
freshly whitewashed plaster walls and tall ceilings, filled with
cookbooks and old furniture and Bubbie's baby grand piano.
When Isabel was growing up, the rolling ladder against the
tall built-in bookcases had been her stairway to a different
world. That was what books had offered her—all the voyages
she wanted, to different realms. Even as a tiny girl, she'd been
the consummate armchair traveler, seeing the world from the
safety of her own home.

Now she was a steward of this place. For her, Bella Vista
lived and breathed with the essence of life, representing security and permanence in a world that had not always been
kind to her. Her mission was to revive the place, resuscitate it
after the hard times. Her grandfather's accident last year had

shaken Isabel's foundations. Magnus was a father figure and besides Tess, her only family.

Isabel still loved to pore over photographs of castles on the Rhein, Ayers Rock in Australia, Italy's Amalfi coast. Sometimes, gazing at the pictures, she would feel a yearning deep in her stomach. Yet when it came to actually traveling to those places, something always made her balk. To her, adventure was always more appealing within the pages of a travelogue.

Tess pulled a stack of new-looking books from a shelf and set them on the lid of the piano. "I met Mac for the first time when I was working in Krakow. I was tracing the origin of some paintings that had been hidden by the Nazis, and he was doing an article on restoring Nazi plunder. I'm actually a footnote in one of his books." She flipped open a thick volume called *Behind the Iron Curtain*. "He talks about the Krakow treasure here."

Isabel felt a surge of admiration for her sister. They had grown up separately, in completely different circumstances, Isabel at Bella Vista, and Tess traveling the world with her mother, a museum acquisitions expert. Isabel could easily picture Tess examining old artifacts, ferreting out the truth about them. She'd had a high-level position finding lost treasures and researching their origins at an auction house in the Bay Area. In fact, her expertise had been instrumental in saving Bella Vista from bankruptcy.

But along with the estate's reversal of fortune came a good deal of unwanted attention. She very much doubted Cormac O'Neill would have anything to do with her grandfather if not for the stories Tess had uncovered in her research. And then there was the lawsuit...brought by Archangel's most wily lawyer, a woman named Lourdes Maldonado. She was a neighbor and friend—*former* friend—who was suddenly looking for some kind of settlement.

"You've had such an amazing career," she said, pushing aside the troubling thought. "Do you miss it?"

"Every once in a while, yeah. I did have a good job in the city. It was great for a long time. But I found something better here." Tess's face softened, as it always did when she thought of her fiancé. "I know, I'm ridiculous. Honestly, Iz, I never knew love could feel this way. You'll see, one of these days. When the right guy comes along."

"Not holding my breath," Isabel said.

"Not even for *this* guy?" Tess handed her the Iron Curtain book.

Isabel took it from her and turned it over in her hands. She studied the author photo on the back. It was an extremely cleaned up version of the grubby, swearing traveler covered in beestings. "Oh, my."

"You're welcome," said Tess, her eyes gleaming. "I mean, obviously we didn't pick him for his looks but it can't hurt, right? If we're going to have someone running around researching the family history, it's nice that he's eye candy. He's single."

"That means there's something wrong with him. Or he's a commitment-phobe."

"Neither," said Tess, her smile disappearing. "He's a widower."

CHAPTER FOUR

"I'll show you to your room," Isabel said, approaching Cormac, who was taking his luggage from his Jeep.

He turned and shot her a grin. "I bet you've always wanted to say that, right? 'I'll show you to your room.'" He spoke with crisp formality.

"Right," she said. "I mean, right this way." She mimicked his formal tone.

"Thanks. And thanks for helping me this morning. I'm guessing a trip to the urgent care place wasn't on your agenda today."

"It never is. How are you feeling?"

"Fine. Nothing like a shot of artificial Adrenalin to get the day started. I took a hike around the place and made a few calls. Your grandfather around?"

"Always. He likes tinkering in the machine shop, or being out in the orchard with the workers. I'm sure he's eager to meet you." She led the way to the entry. It was looking grand these days, a lovely archway framing a view of the big sunny central patio. The wings of the hacienda curved generously around the brow of the hill upon which the house sat, the whitewashed walls expansive and cleanly cut against the blue sky. In the center of the broad, open space, a fountain burbled, the water flashing in the sunlight. Flowers bloomed in pots and espaliers along the walls. Two cats—Lilac and Chips— prowled around, Lilac shadowing the dark gray tabby as if to keep him away from the fountain. The workers were finishing up the pergola, creating a shaded area for café tables.

"This is fantastic," said Cormac. He glanced down as Chips, the older cat, rubbed up against his ankle. "Hey, buddy."

"That's Chips. The white Siamese is Lilac, our latest rescue. We call him Lilac because it was springtime, and the lilacs were in bloom, and he has that unusual color. He takes a bit longer to warm up to people."

Cormac leaned down to stroke Chips, who turned his head this way and that, his eyes shut in pure indulgence. Then, with slow dignity, he padded away. "Is that guy okay? He seems a bit unsteady."

"Chips has a kind of feline Parkinson's, so he has trouble getting around," said Isabel.

"The white one seems to look after him," said Cormac, watching Lilac swirl carefully around the older cat.

"He does," said Isabel. "Chips rescued Lilac, and now Lilac takes care of Chips."

"He rescued him?" Leaning on his cane, Cormac bent and stretched his hand out toward the white cat. Lilac perked up and sidled closer.

"Well, he brought him home one day and we started feeding him. At first I thought Lilac might be feral. He was so skittish, wouldn't let anyone but Chips near him. The two were inseparable. Then I noticed that Lilac knew what to do with toys, and seemed to understand what a bowl of kibbles is, so I figured he wasn't wild after all. He must have been dumped."

To Isabel's surprise, Lilac rubbed his head against the guy's hand. Cormac scratched his finger between Lilac's tipped ears. "We've all been there, buddy. Who dumped you?"

"It happens, unfortunately," Isabel said. "An owner moves or passes away, and a cat gets turned out into the wild. Lilac just got lucky that Chips brought him home one day. And now Chips is the lucky one. Lilac once saved him from drowning."

"Seriously?" He straightened up, steadying himself with the cane.

She nodded, shuddering a little at the memory. "We heard Lilac yowling on the patio one day, and came out to find that Chips had fallen into the fountain. He would have drowned, but Lilac got our attention."

"They both got lucky," Mac said. "Whaddya think, guys? Am I going to get lucky, too?"

Isabel assumed it was a rhetorical question, so she said nothing.

"Tess told me I was going to like it here," he told her as the cats wandered away, making the rounds of the patio. "She says it's like living in a dream."

"Tess said that?" Isabel couldn't conceal a smile.

"Yep."

"Well, she wants you in Erik's room. It hasn't been updated yet, but Tess thinks you'll like it."

"Who's Erik?"

"Our father. He passed away before either of us was born. I'm sure you'll get the whole story out of Grandfather." She led the way into the vestibule and up the winding staircase, which split into two at the landing like great wrought iron wings, echoing the outer curves of the house. Bella Vista had originally been built for a large extended family and a staff, as well. Its three stories were filled with room after room, which Isabel was transforming one by one into guest quarters.

They went down a wide hallway to a room on the end. She could tell Ernestina had freshened it up. The linens looked crisp and smelled faintly of lavender, and the dormer windows were open to let in a breeze. A bowl of fresh fruit sat on an antique washstand, and the fixtures in the adjoining bathroom gleamed.

"After my father died, my grandparents never changed anything in here, just closed it off," she said, turning to Cormac. He was so close behind her that she nearly ran into him—into that broad chest. He smelled even more manly than he had this morning.

As Isabel grew older, she had begun to understand why her grandparents had simply closed the door to Erik's room. Even though Ernestina, the housekeeper, kept it aired out and dusted, the tragedy of his death seemed to hang in the atmosphere. There was a poignant sense of unfinished business, an unfinished life. Everything was frozen in time, as if he had just stepped out, never to return. She wondered if Cormac O'Neill noticed that, or if it was just her, imagining a connection with a man she'd never known.

Cormac set his large bag on a cedar chest at the end of the pine post bed. Erik's boyhood room was still festooned with AC/DC posters, sports equipment, college pennants, old yearbooks, French and Spanish textbooks. Cormac went over to the built-in bookcase and ran his finger along the spines of the books there, some of them bleached by the light.

"Your dad liked books," he commented.

"That's what my grandparents said. When I was young, I made it my mission to read every single volume in this bookcase."

"Why? To get inside his head?"

"As much as you can get into the head of a person you've never met. I made a valiant attempt. My favorites were *Kon Tiki* and *Treasure Island*."

"Good choices. I loved those books." He pulled out a copy of *White Fang* and opened to the inside cover. There was a bookplate on which Erik had written his name, the letters slanted in a careless or perhaps hurried scrawl. Cormac replaced the book and moved on to a row of travel books about Zanzibar, Mongolia, Tangier, Patagonia. "He was a fan of traveling. Or travel books."

Isabel nodded. "He went to the University of Salerno in Italy, as part of the exchange program with UC Davis. That's where he met my mom."

"Are the French and Spanish books his, too?"

Isabel nodded. "According to Grandfather, Erik was a gifted student of languages. He grew up speaking Danish with his parents, Spanish with the workers and French because he loved it. And Italian, because he loved my mother."

"Your mom's Italian?"

"She, um, she died in childbirth. Giving birth to me." Isabel's own mother was yet another ghost in the house.

She caught Cormac's flash of stark sympathy, which made her feel slightly apologetic, given what Tess had just told her—that Cormac O'Neill was a widower. "I know, this makes me Little Orphan Annie, but honestly, my grandparents were wonderful parents to me. If you lose someone before you know them, does it count as a loss?"

He hooked his thumbs into his back pockets and looked out the window. "Every death is a loss," he said quietly.

"Of course. I'm just saying, it didn't hit me the way it did Erik's parents. Or Francesca's. That was my mother's name—Francesca."

Cormac went over to a faded round dartboard and examined some papers stuck in place with a dart. "Looks as if Erik knew how to get in trouble, too. Aren't these unpaid speeding tickets?"

"Yes. He drove a Mustang convertible."

Cormac moved on to a display of ribbons. "What are all these for?" he asked.

"Okay, so he was a typical boy in every way—but he had this quirk," she said. "He was a master baker. He won the Sonoma County Fair Blue Ribbon for the youth division from 1978 to 1982 in several categories." She touched one of the fading ribbons. "Going through this stuff is like putting together a puzzle—but an imperfect one. I have all these artifacts—the things he left behind, photographs, stories from my grandparents and people who knew him. But *I* never got to know him, so that picture will never be accurate." She opened a drawer of an old wooden desk. "My favorite artifact—his recipe collection." Though she didn't say so, this was when she felt closest to Erik—when she was following a recipe he'd put a little star by or annotated in his messy handwriting.

Cormac plucked a photograph from the drawer. "He's a grown man in this picture."

It was her favorite shot of Erik, one she used to take out and study when she was growing up. The photo showed him standing on Shell Beach, out on the Sonoma coast, with the cliffs sweeping up behind him and the ocean crashing around his bare feet. He was smiling broadly, maybe laughing, in the picture. He wore a red baseball cap turned backward, board shorts and no shirt. The camera had frozen him in a moment of freedom and joy.

"He's younger in this picture than I am now." She shook off a wave of regret, then shut the drawer with a decisive shove. "So, do you want a quick tour, or...?"

"Sure." He turned and grabbed his cane.

"What happened to your leg?" she asked.

"I wish I could say I trashed my knee while doing something awesome, but it happened at JFK airport when I was running for a flight." He shrugged. "It'll be okay."

In the middle of the second floor were the two biggest suites, one facing north, the other south. "We just finished remodeling them," Isabel said. "Careful, I think the paint might still be wet on the doorframes."

He scanned the new furnishings, the bright walls and window seats. "It's great, Isabel."

"Thank you. This has been a labor of love, for sure."

"What's up those stairs?"

"Third floor. My room, a few more guest rooms...."

Leaning on the hand rail, he went up the stairs. Isabel told herself to get used to this. Grandfather had invited the guy to explore their lives, and she supposed that meant he would be poking around every room of the house.

She showed him the guest rooms on the third floor, including the suite where Erik and Francesca had lived after they married. Though currently unfinished, this was going to become the honeymoon suite, romantic and private, appointed with luxurious fabrics and a special dressing room for the bride.

"And this," she said, opening a door to a small sunroom, "was my grandmother's domain. It hasn't been refurbished yet, either. I'm not sure what to do with it." Although Bubbie had been gone for ten years, her presence could still be felt in the closed-off room. Her sewing machine stood in the corner, still threaded, the needle raised as if awaiting orders. Under the long bank of windows was a faded daybed where Bubbie had lived the final days of her illness. She had spent time doing the things that mattered to her—simple things—visiting with family and friends, writing letters, gazing out at the beautiful view, enjoying a cup of tea with a buttery cookie, reassuring Isabel and Magnus of her love.

But Bubbie had never divulged the biggest secret of her life.

Regarding the sunroom, Isabel felt a surge of inspiration. "I'd love to turn this space into something Bubbie would appreciate," she said.

"Need any suggestions?"

Not from you, she thought. "I'd love it to be a place of dreams, somewhere to sit and think."

"Thinking gives me a headache."

She gestured at the row of windows. "You'd probably like a universal gym and giant speakers blaring heavy metal music."

"Hey, thanks for reducing me to a cliché. Actually, I was going to suggest yoga mats and gong music."

The suggestion surprised Isabel. She could instantly picture a yoga retreat here. Maybe having Cormac O'Neill poking around and commenting on everything might turn out to be the start of something good.

Yet the thought of a stranger covered in beestings, staying in the house, swearing like a reject from a busy restaurant kitchen, was unsettling.

"Shit, oh, man." As if he'd read her thoughts, he staggered and grabbed the doorknob.

"What's the matter?" She clutched at his arm. "Are you all right?"

"Yeah, sorry, I'll be okay. Post Adrenalin letdown," he said. "Feels like vertigo."

"What can I do?"

"Maybe a rest and a shower."

She escorted him back to Erik's room. "All right," she said, feeling flustered again, "you should find everything you need here."

He paused, studying her. "I already have."

★ ★ ★

Cormac O'Neill had been to a lot of places in his life, too many to count. But as he stood at the window of his room at Bella Vista, he couldn't recall a place that rivaled the beauty of the Sonoma hacienda. Looking out at the orchards and fields, he felt a million miles away from the war-torn places of the world, the airports and grimy cities, the long barren stretches of scorched earth in the foreign lands he'd visited. During his career, he had lived in mud huts and tents, in hovels and out in the open, being eaten alive by bugs or shivering in an unheated room. He could do worse than a luxurious villa in Archangel, that was for sure.

Staggering off an overseas flight at SFO this morning, he'd borrowed a buddy's Jeep, gulped a double shot of espresso and had driven straight from San Francisco to Archangel, hoping to relax and sleep off the jet lag. Instead, he'd encountered the skittish and suspicious Isabel, who had kneed him in the groin. Next came the swarm of bees and the trip to the ur-gent care place. He wondered what the next disaster would be.

When Tess had told him about the book project, she hadn't mentioned hostile women and swarms of bees. In fact, she'd characterized it as a working vacation of sorts, a way for him to recover from his bum knee by soaking up the charms of Sonoma County.

In contrast, Bella Vista was lush and seductive, the landscape filled with colors from deep green to sunburned-gold. Gar-deners, construction workers and farm workers swarmed the property. Isabel Johansen was in charge; that had been clear from the start. Yet when she'd shown him to Erik's room, she'd seemed vulnerable, uncertain. Some might regard the room as a mausoleum, filled with the depressing weight of things left behind by the departed. To Mac, it was a treasure trove. He was here to learn the story of this place, this family, and every detail, from the baseball card collection to the dog-eared books about far-off places, would turn into clues for him.

And holy crap, had Isabel looked different when she'd given him the nickel tour. Unlike the virago in the beekeeper's getup, the cleaned-up Isabel was a Roman goddess in a flowy outfit, sandals and curly dark hair.

Mac reminded himself that meeting Magnus Johansen was the whole point of this trip. At the moment, he didn't feel like meeting anyone. The meds he'd been given, combined with the letdown after the shot of epinephrine, made his brain feel like cotton candy.

Rummaging through his duffel bag, he broke out the cream from the pharmacy and dabbed some on the itchy welts covering his arms, legs and hands. There were bites on his back he couldn't reach, so he scratched himself on the bedpost, seeking relief.

He hoped the bees were not an omen of mishaps to come. He could always hope this morning's disasters were an anomaly. His plan was simple. He would gather information about Magnus Johansen, a war hero turned orchardist, then settle in and write the story. It was what he did, what he was good at—telling other people's stories.

The PR people who worked for his publisher liked to make much of his background. He'd been raised with five brothers by parents who worked in the diplomatic corps, traveling to the far corners of the world, their mission to spread peace and understanding. It all sounded exotic and glamorous, although for a kid, the reality had been far different—an endless succession of airports and foreign hotels, stifling tropical heat and painful immunizations and a new school every other year. The upbringing had taught him much about the world; he'd learned a few languages and had figured out how to be ready to go at a moment's notice. But his way of life had never taught him how to stay in one place. The concept of home was foreign to him.

He went into the immaculate bathroom and took a quick shower in the old-fashioned claw-foot tub. There were perfumed soaps and fancy shampoo and lotions. Damn, it felt good to shower off the travel and the jet lag. He wanted to stand there all day, but he was here for a job. He put on clean shorts and a shirt, then put the knee brace back in place. The zipperlike surgical scar wasn't pretty, but at least his knee didn't feel as though it was on fire anymore.

He was supposed to be taking care of himself after his injury. The doc said his knee would never heal if he didn't follow a program of physical therapy and exercise.

There was a knock at the door. "Hey, Mac," said a voice. "It's me, Tess."

Leaning on his cane, he hobbled over and let her in.

She was as pretty as ever, red hair, tall and willowy. Actually, she was even prettier than he remembered. He didn't recall the brightness of that smile. "Tess Delaney. Fancy meeting you here."

"It's great to see you," she said. "We didn't know when you'd get here."

"I caught a flight from Taipei on standby. Borrowed a set of wheels in San Francisco and here I am."

"Wow, that was quick. Oh, my gosh, it's been too long." With that, she gave him a brief hug. "I'm really glad we stayed in touch, Mac. Thanks for coming." Her eyes sparkled as she grinned at him. "What?" she asked. "You're looking at me funny."

"You look really good, Tess. Glowing. Hey, are you—"

"About to marry the love of my life, yes. And no, I'm not pregnant. Just...in a different place than I was last time I saw you. A much better place, literally *and* figuratively."

He sensed a mellowness about her he didn't recall from before, as if her sharp edges had been softened. Maybe it was this place—Bella Vista. Maybe it would soften him, too. Except he didn't need softening.

She stepped back and regarded him from head to toe. "You don't look so hot. Isabel said you got stung."

"*Stung*'s the word for it," he murmured. "I'll be okay. She was nice enough to take me to a clinic."

"Good. My sister's super nice."

"I'll take your word for it."

She set her hands on her hips. Tess had put on a little weight, and the curves looked good on her. She'd been really skinny in Krakow, skinny and stressed out. "She said you got off on the wrong foot this morning."

"Ha-ha."

She checked out his knee brace. "What happened?"

"Torn ligaments. I'll heal."

"Are you hungry?"

"You know me. I can always eat."

"You came to the right place. Let's grab something for you from the kitchen, and then we'll go find Magnus."

The "something" turned out to be a wedge of the most amazing cake he'd ever tasted. It had cream in the middle, a crust of honey and almonds on top. He crammed half a wedge into his mouth and moaned aloud. "Damn, that's good," he said around the mouthful. *"Damn."*

"I already ordered it for my wedding breakfast," said Tess.

"It's called *Bienenstich*—bee sting cake," said Isabel, coming into the kitchen. "Appropriate, under the circumstances."

He turned to face her, his cheeks stuffed with food like a chipmunk's. Then he swallowed the bite of food. "It's delicious. Did you make it?" he asked, not taking his eyes off her. She didn't look much like her sister. While Tess had red hair and freckles, Isabel had olive-toned skin, dark eyes and full lips, like a flamenco dancer or maybe an Italian film star swathed in veils.

"I did," she said. "It's a German tradition. You should have coffee with it." She went over to an espresso machine that resembled the chrome front of a Maserati, and got to work.

Coffee. Oh, God.

He took out his phone, which was also his work computer, voice recorder and general organizer of his life. "I'm not getting a good signal here. Is there a wi-fi password?"

"I should remember that," said Tess, "because we just upgraded. When I first got here, you couldn't even get a signal. Isabel, do you remember the password?"

"'CATSEX!!' all in caps, with two exclamation points." She shrugged. "I didn't pick it."

"Isabel's the best cook in the world," said Tess, raising her voice over the grind and hiss of the espresso maker. "We eat like this all the time at Bella Vista."

He connected with his phone and scrolled through a depressingly long queue of unanswered emails. A freelancer's dilemma— you were never really free. You just moved from one assignment to the next. He deleted a few nonessential notes, then pocketed the phone and helped himself to another piece of coffee cake, feeling charitable now toward the bees that had produced the deep, rich honey that flavored the topping. Seriously, he couldn't remember the last time food had tasted so good to him.

After the espresso machine spewed forth a cacophony of grinding, whistling and a deep-throated gurgling, Isabel set a frothy cappuccino in front of him. The rich aroma rose on a wisp of steam.

"Okay, that settles it." He wiped his mouth with a napkin. "I'm never leaving."

"Ha," said Tess. "You never stay."

She knew him better than he thought. The longest he'd ever lived in one place was during college. After that, his permanent address was his literary agent's Manhattan office.

Here, he felt like a stranger in a strange—and extremely seductive—land. In contrast to the places of his past, Bella Vista seemed weighted by a sense of permanence—the old country house with its courtyard and patios, the rustic stone barn and machine shop, outbuildings and weathered work sheds, the acres of age-gnarled apple trees, now covered in springtime blooms. He wondered what it would be like to watch the seasons change all in one place, year after year.

"You say that like it's a bad thing," he told Tess.

She gave a dismissive sniff, then turned to her beauteous sister. "He never stays. Mac is a rolling stone."

Isabel offered a bowl full of raw sugar crystals. "Good to know," she said.

"I'm wounded," he said, adding sugar to his coffee. "Why is it good?"

"I like to understand who I'm dealing with. So do you prefer Mac or Cormac?"

"Either." The piercing mechanical whine of a saw came from somewhere outside. "You've got a lot of work going on around here," he said. "If this is a bad time—"

"It's a perfect time," Tess interrupted.

He sensed what she wasn't saying. Magnus Johansen wasn't getting any younger.

When the shrieking of the power saw stopped, Tess asked, "So what do you think about Isabel's project?"

What the hell did he care? The whole idea of running a vast estate, regardless of how historic it was, felt like way too much of a commitment to him.

"She's turning the place into a destination cooking school. Did she tell you?" Tess beamed with pride.

"She's standing right here," Isabel reminded them.

"Cool idea, huh?" Tess asked, ignoring her sister.

"If you're into cooking," said Mac. "And school."

"I take it you're not," Isabel said.

"I'm here for Magnus," he said. "In the meantime, I'll try to stay out of your way."

"Ernestina told me he's out with the workers in the new section of the orchard." She looked him up and down, her gaze hard to read. "It's a few hundred yards away. Can you walk that far?"

He nodded, gripping his cane as he studiously ignored the twinge in his bad knee. "Sure, let me grab my camera."

"You're a photographer, too?" asked Isabel when he returned with his gear. "It looks like a bazooka gun."

"I take a lot of my own pictures," he said. He'd found, in his work, that putting the camera between himself and a subject sometimes created a necessary boundary. Or if that wasn't needed, it was a way to capture a moment, a mood or nuance when words weren't enough.

The three of them stepped through a set of French doors leading to the central patio, which was swarming with even more workmen. Isabel led the way, descending a set of yellow limestone steps. He couldn't stop himself from checking her out from behind. He kind of wished she wasn't wearing all that flowy stuff because he suspected there was something much more interesting underneath.

Pretty women were one of his several weaknesses. There was something about long hair, shapely legs, tanned skin, smooth and soft… He couldn't remember the last time he'd held a woman, inhaled the scent of her hair, pressed his lips to the pulse in her neck. He nearly stumbled over a tree root as he imagined what Isabel Johansen smelled and tasted like.

She turned back, scowling at him. "Are you all right?"

"Fine," he said, clearing his throat. "Just taking in the atmosphere."

They came upon a crew of workers with long-handled pruners. Speaking in Spanish that sounded smooth and natural, Isabel asked one of them where Magnus was.

One of the guys gestured at the end of a row of trees and waved. "He's over by the new trees from the nursery beds."

They headed down another row of trees. At the end of the row, Mac could see an old man silhouetted against the hillside, a ladder on one shoulder and a cane in his other hand. Tall and slender, in overalls and a work shirt, white hair sticking out from under a flat cap, Magnus Johansen moved with the ease of a much younger man.

Isabel called out to get his attention and he stopped, setting the ladder on the ground. He took off his cap and waved it at them.

Mac paused to take a candid picture while Isabel and Tess walked ahead, framed by the rows of arching trees in bloom. A timely breeze created a flurry of petals that filled the air like an unseasonable snowstorm. The camera lens captured the tableau of the old man and his two beautiful granddaughters, the moment gilded by sunshine filtering through the leaves. *Nice.*

Mac put the cap back on the lens and approached him. "Cormac O'Neill," he said, shaking hands. "Good to meet you in person."

Magnus's grip was firm but brief. "I'm very glad you're here, and on such short notice," he said with a subtle lilt in his speech hinting at his Danish heritage. "Welcome to Bella Vista. I see you've met my granddaughters." Though his face was pale, there was a glow of pride in him when he looked at Tess and Isabel. "I hope they gave you a proper welcome."

Cutting a glance at Isabel, Mac thought about the knee to

the groin and the attack of the killer bees. "Yep, she made me feel right at home."

"You've come at a busy time. But the springtime is my favorite."

"The scenery here is amazing," Cormac said. He surveyed the area. The weather was almost unbearably perfect today, a stark contrast to the scorching deserts, barren tundras and steamy jungles he often had to visit on assignment. In addition to the construction crew at the house, there were people in every section of the orchard, some working alone, some in teams. Farming was as foreign to Mac as picking out draperies. "And your home is beautiful."

"Yes. I have enjoyed much good fortune in my life."

It was a startling statement, given what little Mac knew of the man. Magnus Johansen had lost his family in the war, and had outlived his only son and his wife. He had survived a head injury not so long ago. And yet here he stood, elderly but still proud, beaming at his granddaughters. Mac was suddenly more interested in Magnus, anxious to find out how the man had endured all that, yet could still call himself lucky.

"So," said Magnus. "We must get to know one another."

"My thoughts exactly."

"I've read some of your books. I'm honored that you're going to be writing about me. I warn you, though. I have a very long story to tell."

Mac's gaze kept straying to Isabel. She clearly didn't like him, and despite what his libido was telling him, he didn't like her, either. Still, there was something about her, not just the slender ankles and the pretty dark hair, but some vibe that drew him, even as he told himself she was a complication he didn't need in his life.

"I've got time," he said.

CHAPTER FIVE

"So how do you prepare for your first interview with your subject?" asked Isabel the next morning.

After dragging himself out of bed, Mac needed coffee, not questions. He noticed a soft hissing sound coming from the espresso machine. "So that magic cappuccino you made me yesterday—was that a one-time event or can I get another?"

"Depends on how you ask."

"Please. Begging here. Charge me anything you like. Put it on my tab."

"I might just do that." She didn't smile, but her eyes were light as she ground some coffee beans into a one-shot filter.

Mac inhaled the aroma and watched her expertly pull the shot and then steam the milk with a wand. He liked watching her work, each movement economical, efficient. He liked watching her, period. What the hell? If he was going to be stuck in paradise for a while, he might as well enjoy the view.

"You and Grandfather can have coffee on the patio, and then get to work on your project. It's quiet out there until the workmen arrive. After that, he can show you more of Bella Vista."

"Thanks. Will you and Tess be joining us?"

She hesitated, glanced back over her shoulder at him. "It's Grandfather's story."

"You're part of it. Just figured you might want to hear what he has to say."

"Oh. Well, I suppose…."

"Sure we do," said Tess, coming into the kitchen. She was wearing some crazy headpiece, a white net thing with a big fake flower made of feathers. Noticing his stare, she said, "Do you like my fascinator?"

It looked weirdly similar to Isabel's beekeeping veil. "Your *what?*"

"My fascinator. I'm trying out different looks for the wedding." She turned her head this way and that. Tess was a pretty woman—and who didn't like a redhead—but the lopsided headgear didn't do much for her.

"I never give fashion advice before I've had my morning coffee," he said.

Isabel set a perfect bowl-shaped cup of cappuccino in front of him. "Good answer."

"Bless you," he said, savoring the first creamy sip.

Tess picked up a painted serving tray. "Let me help you carry."

"Thanks." Isabel held the door leading out to the patio. Mac followed with his coffee and his cane, and a satchel of files and photographs he'd stayed up late studying last night. Magnus sat at a wrought iron and tile table with his coffee, the two cats swirling around his ankles. "Grandfather, is it all right if we join you for a bit?"

"Of course. Particularly since you've brought sustenance." He eyed the tray of food.

It looked like a food magazine layout, featuring a variety of cheeses with fresh berries on brightly painted Italian pottery, and a tiny glass container of honey with the smallest spoon he'd ever seen.

Isabel laced a thread of honey across the cheeses. "These are my favorite honey and cheese pairings. Comté, Appenzeller and ricotta. I had my first honey harvest last summer—a small one. That's when I realized I needed expert help with my beekeeping."

"Sorry I wasn't your guy," said Mac.

"Please, sit down and let's enjoy the morning." Magnus gestured at the chairs.

It was all Mac could do not to wolf down the whole snack tray. But he'd been trained by the best, his redoubtable mother, who had taught her six sons diplomatic protocol and etiquette as if it were her job. He made himself a small plate, sipped his coffee and settled in, curious to find out more about Magnus, his beauteous granddaughters and the place they called home.

Magnus smoothed his weather-beaten hands over the legs of his trousers. "So. Here we all are. It is hard to conceive of, my life in a book. I don't know where to begin."

"It doesn't matter," Mac said. "Whatever crosses your mind."

"Bella Vista," Magnus said without hesitation. "This place is always on my mind. Perhaps I even imagined it before I realized it was quite real." He flexed his fingers, resting them on his knees, and said, "When I was a boy in Denmark, we would go to the cinema on Saturday afternoons, and naturally my favorites were the films about cowboys and Indians in the Wild West. I always envisioned America as this vast, unsettled land, a place of endless opportunity. It never looked like this in the picture show. My schoolmates and I yearned to come here, but I never thought I would. It was more like a place of dreams."

In an odd way, Mac could relate. He, too, had grown up far from the States, and he, too, had been drawn to its larger-than-life, practically mythic aspect. His impressions had been formed by watching old VHS tapes of Nickelodeon series. Instead of the Wild West of Magnus's imagination, he had been filled with mental pictures of schools populated by perky girls with ponytails, a row of candy-colored lockers and stern but good-hearted teachers capable of solving a spunky kid's problems before each thirty-minute segment was up.

"Do you recall when you made the decision to come here?" Isabel asked.

The old man rested his hands atop his cane. "There was no decision. It was an act of desperation. And survival."

Mac put his phone on the table. "I've got a digital recorder app. Do you mind?"

"No, of course not. That is why you're here."

From the corner of his eye, Mac could see Isabel stiffen, but then she settled back and waited quietly.

"It was not something my family aspired to or wanted for me. We would have been content to live out our lives in Denmark. We—my parents, my grandfather and myself—were comfortable in Copenhagen," said Magnus. "We had all that we needed. We weren't wealthy, though we were certainly comfortable. My father worked as a civil servant. My mother kept house, and her passion was for growing things. She prized her apple trees, and the whole neighborhood loved the Gravensteins she cultivated. Not the most beautiful fruit ever to grace the table, but surely the tastiest."

He leaned back in the chair, his pale eyes looking into a past Mac could only imagine. "I was but a boy when the Nazis arrested them and took them away. A youngster still in his school years doesn't get to decide anything, least of all whether or not to emigrate to America. It was all I could do to avoid getting caught myself."

"Do you know why they were arrested?"

"For harboring a Jewish man and his daughter. My uncle Sweet and little cousin Eva. We weren't really related, of course, but that is the story we gave out."

"Eva...the woman you eventually married."

"Yes," he said, smiling at Isabel. "My Eva. Although in 1940, when she first came to live with us at the house in Copenhagen, I considered her a pest. Sweet was born a Dane, same as my father, but his wife was a member of the *chalutzim*—that is the Hebrew term for *pioneers*. Thousands of them came to Denmark from eastern Europe or Germany, and they were welcomed by the Danish and by King Christian. They had come for agricultural training, the goal being to eventually move to Palestine. But Sweet's wife had no interest in farming." Magnus's mouth turned briefly into a curl of disgust. "She wanted only to be rich and comfortable, and she believed Sweet would give her that. He didn't seem to care for money, though. He was a photographer, and a good one at that. He turned the basement of our house into a darkroom."

"So he took these pictures?" Mac opened a file folder to four fading snapshots, turning them so Magnus and the two sisters could see.

Magnus nodded. "Yes, I brought one large case along when I came to America after the war, and those photographs were tucked into the lining."

"Talk about life in Copenhagen at the start of the occupation. What was it like, having another family living with you?"

"At first, life still seemed...normal. Routine. From my perspective as an only child, it was good fun having a playmate.

Yes, it was routine, until Sweet and Eva disappeared into the night."

"Were they warned that there was going to be a roundup of the Jews?" asked Mac.

"You've done some reading, then," said Magnus. "But in fact, some years later, in the autumn of 1943. No, the reason Eva and her father had to leave was that the Germans found out my father's greatest secret."

Secrets seemed to run in this family, Mac thought, looking from one sister to the other, two beautiful but very different women who hadn't known each other while growing up.

"What precipitated their leaving, then?" Mac asked Magnus.

"An agent affiliated with the Danish underground was caught and tortured. We had to assume the operation was compromised. Eva and her father had to leave in secret well in advance of the official action. They were sent up to a small coastal town called Helsingør—you would know it as Elsinore, from the Shakespeare play. Shortly after that, the soldiers came to search the house, but by that time, there was nothing to find. The Nazis were furious that the tip-off failed to yield any results, and they took my parents in for questioning."

Now Magnus closed his eyes and held himself very still, so still that Mac thought he might've drifted off to sleep. He exchanged a glance with Isabel. She sat unmoving, her fingers braided together, tense.

Then Magnus opened his eyes. "I never saw them again. From that night onward, I was on my own. Which is my long-winded way of explaining what I meant when I said I didn't make a decision of any sort about my own future. I simply reacted, determined to survive, as any wild animal might do. I lived by my wits—or lack thereof—from day to day. So in that sense, it wasn't a decision that brought me to America. It was happenstance—and sheer blind luck, although I do not recall feeling at all lucky that day."

He shook his head, paused to sample the honeyed cheese with some bread. "From today's perspective, it is easy to look back and deride ourselves for not seeing the storm coming. But you understand, we were simply Danes, living our lives and going about our business. It was quite some time before I even grasped that there was a division between Jews and Gentiles. We were all Danes first. Denmark did not force Jews to register their property, or to identify themselves, and God knows, they were never made to give up their homes and businesses."

"That came later, didn't it?" said Tess, regarding him with soft-eyed sympathy. She reached up and took the feather thing out of her hair and set it aside.

"It all came about gradually as the Germans tightened their control. They broke their promises one by one, replacing each edict with another. The Germans even claimed the Jews of Scandinavia would not be included in their Final Solution. But by that time, everyone knew that was a lie."

PART II

"For the bee, honey is the ultimate reality. It represents the fulfillment of her life mission, the triumph over her enemies, the continuity of the hive, the justification for working herself to death. Honey is to bees what money in the bank is to people—a measure of prosperity and well-being. But there is nothing abstract or symbolic about honey, as there is about money, which has no intrinsic value. There is more real wealth in a pound of honey, or a load of manure for that matter, than all the currency in the world. We often destroy the world's real wealth to create an illusion of wealth, confusing symbol and substance."

—William Longgood, *The Queen Must Die*

SUMMER FRUIT
WITH HONEY DRESSING

If possible, get the ingredients at your local farmer's market. Food tastes better when you know where it comes from.

⅓	cup honey	2	cups melon cubes
⅓	cup lemon or lime juice	2	cups green seedless grapes
6	fresh mint leaves, finely snipped	1	cup fresh blueberries
		1	cup fresh pineapple chunks

Use a whisk or hand mixer to whip the honey until it turns thick and opaque. Add the lemon or lime, then stir in the mint leaves. Combine the fruit in a large glass or pottery bowl. Pour the honey mixture over and stir gently to coat. Serve immediately with a clear flute of sparkling water or Prosecco.

[Source: Original]

CHAPTER SIX

Copenhagen, 1940

"Here, let me fix your hair again." Magnus's mother licked the palm of her hand and smoothed it over his head. "This cowlick will not be tamed."

He gritted his teeth, enduring the grooming in order to get the picture taking over with quicker.

"Goodness," Mama said, "you're taller than me all of a sudden. When did that happen?"

"He's going to be taller than all of us," said Farfar, his grandfather, reaching out to straighten Magnus's tie. Even though it wasn't a Sunday, they were all wearing their Sunday best. The starched and creased collar cut into his neck.

Uncle Sweet had set up a big cube-shaped black camera on a tripod, its accordion-fold lens aimed at the apple tree in the backyard, where they were gathering for the family portrait. Sweet wasn't really Magnus's uncle, and Sweet's daughter, Eva, wasn't really Magnus's cousin. Yet Magnus had long known him as Uncle Sweet. His real name was Sigur, but everyone called him Sweet. Papa said they'd come up through school together as boyhood friends, the way Magnus was with Kiki Rasmussen, his best mate.

Sweet was a photographer, making his living by taking pictures of people and buildings. He used to have a studio and picture laboratory in Strøget, but he closed up shop soon after the Germans invaded Denmark and overran the city. Papa said this was because Uncle Sweet was Jewish.

"All together, now," he said, motioning Magnus and his parents and Farfar to their places under the tree. "You, too, Eva. How pretty you look, with those ribbons in your hair."

Unlike Magnus, Eva seemed to like getting all dressed up. She preened as she stood next to him. Then Uncle Sweet got into the picture, and fired the shutter with a button on a cable attached to the camera. He repeated this several times until he was satisfied.

"Good work, everyone," he declared, clapping his hands. He had a funny grin and dark hair that stuck out over his ears. Magnus had always thought he looked like a tall, skinny clown. "I'll go to the basement and process the plates. Eva, hang up your good clothes and finish putting your things away in your new room."

"Yes, Poppy." Flipping back her fat, dark pigtails, she followed him into the house.

Papa had explained to Magnus that Uncle Sweet and Eva had been put out of their house, and were coming to live with them. For safety's sake, they had to pretend they truly were family. The photograph was meant to promote the illusion. It would be displayed on Mama's pianoforte, along with the other family pictures.

"How long will they stay with us?" Magnus asked his mother.

"For as long as they need to, I would imagine." Her mouth turned down at the corners. "That poor little girl. I don't know what her mother can be thinking, abandoning her family."

Sweet had a beautiful wife named Katya, but Magnus had always thought her a bit strange. She rarely joined in the picnics and parties with Magnus's family, and she was always complaining that Sweet didn't make enough money. She loved pretty things and said he never bought her enough of them.

"Does that mean Eva's mother won't be coming to live with us?"

Mama looked as if she'd tasted something sour. "No, she will not. She ran off with a German officer."

"Why do you say she ran off?" he asked his mother. "Last week, Kiki and I saw her through the window of the Crown Prince tea room, and she wasn't running."

"It's just an expression," Mama said. "It means she no longer chooses to be with her family." Her mouth turned even harder and more disapproving.

"Because the German officer can give her fancy things so she would rather be with him," Magnus concluded, repeating a snippet of gossip he'd heard.

"As I said, I don't know what she must be thinking. Just don't speak of it in front of Uncle Sweet and Eva. It makes Eva very sad."

"I would never say anything," Magnus promised. He tried to imagine what it would be like, seeing his mother with some stranger, and a German at that. The very idea made his skin crawl.

Uncle Sweet had turned the basement into his workshop and laboratory. Magnus was fascinated by his collection of cameras, big and small, and by the workings of the darkroom. Sometimes Sweet would let him watch as he created a print, the image appearing onto the paper in the chemical bath, like a ghost emerging from another world. Most of the pictures commemorated life's events—marriages and birthdays, new babies and commencements. Some of his clients had their pictures made with horses or dogs, or surrounded by gardens.

As far as Magnus knew, that was the extent of his work.

He found out Sweet's secret one day not long before Christmas. The first good freeze had arrived in Golden Prince Park, and Magnus wanted to go skating with his schoolmates. His skates still fit, but the blades were dull. He clumped down to the basement to find the whetstone, bringing a lighted candle with him. They had an electric torch, but thanks to the war, batteries were hard to come by.

He shut the door behind him so his mother wouldn't complain about the draft. The smell of damp stone mingled with the sharp reek of Uncle Sweet's chemicals. Magnus set the candle on a shelf and looked around for the stone to sharpen his skate blades.

There were tools stored in a wooden chest under the stairs. He dropped to his knees to begin the search. At the same moment, the basement door swished open and then quickly shut, the movement blowing out Magnus's candle.

Three shadowy figures came down the stairs, lighting their way with an oil lantern. Magnus froze. He didn't dare breathe.

"Were you seen?" asked Magnus's father. *Speaking English.*

"Doubtful," said an unfamiliar voice. "And would it matter, when I'm dressed like your dotty old grandmother?"

"Can't be too careful," said Sweet, also speaking English. "The Germans are like watchdogs. They never sleep."

Magnus had been studying English in school since he'd been begun losing his milk teeth, and he understood it perfectly. Each night, they listened to broadcasts in English on

Farfar's shortwave radio. But what was an Englishman doing in the basement?

Magnus should have made his presence known. But it all happened so fast, and he was so startled that he simply froze, riveted to the spot under the stairs.

"If they never sleep," the stranger said, "then won't they catch on?"

"Not with the travel permit we're going to create for you," said Uncle Sweet. "You'll be able to go anywhere without being questioned."

Magnus poked his head up between the risers of the stairs in time to see the stranger take off his head scarf and shawl. He was a dark-haired man, his features in shadow. "How long have you gentlemen been with the Princes?"

Magnus pressed his lips together to stifle a gasp. The Princes were a shadowy organization of intelligence officers from the Danish army. Although nothing could be proven, rumor had it that the Princes regularly channeled reports to London, at great risk to themselves. The idea that his father and Sweet secretly worked for the group gave Magnus a thrill of fear.

"We have no knowledge of this group," his father murmured. "If we don't know the answer, then it can't be tortured out of us."

Magnus pressed his lips together even harder.

"Please, take a seat on this crate for the portrait." Uncle Sweet got his camera ready on a tripod and held the flash bar high up in the air.

"Hold still. Neutral face. Don't smile," said Magnus's father.

The flash fired, its glare shining on the man's face. He needed a shave. He wore a plain broadcloth shirt and dark colored pants. Sweet closed the black curtains around the darkroom and quickly went to work.

The stranger set a long flat wooden box on a pair of sawhorses and lifted out what appeared to be a firearm made of pipes. Magnus clamped his jaw to keep his teeth from chattering.

"Here it is," the Englishman said. "The STEN gun, as promised. British made, very simple and powerful. It will fire ten rounds per second. I'm told you can take it apart and make a draft of each individual piece."

Magnus's father nodded. He picked up a piece of the disassembled gun. "You see how this looks? It could be anything. A part for a clock. A mechanism for a tire pump. Taken bit by bit, a gun is unrecognizable. Even a trained eye would not know this is the trigger of a lethal weapon. On the sketches, each element will be measured and labeled as a sewing machine part."

"Sewing machine?"

Papa shrugged. "As I explained, piece by piece, the production drawings will look innocent enough."

"And you have a manufactory in place?"

Another nod. "Assuming the materials have been rounded up, we will have the resources to manufacture thousands of these."

"Good, then—"

"I would not call it good. But necessary in these times."

"Yes, of course. We're all aware of that."

Sweet drew back the curtain of the darkroom area. "The papers are ready," he said.

"Your identity papers will designate you an apple farmer," said Papa.

The man smiled, his eyes crinkling at the corners, and he looked pleasant, but nervous. "Back home in Shropshire, my family has an orchard," he said.

"Appropriate, then," said Uncle Sweet.

"You see, I'm not simply a courier of submachine guns,

but a farmer," the Englishman said. He seemed a bit defensive after Papa snapped at him.

"We all do what we must," Sweet said.

"And you've done this before," the man said. "I don't mean to seem ungrateful, but—"

"We understand," said Papa. "I promise, the document will be undetectable, even under scrutiny."

"How can you make such a promise?"

"I'm a civil servant," said Magnus's father. "I have access to all the tools." He brandished something that looked like an official stamp or seal. "Just use your common sense. It's a dangerous business we're in these days."

"No more dangerous than letting the Nazis take over all of Europe. The Germans are bringing in munitions for storage, knowing the Allies won't bomb Copenhagen. We can't allow the Nazis to turn your city into a satellite of their base of operations."

"Good man," said Uncle Sweet. He smiled briefly, but there was always a sadness in him. Magnus supposed it was because of everything he'd lost—not just his business and his home, but his wife. Even though she had done a terrible thing, Magnus knew Sweet missed her. Sometimes at night, Uncle Sweet would get into the aquavit from Farfar's cut crystal bottle, and he would lament that he should have taken better care of his Katya. Mama got short with him, and said Katya should have taken better care of her family.

"All right, then," said Papa, inspecting the document they had created. "You are officially an undercover agent. Not, of course, that there is anything official about it."

"Pray we stay that way," said the stranger.

"It will take more than prayers," said Papa.

The Englishman stepped into the light, and Magnus noticed that he had a deep scar angling from his jaw down the side of his neck. "Your help is appreciated," he said quietly. "I know what you're risking."

"No more than you are," Papa said, and Magnus felt a welling of pride in his chest.

"All right, then," said Sweet. "You can leave by the back door. There's a work barrow for you to use in tonight's operation. Good luck."

The three of them left the basement, their shoes kicking dust through the stairs. Magnus's nose tickled, and he held his breath, suppressing a desperate sneeze. They seemed to take forever to leave. Just as the door shut, he burst out with the sneeze.

The footsteps outside the door stopped. "Did you hear something?" asked Uncle Sweet.

There was a long pause. "It was nothing," Papa said.

CHAPTER SEVEN

"And that," Magnus told his rapt listeners, "is how I learned my father and his friend Sigur—my uncle Sweet—were involved in the resistance effort. It was quite a moment for me, finding out my mild-mannered father had a secret persona. Discovering his secret was like revealing Clark Kent's hidden identity as Superman. Very exciting. In my mind, my father went from being an ordinary civil engineer to a war hero."

"Your father claimed he wasn't risking anything more than the British guy was risking," said Tess. "That's not true, though. He put the whole family at risk."

Magnus's smile of memory disappeared. "Times were different then. Early in the occupation, life continued to seem normal for a time, so perhaps we didn't understand the risk. It wasn't until later that we grasped the danger and seriousness of the underground activities. In all, the Danes manufactured about ten thousand submachine guns, and many of those originated with my father's production drawings. He drew everything down to the last detail, and then mislabeled the parts in code so they would appear to be anything but weapons. For all the Jerries knew, the drawings were entirely mundane—parts for bicycles or sewing machines. The guns were then assembled in various places throughout the city—bicycle shops, small machine shops, pump repair facilities—under the pretext of being something else altogether."

Mac scrolled to a website on his laptop. "So these production drawings that were preserved by the Danish Historical Society were made by your father?"

"The ones labeled *Bruder Petersen*—Petersen Brothers—likely came from him. The Petersen brothers were two boy detectives in a series of novels we used to read as youngsters, so it was actually a nonexistent company." He studied an enlarged drawing on the screen. "This one is labeled 'rocker arm for pump relay.' In actuality, it is a STEN gun trigger. I assume that after my father drew, measured and labeled each individual part, someone else was in charge of the assembly."

Isabel exhaled a shaky breath, not even realizing she'd been holding it as she'd listened to the story. The tension her grandfather had described while hiding beneath the cellar stairs had been palpable.

On the table lay a few pictures of Magnus as a boy; she'd seen them before. He was tall and good-looking, neatly dressed and solemn, his eyes large and darkly fringed, making him appear almost too pretty for a boy. Yet as often as she'd seen the photographs, she had never quite been able to connect the teenage boy with her grandfather. Now the youngster came to life in her mind, a kid avidly reading a comic book, or looking forward to ice-skating with his friends, or crouched beneath the basement stairs, too frightened to speak up.

"That's such an extraordinary story. Why have you never told me this before?" she asked him.

He reached across the space between them, patted her hand.

"Life is long," he said. "I have so many moments to remember, large and small, and I haven't thought about that incident in decades. I suppose, considering what came after my discovery in the basement, it never occurred to me that this would be of interest to you. Or to anyone."

"Of course it is," Tess assured him. "Your father and his friend must have been incredible."

"I'm sure they regarded themselves as ordinary men, simply doing what was right in order to live with themselves. But yes, they were heroes in my eyes."

"In anyone's eyes," said Isabel. "I like to think I'd be that kind of person, the one who would dare to put myself at risk."

"Let us hope you never have to find out," said her grandfather. "I was very proud of my father, and I miss him to this day." Magnus's eyes looked into something distant and unseeable. "However, sometimes I can't help imagining how our lives would have unfolded if he had not embraced the cause. You see, many of our friends and neighbors simply kept their heads down and endured the occupation, then returned to normal routine after the war. Of course a big part of me, the part that desperately needed my parents and grandfather, wishes Papa would have chosen that path rather than risking himself. Risking the whole family, when it comes down to it."

"You're only human," said Tess. "Of course you wished that."

"Did you know what resistance group your father was affiliated with?" asked Mac.

"He wasn't with the Princes, since he was a civilian, although I believe he did identity work for them. There was a faction of the resistance known as the *Holger Danske*. It wasn't terribly well organized, but they got things done—underground activities, rescues, acts of sabotage. I believe that was his main connection."

Isabel studied the "family" picture taken by Uncle Sweet so long ago, angling it toward the fading light. Grandfather was just a gangly boy on the verge of becoming a man, yet he had a face she recognized. He was standing next to his own grandfather—the beloved Farfar, a distinguished physician and a widower. His mother sat in an old-fashioned tufted armchair, which looked incongruous in the outdoor setting. With a faint smile on her face, she was flanked by his pretend uncle and cousin, a slender girl with her hair in pigtails. She looked directly into the camera, her guileless expression heartbreaking to Isabel, because the girl in the photograph had no idea what would soon happen to her. Finally her gaze went to Magnus's father, Karl Johansen, who stood with one hand on his wife Ilsa's shoulder, comb furrows in his hair, his tie perfectly straight.

The idea that the Johansens had sheltered a Jewish man and his daughter made Isabel proud, too. Yet she could relate to her grandfather's wish. Suppose his father had done nothing to resist the Nazis. The family's entire future would have unfolded in a different direction.

Mac stood and checked out the photograph over her shoulder. "They were hiding in plain sight," he said.

Magnus nodded. "At first, I'm certain we—everyone—underestimated the danger. Reports of atrocities were just that—reports. Everyone found out about *Kristallnacht* when it occurred in 1938, but the world shrugged its shoulders. Most people believed the Night of Broken Glass was a disgusting spectacle, but an isolated event. The extent of the Nazis' activities was still not fully known. Look at us in that picture. None of us knew what was around the next corner."

"You look so much like your father," she said. "I'm sorry you lost him."

"I lost everything," Grandfather said, bracing his hands on

the chair arms and levering himself up. "I'm tired. I believe I'll go inside and read my paper."

Isabel exchanged a glance with Mac, who pocketed his phone and stepped back.

"Are you all right, Grandfather?" asked Isabel, going to his side. "Do you want me to help you?"

He gently touched her cheek. "I am fine," he said. "Fine. It's curious, the way reliving the past can be so draining. It will be good to be alone with my memories for a bit, and to get some rest."

"Are you sure? I can get you a glass of chamomile tea on ice, maybe a *honig kik*—your favorite cookies—"

"Such a worrier," he said with a chuckle. "How did I manage to raise such a worrier? I forbid you to hover. You stay here and entertain Mr. O'Neill. Theresa, you can help me inside. We will talk some more tomorrow, perhaps."

She stood and watched him go, with Tess walking slowly by his side. Though shrinking with age, he still had a proud bearing as he moved. Her heart was filled with love for her grandfather, yet there were questions, too. She knew the conversation was only one of many he would be sharing in the weeks to come.

Turning back to Mac, she said, "Just so you know, I'm not going to entertain you."

He grinned. "And I was so looking forward to that." He gathered up the photos and papers, tucking them into a clear green envelope with a string closure. "Your grandfather has quite a story to tell."

"I always knew it, but he never spoke of it in such detail, like the story he told about the basement. I worry, though. He's going to relive the loss of his family and lord knows what else."

"He'll let me know if it's too much for him."

Mac sounded very sure of himself. Isabel studied him in the rich golden sunshine, watching the play of light on his face, the breeze in his hair, his big hands as he gathered up his notes and gear. His dog-eared spiral-bound notebook was already filled with several pages of notes in his squarish, precise handwriting. She'd watched him writing as Grandfather talked; he seemed to have the ability to listen and compose simultaneously.

"Everyone knows people suffered during the war, but hearing him talk about things as he lived them really drove that home."

"He'll be okay. People process trauma in their own ways."

She thought about the few things Tess had told her about Mac's past, and wondered how he'd dealt with his own trauma. He was a widower. It was shocking to contemplate the idea that he'd been married, that his wife had died. In her mind, she'd always pictured a widower as someone like her grandfather, not a young, vital man who exuded sex appeal. Mac looked older than Isabel, but not much older. Maybe thirty-five to her thirty.

She wondered what had happened to his wife. Tess hadn't been able to answer that question, saying she'd never met the woman, but judging by her name—Yasmin—assumed she was foreign, perhaps Middle Eastern.

"Something wrong?" he asked.

She realized she'd been staring at him. Though tempted to ask him about his past, she felt the need to keep her distance. She barely knew the guy. "I'm... You seem pretty sure of yourself. Pretty sure he's going to be able to talk about these things."

He flashed a half grin. "Trust me, I'm a professional."

"That's what Tess says."

"Then trust *her*. She's your sister."

Isabel nodded. "Yes, but we haven't grown up as sisters. It's...complicated."

"I don't have a sister myself, but I've heard it's always complicated."

"Tess and I met only recently. Did she explain that to you?"

"She said neither of you knew about the other when you were growing up."

"We connected with each other when she came here a year ago, and she changed everyone's lives."

"Seems like Bella Vista—and you and your granddad—changed *her* life."

Her heart skipped a beat. "What a nice thing to say."

"Sometimes the truth is nice. A lot of the time, actually." He moved the wooden chairs out of the pathway. "Does this mean I'm forgiven for losing your colony of bees?"

"Never," she said.

"That's harsh."

"Oh, yeah, that's me. A harsh woman."

"My favorite kind."

"Really?"

He gave her a long, considering look. Then he said, "We'll see."

"How's your knee?" she asked suddenly. "Are you up for a short walk?"

"With you? Hell, yes."

She turned away quickly, pretending not to be flattered by his enthusiasm. "We can go to the top of that hill with the big oak tree. There's something up there that might give you some insights about my grandfather...and me. You might find it kind of grim, but it's part of the story."

"I can handle grim," he said simply.

Though tempted to ask him about the grim things he could handle, she'd save those questions for another day. She led the way up the slope, stepping over the ankle-high grass in the meadow, covered in budding lupine.

"It's the family plot," she said when they arrived. The rectangular area was west-facing, bathed in afternoon light and surrounded by a wrought iron fence. There were three simple headstones of weathered rock. Oscar Navarro, the caretaker, kept the grass mowed, though wildflowers were left to bloom around the stones—egg-yolk-yellow California poppy, purple sage and tiny delicate wild iris. Not far away was a spreading California oak, its long branches creating a broad shaded area. "See what I mean?" she asked. "Grim."

"It feels peaceful here," he said. "A resting place. And it's sad, yeah." He regarded the carved stones. "Your grandmother Eva, your mother, Francesca, and your father, Erik."

"The family plot," she said. "It doesn't really make me sad anymore. I don't associate this spot with the people I've lost."

"Still… Isabel, I'm sorry. Real sorry."

"Thank you. I never knew either of my parents, but my grandmother, Bubbie…" Even now she couldn't find the words to express how much she missed her. Sometimes when she closed her eyes, she could still feel Bubbie's hand expertly brushing and braiding her hair while singing a soft song in Yiddish about a cherry tree.

"You want to talk about it?"

"I don't know. When Tess first told me about this project, just yesterday, in fact, I didn't want to talk about anything."

"But now…?"

"It seems like something my grandfather wants. But his story is entwined with my own…" She bent and picked a sprig of sage, inhaling the savory scent of it.

"Then how about you tell me. Make me understand why

you don't want me here, asking personal questions about your grandfather, your family."

His frank request startled her, yet oddly enough, she didn't feel defensive. She chewed her lip, wondering if she could possibly trust him.

He regarded her thoughtfully, then lifted a hand, palm out. "Go ahead. I'm not here to pass judgment. Swear."

She couldn't tell if his reassuring manner was genuine, or a journalist's trick. *Please be genuine,* she thought. "As I said, it's a bit complicated. Tess and I are half sisters. We were born on the same day."

"That's cool. But how is sharing a birthday a complication for the two of you?"

"Not just the same day." She took a breath, cut her gaze away from him. "The same *year.* To different mothers who had no idea the other one existed. That's why we grew up apart. My grandparents raised me here at Bella Vista, and Tess and her mother lived all over the place, in big cities, mostly."

He folded his arms across his chest, and she watched him process the information. "Oh. Well. Unusual circumstances make for a good story, anyway."

"We're not just a 'story,'" she said, bridling.

"I get that," he said. "But I still don't see why it's a problem for you. Nothing you've told me is going to reflect badly on you. Or your grandfather. Your dad...maybe."

The tension she'd been holding inside unspooled just a little. Sometimes, when people heard about the unorthodox situation, they acted as if Tess and Isabel were somehow defective, having a rogue of a father who'd been careless enough to get two women pregnant, and then get himself killed in a mysterious car wreck.

Mac studied Erik's name, carved on the headstone, with a phrase:

Erik Karl Johansen, beloved son. Measure his life not by its length but by the depth of the joy he brought us. He jumped into life and never touched bottom. We will never laugh the same again.

"Our father was a bit of a rogue," Isabel said. "More than a bit. Sometimes I wonder what he might say in his defense. 'He jumped into life and never touched bottom,'" she read from the headstone. "I once asked Grandfather what he meant by that, but all he ever said was that Erik had a huge appetite for life."

"He gave the world two daughters. I can't imagine your grandfather would have any regrets about you and Tess. And after all this time, the fact that your dad was banging two women doesn't seem like much of an issue."

Had he really said *banging?* How very refined of him. "Has Tess told you anything else about Erik?"

"Nope. Something tells me your sister is preoccupied with other things these days."

"The wedding. I love that she's having so much fun with it."

"I never took her for the marrying type."

"Really?"

"She was such a go-getter. Always seemed married to her career."

"That was what she was like when I first met her, too," Isabel agreed. "Now she's going to be a wife and a stepmother, and probably a mother one day. I suppose it just goes to show you—love can change everything."

"Very nice," he said. "You're a hopeless romantic."

"No, just a keen observer." She suddenly felt uncomfortable under his gaze. "So about Erik—our father. One thing you're bound to find out from Magnus is that my grandmother, Eva—Bubbie—was not Erik's birth mother."

"He was adopted?"

"Yes. Grandfather is very open about it—lately. But for the longest time, no one knew." Isabel took a breath, then said in a rush, "Grandfather was his birth father."

"Oh. So he was—"

"Please don't say 'banging' again," she said. "He will have to be the one to explain, and you'll have to figure out how it fits into the story you're writing. Erik's birth mother was a woman named Annelise Winther."

Mac said nothing, just stood there, his arms still crossed. She couldn't help but notice how good he looked in a white T-shirt and jeans, his coloring deepened by the sunset. Finally, he asked, "Is she still living?"

"Yes. She lives in San Francisco."

"Do you know her?"

"Thanks to Tess, I do now. Annelise is another survivor from the war years in Denmark," Isabel explained. "She and my grandfather knew each other during the war. She's actually...kind of wonderful. I'm hoping to get to know her better."

"So you're saying this woman had a baby, and Magnus and Eva raised him."

"They did. We figured it out last year as we were going through old records and learned Bubbie could never have children. It was all a huge secret at the time."

"That sort of thing was a bigger deal back then."

"True. Now Grandfather wants it all out on the table, for my sake, and for Tess. You're going to have to ask him what sort of arrangements they made in order to pull it off, because it seems they were very careful. Even the Navarros— they've lived and worked at Bella Vista for decades—claim they never knew."

"And let me guess. Tess had a hand in figuring all this out."

She nodded, feeling a flicker of surprise—at herself. She was giving up information like a singing canary. There was something about the intent way he listened that made her want to talk. Another reporter's trick? Or was he actually a good listener? A rare trait in a guy.

"Tess is very good at research," she continued. "In all the mountains of old family papers and records, she came across a medical file from the 1960s. From that, we figured out that Eva could never have children." Isabel's heart filled with sympathy for her lost grandmother. She could too-easily picture Bubbie as a hopeful young wife, getting the news that she had uterine cancer and needed a hysterectomy. In one cruel moment, the news would have taken away any dreams she'd had of having babies of her own.

"How much is it going to bug your grandfather when the subject comes up?" asked Mac.

She thought about it for a moment. "Ever since his accident last year, he's been adamant about telling us everything. He seemed almost relieved when Tess and I asked about Erik's birth mother."

"Ah. Then you're thinking it's going to bug *you*."

Ouch. "Bubbie was the only mother I ever knew. To find out, after all this time… I'm still getting used to the idea. And now it feels very strange that you plan to publish this whole story about my family. I keep trying to convince myself it's not disrespectful." She stared down at Bubbie's headstone, wishing she could feel her presence once again, hear her voice, listen to her sing the cherry song one more time.

"In my experience, people are more comfortable with the truth than any lie," said Mac. "Eventually."

She leaned down and plucked a dockweed from the base of one of the stones, and then started down the hill toward the house. "I realize that. The fact that my grandfather had a baby out of wedlock is a key part of his story. I don't understand why he did what he did."

"Have you ever asked him?"

"No."

"You should. It's remarkable how much you can learn simply by asking."

"Good point, but try asking *your* grandfather to explain something like that."

"No, thanks. My granddad was a Freudian analyst. He probably would have liked the topic way too much. I never really knew my other grandfather. He owned a pub in Ireland, died when I was a little kid."

"And the Freudian grandfather?"

"Total nut job, but he was a good listener."

So are you. The thought crossed Isabel's mind, taking her by surprise. "My grandfather has always been big on loyalty," she said. "You'll see that as you get to know him. When I found out about him and Annelise, it totally threw me off. It was hard to imagine Grandfather betraying his wife. He was—he's always been—my moral compass."

"Whoa. That's a lot to ask of someone."

"True. I'd hate to be someone's moral compass," she admitted.

He held open the wrought iron gate leading to the courtyard. A visceral hip-hop tune was playing on the workers' radio. "I bet you'd be pretty good at it, Isabel."

Her head snapped up as she passed through the gate in front of him. "You don't know me."

"No," he said, his voice like the breeze, a soft caress. "But I want to."

PART III

One week after she emerges from her cell, the queen bee leaves the hive to mate with several drones in flight. To avoid inbreeding, she must fly a certain distance away from her home colony. Therefore, she makes several circles around the hive for orientation, so she can find her way back.

She leaves by herself and stays away for thirteen minutes. In the afternoon, hovering twenty feet above the earth, she will mate with anywhere from seven to fifteen drones. If foul weather delays this crucial mating flight for more than three weeks, her ability to mate will be destroyed. Her unfertilized eggs then result in drones.

HONEY LAVENDER LEMONADE

The best honey comes from a source you know, and is processed without heat. Raw, unfiltered honey retains its royal jelly, bee pollen and propolis—three major sources of antioxidants, vitamins and minerals.

1	cup of locally produced, raw organic honey	1	cup fresh squeezed lemon juice
2½	cups water		Additional water, about 2 cups
1	tablespoon dried culinary lavender		Ice cubes or crushed ice

Combine honey and 2½ cups of water in a saucepan and bring to a boil, stirring to dissolve the honey. When the mixture reaches a boil, stir in the lavender and remove from heat. Let the mixture steep for 20 minutes.

Strain the lavender from the liquid, then add the fresh lemon juice and an additional 2 cups of water. Use sparkling water if you wish. Pour into glasses full of ice and serve, garnished with a sprig of lavender or mint.

[Source: Original]

CHAPTER EIGHT

"Isabel? Someone's here to see you." Ernestina Navarro stepped into Isabel's study, a small space tucked into an alcove near the main kitchen. One wall was lined from floor to ceiling with bookcases crammed with cookbooks, which she'd been collecting ever since she was a little girl. The other walls were pinned with pictures she'd collected as inspiration for the renovation, and with lists and ideas for the upcoming wedding. There was a needlepoint sampler from an old family friend with the phrase "Live This Day" embroidered in the middle.

Isabel looked up from the mood board she'd been studying for far too long. The day after her uncomfortable conversation with Cormac O'Neill, she had escaped into work. But she couldn't escape her own thoughts. He had a way of saying things that stuck with her, turned over and over in her mind as she speculated on the meaning.

You don't know me.

No, but I want to.

Focus, she commanded herself. There was plenty to be done, anyway. The task in front of her was to study the mood board in order to pick colors and finishes for the two guest suites at the end of the second-floor hallway. Only a year ago, she'd had no idea what a mood board was. Now she was intimately familiar with the device, used by designers to present options for colors, textures and patterns. Isabel discovered that she could look at mood boards all day, and still not make a decision.

The designer in charge of the guest rooms at Bella Vista offered far too many choices. Should the upholstery be navy graphic or ecru abstract? Sandy-brown or celery-green on the walls? Wrought iron or glass sconces? And that was just for one of the suites. Isabel found it all bewildering, though she knew the details were important.

"Thanks," she said to Ernestina, and swiveled to face her computer screen. She typed a quick note to the designer, telling him to go with the navy, the sandy-brown and the wrought iron. *There,* she thought, pushing back from the desk. *Done.* "Who is it?"

"Jamie Westfall."

"Oh, good. The beekeeper." Sliding her feet into sandals, she made her way down the hall to the main entryway. It was too bad he hadn't shown up in time for the whole swarm drama. But it was springtime and there was still plenty of work to be done.

She stopped in the foyer, startled by the sight of her visitor.

Jamie Westfall was a woman. A very young woman. With tattoos, short, razor-cut, purple streaked hair...and what was almost assuredly a baby bump. The girl was long-legged and thin, wearing tight shorts and a Queensrÿche T-shirt stretched over her protruding tummy.

"Hi, I'm Isabel," she said, mentally regrouping. "I sent you a message the other morning."

"Yes." The girl offered a fleeting smile and ducked her head. "Sorry, I didn't see it in time to help you out."

"That's all right. The swarm got away. But I've still got some overcrowded hives that need to be divided, and I'm quickly finding out that I'm in over my head. I'd love to get your advice about my hives."

"Sure, I can try to help you out." She seemed soft-spoken, almost bashful in contrast to her hair and tattoos.

"Let me get you something to drink, and then we'll head out to the hives. I've got a pitcher of lavender lemonade made with Bella Vista honey."

"Sounds great. Thanks." The girl looked around, wide-eyed, her gaze skimming over the surroundings of the foyer—a rustic table set against the wall, where eventually a guest book would go. Above that hung a large mirror Tess had found at a flea market, and on the opposite wall hung the main focus of the space—a stunning, mission-era scene painted by Arthur Frank Mathews. It was an original. Isabel didn't even dare ask Tess about its value. She was certain the number would stress her out.

"Um, could I use the restroom?" asked Jamie.

"Yes, of course. It's just there, down that hallway." Isabel pointed. "Take your time. I'll go get the lemonade."

As she went to the kitchen and poured the drinks, Isabel readjusted her mind around the beekeeper. She'd been expecting a guy with a battered pickup truck plastered with Ag Extension stickers. Not a teenage pregnant girl.

Setting out some honey shortbread cookies to go with the lemonade, she flashed on memories of her grandmother, offering refreshments to anyone who was lucky enough to come through the kitchen door. As a working farm, Bella Vista was always busy with workers, some seasonal and others permanent. *In my kitchen, everyone is family,* Bubbie used to say, beaming as the orchard workers, mechanics or gardeners gladly wolfed down her baked goods.

Knowing now what she did about her grandmother, Isabel wondered if there was a broader meaning to Bubbie's pronouncement.

Jamie came into the kitchen and set down her frayed army-surplus messenger bag. She looked scrubbed now, the hair framing her face damp. "It's really beautiful here," she said, looking around the kitchen. "What a nice place."

"Thanks. I've lived at Bella Vista all my life. I went away briefly for school, but... I had to cut it short, and ended up right back here." Isabel often felt awkward, explaining that she'd never been anywhere. It made her feel incomplete, somehow. She handed Jamie a glass of lemonade. "Should we go take a look at the hives?"

"Sure."

The girl's car was parked in a graveled side lot next to Cormac O'Neill's Jeep. Jamie's old hatchback had definitely seen better days. The passenger door was marred by dents like unhealed bruises, the spots primed with putty-colored Bondo. The front seat held a battered guitar case secured in place with a seat belt. The back dash was crammed with clothing and a couple of rumpled pillows. Overflowing cardboard boxes covered the back and passenger seats. One large crate was filled with empty canning jars.

"I'm, uh, kind of in transition," Jamie said. "Haven't really settled in yet."

"Oh!" Isabel flushed, knowing she'd been caught staring. "Settled...you mean you're just moving to town?"

"That's right. I'm hoping there's enough work locally to keep me busy."

"Well, I think you're going to love Archangel. And I can keep you as busy as you want to be, because I've got big plans for Bella Vista honey. The hives are over there, on that east-facing slope by the milkweed."

"Great," said Jamie. "Milkweed's the best."

"I was thinking it might be too windy and exposed over there."

Jamie slowly turned to study the area, shading her eyes as she surveyed the orchards and gardens, the stone-built outbuildings, the patios and arbors. "This is really nice," she said. "I don't think wind will be a problem here."

Isabel felt a welling of pride. Bella Vista really was that beautiful, and the renovations were designed to enhance the setting to create an irresistible destination.

"I'm glad you like it. It's been a busy year for me, but I don't want to give up on my bees, so I'm hoping you'll take on the project."

"That's why I came," said Jamie, surveying the view.

"I'm launching a farm-to-table cooking school, and honey will be one of our key ingredients. Over there—" she indicated the long green meadow with a pathway connecting the patio to the stone and timber barn "—that's the event space. The barn's been converted into a hall for banquets and dancing. My sister's getting married this summer. Our first event."

"Cool," said Jamie.

"Needless to say, there's honey on the menu. That's Tess's theme for the whole affair. All the planning is fun, but tons of work."

She saw Jamie's attention turn to an oak tree in the meadow, its branches spread as wide as it was tall. There, Magnus sat in the shade with his new constant companion. Mac was seated backward on the chair, his arms folded over the back as the old man talked. After getting together just a few days before, the two of them were already inseparable. It was gratifying, and maybe a little unsettling, to observe the fast-growing intimacy between the two men. "My grandfather. And our houseguest, Mac. A guy who's working with him on a project."

She wondered what they were talking about. Mac seemed so easy and affable in Grandfather's company. Yet judging by her conversation with him yesterday morning, she had concluded that he was not a morning person. Come to think of it, he wasn't particularly an afternoon or evening person. Maybe he was cranky all the time. She'd already resolved to keep her distance and let him get on with the Magnus project. She had enough on her plate. But she couldn't deny that Mac was distracting. Very distracting.

"My grandfather's always been really good about letting the milkweed grow," she said. "He's never considered it a blight like some growers do."

This time of year, the purple blooms were busy with life—not just the bees, but butterflies and ladybugs, skippers and emerald-toned beetles, flitting hummingbirds and sapphire dragonflies. The sun-warmed sweet haze of the blossoms filled the air.

"When I was a kid," said Isabel, "I used to capture butterflies, but I was afraid of the bees. I'm getting over that, though." The bees softly rose and hovered over the flowers, their steady hum oddly soothing. The quiet buzzing was the soundtrack of her girlhood summers. Even now, she could close her eyes and remember her walks with Bubbie, and how they would net a monarch or swallowtail butterfly, studying the creature in a big clear jar before setting it free again. They always set them free.

As she watched the activity in the hedge, a memory floated up from the past—Bubbie, gently explaining to Isabel why they needed to open the jar. "No creature should ever be trapped against its will," she used to say. "It will ruin itself, just trying to escape." As a survivor of a concentration camp, Bubbie only ever spoke of the experience in the most oblique of terms.

A dragonfly hovered in front of Jamie. She put out a hand and it alighted, gently fanning its wings.

"My grandmother used to warn me that a dragonfly would sew up your lips if you said a swear word," Isabel remarked.

Jamie offered a fleeting smile. "Did it stop you from swearing?"

"Gosh, yes, are you kidding? I still watch my mouth."

"I don't. I probably should." The dragonfly on the back of her hand darted off. "Is there water nearby?"

"Angel Creek. It flows across our property and the neighbor's—Dominic Rossi. He's going to become my brother-in-law this summer. He's great—a grower and winemaker."

The girl squinted at Isabel. "You married?"

"No. Happily single." Her standard answer. "You?"

"Oh, hell, no." She smoothed a hand down over her belly. "It's just the two of us."

The girl hardly looked old enough to be having a baby. "That's exciting. Congratulations."

"Thanks. Needless to say, this wasn't planned. I'm still trying to get used to the idea." She watched a bee struggling in the blossoms, buzzing furiously as it tried to extricate itself. "I used to try to free them," she said, watching the weathered bee's tattered wings. "But they always dive right back into the stickiness and get stuck again. They can't resist."

The girl moved from hive to hive, lifting the occasional lid, seemingly lost in thought. "Judging by that swarm you described, you have some overpopulated hives. I can split them for you."

"I would love that. I've been reading up on how to do it. The process seems complicated."

"It's not, but you need to know what to look for. You have to pick the right frames to move to the new hive, and you have to find the queen to move with them. And then you can't put a new queen in too soon. I like to wait three days. Sooner than that, and the other bees might kill her."

"Yikes, really?"

"It happens. But after a few days of being queenless, they'll accept a new one. It's all about the timing."

"Great. I'd love to get your help with this. What's your schedule like? Do you have time to work here?"

"I have tons of time," Jamie said. "I haven't gotten many calls for my services and I've been thinking I might have to move on." She watched a small cluster of bees as if mesmerized. "I'd love to help you."

"Do you think I should move that row of hives closer?" Isabel gestured at the row of pastel-painted hives in the distance.

Jamie lifted her chin, her nostrils flaring slightly as she seemed to sniff the air. Isabel noticed a slight shadow on the underside of her jaw. A smudge of dirt? A bruise? Maybe just a shadow. "You're good right here," Jamie said. "I like where the hives are." She tipped back her head and took a long drink of her lemonade. Isabel studied the spot on her jaw again, but this time, Jamie caught her. "Something wrong?" she asked, wiping her wrist across her mouth.

She hesitated, not wanting to pry. Sometimes, though, prying was called for, she decided, thinking about her own experience. Back when she was Jamie's age—the girl looked to be nineteen or twenty—having someone ask the right questions might have changed everything for her. "Looks like you hurt yourself."

Jamie's fingers—the nails embedded with dirt—gently skimmed the spot on her jaw; obviously she knew just what Isabel was referring to. "Nope," she said, and rattled the ice cubes in her glass.

Then who did? But Isabel didn't ask that. They'd only just met. She had a feeling about Jamie Westfall. She wanted to get to know her better. "Let's go back to the house." As they started walking, she asked, "So why bees?"

"I grew up near Chico. I worked on a berry farm when I was in high school, and there were hives. I started working them and never looked back. It was kind of like falling in love, even though I don't think I've ever been in love. All I know is I would wake up every day, and I couldn't wait to check the hives. Then I got into harvesting and processing the honey. I started selling organic honey at farmer's markets, and that's been it for me ever since."

Isabel could relate to the light she saw in Jamie's eyes. Passion for a pursuit was the best feeling. "Kind of like falling in love" was a good way to put it. Although, like Jamie, Isabel had never been in love before, even though she had once deceived herself into thinking she had been.

"And now you're looking to make a go of it in Archangel."

"That's the plan. I, uh, I sing a little, too, and play guitar."

Isabel led the way back into the kitchen. "I'd love to hear you one of these days. I'm sure we can work something out. Where do you live, Jamie?"

There was a beat of hesitation. Two beats.

It took only that long for Isabel to connect the dots—the crammed car, the rumpled clothes, the exhausted, unwashed look of her. The girl was homeless.

"I haven't actually found a place yet." Jamie put her glass in the sink and washed her hands, slowly and luxuriously, as though savoring the warm water and lavender soap.

"Yes," Isabel said, not allowing herself to pick apart the decision. Her gut was telling her what to do. "You have."

Mac sat straight up in bed, chased by a nightmare. "We had a deal," he heard himself saying, "a deal, motherf—" He stopped talking to the nightmare and slammed himself back down on the pillow. He was drenched in sweat, the cold clammy residue of panic.

His head was foggy with images he wished he couldn't see. People often said they envied him, having a job that gave him the freedom to travel the world, taking pictures and writing articles and books, taking pictures of things most people would never get to see. But freedom had its price. In pursuit of a story, sometimes he was forced to look into the face of hell, to see and hear things that made nightmares seem like fairy tales—like watching his wife murdered in cold blood.

He took another breath, reminding himself to concentrate on the here and now—a sunny room in a beautiful house, rich smells emanating from somewhere downstairs, the sound of…singing?

Yeah, someone was singing. And making breakfast. He was definitely not in hell anymore. He tugged on a pair of shorts and brushed his teeth, then grabbed his cane and wandered down to the kitchen to find the source of the singing.

The kid on the barstool, strumming a guitar, was a ringer for a younger, more tattooed Alanis, with a raspy, soulful voice and an unhurried touch on the strings of a battered acoustic guitar. Magnus was seated in a flood of morning sunlight at the end of the kitchen bar. Nearby, Isabel was creating something with grilled bread and a pan of eggs poaching in tomato sauce. It smelled incredible.

"This could turn me into a morning person," Mac said, walking across the kitchen. The saltillo tile floor felt cool and smooth under his bare feet. "I'm Cormac O'Neill. Mac."

The girl put aside the guitar. Despite the hair and the tats, she had a timid look about her. "Jamie Westfall," she said.

He recognized the name. "The beekeeper."

"I thought Mac was you when he first showed up," Isabel said, placing a slice of grilled bread in a shallow dish, and serving up the eggs and tomatoes. She had an artless, graceful way in the kitchen. Mac could watch her all day, a woman in her element. "The name Jamie threw me off," she explained to the girl. "One egg or two?"

"Two," Mac spoke right up.

Isabel shot him a look. "Ladies first."

"None for me," Jamie said apologetically. "Maybe a piece of toast with honey. I...don't have much of an appetite in the morning."

"I'll have hers," Mac volunteered.

"It smells delicious, Isabel," said Magnus.

"Can I help?" Mac asked.

Isabel's look softened. "Set the table?"

"Sure." He found the silverware and a supply of napkins.

"Jamie has agreed to stay at Bella Vista and work here," Magnus said. "We officially have our own beekeeper."

"Jamie's going to oversee the honey production, too," Isabel said. "She thinks we'll have plenty for the cooking school, and a surplus for Tess's shop."

"An on-site beekeeper and resident musician," Mac said. "I like it here more every day."

"Bella Vista has always housed its workers," Magnus continued as if he'd sensed the question Mac didn't ask. "*Los piscadores* are vital to the orchard's success, and we make sure the housing for guest workers is top-notch."

Jamie offered him a bashful smile. "I appreciate it. I love my little cottage."

"It's yours for as long as you care to stay," Magnus said. He tucked a napkin under his chin. "Isabel, thank you for this delicious breakfast. Eat up, Mr. O'Neill. We have a lot of matters to discuss today."

"I've enjoyed our rambles so far," Magnus said, leading the way through a long section of the orchard. "It appears I have more to say than I originally thought."

"Most people do," Mac said. "Memories are like a series of locked doors, and once you manage to get one open, it leads to another, and then another and so on. The hard part is finding the key to that first lock and getting through it."

"You're rather wise for a young man," Magnus said.

"I've done my share of dumb things." He felt a twinge, thinking about his next assignment after this one. He had made a promise to explore and investigate his worst mistake, and there was no getting out of it.

"As we all must, I suppose," said Magnus. "How else does one learn wisdom?" He pointed out a row of painted shotgun-style cottages set shoulder to shoulder down one side of the orchard. A couple of them had cars parked behind them and laundry pegged out on clotheslines. "The guest worker housing is down there. When I first came here, there was no electricity or indoor plumbing. These days, they're quite comfortable."

"Isabel gave me a bit of history about her father."

"Did she now?" Magnus picked up his pace, his cane thumping on the ground. "I wish she'd had a chance to know Erik. He was my heart, right up until the moment he shattered it. I miss my son every day, but then I see glimpses of him in his two daughters. It's a sadness, yet this has only made me look deeper to find the joy." He paused to watch a bird circling the meadow. "Some days, it's hard to find."

"I'm very sorry."

"He came to Eva and me after we had given up the dream of having a child," Magnus said. "I gather Isabel explained that Erik was adopted."

"She did."

"His birth mother, Annelise Winther, is a wonderful woman, her generosity beyond comprehension. Our arrangement was…unorthodox, to say the least."

Mac would like the old man to say *more,* but he didn't

push. Often, the most important part of a conversation was the waiting.

Magnus flexed his hand on the head of the cane, the fingertips gripping its rounded head. It was a working man's hand, strong and rough, now spotted with a patina of age. "Sometimes I wonder if losing Erik was a punishment. And then, of course, I must dismiss this thought. Things happen as they are meant to happen. There is no grand plan, just flawed human beings bumbling through life."

He turned abruptly and led the way along a gravel track to a humble-looking stone and timber building with several bays and rolling doors. Flowering vines climbed up the crumbling stone walls. Inside, the sweetish smell of motor oil and old rubber hung in the air. The sunlight through the windows illuminated several work bays and an impressive array of equipment and vehicles. Somewhere, a radio was playing classic rock, and swallows nested in the high rafters. There were a couple of cluttered desks, a long wall and bench of tools that could make a grown man cry.

"Fantastic. It's every guy's dream to have a place like this," Mac commented.

"I knew you'd like my machine shop. In my younger days, I would be banished here for my nightly pipe."

"These days, it's called a man cave."

"It was once a barn, which accounts for the height of the rafters. My foreman runs the place. We don't do as much work here as we used to. When I came here right after the war, the nearest mechanic was in Petaluma. We learned to fix everything on our own or do without. Back in Denmark, I developed an aptitude for mechanical things."

Mac made a mental note to ask about that later.

"I've been accused of hoarding by my late wife, and lately by my granddaughters," Magnus said. "The habit is hard to break. During the war, I had little more than a knapsack filled with a few keepsakes and scavenged possessions. Once I settled here, I found it hard to let anything go. The habit has served me well enough. I've always got the right tool for the job."

Mac spent a long time poking through the dusty, oily wonders in the shop. There were tree shakers, catchalls and trailers, tractors and mowers in different sizes, conveyer carts and bin carriers, parts and supplies old and new.

Then, in an out-of-the-way, cluttered corner that looked as if it hadn't been disturbed in a long time, he spotted a big shape shrouded in a dusty padded canvas tarp. "What's that back there?"

Magnus hesitated. He removed his glasses and polished the lenses on his shirttail, then put them back on. "Something I haven't thought about in decades. If you can make your way back to that corner, you're welcome to take a look."

Mac cleared a path between the crammed shelves and repairs-in-progress. A wall calendar from 1984 gave him a clue that Magnus hadn't exaggerated about the decades. He lifted a corner of the tarp, folding it back to reveal an ancient scooter. "This is a Vespa," he said, intrigued.

"Indeed, it is. The scooter belonged to Francesca—my son Erik's wife."

"Isabel's mother, right?"

"Yes. Francesca was the loveliest girl you can imagine."

Mac was silent, checking out the scooter from stem to stern. Judging by the shape, the placement of the headlamp and some other details, it was a model from the fifties. "This is cool. I worked at a Piaggio shop in New York when I was in school, so I know a bit about them. Do you know where it came from?"

"She had it shipped from Italy. She was born and raised in

a little hill town there, and when she met Erik, she came to America to marry him—against her family's wishes."

"Why against their wishes?"

He shrugged. "They must have been old-fashioned, very traditional Catholics. Erik's mother—my Eva—was a Jew. Francesca spoke very little of the break with her family. She never received letters or calls from anyone, so we didn't pry. But she did say the scooter had belonged to her father. That would account for it being so old. It ran quite well, though, and Francesca kept it in good repair. She used to drive it to the farmer's market and come home with the wicker panniers filled with produce."

An appealing mental picture popped into Mac's head—a young woman with bare suntanned legs and long hair, puttering into town on the scooter. In his mind's eye, the woman looked just like Isabel.

"And you've kept it all this time," he said to Magnus.

"I always intended to keep it running, and to eventually give it to Isabel. Eva wouldn't allow it, though. She claimed it was too dangerous."

In light of what had happened to Erik, that was understandable, Mac thought.

"Eva and I never would have survived the loss of Erik and then his wife, two days after his death, if it hadn't been for Isabel. She became our reason for living." Magnus touched the handlebar of the scooter, pressing the button, which of course made no sound. "These days, I find myself wondering if I protected Isabel from too much."

Mac reflected on his rough-and-tumble childhood with his brothers, being moved all over the globe as their parents' assignments changed. He'd enjoyed a decided lack of supervision, which sometimes led to trouble.

"I brought her up as best I could," Magnus said. "I gave

her love, but did I teach her to live? No, she will have to discover how to do that on her own. She has found a measure of happiness here at Bella Vista. But she is not at home in the world. I was too preoccupied with protecting her from it."

Mac brushed the dust off the leather seat of the scooter. "I'm sure you did a great job," he said. "The rest is up to her. It's never too late to make a change."

As evening gathered in a lavish orange sweep across the orchard, Mac spread his handwritten and typed notes on one of the long tables in the central courtyard. It was impossible to stay inside in weather like this. He wasn't used to the almost unreal perfection of the climate here, the palpable sweetness of the air, the utter quiet disturbed only by the songbirds and sighing breezes. He was more accustomed to the grit and smog of cities, the hot air filled with the sounds of chugging engines, honking horns, shouts and sirens. Even the rural areas he'd seen lacked the special silence of Bella Vista. The places he'd visited, many of them in developing nations, were filled with the grind of generators, the sounds of squabbling families and barking dogs—day and night.

In the initial stages of any project, he always reminded himself to approach the story with a beginner's mind. Despite the insistence of English teachers through the ages, he never came up with a theme first. Who the hell knew what the theme was until you did the work? Instead, he organized his thoughts around a timeline, knowing that if he did the hard, honest work of getting the narrative down, word by word, the real story would emerge.

He was already seeing glimmers and flashes of Magnus Johansen's theme—endurance and commitment, a habit of holding on to things, like that scooter, which was a classic diamond in the rough if Mac had ever seen one. The more he talked with the old man, the closer he would come to the essence of all that had transpired.

"This is the contractor's work table," said Isabel, crossing the patio toward him. Charlie, the German shepherd, trotted at her side, and the two cats slipped along in her shadow.

"Uh-huh," said Mac. "Everyone's gone for the day. I didn't figure they'd mind."

She pursed her lips in that way she had, making annoyance look sexy. "If you need more space to work, there's a foreman's office down there." She gestured at a distant building down by the main road.

"I don't. I just like being outside. Look where you live. Jesus, it's a piece of heaven." The wildflowers in the surrounding fields had closed their petals for the night, and an owl swooped across the meadow, already on the hunt.

"You think so?"

"Hell, yeah. You've got apple orchards and fresh air, a doting grandfather, a smart dog and two unusual cats that follow you around. Oh, and honeybees, let's not forget that. If you suddenly burst into song, then I'll know I'm watching a Disney movie."

Her pursed lips softened into a smile that became a small laugh. "No danger of that. I never sing where someone might hear me. But thank you for thinking my dog is smart and that Chips and Lilac are unusual. I'm sure they'd take that as a high compliment."

"You're lucky to live here."

"I think so." She stood looking out at the landscape and buildings silhouetted against the sky. "That barn over there— when I was about eight years old, I made a pair of wings out of cardboard and duct tape and jumped from the hayloft, convinced I could fly."

"Bet that didn't end well."

"I landed in a pile of loose straw. Once they figured out I wasn't hurt, there was hell to pay. That barn is now called the Ballroom. It's our event space for weddings, gatherings, farm-to-table dinners, reunions…. Tess's wedding is the first event."

"You think big," he said. "I like that."

Her smile widened, and she approached the table. "When the project is finished, I think this part of the garden might be a favorite gathering place for the guests. At the bottom of the stone stairway, we're building an outdoor shower."

"Everybody loves an outdoor shower. But you're missing a key item."

Crossing her arms over her chest, she scanned the area again, and then scowled at him. "Missing what?"

"The swimming pool."

"But there's not—"

"I noticed. A glaring omission. You need one."

Her frown turned to worry. "A pool? That wasn't in the plan…"

"Kidding," he said. "Sort of. Who doesn't like a swimming pool?"

"Darn it," she said.

"What?"

"Now I totally want one."

"Then you should have one."

"I like the way you think. A swimming pool. Sure, what's another hundred grand?"

"Wouldn't know. I never saw the first hundred grand." What would he do with a sudden fortune? Probably what she was doing, building a dream. Except his dream looked a lot different from hers. She was dug in here for good. He couldn't imagine staying in one place for more than five minutes, let alone his whole life.

"I feel very fortunate, being able to create the cooking

school. I imagine Grandfather told you Bella Vista was on the brink of foreclosure, until Tess came along and worked her magic. Except it wasn't magic. It was just knowing what to look for, and where to look."

"Yeah, your granddad says it's his favorite part of the story."

"It was amazing to suddenly find myself without any financial worries," she said. "Sometimes I can't believe it's true."

"It must have changed your life."

"Well, yes and no. I've never wanted more than I have—friends and family, Bella Vista, my cooking."

"You didn't run out and buy a fancy car or boat?"

"Is that what you'd do?"

He grinned. "Yeah, probably."

"You would not."

"Hard to say. I've never found myself in your position. Come on, tell me how you spoiled yourself."

"I had a brief flirtation with a pair of Hey Lady shoes, but I'm much too practical for four-inch heels. Besides, I've always been focused on practical matters. Something…respectful, to honor my grandparents' heritage."

"That's cool. I still think you should get the shoes, though. Not to mention the pool."

She took out her smartphone and tapped the screen. "A swimming pool. I can't believe no one suggested it."

"The landscape designer didn't propose it?"

"No, and it's a wonderful idea. I'm adding one to my wish list."

"You have a wish list?"

She glanced up, and the soft smile on her face did funny things to his insides. "Sure. Doesn't everybody? Don't you?"

"No. Not on my phone, anyway."

"But you *wish* for things, right? You hope and plan?"

"Things? You mean like a Leica camera, or my favorite nail clippers the TSA confiscated at the airport?"

"Very funny. Anything."

"Lady, the things I wish for can't be provided by a contractor with hairy armpits."

She narrowed her eyes at him. "You don't like talking about yourself, do you?"

Bingo. "What else is on your list?" He took the phone from her hand.

"Hey, give that back." She grabbed for it, but he held it out of the way, teasing.

"You really do have a list," he said, glancing at the screen. "That's cool."

"It's none of your business. Give it back."

"Let's see—swimming pool, wood-fire pizza oven, solar panels for charging the electric Tesla, endowment for the nonprofit foundation? For what?"

"That's also none of your business, but it's no secret. I'm setting up a scholarship program so aspiring culinary students can study here at no cost."

"Nice. I like that." He scrolled down the screen, all the way to the bottom. "Everything on here is for the cooking school. Don't you want, like, Botox or designer earrings?"

"Thank you for trivializing me. Are you saying I need Botox?"

"I heard it works on frowns."

"Hey—"

"Ravello," he read from the screen. "As in Ravello, Italy?"

She put her hands on her hips and looked into the distance. "It's where my mother was born."

"How come it's the last thing on your list?"

"Because in case you haven't noticed, I'm busy getting the

cooking school ready and planning my sister's wedding. I barely have time to get a haircut, let alone travel to Italy."

"Why would you need a haircut? Your hair is gorgeous." She was rooted firmly in the soil of Bella Vista. The wedding, the cooking school, creating a vibrant community at the estate— this was her future, and it was all happening right here.

She blushed—*blushed*—and touched her long, thick braid. "Bees tend to get tangled in long hair."

"You just hired a beekeeper. So you don't need to worry about the bees anymore."

"I *like* dealing with bees."

His welts still itched, days later. "Then what is *she* here for?" He gestured at the distant slope where the hives were set amid the grass and milkweed. It was twilight, the sky a rainbow arch of deep pink and purple, the beekeeper a slender black silhouette as she moved among the hives. "She didn't have much to say to me this morning. In fact, she seems to have that raging-tattooed-chick thing going on."

"Do raging tattooed chicks scare you?"

"No more than angry bees."

The girl was using a smoker to calm the bees, and against the sky, the puffs of smoke from the funnel turned to pink wisps. "She's splitting the hives. Mine are overpopulated, and that causes swarming. I'd take you over and show you, but I suspect you want to keep your distance from the bees."

"Good guess."

"Even though I just met Jamie, I have a good feeling about her. She needed a place to stay, and I offered her room and board at Bella Vista for as long as she needs it. I'm hoping she's the perfect person to work the hives and take over the honey production."

"You've taken in two strays in the same week," he commented. "Not to mention those cats of yours. Is this a regular habit with you?"

She made a lingering study of him, and he liked the touch of her gaze. "Depends on the stray," she said.

"Got it. So, back to this list." He consulted her phone again. "If Italy was on *my* list, you can bet it wouldn't be at the bottom."

"You said you didn't have a list."

"I don't write stuff down. That doesn't mean I don't have a list," he said, then deflected the topic back to her. "What's Ravello like? I've been to the Amalfi coast, but haven't made it up the cliffs to Ravello. I've heard good things." All of a sudden, it was incredibly easy to picture the famous hill town with its cobblestone plazas, old men smoking in front of the *farmacia,* the pottery shops hanging out their wares, the smell of lemons everywhere. It was even easier to picture himself on a Vespa like the one Magnus had shown him in the machine shop, with Isabel behind him, that long hair streaming in the breeze. Yeah, he had a list. He carried it around in his head everywhere he went. Maybe he'd tell her about it one day.

She set her hands on her hips and looked out at the distance. "I couldn't tell you what it's like. I've never been to Italy."

He was sure he hadn't heard right. "Wait, what? You've never been…?" Impossible. Italy was one of those places in the world everyone should visit. "Well, that's just wrong. I have no idea how you can keep yourself from going, especially since there's a family connection."

"Not much of one. It's just a place my mother left, a long time ago. My grandmother told me she came to Archangel with my father after knowing him only six weeks. Her family rejected her because Erik wasn't Catholic. No one from the Italian side of the family came to the wedding." She sighed, and he had a crazy urge to kiss the sadness from her eyes.

Her story was consistent with what Magnus had told him. "No accounting for the way people can be," he said.

She nodded. "Bubbie liked to think they would have reconciled after I was born, but with Francesca gone, I suppose it must have been too painful for them. When I was a girl, I used to wonder if my Italian relatives ever thought about me, if they might want to meet me one day. Maybe if my mother had lived, she might have reached out to them and reconnected." She absently twirled a finger in a lock of her hair. "The answer to that is just...lost."

"You could reach out," he suggested. "Nothing should stop you from going there whether you go in search of your family or not. Italy's awesome. My God, the food, the people, the wine, the landscape... Damn. It's magic. You have to go."

She led the way back to the house, walking quickly and purposefully. "I'm not much of a traveler. I don't even have a passport."

"Seriously? Okay, now *that* needs to be on your list." He quickly typed it into her phone.

Pausing on the patio, she looked up at him with a scowl. "Since when are you in charge of *my* wish list?"

"Since you said you wanted to go to Italy and you don't have a freaking passport."

"Let's let that be my problem, shall we?"

"It doesn't have to be a problem at all. Just get a damned passport."

She tossed her head, showing off that long, pretty braid. "You're very exasperating."

"And *you*—"

"What are you two bickering about?" Magnus walked over to them with a tray of small glasses. "Bickering is not a good pairing with port wine. This is an old vintage. Appropriate for our project, no?" He set down the tray and lifted one of the small, stemmed glasses. "Cheers. To a beautiful evening in springtime. To a remembrance of the past, and to a dream of the future."

Magnus took a seat at the table. The evening light spread over the surrounding orchards and gardens, turning the stucco walls of the villa the color of fire.

Mac felt slightly sheepish as he lifted a glass and touched its rim first to Magnus's and then to Isabel's. With her, bickering felt pleasantly like flirting. Then he reminded himself that flirting was fine, but with a girl like Isabel, it was a dangerous game. There was something about her that made him wish they were a better match.

CHAPTER NINE

"When I woke up this morning, I realized I'd been dreaming about chair tiebacks," Tess said, coming into Isabel's teaching kitchen with Dominic, her fiancé.

"What are chair tiebacks?" asked Dominic. "And why do I sense they're important?"

Isabel, who was on a ladder inspecting the position of an overhead mirror, shared a look with her sister. "Chair tiebacks are one of the ten thousand style choices Tess has to make for the wedding."

"Is it something I can help with?" he asked.

Isabel came down the ladder. "Doubtful, unless Tess is going to be happy with plaid or camouflage."

Tess showed him a set of photos in the wedding planner's massive binder. "Behold—chair tiebacks."

"Without which, the wedding will be a disaster," he said with a grave expression.

Tess shot him a glare and he backed away, palms facing out. "I just remembered, I've got work to do at the winery. See you around, Isabel."

As he strode away, Tess called after him, "Chicken."

"That's me. Later, babe." He waved, and then hurried off.

"Am I being a bridezilla?" Tess asked Isabel. "Tell me I'm not being a bridezilla."

"Of course you aren't. You're being stylish. Bella Vista is going to look incredible, and I totally support your obsession with having everything exactly as you want it." She set down a colander full of freshly picked plums—the first of the season—and started polishing them, one by one, checking the overhead mirror, which was a key part of the teaching kitchen. The mirror would offer guests a bird's eye view of the cooktop island, with its commercial gas burners and large prep area. "So, have you had a chance to visit with Jamie?"

"Ah, our resident beekeeper. I had tea with her this morning, and we walked down to the shop. She's a bit bashful."

"Was I too impulsive, inviting her to stay without asking for references?"

"Probably. But something tells me it's going to be fine."

"She's pregnant," Isabel said. "And homeless. Did you talk about that?"

"No, but I have a feeling you'll be discussing that with her."

Isabel nodded. "She seems kind of lost. I'm guessing she isn't getting prenatal care. I know we just met, but I already feel responsible for her."

"Ah, Isabel. You're totally cool, you know that?"

"I'm not cool. Just…responsible."

"Well, let me know if I can do something to help." She showed Isabel a picture. "I like the organza tiebacks. They're pretty and ethereal."

"Lovely. I think those are the ones."

"Me, too. And hey, can we invent a signature cocktail for the wedding, using honey?"

"I'm working on one made with honey syrup, apple juice and calvados. Garnished with an apple slice, of course."

"Really? Isabel, that sounds fantastic. I can't wait to see what you come up with. But seriously, you *have* to tell me when I've overstepped and strayed into wedding hell."

"Just enjoy being the bride. You deserve it."

Tess beamed. "I'll tell you what I *don't* deserve. You. And Dominic. And this life we're about to start together. How did I get so lucky?"

"Was it luck?" Isabel asked.

"You're feeling lucky today?" asked Mac, coming into the room. In age-worn shorts and a slightly rumpled T-shirt from a surf school in Bali, he looked relaxed and casual, as if he already belonged here. He stole a plum from the bowl and started eating it—very slowly.

Isabel's heart skipped a beat.

"I'm lucky every day," said Tess. "Don't get me going on how excited I am about my wedding. I'll start being so sweet, you'll slip into a diabetic coma."

"You? Sweet?" He finished the plum and used his T-shirt sleeve as a napkin. "Since when? I don't remember you ever being sweet."

Tess sniffed. "People can change. All it took was finding my soulmate. Simple. And don't roll your eyes. I used to be a skeptic, too. When the right person comes along, you'll see what I mean."

"Tess." Isabel shot her a warning look. Tess knew the guy was a widower. Why would she make such an insensitive comment? Suppose he'd already found his soulmate, and then lost her?

"I'm just saying." Tess lifted her shoulder in a defensive shrug. "Look, when I first came here, there was no one—and

I mean no one—more cynical than I was. Now I'm so crazy in love, it's ridiculous."

"A walking, talking greeting card," said Mac.

"And proud of it."

"I'm happy for you," he said. "It'd be great if what you've got is contagious. But it doesn't work that way."

You're right, thought Isabel. She had read the rest of the "What To Do When He Doesn't Notice You" article and had come to the conclusion that she was not the target audience for that sort of advice. She didn't actually want to be noticed, not in that way, not by Mac or anyone else. She had other things to do. At least a hundred other things.

She went to the walk-in pantry to fetch some dried cardamom for tonight's dessert. There was one shelf that was too high to reach. At some point, someone—probably Bubbie—had created a display of family photos—shots of Bubbie, pictures of Erik as a boy, red-haired and smiling, having no clue about his fate, even a rare photo of Francesca in a pretty dress that looked as if it had been designed by a real couturier.

When Isabel was little, she used to make up conversations with the people in the photos, asking young Erik which trees were his favorites to climb, or seeking advice from Francesca about how to braid hair. She remembered gazing into that flat, frozen face, looking for the person inside. Her mother had a very small, round mole at the crest of one cheekbone, and Isabel used to wish she had one, too. Bubbie recalled that Francesca was left-handed, and Isabel had always taken pride in being left-handed, as well.

Her gaze lingered on the photos a moment longer; then she returned to the kitchen and said to Tess, "So, I told Mac about Erik's birth mother."

"Well, he'd need to know that, wouldn't he?" Tess said briskly. Having never known Bubbie, she was more philo-

sophical about the drama of their father's parentage, and probably saw things from a different perspective.

"Grandfather has never had much to say about the situation," Isabel told Mac.

"Perhaps because you never asked," said Magnus, joining
them from the main house.

Isabel whipped around to face him, her hair flying. She
knew she should probably bow out at this point, but then she
found herself saying, "I've never been good with awkward
conversations."

Mac took another plum from the bowl and bit into it. "I
am," he volunteered. "I'm good with them. I'll ask any awkward question you want."

Charming, Isabel thought.

"What shall we discuss today?" Magnus asked. "Eva, perhaps?"

"Sure," said Mac.

"Very well. We can talk in the lounge room," Magnus suggested. He glanced at Isabel and Tess. "You're welcome to join
us, my girls. Perhaps you'll get some answers to the questions
you're so reluctant to ask."

"I'm not sure I'm ready to hear about your complicated ro-
mances," Tess said.

"Romance is simple," Magnus said, a twinkle in his eye.
"*Life* is complicated. But I suppose that is something we all
find out on our own, yes?"

Isabel had a busy day lined up for herself. In addition to
working with the contractor, she hoped to spend more time
with Jamie, who was constantly busy with the apiary, divid-
ing the hives and creating new ones. The teaching kitchen
was still a work-in-progress, and her web designer was coming for a meeting. They were going to search for a photographer to shoot photos and video for the cooking school website.

Yet she found herself following them to the lounge. She had

vivid memories of her grandmother here in this high-ceilinged room. Bubbie had been a great reader, and she would sit for hours, lost in a book, the light from the tall arched windows falling over her.

Isabel was burningly curious about what her grandfather might have to say about his long marriage, filled with love and tragedy and secrets he'd only recently begun to disclose.

Mac set his phone in record mode and took a seat on the sofa, stretching out his long, lean legs as he flipped through his notes. He massaged his knee with both hands.

"Feeling better?" asked Grandfather.

"Yeah, thanks. I don't need the brace anymore."

"Wonderful. You'll be good as new in time for the wedding."

Mac lowered his gaze, but not before Isabel saw a flash of doubt in his eyes. He intended to be gone well before the wedding; he'd made no secret of that. She hoped Grandfather didn't become too fond of Mac's company.

"So, then," said Mac. "You were married for fifty years. Lucky man."

Grandfather nodded. "My Eva. It is hard to remember a time in my life when I didn't know her." He picked up their framed wedding portrait from the mantel. They were impossibly young, posing stiffly for the camera. Magnus looked strong and proud, Eva delicate, shrouded in an old-fashioned veil that framed her deep-set eyes and controlled smile. Knowing what her grandmother had survived during the war, Isabel imagined a haunted quality in the young bride's expression.

"There is nothing I wouldn't do for her," said Magnus. "I loved her deeply."

Then why did you betray her? Isabel wondered. *Why did you father a child with another woman?*

"However," Magnus continued, setting down the portrait, "it didn't start with love. It started with a promise I made."

PART IV

On the first day of foraging in a new area, scout bees are sent out first to taste the nectar and pollens. If any are adversely affected they will be expelled from the hive immediately, and the colony will avoid the area.

In addition, once foraging begins, nurse bees in the hive clean foragers each time they return. These strategies protect the colony from mass exposure to…any contaminants they encounter.

—Soil Association [www.soilassociation.org]

PIERNIK

Piernik is a moist, sweet honey bread that is delicious served toasted with a bit of butter and a cup of tea. Thanks to the intense spices, the bread has a long shelf life.

It's an old Polish tradition to bake piernik to welcome the birth of a baby girl. The loaf is then buried underground to preserve it. The bread would be brought out and eaten at the girl's wedding.

These days, this is not recommended.

½	cup of soft butter	3 to 3½	cups flour
1½	cups honey, warmed in a pan or in the microwave	½	cup of vegetable oil
1¾	cups of sugar	6	eggs, separated
1	tablespoon ginger	1	tablespoon cinnamon
1	teaspoon cloves	1	teaspoon nutmeg
2	cups of dried fruits and nuts: raisins, candied orange peel, walnuts, dried apricots, dates, etc.	1	cup of dark beer
		2	teaspoons baking soda

Beat together the butter, oil and warm honey. Add the egg yolks one at a time. Beat in the sugar and spices. Then add the beer, baking soda and flour alternately. Finally, fold in the beaten egg whites and fruits and nuts.

Bake in buttered loaf pans for about an hour, until the tops begin to crack and the cake tests done.

Yield: 3 loaves or 6 mini-loaves.

[Source: Traditional]

CHAPTER TEN

Copenhagen, 1941

"Poppy says we have to go away," Eva said to Magnus, coming out to the kitchen garden where he was doing chores. His mother had set him to weeding. Since the Germans had taken over the year before, food supplies were scarce, and Mama was determined to have a good yield of tomatoes and beans this year.

"Yes," said Magnus, thinking about the secret goings-on in the basement.

"Why do we have to go?"

He didn't think she knew about the secret. Maybe his mother didn't know, either. After the incident he'd witnessed in the basement, Magnus had snooped and discovered that Uncle Sweet and his father were deeply involved. They made a good team. Papa went about his business, going to the office every day with his leather satchel and his bowler hat, returning home at suppertime to read the newspaper, question

Magnus about his day and give his wife an affectionate hug. Then he would settle down with his "cousin" Sweet and little Eva, ending the day with a satisfying meal.

Now Magnus knew there was more to him than that. His father—quiet and reserved, never one to make waves, was an underground hero.

"Your father and my father don't trust the Germans to leave people alone," he told Eva.

She picked up a stick and poked it at one of his mother's three willow skeps.

"Hey, stop it," Magnus said. "You shouldn't disturb the bees."

"I'm not disturbing them. I just want to see."

"They don't know that. If you bother them, you might get stung."

"I saw your mother getting the honey out. She didn't get stung."

"Because she knows what she's doing," Magnus said, exasperated.

"Where do the bees go in winter?" she asked.

"They don't go anywhere. They just stay in their hives. All the worker bees cluster around the queen bee for warmth."

"How do they know when it's springtime and they can come out?"

"They can tell when the outside temperature heats up. You can get them to come out by carrying the skep to a warm place, but it's not a good idea. You don't want them coming out unexpectedly. If they think the hive is under threat, they'll attack."

"Oh. I'll leave them alone, then."

Magnus wished she would leave *him* alone. Instead, she leaned over his shoulder as he dug out a weed. "What's censorship?"

"It's when people aren't allowed to read the truth," Magnus said. "The Germans have been censoring the newspapers to hide what is really going on in the world."

"Papa says the truth can't be hidden, not for long. It always comes out." She watched a cluster of bees around the entry of one of the hives.

Magnus wondered if she was thinking of her mother, who never called or came to see her anymore. He worked in silence for a while, grateful that his own parents were loyal to each other, and brave enough to open their home to Uncle Sweet and Eva.

"Papa told me we don't go to temple anymore because the Germans hired some thugs to set fire to the synagogue," she said.

"Yes, they couldn't censor that news because people saw it happening."

"The local police stopped them. The police are on our side, aren't they?"

"Yes."

"Then why do we have to leave Copenhagen?"

"Because the Germans might take over the police, and then we won't be so safe."

Eva plucked a dandelion that had gone to seed. Forming her lips into a perfect O, she blew the tiny seeds into the wind. "I don't want to leave," she said, bending to pick up another dandelion head. She blew the seeds again. "I like it here. I like you."

Hearing her words made him feel a little funny inside, pleased and embarrassed all at once.

She picked a third dandelion and puckered her lips.

"Hey, cut that out," said Magnus. "You're spreading weeds."

"It's beautiful, the way they float on the breeze," she said, watching the flurry of seeds. "Like thousands of tiny umbrellas. Or parachutes, more likely."

"All I see is a silly girl spreading weeds in my garden."

"They're like tiny paratroopers," she said, watching the seeds with a thoughtful expression. "The paratroopers land behind enemy lines, don't they? Poppy says that's what they do, down where the fighting is."

"So I've heard."

"The Germans want all the Jews dead," she said bluntly, her voice expressionless.

His stomach clenched into a knot. "Who told you that?"

"I heard Poppy talking about it to your father. He said he tried to convince my mama to come away with us, but she doesn't believe him. She says if she's nice to the Germans they'll be nice to her."

Magnus stabbed the spade into the earth, digging out a dockweed. He had no comment about being nice to Germans.

"I'm scared," Eva said.

He had no reply to that, either. He couldn't tell her not to be scared. He couldn't tell her she was being silly, because for once, she wasn't.

"If something happens, will you take care of me?" she asked baldly.

He had no idea how he could do such a thing, but she looked so worried. "I'll do my best," he said.

"Promise?"

"Yes."

"Forever and ever?"

"Yes."

"Good. That makes me feel better."

It shouldn't, he thought. The truth was, he felt as scared as she did. Promises were easy to make, easy to break. But he meant to keep this one.

★ ★ ★

The garden flourished that summer because Magnus's mother was determined to feed her family despite the depredations of the distant war. In the fall, there were beans and tomatoes and pickles to can, and jar after jar of applesauce. Mama's hives yielded fresh honey, and then willow skeps were winterized. The bees would not come out until the air warmed and the sun appeared. Some days, he could believe life was normal, but then he would wander out and see something—a stupid decree pasted on a bus kiosk, a Jewish business abandoned and boarded up—and he would remember the country had been invaded.

Just after Christmas, Uncle Sweet and Eva disappeared. Magnus woke up one gray, chilly morning to a house that was preternaturally quiet. He tiptoed into the room Eva and Sweet used to occupy. It was bare; the two turned-wood bedsteads and washstand empty, the cupboard where they kept their things empty.

"Where is Eva? Where's Uncle Sweet?" he asked his mother at breakfast.

She served him a bowl of porridge and stewed apples. "Off to a safer place. They had to get out of the city. The… authorities…" Her voice trailed off. Her mouth was set in a grim line. "These are difficult times."

"Where did they go?"

"I don't know. I truly don't. It's best if we don't ask."

Something in her tone raised goose bumps on his skin. He thought about something he'd overheard in the basement. *If we don't know the answer, then it can't be tortured out of us.* "When will we see them again?"

"God only knows." She held him close, just for a moment, for three heartbeats, perhaps. Then she smoothed his cowlick with her hand and followed it with a kiss, something she did every day. She smelled of floral cologne and of cinnamon from her baking, a comforting scent.

Magnus tried to eat, but he had no appetite. He kept thinking about the promise he'd made to keep Eva safe.

For the next few days, he could hear his parents at night, their worried murmurs a constant hum in the house. Something was happening, something bad.

Then one icy night, when he was out in the back getting wood for the stove, the Germans came. Magnus could hear them inside, their heavy boots stomping through the house, harsh voices questioning. Huddled in terror, he listened to the ransacking of his house—the only home he'd ever known. Instinct kept him hidden; he wondered if they'd found his father's materials in the basement. He waited, crouched in the dark, until the noise subsided. The grinding gears of a truck filled the air. Then he forced himself to wait some more, and he went in.

The house had been ransacked. Valuables, liquor, food, everything. The Christmas tree lay on its side, its candles setting fire to the drapes and furniture. Coughing, he grabbed the hidden cache of valuables his parents had stowed under a trapdoor beneath the parlor rug, and then he ran.

His friend Kiki Rasmussen took him in for a time. They shared a room, and sometimes it seemed like fun, staying the night with his best friend, whispering secrets in the dark. But most of the time, Magnus felt choked by the hot lump of tears in his throat, and he would bury his face in a pillow and cry until he felt as if everything had drained out of him. Kiki's parents went to the *Hauptsturmführer* and demanded to know where the Johansens had been taken, but no one would tell them. Rumors rushed like a winter storm through the city.

People were taken away, families torn apart, homes ruined by the German invaders.

On a bone-cold January day, Magnus walked across the bridge over Sankt Jørgens Sø, a city lake favored by ice-skaters. He had no interest in skating, though, as he trudged toward the center of the city. The Nazis had set up barriers made of sawhorses wrapped in barbed wire, blocking off the side streets near the bridge, which channeled traffic down the main boulevard, making it easy for Magnus to blend in. He wore his school uniform and a plain wool coat that was too large for him, a hand-me-down from Kiki's older brother. His green knitted cap was warm, but scratchy. All of Magnus's clothing had been ruined in the fire.

Behind him, he pulled his old bladed sled, the one he and his father used to coast down the slopes in Golden Prince Park. On the sled was a heavy box tied up with a bit of string. The chunky ice and partially exposed walkway were sure to dull the blades, but Magnus didn't care.

His gut burned with a fury so hot, he scarcely felt the cold as he approached the building, once the headquarters of the Royal Dutch Shell company. Now the entire place housed the *Geheime Staatspolizei*—the Gestapo. The outside walls were painted with gray and green blotches to camouflage it from British air raids, and there were helmeted guards in long overcoats stationed at the U-shaped opening.

Though it was barely three in the afternoon, darkness crowded down from the winter sky, and the windows glowed with lights from within, offering a deceptive warmth. He could see offices and conference rooms through the windows of the building. Some of his friends' fathers used to work at *Shellhus,* but it was all different now. These days, the place was overrun with uniformed foreigners on a mission to keep the

Danes from disrupting their war effort. It was no secret that they used any means necessary, including torture.

Magnus couldn't bear to think that his parents might have been brought here, tortured here. He stopped on the sidewalk outside the building and watched a room filled with German soldiers having a meeting, as they did each afternoon since Magnus had started covertly watching the place. They all looked very serious as they shuffled through papers and smoked fancy, machine-rolled cigarettes. On one wall, a cheery fire burned in a fireplace, lending a warm glow to the scene.

Someone bumped him from behind, and he nearly stumbled over the sled. Holding its rope tighter, he turned. "Excuse me," he said, regarding a street sweeper. The guy scowled at him, his unshaven face grim, his gray canvas coveralls stained. He reeked of aquavit and stale cigarettes. He had a twig broom and long-handled dustpan filled with bits of trash.

"Watch yourself, boy," he said, whistling through the gaps in his teeth. He jerked his head in the direction of the *Shellhus*. "Nothing but trouble that way."

Magnus sidestepped the guy and walked boldly up to one of the guards stationed at the entranceway. "I have a delivery for Colonel Achtzehn."

The helmeted soldier fixed him with a stony look. "Leave the parcel here. It will have to be inspected."

An inspection. Magnus hadn't counted on that. "It's a gift from my school," he said, offering a bright-eyed, eager look. "The Jeanne d'Arc School, where he gave a historical presentation on Friday. May I be allowed to deliver it in person?"

"Let's have a look." The soldier used a utility knife to cut the string of the box and lifted the flaps. "What the hell is that?"

"Honey from the garden," Magnus said. "It's a great delicacy. It should be taken inside immediately before it gets ruined by the cold."

"I'll deliver it myself," the guard said.

This wasn't working out the way Magnus had planned it. "Yes, but—"

"Off with you, boy. I'm sure Colonel Achtzehn will send his compliments to the headmaster." He picked up the box and strode into the courtyard.

Magnus stared after him until the other guard made a shooing motion. "Go on with you, then."

Magnus dragged the sled away, passing the street sweeper, who was swirling his twig broom around the gutter. Rounding the corner to a car park, he ditched the sled. Then he scurried across the road, blending in with shoppers and school kids and office workers dodging traffic. With a quick motion of his hand, he took off the green cap and let it drop behind a bus stop. Retrieving the school knapsack and brown cap he'd left in a doorway, he went on his way. He had an urge to linger and try to catch a glimpse of the meeting in the *Shellhus,* but he didn't dare, in case they came looking for him.

Ahead of him was the bridge over the lake. It was nearly dark now, and the crowd was thinning. For the first time since he'd approached the *Shellhus,* he dared to exhale a long sigh of relief. He realized his heart was pounding crazily. He was shaking, and not just from the cold. And for the first time since his parents had been arrested, he felt a small, tight smile—more of a smirk—curve his lips.

When he was just a few steps from the bridge, a large, gloved hand clapped over his mouth and an arm wrapped around him from behind with such force that Magnus lost his breath. He felt himself being dragged behind the wood and barbed wire barrier, into the recess of a doorway. He struggled and tried to scream. His assailant smelled of aquavit and tobacco, and the cold reek of winter.

"Settle down, you," said a voice that was rough with fury. It was the street sweeper's voice. "Don't you make a sound, or I'll slit your throat, don't think I won't. Understand?"

Magnus nodded his head vigorously. He couldn't make a sound anyway; he was too scared.

"I saw what you did," the guy said.

"I… I didn't do anything," Magnus protested, his voice quivering. He wasn't going to cry. He'd cried enough tears for his family. Some smelly old street sweeper wasn't going to make him cry.

"That's a lie," the man said. "I watched you, and then I watched what happened after. Saw it all through the window." He turned Magnus around, digging a thumb into his upper arm. "There was a *beehive* in that parcel you delivered."

Despite his fear, Magnus felt a stab of pride. It had been his mother's best hive, housed in a woven straw skep with an opening at the bottom. Under dark of night, he had sneaked back to the Johansen family home, and had taken it away.

"Do you *know* what happened when the hive was brought into the office?"

Magnus hung his head. "No."

"Would you like me to tell you?"

Magnus said nothing, knowing the man was going to tell him, anyway. He wondered what the punishment was for getting caught at such a prank. When it came to the Nazis, you never knew. He'd heard a rumor that in Germany, they shot people just for going to temple.

"I'll tell you what happened, you foolish little scamp. The bees poured out of the hive in a huge swarm."

"Sir, that is because the warm air brought the bees out, and they sensed the hive was under attack."

"People got stung. There was a mad rush for the door. It was insanity for a while."

Magnus kept his head down, this time to hide a smile of triumph.

But the street sweeper saw. "You think this is *funny?*"

Magnus snapped his head up and glared at the man. "I think they deserve worse than being stung by bees. I'm just getting started."

The man gasped, and Magnus realized he'd said too much. But his fear had turned to defiant anger.

"Then you'd better listen to me, and listen closely," said the street sweeper, grabbing the front of Magnus's shirt.

He tried to wrench away, but the man held fast. "Why should I listen to you?" Magnus demanded.

"Because I know what I'm doing. If you intend to perform acts of mischief against the Nazis, at least do something that counts." He pushed Magnus away with a contemptuous shove.

Magnus gaped at him, digesting this advice. "I beg your pardon?"

"You heard me. You think you're the only one who doesn't like living under German rule? You're not alone in wanting to disrupt the Nazi war effort—by any means necessary."

"You mean…you're against the Germans, too?" Magnus asked, amazed and relieved.

"Any self-respecting Dane is," said the man. "But don't waste your time and effort with child's play. A *beehive*. What if you'd been caught today? You'd have been locked up forever, and for what? So a few stupid Gestapo officials could get stung by bees?"

"It's…like I said. I'm just getting started."

"Then it's time you learned how to do some real damage."

CHAPTER ELEVEN

"And that," Magnus said to Mac and Isabel, "is how I met the Teacher."

Mac was blown away by the story. He scribbled several questions on the list he was keeping, because he knew there would be many. His literary agent had promised the scope of this project would reach beyond an old man's memoir. He couldn't wait to hear more.

"The street sweeper was a teacher?" asked Isabel.

"No, that was his code name. I never knew him by anything else. For security, no one used their actual name. So this man was the one who brought me into the resistance. And although he wasn't a teacher, I learned much from him. He showed me how to hide in plain sight, how to use hot weapons and cold weapons, how to handle dynamite and set homemade bombs."

"Hot and cold weapons?" asked Isabel.

"A hot weapon is one that fires or ignites—a gun or incendiary. Cold weapons are made of metal or wire. Not the sort of thing a schoolboy learned in class, but I probably owe that man my life. He taught me to fight back, and he taught me survival tactics." Magnus took off his spectacles and pinched the bridge of his nose. "Later that year, the Nazis gunned him down. I witnessed the incident and barely escaped with my life."

"You saw a man being murdered?" Isabel whispered the question.

He nodded. "I wish I could tell you it was the only time. Before his death, he gave me shelter and did his best to locate my family. But I never saw my parents again, though I refused to stop looking high and low. My grandfather—my beloved Farfar—was gone, too, and to this day, I've never known his fate. Kiki's family said I could live with them, but I didn't want to put them in danger, and I knew I would, because I was committed to the resistance effort. I lost my childhood that year. I never felt like a boy again."

"I'm sorry, Grandfather," Isabel said. "I wish I could take the terrible memories away from you."

He patted her hand in a way that made Mac's heart lurch. "You do, my darling. Every day."

Mac could tell Magnus was exhausted. The old man's shoulders slumped a little, and the lively light in his eyes had dimmed. "Tell you what," Mac said. "How about we take a break here?"

"Yes," said Magnus. "I'd like that. I think I shall listen to some music."

Isabel handed him an iPad and set of headphones. He opened the music program and tapped an icon, looking up with a slight smile. "Whoever thought it could be so easy to hear a Carl Nielsen symphony?"

"Is he a favorite of yours?"

"Indeed, a native born Dane. When I hear the music, I

can picture the old country with perfect clarity—the islands and the meadows, the light and the chill air of the forests and farms. There is nothing quite like the bracing scent of the sea on a cold, clear morning."

"Did you ever go back for a visit?"

"No. When I left, I knew it would be forever. There is nothing back there for me, nothing but memories, and they stay with me wherever I go."

"I'll have someone bring you a mug of tea," said Isabel. *"Alt vil være okay,"* she told her grandfather, garnering a look of surprise from Mac.

"Ja, jeg ved." Magnus nodded and gave her hand a pat, then put on the headphones and closed his eyes. Mac walked outside with her.

"You could tell he was tired, couldn't you?" she said.

"Sure. Sometimes just sitting still can be exhausting, when you're reliving times like that."

"Yes, emotionally exhausting. It's too easy to forget he was just a young teen when his family disappeared and he joined the underground. Dredging up all this trauma can't be good for him. It's exactly what I was worried about when you came here for this project." She lifted her chin, sent him a challenging glare.

She had no idea how sexy she was when she looked at him like that.

"Listen, the last thing I want to do is upset the guy. If it's having a negative impact on his health, I'm out of here."

"Really?"

"Hell, yeah, really. I don't make a practice of tormenting my subjects."

"So…if you thought it was bad for Grandfather, you'd abandon the project. There would be no book."

"Correct." He watched her digest this information. It was

kind of heartbreaking, seeing how torn she was. He had a crazy urge to touch her, pat her hand or her shoulder or… something.

"But he wants this. He wants a record of his life."

"I can make you this promise. I'll write it well. I'll write the truth and I'll be respectful about it. He's been living with his memories whether or not he's spoken of them out loud. You heard what he said—they're always with him."

"Do you think it's *good* for him to talk about it?"

"Does he seem like he's going to drop dead when he talks to me? No. He's a sturdy old guy, Isabel. Tess told me he survived a head trauma last year, so I don't think a trip down memory lane is going to do him in. He's a grown man. If he changes his mind about doing this, he'll tell me."

She nodded, appearing to concede his point. "But the more he tells us, the more confused I get."

"Sounds as if you're the one who's bothered by all this digging into the past, not your grandfather."

Her gaze skated away. "I'm not bothered. Just…confused. He loved Eva, but then there's the whole question of Erik's mother."

"Annelise Winther," Mac said. "The birth mother. I'd like to meet her."

She glanced up at him. "I imagine you will. She comes to visit sometimes. She and Magnus reconnected after his accident last year. She'll be here for Tess's bachelorette weekend."

"Seriously?"

"She's the world's oldest living bachelorette."

"So what's a bachelorette party like? I've never been to one."

"Because it's girls only. Food and presents—the sillier and the prettier, the better. I love giving parties." She offered a shy smile.

Again, he had the urge to touch her. She was just…delicious

to him. He couldn't understand it. He'd never felt so drawn to a woman—her scent, her soft curves, the curls of hair framing her face, the fullness of her lips. It was something more than attraction. She moved him—the way she cared so much about her grandfather and Bella Vista, her earnest dedication to her family and friends. Her unbelievable cooking. The tiny pulse beneath the delicate skin of her throat. She bothered the hell out of him, too, because his attraction to her wasn't something he could rationalize or control. He loved talking to her, even when she was griping at him. He liked the softness that came over her face when she was in the garden or with her grandfather. He just *wanted* her.

This development was totally unexpected, not to mention inconvenient as hell. He had come here on a job, and once that was done, he'd be leaving. Getting into some kind of emotional entanglement was the last thing he needed. He wasn't good at relationships. He'd proven that again and again.

This could be different, he caught himself thinking. And then Mac came to a startling realization—the thing that was so wrong about the whole situation was that it felt so right.

"...impossible to imagine how hard it must be for a woman to make that choice," Isabel was saying.

"Sorry, what?" Mac gave himself a mental shake. *Focus.*

"I was talking about Annelise Winther," she said, sounding slightly exasperated. She quickened her pace toward the tool shed. "I've been trying to imagine what it's like to make that choice."

"To give a baby up for adoption?" He reined in his thoughts and picked up on the conversation again.

"Yes. Because it's—" She came around the corner, and there was Jamie, carrying a box of beekeeping gear. "Oh, hey, Jamie." Isabel looked flustered, and Mac couldn't understand why.

But when Jamie set down the box, he did. The girl smoothed her hand over her belly in that universal way women seemed to have when they were pregnant. When she looked up at Isabel, her eyes were haunted. "I've been imagining exactly that a lot lately," she said.

She was an odd little character, intense, with a distrustful flicker in her eyes when she looked at him. Isabel had taken her in with open arms. Yet another thing to like about Isabel, not that he was looking for things to like about her.

"Oh, gosh, I was talking about something that happened in my family a long time ago," Isabel said. "Not—"

"It's okay, really."

"If there's something I can do to help, you'll tell me, right?"

Jamie stared at the ground. Mac sensed the girl had plenty to say. But not in front of him, that was clear.

"I need to get to work," he said, stepping away from them. "See you around."

Isabel watched Mac go, his lanky form moving with an easy grace, though he still favored the injured knee. She still wasn't convinced that he should stay and pursue his project, but at the same time, she didn't want him to go. And as he'd said, it wasn't her decision to make.

Jamie let out a gust of air as if she'd been holding her breath.

"Are you all right?" asked Isabel. "Feeling okay?"

"Yes. No. I don't know." She raked a hand through her spiky hair. "Feels as though an alien has taken over my body. Not that I know what that feels like, but it's what I'm imagining."

"How can I help?" asked Isabel.

She indicated the box of new racks she'd ordered for the hives. "I need to check the supers and make sure we got rid of the mites we found last month. I was going to treat for mites one more time, just in case."

"Well, of course I'd love to help with that," Isabel said, "but I was talking about you. What can I do to help you?"

Isabel carried the gear as they walked together up the path toward the apiary. In the bright, hot sunshine, the hives were boiling with activity. Bees hovered in the milkweed and lavender, in the yarrow and thyme. The low, humming sound they made still felt unsettling to Isabel, but it seemed to have a calming effect on Jamie.

When Jamie was around the hives, she was deeply in her element, confident and graceful in her every move. She used only natural ingredients to control pests—thyme oil and powdered sugar. She had an uncanny sense about when and how to replace queens, and the new hives she'd installed already seemed to be thriving.

"Here's the thing," Jamie said as they moved among the hives, checking bottom racks and supers. "I know I need to get real with myself, and the reality is, I can't raise a baby. I can't. I don't have anything to offer it. If you hadn't let me stay here, I wouldn't have a place to live. I have just enough money to get by, and I…it's simply not in me to bring a baby into the mess I've made of my life."

Isabel winced, hearing the ache of regret in the girl's voice. "Don't sell yourself short. You're strong and healthy, and you have all the love in the world to give."

"That's nice of you to say. But I can't let myself be stupid about this, or make a stupid decision. God knows, I've done plenty of that already."

"Question—and feel free to tell me to butt out if it's too personal. What about the baby's father? I mean, you said you weren't together, but maybe he'll step up and support you."

Jamie shot Isabel a dark look. "He was the worst, you know?"

Isabel thought of the bruise she'd seen on Jamie's jaw. "He's not in the picture, then."

"Nope."

"And...sorry about the third degree. Are you safe?"

She nodded. "I am now."

"Was it some guy in Napa?"

Jamie ducked her head, but not before Isabel saw something—a flash of insight she didn't understand—in the girl's eyes. "Yeah," Jamie said. "In Napa."

"So you were living there? Working there?"

Again that flash. "I had a gig singing in a small restaurant. And I was supplying organic honey for the culinary school, and for some restaurants. The cooking school there is a big deal, you know?"

"I do know." Isabel hesitated, then admitted, "I was a student there when I was about your age."

"And?"

"And it didn't work out for me there, either. Wasn't really the right thing." Isabel had gone to culinary school with such hopes. How quickly that had all turned upside down.

"Yeah? What was wrong with it?"

Isabel sighed. "Long story. And you're trying to change the subject."

"Look, he's not going to come looking for me, if that's what you're worried about," Jamie said firmly.

"I'm worried about *you*."

"There's no need. My...the guy...he was nice at first, but he turned mean. Like, really mean."

Isabel felt a leaden sensation in her gut, remembering all too well how it felt to realize someone you trusted, maybe even loved, had turned on you. "So you left him," she said. "Good for you."

Jamie nodded, then tossed back her head, almost defiantly.

Her eyes were hot with self-loathing. "You don't get it, Isabel. I didn't leave. It wasn't good for me and I knew it but I still didn't leave. The only thing that got me out of my predicament is that he threw me out. I'm an idiot."

"No, you're not. You're..." *Like me,* thought Isabel. Sometimes a perfectly rational, intelligent person made stupid decisions. "Please don't be so hard on yourself," she said.

"Forgiving myself doesn't change my situation. I just can't figure out how in the world I'm going to raise a kid."

"It's the biggest commitment you'll ever make, and it's great that you're taking it so seriously."

She nodded, using a hive tool to pry apart the stacked supers of a hive. "I never thought I'd be in this position, you know? But now that I am, I've got to figure out what I'm going to do."

"You have time to think this over and weigh all the options," said Isabel.

Jamie nodded. "I'm glad there's time. But there's definitely a deadline, and I'm not ready to be a mom. I might never be ready. I knew right away that ending the pregnancy wouldn't be the right option for me, so now I really only have two choices—to keep the baby, or to give it up for adoption."

"I've never liked that phrase—'giving up' a baby. It doesn't really describe the situation." Isabel paused, thinking about her grandparents. Annelise Winther's actions had changed her grandmother's life forever. She hadn't given up a baby. She'd given Magnus and Eva a priceless gift.

"A kid needs a family," Jamie said, and the pain in her voice was hard to hear. "A mom and dad, a stable home."

"Families are made in lots of ways," Isabel pointed out. "I was raised by my grandparents. My sister, Tess, is getting an instant family with Dominic. And she was raised by a single mom."

"I know, and I have nothing but respect for single moms, but I don't want that for this baby."

"There are plenty of resources and help out there," Isabel said. "Listen, I've never been in your position before, but I promise you one thing—life gets better when you let people in."

"Not if you let in the wrong people."

She had a point.

"And by the way," Jamie said, "I don't exactly see you taking your own advice."

"What's that supposed to mean?"

"Like you don't know. That guy—the writer guy—he's totally into you and you act as if you don't even care."

Yikes, was it that obvious? "Jamie, we're talking about you. Would you be willing to meet with someone who's an expert in this area? I can be your friend, but I can't advise you about something this big."

Panic flared in Jamie's face. "I, um… I'll think about it. Hey, listen, I was going to finish up here and then head into town to do some errands…."

Isabel sensed the girl pulling back. "Of course. I'm being pushy, aren't I?"

Jamie narrowed her eyes and pulled her mouth into a tight bud. "You're being kinder than anyone's ever been to me," she said curtly, and slid the rack back into the hive.

CHAPTER TWELVE

A loud yell in the night awakened Isabel. She hadn't been asleep, anyway; she'd been staring into the darkness, thinking about Jamie. She had been in the girl's place before, if only briefly, and she recalled the surreal wonder and dread that had taken her over on discovering she was pregnant. Although it had come as a shock, although she hadn't been ready, she'd been awash with emotion.

Reacting to the noise, Charlie scrambled to his feet and gave a wary *woof.* Isabel lay still and listened, but didn't hear anything more. Maybe Grandfather was up late, watching TV. Still, sleep eluded her. She could only imagine how thoughts of the baby must consume Jamie. Isabel could too easily put herself in that place—young, pregnant, broke and frightened. And alone, so very alone. She never saw Jamie talking with anyone on her phone or going to visit friends. Isabel had not been homeless; nor had she lacked for family or friends. But she shared a key issue with Jamie. She'd been with a man who had turned on her.

And now Calvin Sharpe was back, more successful than ever, planning his next destination restaurant right here in Archangel. Isabel hated herself for not filing a complaint against him when she'd had the chance. The statute of limitations had run out, and it was too late. Yet hearing about Jamie's experience made Isabel wish she'd found the fire to fight back. Men who hurt women should not be allowed to get away with it.

The yelling started again, and this time she was sure it wasn't her imagination or a TV. Charlie trotted down the hall and Isabel followed. The noise was coming from Mac's room.

"Anything, you motherfuckers, we had a deal. We had a *deal.*" Mac sounded furious, his voice angry enough to cause her to flinch.

Was he on the phone with someone? In the middle of the night?

"Hey," she said, rapping on the door. "Hey, Mac, is everything okay?"

The door was ajar and Charlie surged into the room. It was completely dark inside. Mac wasn't on the phone, but on the bed, slamming his fist down repeatedly.

"We had a deal," he said again.

Isabel flipped on the light. "What's going on?"

He swung toward her, his eyes staring. It was eerie, the way he stared right through her. It took her only a second to realize he was in the middle of a nightmare.

"Mac," she said. Then more sharply, *"Mac."*

"No," he said, still with that blank look. "No, don't...."

"Mac, wake up." She crossed the room and touched his arm.

He yanked his arm sharply away. The sudden movement should have caused her to panic, but for some reason, she didn't. Instead, she felt an odd tenderness toward him. He seemed lost, vulnerable.

"Hey, it's okay," she said. "I've heard you shouldn't wake someone from a nightmare, but how about you wake up on your own?"

Charlie whined and scratched the floor. Mac glared wildly around the room. He said something in a language she didn't understand. Then he blinked and lay back on the bed, a sigh escaping him like air from a tire. "Who the hell turned on the light?" he grumbled.

"You were having a nightmare."

"Oh…shit. Sorry."

She couldn't help but notice he slept in the raw. It was hard to keep herself from staring. "Are you all right?"

"Yeah." He propped himself on one elbow and rubbed his stubbly cheeks. "Yep, I'm fine." He appeared to take his time pulling the sheet over himself. "That's twice you've seen me naked," he said, "and we haven't even had our first date."

"What makes you think we're ever going to have a date?" she asked.

"You were checking me out. You like me. I can tell." He reached out and scratched the dog's ears. "Right, old boy?"

She carefully lowered herself to the end of the bed, self-conscious about the old Giants jersey she wore as a nightshirt. "So you have nightmares?"

"Yeah, sorry about the noise. Did I wake your granddad?"

"Doubtful. He takes his hearing aids out at night. Is there anything I can do?"

He gave her a tired grin. "Crawl in bed with me."

She glared at him, then got up and tossed him a terrycloth robe she found hanging on the back of the bathroom door. "Meet me in the kitchen. I'll make you a sandwich."

"You don't need to make me a sandwich."

"But I'm going to." She left the room before he could protest further. In the kitchen, she layered grilled pancetta, tomato and lettuce on toasted thick slabs of sourdough. She added some chopped cornichons, Dijon mustard and fresh snipped tarragon to the mayo, just to show off. Around Bella Vista, her PLTs were legendary.

Mac wasn't wearing the robe when he came downstairs. He'd thrown on a pair of lived-in cutoffs, faded in all the right places, and a rumpled but clean T-shirt with a logo from a kiteboarding resort in Australia.

She cut the sandwich into quarters and set it on a pottery plate, along with a side of grapes and parmesan chips, and a beer in a frosty mug.

He regarded the small feast on the table. "I hope you don't mind if I moan in ecstasy while I eat this."

"I'd rather you didn't," she said, helping herself to a quarter of the sandwich. "Cook's tax," she explained.

"Fair enough. Thanks, Isabel."

She didn't know why it felt so pleasant, sitting here with him, or why she'd been so keen to fix him a midnight snack. He'd looked scared and lost in the grip of the nightmare. She supposed everyone did, but seeing him that way was strangely touching.

He sat at the old pine kitchen table with his leg sticking out to the side. Even in the dim light, she could see the crescent-shaped scar on his knee.

"You're not using your cane."

He shrugged. "Hate that thing. All the walking around I've been doing with your granddad is good exercise for the knee. I think it's helping."

"Are you supposed to be doing physical therapy?"

"Yep." He took a gulp of beer. "Massage and whirlpool, too. I did it right after surgery but didn't keep it up. Who has time for that?"

"If you want to heal properly, you'll make time." On impulse, she went to the pantry and found a jar of coconut oil. Then she oiled her hands and took hold of his knee. "Grandfather had a knee replacement years ago. I'm convinced he walks like a champ now because he did all the recommended therapy."

"Hey—"

"Relax. This won't hurt a bit. I did it for Grandfather all through his recovery." She used the connective tissue massage techniques she'd learned for Magnus, rotating her thumbs along the length of the scar. She couldn't recall the last time she'd touched a man intimately. And she couldn't recall it *ever* feeling like this. "The guest suite on the main floor has a whirlpool tub. You should use it."

"You really don't have to do this," said Mac.

"True. I could just let you hobble around Bella Vista the whole time you're here."

"Why are you being so nice to me?"

She kept her head down, thumbs circling the ridged scar. "Why is it so hard for you to let someone take care of you?"

"I've never needed that."

"Have you ever *wanted* that?"

He stared down at her massaging hands and took another swig of beer. "I might be open to the possibility."

Making Mac a sandwich in the middle of the night had distracted Isabel from her troubling thoughts about Calvin Sharpe. But they came crashing back the next day when Tess's bridesmaids and city friends came to Bella Vista for the bachelorette party and bridal shower. One of the bridesmaids raved about the fabulous meal she'd had at CalSharpe's in Napa.

Just the mention of him set Isabel's teeth on edge. Her grandfather claimed he didn't want to leave this world with regrets still on the table. Well, neither did she. And she didn't want to wait until she was eighty to unburden herself.

She refused to let herself be dragged down by her own painful history and her failure to speak out against Calvin Sharpe. Everyone had a past, she reminded herself. Everyone had pain. But not everyone had to stay hidden behind it.

She joined Tess's friends on the patio. They were getting together to head over to Dominic's vineyards and estate winery. His sister, Gina, would be hosting the bridal shower at the winery, and the women were armed with gift bags and boxes festooned with brightly colored tissue paper and ribbon.

The girlfriends from Tess's former life in the art world of San Francisco embraced the charms of Bella Vista. The women were chatting and fawning over Charlie, who shamelessly basked in the attention. The cats were more tentative, but Suzanne and Kelly had a way with them, even with Lilac, the shy one. Lilac, as usual, stayed busy keeping Chips away from the fountain.

"Okay, I take back everything I said about Tess moving away from the city," said Lydia. "It's so beautiful here, it makes my eyes hurt."

"In a good way, I hope," said Neelie.

"Tess was telling us about the cooking school," Lydia said. "And I have just one question— Where do I sign up?"

Isabel grinned. "A week after the wedding, our website is going live."

"Where is the bride-of-the-moment, anyway?" asked Lydia.

"Finishing up her dance lesson. We weren't allowed to watch," said Oksana.

"I'll go get her," said Isabel.

Tess and Dominic were learning a special wedding tango to perform as their first dance at the reception. Isabel headed out to the timber-and-stone building that had been converted into the ballroom and banquet hall for events. It looked beautiful even before the florist did her magic. Tess's former job with an international auction house had come into play as they styled the space. She had managed to hunt down unique treasures to make the place special. Vintage chandeliers and coaching lanterns with crystal chimneys, Irish lace and antique furniture added a touch of elegance, juxtaposed against the old stone floor and exposed beams.

Look what we created, thought Isabel, feeling a wave of pride and happiness. The light, airy space would soon be filled with friends and family on a joyous occasion, and that was only the beginning.

For the dancing practice, the tables and chairs had been moved to the periphery of the room. The final strains of *"Por Una Cabeza"* drifted from the stereo as they executed their final move, a glide, followed by a breathless pause and then a classic pose, with Tess draped over her bridegroom's strong arm. The tall, dark bridegroom towered protectively over his bride, willowy and pale in his embrace. It made a beautiful picture even before the two of them were dressed in their wedding finery.

Standing unseen in the doorway, Isabel felt the burn of an unexpected lump in her throat. She was truly happy for her sister. In Dominic's arms, Tess had been transformed from a tense, even angry woman into a lovely bride whose heart was blossoming like a summer rose. Yet for Isabel it was bittersweet, because Tess's newfound happiness held up a mirror, forcing Isabel to take a good, hard look at her own loneliness.

The strains of the tango music faded, and a soft, dry clapping of hands ensued. "Bravo, you two," said the dance teacher in her lilting accent. "Good job. You are going to be spectacular."

Isabel joined in the clapping as she walked into the room.

"I didn't peek," she said, "but I trust your teacher." She looked at the instructor. "When Tess told me you had a career as a teacher, I didn't realize it was ballroom dancing."

As the next track started to play on the stereo, Annelise Winther turned down the volume. "And I never dreamed I would have the pleasure of teaching the tango to my granddaughter and her bridegroom," she said. "The ballroom dancing was a sideline for me," she added. "During the day, I taught art to children in San Francisco."

Isabel went over and gave her a hug. Annelise was still sturdy despite her years. "I'm glad you're back for a visit," Isabel said, though she still felt a hint of awkwardness around Annelise. Both women were still adjusting to the idea of their family connection. "Did you sleep all right?"

"Indeed I did," Annelise said, beaming. "You've transformed Bella Vista into a place of dreams, Isabel. The refurbished rooms are absolutely beautiful."

"Thank you. It's a labor of love."

"Yes, I can tell. I'm excited for you. It's wonderful to picture all the events you'll host here, all the memories that will be made."

Dominic leaned down and kissed Annelise's cheek. "Thanks for sorting out my two left feet. I'd better go. I heard a rumor that a half dozen gorgeous ladies are coming to the winery for lunch."

"And bringing presents," Tess said. "Do you *know* how much I love presents? I made a rule that I didn't want anything practical."

"I'll brace myself," he said.

After Dominic had left, Annelise looked pensive, then went and got something out of her tapestry bag. "I wanted to give this to you without a crowd around, because it's very personal," she said, holding out a simple, long white case. "It will be the 'something old' you wear on your wedding day."

Tess's face turned pale as she took the box from her. "You tried to give this to me once before, and I couldn't take it."

"I'm trying again." Annelise gave her a soft smile. "Now you have a good reason to accept it."

"For heaven's sake, Tess, what is it?" Isabel crowded in close to see.

Tess opened the box and reverently took out a lovely antique necklace with a pink stone pendant. "It's a lavaliere that belonged to Annelise's mother in Denmark," she said. "Our great-grandmother."

"It's beautiful." Isabel turned to Annelise. "What a lovely gesture."

"Tess recovered it only last year, and she brought it to me. In fact, this necklace is the reason we've all been reunited. It's funny, isn't it, how one small turn of events can set us on a new path," Annelise said. "If I hadn't seen Tess on that History Channel episode about stolen Nazi treasures, we would not be together now. This was my mother's favorite, a gift my father brought from his travels in Russia during Romanov times. I tried to give her the lavaliere once, but she wouldn't take it."

"She will now," Isabel stated. She turned to Tess. "You will, and no arguing. It looks so bride-ish. Or bridelike. Whatever."

"We won't take no for an answer," said Annelise.

Tess nodded. She seemed to be having trouble speaking. "I will, and I can't thank you enough. But on one condition."

"What is that?" asked Annelise.

"Isabel has to wear it on *her* wedding day, too."

Isabel flushed. "Don't be ridiculous."

"Swear," said Tess. "For God's sake, it's a genuine Fabergé. I authenticated it myself."

"Fine, I swear, but it's premature to talk about my wedding day when I'm not even dating anyone."

"That's very silly," said Annelise. "A pretty girl like you should be enjoying the company of suitors."

"We could say the same of you," Tess pointed out. "Why didn't you ever get married?"

Annelise pursed her lips, and a darkness shifted into her eyes as though she'd just stepped under a cloud. "That is a story for another time."

As if sensing she'd trod on delicate ground, Tess said, "The lavaliere is precious to us all, and I'd be honored to wear it on my wedding day. Could I try it on?"

"Of course."

Isabel helped her fasten it. The gorgeous, ornate pendant lay upon her throat, a perfect match for her Irish redhead coloring. "It's wonderful," she told Tess.

"My mother always loved the color pink," said Annelise. "She wore this often, and I used to love the way the stone seemed to absorb the warmth of her skin."

"I don't know what to say." Tess gently touched the cabochon stone.

"Say you'll wear pale pink nail polish to match."

Tess laughed. "Done. Let's go show the girls."

Her sister's joy swept Isabel's melancholy away. In this moment, there was no room for anything in her heart but hope and happiness. Weddings had a way of doing that to a person.

The weekend was filled with silly games, gossip, copious amounts of food and drink, and plenty of laughter. Annelise and Jamie Westfall had taken a liking to each other, and even the two of them joined in the fun. The single bridesmaids fawned over Mac, no surprise given his looks and affable personality. Yes, despite his gruffness with Isabel, he did know how to turn on the charm.

"You look like something that should be jumping out of the cake, not serving it," said Neelie, accepting a thick slice of Italian cream cake from him after dinner.

"Tempting," he said with a grin. "I've been thinking about a career change."

"I work in HR at Sheffield Auction House," said Oksana. "You should send me your resume."

Isabel tried to seem amused by the flirting. Instead, she found it irritating.

"The invitations came today," Tess said. "Wait until you see."

The women gathered around a fancy box filled with paper goods. At the top of each invitation was a stylized logo of a traditional bee skep.

"'The Beekeeper's Ball,'" said Jamie, studying one of the letter pressed cards.

"I didn't want the traditional wording, you know?" Tess explained. "Mr. And Mrs. So-and-So request the honor of your presence at the marriage of their daughter, blah, blah, blah… It doesn't apply in our case. Dominic and I came up with the Beekeeper's Ball because everything we're serving has honey in it."

Jamie offered a tentative smile. "That's really cool."

"You're invited, you know," Tess added, handing her a card. "Everyone at Bella Vista is, of course."

"Oh." The girl looked a bit flustered. "I'm not… I don't—"

"Just say yes," Lydia advised her. "Tess is super bossy. She won't take no for an answer."

"True," said Tess. "And I'd love it if you brought your guitar."

The night ended with Jamie performing a few songs. She really had a lovely voice, soulful and sincere, and she played guitar with simple clarity. The next day the bridesmaids headed back to the city, and Tess was the proud owner of quirky gifts—an absinthe spoon, an aebleskiver pan, silk and lace underthings, a pizza stone, asparagus tongs and several honey wands.

Annelise stayed on at Bella Vista. She and Magnus spent quiet hours together, taking slow walks in the gardens, browsing through the farmer's market in the town square of Archangel, sipping coffee or playing bocce ball in the small city park. She had agreed to contribute to the book Mac was working on, and both Isabel and Tess were eager to hear her input. She was part of Grandfather's story, but more importantly, she was family.

Isabel was not about to judge either her or Grandfather for what had happened. Still, she did want to understand.

They all got together one evening as Tess was closing up Things Remembered, the antiques shop she had founded after moving to Archangel. The shop was situated in a vintage building at the junction where Bella Vista Drive joined the main road leading to town. Years ago, Eva Johansen had run a farm stand on the shady corner. Now refurbished and painted bright white, it had the feel of an old-time general store, but it had an exquisitely modern flair, thanks to Tess. Tourists and locals could stop and browse through the treasures, or pick up fresh produce from Bella Vista and the surrounding farms.

In one corner of the shop, there was a seating area by an old iron stove. Nearby was a special collection housed in vintage glass cases marked *Not for sale. For display only.* The exhibit featured a collection of old papers and artifacts Tess had found over the past year while sorting through Magnus's affairs. Most of the objects were related to farming and country life in the past century, old photos and mementos of Bella

Vista, and some even went back to Magnus's war years and his Danish boyhood.

"Wow, looks like a gold mine," said Mac, checking out the lighted display.

"I'd forgotten about most of these old things, but we now have a wonderful curator." Magnus beamed at Tess.

"Thanks," said Tess, finishing up the day's till at her desk. "It's still a work in progress. The local historical society is helping. Eventually it will become a community project. I'm hoping one day to give the exhibit its own space next to the shop."

"Magnus told me about this," said Annelise. "I've brought you a number of items to donate to the collection."

Isabel set down a tray with a Belleek china teapot and a batch of buttery madeleines she'd baked that afternoon. She had a cut crystal decanter of vintage sherry as well, and tiny colored glass goblets.

"There's something I want to tell you," Magnus said. "When I told Annelise that Mr. O'Neill is writing my story, I gave her the option to kill the project."

The two of them shared a long look. Isabel could only imagine the memories that passed between them in those drawn-out seconds. Magnus held his goblet up to the light, then took a sip. Annelise folded her hands in her lap. "I will tell you what I told Magnus. I would never stand in the way of someone telling the truth about his life."

He patted her hand. "You are part of the story. I shouldn't like to force this on you."

A succession of emotions shone in her face. Isabel could practically feel the old woman hovering on the edge of a decision. Mac waited, unmoving.

Annelise reached forward and took a glass of sherry. She drank it all in one gulp. Finally, she said, "Of course you must pursue this." Turning to Mac, she added, "You understand, I assume, that my own contribution will not be easy for any of you to hear, nor will the telling be easy for me. But the past matters greatly, and I want to help if I can."

"Ma'am, if you prefer, I won't include any references to you in the book."

"I appreciate that." She said something to Grandfather in Danish in a rapid murmur.

Isabel caught his reply: *"Jeg har ingen anelse." I have no idea.*

The old lady set her glass back on the tray. She held herself stiff and straight with the posture of a much younger woman. "My story and the story of Magnus are intertwined. If you tell one without the other, it would not be complete."

"I understand," said Mac. "But your participation is entirely optional. If you'd like to take some time to think about it—"

"I have already done so," she said quickly. "The things that happened...they are important. I'm glad you're doing this." Her gaze softened as she looked around at her listeners.

"He will write the story with honesty and respect," Magnus said, his voice sharp and clear, somewhat commanding. "Won't you, Cormac?"

"You have my word," said Mac. He was being very low key, yet Isabel got the sense that he was not missing a single nuance of the oddly tense conversation.

"Mac's a wonderful writer," Tess said. She closed the old brass register and helped herself to a madeleine. Then she touched Annelise's shoulder. "You're very important to our family."

Annelise nodded and patted Tess's hand.

"More than you know," Magnus murmured.

The silence was weighted by unanswered questions. The deep connection between Grandfather and Annelise was almost palpable. How had their lives become so entwined? How had a secret passion turned into infidelity, and then back to love again? How did they live with the past they carried in their hearts?

Magnus stood and used a tarnished key to open the display cases. He took something out and turned it over in his hands. "The handle of this pocketknife is made of ivory. The illustration was done by my grandfather. Etching was a hobby of his." He held it out for everyone to see. The yellowed ivory had a delicate folk art design of bears on both sides. "I carried it with me all the way from Denmark, and it was lost for a number of years. The girls found it in Erik's room."

"I remember that knife," Annelise said. "You carved puzzle boxes with it when we were at sea, on our way to America."

"You came to America together?" Tess's eyebrows shot up.

"We came with a number of people," said Annelise. "We sailed aboard a Norwegian ship called the SS *Stavangerfjord,* packed full of people needing to make a new start. It had been taken over by the German authorities as a troopship during the war, but returned to the Norwegian America Line soon afterward."

"I had no idea you came together," said Isabel, watching her grandfather's face. He smiled briefly, then took a seat next to Annelise.

"I shared a bunk with your grandmother Eva," she said. "And Magnus shared one with Ramon Maldonado, as I recall."

Magnus nodded, turning to Mac. "You've not met Ramon. He isn't well, but perhaps we can visit him on a good day." He stacked his hands atop the head of his cane. "The two of us have been friends since we were boys in the underground."

"Friends?" Annelise shook her head. "I have a different recollection."

"I'm sure Mr. O'Neill would like to hear it," Magnus said, a twinkle in his eye.

Mac spread his hands, palms out. "That's why I'm here. It would be great to hear both your perspectives."

Annelise clasped her hands in her lap, then unclasped them. She patted the carpetbag. "I brought some things for your exhibit." She turned to Mac. "This is a wonderful opportunity after all."

"We're here to listen," he said quietly.

Isabel watched his manner with her grandfather and Annelise. He had a gift for being neutral, yet compassionate. It seemed to put people at ease. It put *her* at ease, which was not the way she was accustomed to feeling around guys.

"When I was a girl," Annelise told him, "the Nazis arrested my parents. My father was a hospital administrator in Copenhagen, and Mother worked as a volunteer nurse there. The Nazis discovered they were part of an organization affiliated with the resistance. From the hospital where they worked, people would be smuggled out of the country by way of the hospital's body bags, or disguised as victims of illness on stretchers. They were betrayed and taken away, perhaps the same way Magnus's parents were—without warning, and then sent to die in work camps without any due process at all. It's likely I would have been taken, too, but Magnus helped me run away." She paused, and shared a solemn look with Grandfather. "He put me on a boat to my grandmother's house in Helsingør. She was a widow who gave music lessons to the village children." She took a breath, turned to Tess and then Isabel. "That is where I met Eva. We became best friends."

"You and Eva were friends in Denmark, too?" Isabel interjected. "I didn't realize you even knew each other." *Friends.* Bubbie and Annelise had known each other, had shared a berth while coming to America.

"If not for the upheaval of war, we would not have met at all. She and her father had gone to Helsingør to keep from being found and deported. It was a little fishing town on a narrow strait. People needing to disappear quickly would sometimes take a boat, even a small dory, across the strait to Sweden. Eva and I met in the autumn at the Wednesday market. She was selling apples, and I made a sketch of her."

Rummaging in the carpetbag, she took out a faded cardboard portfolio bound with string. "This is a sketchbook I managed to keep with me all these years." She unwound the string and paged through the thick, yellowed paper. Then she held out a simple pencil sketch of a girl with large eyes and pigtails, holding a basket of apples.

"That's lovely," said Isabel. It was rendered well, though she didn't recognize her grandmother in the smiling girl.

"Annelise has always been a fine artist," Magnus said.

"A hobby," she corrected him.

"She was an art teacher in San Francisco for many years," he added.

"Forty-five, to be precise, all at the Sherman School." She smiled, her eyes misty with memories. "I think now that I retired too soon. I miss those children every day, even with their noise and their messes. My life is much too quiet these days." She set aside the portfolio. "Now, where was I?"

"Eva, the girl in the picture," Mac said quietly. "You were telling us about your friendship with Eva Solomon."

"Oh. Yes, of course." The old lady blinked slowly, her pale face soft with vulnerability.

Isabel exchanged a glance with Tess. Grandfather and Annelise were both sturdy for their age, but moments like this were a reminder of their great age and their fragility.

"We became fast friends the day I sketched the portrait, and I adored her. But as you surely understand by now, ours was a long and complicated relationship. She was a wonderful person who rose above the things she suffered. Isabel, you were privileged to be raised by her, as I'm certain you know."

Isabel nodded, unsure of what else to say. She was dying to ask why, if Annelise considered Eva such a wonderful person, she would have a baby with Eva's husband. Had Annelise and Magnus actually been in love, or had they succumbed to a moment of passion? She cautioned herself to keep silent. She was learning from Mac that listening could sometimes be the most important part of the conversation.

"So you both lived in Helsingør," Mac prompted.

"We did, for a time. I wish I could recapture those days for you. Everything seemed to be painted by a gilded haze. We were young girls, and despite what had happened to us, we lived each day as children do." Annelise helped herself to a cup of tea, drizzling honey into it. "I believe children have a gift for recovering from even the most terrible losses. Perhaps it's a survival mechanism. Surely we were all deeply scarred by what happened, but life went on and played out day by day. We discovered it was impossible to be hurt and sad every single moment. We learned to find the joy in the small things, and to hold that in our hearts. I believe Eva would agree with me. When I remember those days, I remember the laughter and the sunshine."

Magnus set aside his cane, then settled back in his chair. "Memory is a strange thing. There are moments I can recall with the most detailed clarity, and other whole stretches that exist in an undifferentiated blur."

Annelise took something else from her bag. She wrinkled her nose in apparent distaste. "I have always felt obliged to keep this for its historical significance. It certainly has no sentimental value for me," she said, handing Mac a small booklet with brittle pages. "I consider it a reminder that we can move past our history, but we can never truly erase it. I have given a lot of thought to this project. There are things that happened that I've never disclosed, not even to you, Magnus. Not to anyone. Now I wish to be part of the conversation."

Mac studied the little book, the colors of its cover faded by time. *"Poesiealbum?"* he asked. "Is that a book of poems? Do you mind if I have a look?"

"Help yourself," said Annelise. "It is a bit of ephemera you've probably never encountered." There was a waver in her voice that sounded to Isabel like anger.

"Is something wrong with it?" She leaned over Mac's shoulder as he paged through the fading, handwritten pages. A couple of brightly colored illustrations were stuck between the pages. Mac paused to study one of them. The illustration depicted apple-cheeked children with armloads of flowers, skipping along, their chubby knees rosy...and their clothes decorated with swastikas. Isabel slumped against Mac's shoulder, its solid strength a comfort until she caught herself, and then backed away.

"I don't have cooties," he murmured.

"That's what all the boys say." She turned to her grandfather and Annelise. "I can see why you're not a fan."

"The little pictures are called *Oblaten,*" Annelise explained. "They're a bit like the stickers or trading cards my students used to love. Members of the League of German Girls used to collect and exchange them. The *Oblaten* were quite the commodity, the 'Hello Kitty' of their time."

"Only not so innocent. It's a form of vile propaganda, perpetrated upon children," Magnus said.

"I've never heard of the League of German Girls," said Isabel. Yet for some reason, she knew she'd find out soon enough.

"The League was known in Germany as the BDM," said Annelise.

"Now that," Tess remarked, looking up from her desk, "I've

heard of. I probably came across it in my research. Stands for *Bund Deutscher Mädel.* It's the girls' arm of the Nazi Youth."

"That's creepy," Isabel said.

Mac flipped through the innocent-looking paper album, its yellowed pages filled with childish script. "Okay, not my favorite artifact. Where'd it come from?"

Annelise cleared her throat and winced, glancing away from him. "It belonged to me, long ago."

Isabel's heart dropped. "You mean you belonged to the Nazi Youth?"

"No, certainly not, although I was encouraged to join." She locked eyes with Magnus, and some kind of wordless exchange passed between them. "In truth, I was nearly forced to join."

Grandfather said something in rapid Danish. Isabel didn't understand, but the expression on his face was unmistakable.

"That's shocking," said Tess. "I'm sorry, Annelise. It must have been awful."

"And this?" Mac held up a small triangular-shaped pin with the SS logo and a word across the top. Its rusted pin was attached to the back of the booklet.

"Another terrible memento," Annelise said. "You see, I was only safe in Helsingør for a short while, and then my grandmother died. I had no other family, and knew no one to take me in. There might have been neighbors who would have looked after me, but there was such fear and depredation in those times. I was in a haze of confusion when I ran off after her death. That was when I joined the *Holger Danske,* living by my wits, much as Magnus was doing. As a young girl, I rarely fell under scrutiny from the authorities, and I became quite good at underground activities. Youthful arrogance was my downfall. While carrying out an act of sabotage, I was apprehended." She fixed her gaze on Magnus. "I believe you'll recall the night in question."

"Yes. I was with you that night. I'm sorry...."

"You couldn't have done anything to prevent my arrest." She turned to her other listeners. "After I was caught by the soldiers, I was sent to an orphanage on an island in the Baltic Sea. And it was known—although not to me, as I was so young—that this was a place where certain young girls were forced into Himmler's *Lebensborn* experiment. You have heard of this?"

A chill passed over Isabel's skin. *Dear God.*

Annelise nodded. "It was a horrible attempt to breed a master race. The Germans kidnapped young girls all over Europe, but some came from orphanages. There was an obsession with a certain physical type—Nordic and tall, light-haired and blue-eyed. It was known as 'Aryan' and considered to be racially pure. Everyone knows it's nonsense, but under the Nazis, the program was accepted and state sponsored." She paused again. "I had the misfortune to match their ideal physical characteristics."

The back of Isabel's neck prickled, though she held herself very still. She had a bad feeling about this conversation.

Annelise handed over a picture. "This was taken for an identity card."

Cast in the fading amber of an old photograph, Annelise had been as deadly serious as a marble statue, but extremely beautiful. Even in old age, she was a beautiful woman, taller than most, with cornflower-blue eyes and fine facial bones, her hands delicate and ladylike.

"It's like some horrid sci-fi story," said Tess.

"Except it was no story," Annelise said. "Girls were treated like livestock, forced to mate with selected men—or raped—until there was a pregnancy. Many of the men were SS officers or other ranking officials. There were even special homes for them all over Nazi-occupied Europe. Birthing houses, they were called. The girls were sent to these places to have their babies in secret, yet the Germans claimed it was a privilege to bear children in the name of the Reich. The special homes were run like luxurious resorts, by caretakers who treated us like captive princesses. We were then compelled to give the babies away to Nazi families."

Us...we. Isabel stared at her. The prickling on the back of her neck spread down her arms and to her throat. "You mean you..." She couldn't find the words.

Annelise got up and walked to the window. She folded her slender arms across her midsection.

Magnus hurried over to her with the strides of a much younger man. His stance as he planted himself behind her was protective. He smoothed his hands over her shoulders and murmured something in Danish.

Isabel caught some of what Grandfather said: *"You never told me...."*

Annelise's reply was indistinct. Then, in Danish again, Magnus said, *"You do not have to speak of this to anyone, ever."*

This time, Isabel understood Annelise's response: *"Keeping silent is just as hurtful as telling the truth. Nothing will make it..."* The next word was one Isabel didn't recognize in Danish.

"He's right," she said, speaking to Annelise but sending Mac a look. "You're under no obligation to talk about any of this."

"I understand that. And I've gone through most of my life in silence." She turned back to them, and seemed to grow in stature as she straightened her shoulders. The evening light through the window outlined her slender form. "I believe I would like to be heard now."

Tess went over and gripped her hand. "Really?"

Annelise nodded again. "If I survived the ordeal then I can survive the telling of it."

Both Tess and Magnus urged her to sit down. "I cannot

argue with that," Magnus said, still speaking Danish. "Sit down, love, and take your time."

Love. The endearment filled Isabel with confusion. It felt both strange—and strangely right—to hear her grandfather refer to her as his love.

Annelise was silent for a moment, though her expression became lively and engaged. Finally, she started speaking. "The only way I can bear to think about what occurred is to imagine that it happened to another person, in another life," she said. Her voice was soft and flat-toned, devoid of emotion. Or perhaps, Isabel reflected as the old woman carefully and deliberately folded her hands in her lap, the emotion was buried so deep, it was unreachable.

"At the age of thirteen, I was forced to have a Nazi SS officer's baby," the old lady stated.

Isabel felt nauseated. Her pulse thudded heavily in her gut.

Tess moved her chair closer to Annelise. Her eyes brimmed with unshed tears. She slid her arm around the old woman's shoulders. "We're here to listen."

"I appreciate that more than you know," Annelise said. "What happened to me was not an uncommon occurrence during the Nazi regime. Yet these days, the *Lebensborn* program has been forgotten except by a few."

"That's true," said Tess. "Mac, had you heard of it before today?"

"Yes," he said. His face was stony. "It was a breeding program created by Himmler, but the idea is so outrageous, I never thought about it in actual human terms." His gaze was deep with sympathy as he regarded Annelise. "Until now. Miss Winther, I'm so sorry."

Her folded hands tightened in her lap, though she nodded in acknowledgment. "The child was born at a special clinic about forty kilometers from Copenhagen. The place had beautiful furnishings, lace curtains, nurses in crisp uniforms, embroidered bed linens and lovely gardens. The food was abundant and delicious, unheard of in wartime. That is where I was given the *Poesiealbum*. I never wanted to make a single mark in it, but I complied because the whole time I was forced to stay there, I was plotting my escape."

"I'm glad you got away," Isabel said softly.

"Do you know what happened to the baby?" asked Tess.

Annelise unfolded her hands and took hold of Magnus's. "The infant was taken from me with its umbilical cord still attached. I never saw its face, though I'm quite certain I heard someone announce that it was a boy. I had been given a narcotic drug during labor, probably some sort of morphine, and my memories of those hours are vague and somewhat confusing. This is probably a mercy. I'm sure I would have been forced to bear more children. Another girl at the residence had born two in as many years. This made me absolutely determined to get away. Out of pure necessity and a will to survive, I had developed some useful survival skills."

"You must have been very brave," Tess told her softly.

"Sometimes desperation can look a lot like bravery," Annelise declared. "There was a moment after the birth when the nurses' guards were down and they were preoccupied with the infant. That was the moment I seized to escape from that place with the blood…still running down my legs."

Aching for the captive girl Annelise had been, Isabel felt a tear slip down her cheek. She tried to be discreet as she brushed it away. The image of the terrified girl haunted her.

Annelise must have seen the horror and sadness in her eyes. "Pardon me, but I must speak plainly."

"Of course," Mac said.

"I stole some clothes from the clinic laundry and wheeled a cart of soiled linens off the grounds of the place."

"Please tell us you found help right away," said Tess.

"The birthing house was on an island. I told a local fisherman some nonsense story about needing to get back to the city, and persuaded him to ferry me on his daily run to Copenhagen. Once there, I went to a Catholic church in a farming neighborhood. I had heard some things about it, that it was a safe haven. A laywoman took me into her home and gave me a room in the attic. I slept for days, waking only to drink some soup and water. I left her as soon as I'd regained my strength, not wanting to put her in jeopardy.

"Eventually I found safe haven with the *Holger Danske,* the resistance group I'd worked for before my arrest," Annelise said. "As soon as I'd regained my strength, I rejoined their effort. It was dangerous, but I suppose I was looking to reclaim some sort of power and control over my life. I became a bit of a daredevil, and more vengeful than ever. I played fast and loose with my safety, because at that point, I was beyond caring."

"You're amazing," said Tess. "And heartbreaking."

"No, I am a survivor."

"She turned out to be one of the youngest and best agents in the organization," Magnus said. In Danish, he said to her, *"For the love of God, you should have told me."*

She simply shook her head. "I wanted the entire ordeal behind me as quickly as possible. However, after the war, I made an attempt to seek out the child that was taken from me. This turned out to be an impossible quest. Once the Nazis realized their regime was on the brink of collapse, they were quick to cover their crimes. The children born from this experiment became known as orphans of shame, although they came innocently into the world. Many were abandoned as all the birthing homes were evacuated in a panic, and the records were destroyed. It's assumed that the children survived thanks to the kindness of strangers, but understandably, their heritage was kept secret."

Tess regarded the poetry booklet with a nauseated expression.

"It took me many years to forgive myself, though I always realized nothing that happened was my fault." She sighed. "It was so long ago. A different person, a different life. After I escaped, I discovered Eva had been transported to Theresienstadt, and I realized my own suffering paled in comparison. And my own fortunes improved once I made myself useful to the *Holger Danske*. That was when I encountered Magnus again."

"I didn't recognize her at first," he said. "If I'd known..."

She offered a smile that was full of affection, giving Isabel the sense of a shared secret. "You would have been more civil to me?"

"I was civil."

"Hmph." She turned to Mac. "The very first time we met, he shoved me into a boat—"

"It was either that or be questioned by the brownshirts," Magnus said.

"The second time we met," she continued, "he cut off all of my hair. I'm not sure I've ever forgiven him for that."

Isabel frowned. "What do you mean, he cut off all your hair?"

"He turned me into a boy."

PART V

*Ten thousand forager bees in a typical hive need to coordi-
nate their quest for nectar. They do this through the famed
"waggle dance," which communicates the flight direction
and distance to sources of nectar. The complexity and pre-
cision of these dances is breathtaking, and success relies on
the integrity of a nervous system where each synapse is crucial. It is no surprise then that honey bees have been shown
to have a higher number of neurological receptors than other
insects.*

—Soil Association [www.soilassociation.org]

HONEY BUTTER FRIED CHICKEN

BRINE:

1 pint buttermilk mixed with 2 teaspoons kosher salt and ½ teaspoon pepper

CHICKEN:

1	cup all-purpose flour	2	teaspoons salt
¼	teaspoon black pepper	2	teaspoons paprika
1	free range, organic chicken, cut into 8 pieces	½	cup butter

Make a buttermilk brine for the chicken by combining the buttermilk, salt and pepper in a large resealable plastic bag. Add chicken pieces and chill overnight. Drain before using.

Preheat oven to 400 degrees F. Combine flour, salt, pepper and paprika in a bag and shake each chicken piece to coat it in the flour mixture.

Melt a stick of butter in a big ovenproof skillet. Over medium heat, add chicken pieces in a single layer, turning chicken to coat with butter.

Bake skin-side down for thirty minutes.

SAUCE:

4	tablespoons (¼ cup) butter	¼	cup lemon juice
¼	cup honey		

Melt remaining butter in a small pan and whisk in the honey and lemon.

Turn the chicken pieces, pour on the honey butter sauce, and bake an additional 20 to 30 minutes or until tender. Serve with biscuits and pan juices.

[Source: Adapted from the Mr. Food Test Kitchen]

CHAPTER THIRTEEN

June 1942

"Why do I always have to be the one to go first?" Magnus muttered, his breath coming quick and shallow with nervousness.

"Because you're the smallest," said Kjeld, a boy he'd been bunking with in a boatyard at the edge of the old town near the port. They were camped out in a lap-sided wooden fishing boat, long abandoned and flipped over with its keel pointing at the sky like the dorsal fin of a shark. To the casual observer, the old boats in the yard appeared to be rotting into the marsh on the east side. In reality, the abandoned watercraft had become a rabbit warren of hiding places for supplies, everything from sacks of dried, salted fish to boxes of dynamite to the occasional fugitive on the run from the law. They also briefly sheltered Jews from the Nazis and underground resistance fighters and agents.

"Here's what you have to do," said Kjeld. He was a big

blond-headed kid with crooked teeth and a wicked aim with his throwing arm. Actual firearms were hard to come by, but a guy with good aim managed to do a lot of damage with rags soaked in gasoline, rocks and kitchen matches. Kjeld had been known to break a window at fifty paces with a fist-size river stone. "The German ship will be taking on food supplies at about ten in the morning. You'll be smuggled aboard in an apple barrel. Come and see."

Magnus regarded the barrel with a dubious frown. "I'm to hide in the bottom of that, am I?"

"Yes. Ingenious, isn't it?"

The barrel had a false bottom with just enough space for Magnus to fold his wiry frame into a tucked position. The upper part was filled with wood shavings and apples from the previous autumn's harvest.

When the Germans had first invaded and taken up occupation in Denmark, many promises had been made regarding the safety and security of the Danish people. The rationale—which no one with half a brain believed—was that the Danes under German protection would be shielded from attack by the British enemy.

The real reason for capitulation was simply the law of numbers. The Danish army had no chance against the Nazi war machine.

But that didn't mean there weren't ways to fight back. Ever since meeting the man known as the Teacher, Magnus was learning things he'd never dreamed of.

Before the Germans moved in, he had been a guileless, even well-behaved boy who would have been appalled at the idea of pulling any sort of bold or risky prank in defiance of the authorities. But the night the Nazis had taken his family, they had also taken his innocence.

These days, he had no more scruples than a feral alley cat bent on survival. In the service of the resistance, he had lied, cheated and stolen. He had planted dynamite in warehouses and drilled holes in ships' hulls. He'd never killed a German, but he would do so if he had to.

He just hoped he wouldn't have to.

"And once I'm aboard?"

"Someone else will tell you your objective."

Magnus nodded. No single member of the resistance was permitted to know all the details of an operation. That way if someone was caught, he wouldn't be able to furnish any information, even if he was tortured. Magnus was quite confident that the other boy's name was not Kjeld. It was someone else entirely who told him what he was to do once he made it down to the ship's cargo area.

He was to find a collection of certain marked crates, and to replace the instruction labels on them. This would ensure that the crates would be left at the dock tonight rather than being loaded on transport trucks. He didn't know what was in the crates, probably didn't want to know. They might be filled with anything from office supplies to munitions.

Kjeld helped him into the barrel and loosely replaced the top. Magnus waited in the cramped, dark space, which smelled of ripe apples and packing straw. He was jostled and rolled along, gritting his teeth and pressing himself against the sides to avoid making a sound. He wasn't scared. Concentrating on his mission kept him from feeling afraid. The need for revenge was like a cold, clean blade.

Once aboard, he waited in darkness for a few minutes. It was silent. Time to move. He pushed up on the lid of the crate. It was dark in the hold, but he had a very small battery torch to light his way. Just as he'd been told, there was a stack of marked crates. He replaced the labels with the ones he'd been given, ensuring that the supplies would be misdirected. Someone was going to get into big trouble, but it wouldn't be him. As quick and discreet as a wharf rat, he made his way out of the supply hold and climbed over the edge, landing almost soundlessly on the dock.

Then he went to work on the next part of his assignment. He had been given a code word and told to meet another agent on Gammel Strand, an old street and public market along a beach canal where white-scarved women from the fishing village of Skovshoved sold their fish. He scanned the area along the portside plaza, a busy place at midday. The ever-present soldiers milled at the edges of the crowd. The Danes were used to them now, and for the most part, the two factions kept their distance from one another.

On one corner was a group of people awaiting the horse bus. Petrol was in such short supply that some areas of the city had been obliged to revive the old way of transport—long buses with bench seats and a canopy overhead. The big draft horses harnessed to the rig looked old and weary as they clopped through the streets of Copenhagen. They probably *were* old and weary. The more able-bodied horses tended to be commandeered by the German authorities and shipped to the war zone to pull supply trains.

Next to the bus kiosk was an old stone water fountain set into a moss-covered wall, the stream dripping steadily into a cracked concrete basin. The side of the bus shelter was plastered with the latest Nazi proclamation, which had begun to appear throughout the city. "Effective One July, all Jews without exception must display the yellow Star of David emblem on the right upper sleeve, such emblems to be provided and distributed by the Central Authority. Failure to comply will be considered an act of insubordination. By order of the Reich."

The Danes, whether Jewish or not, despised the proclamation, and rumors were rife throughout the city that they would defy the order by any means necessary.

Magnus waited anxiously until the bus lurched away with its passengers. The plaza still teemed with dockworkers, the women selling fish and people going about their business. Two guys pulled an iron-wheeled ice truck along the quays and offered shovelfuls of ice to the fishmongers.

Magnus was nearing the kiosk when a washerwoman appeared, her drab blue work uniform hanging off her frame, and her clogs stained black with filth. A soiled kerchief covered her head, holding her hair back from her expressionless face.

Great, thought Magnus. Just what he needed, a bystander. Now his contact would have to wait to approach him.

She bent and dipped a sponge in the bucket, but instead of washing the glass window of the kiosk, she wiped a swath of charcoal colored paint across the printed decree. Working quickly, she wrote in big, bold letters. "In a pig's eye."

Then, as calmly as you please, she emptied the bucket of black liquid into the gutter and washed her hands in the water fountain.

Magnus waited at the kiosk, trying his best to suppress a grin of surprise. So this was his contact after all. The code word was *pig*. He just hadn't expected to see it like this. His next move was to casually switch his rucksack full of schoolbooks from one shoulder to the other to acknowledge the contact. Moments later, the girl returned to the kiosk, setting down her bucket and scrub brush.

He stared up at the clock on the facade of one of the tall, colorful buildings, pretending to check the time. "That was cheeky of you."

"I do what I can." Her voice was soft. She sounded younger than she looked. She probably *was* younger than she looked. But like him, she might have had to leave her childhood behind just to survive. Her pale skin, stretched across her cheekbones, was streaked with dirt, and her expression was set in a frown. She held her jaw firmly, as if clenching her teeth. The German occupation took its toll in ways he was only just discovering. Although there was no direct warfare and fighting, the strain and uncertainty of day-to-day life under Nazi rule pressed down on the spirit. Her expression exuded anger and distress.

Magnus wondered what trouble the woman—just a girl, really—had endured at the hands of the Nazis.

"I don't suppose it's helpful to tell you how dangerous it is, baiting the Nazis like that," he said.

"Everything is dangerous these days," she replied in a flat, matter-of-fact tone.

"Do you have a message for me?"

"You're to go to the east harbor and find the *Selfors*," she said. "A supply ship. Do you know it?"

He had just come from the harbor, having risked his neck in that apple barrel to change the labels on the shipping crates. "Of course."

"Go to the shipmaster's office on the dock there. He will have a parcel for you. It's to be delivered to the Ivarsen Brothers' shop on Linden Street."

Magnus felt a dark surge of pride. He knew the task was related to the making of firearms, the very job his father had done before his arrest. Somehow, participating in the illicit activity made him feel closer to his father. He wondered every day what had become of his parents after the night they'd been taken away, even though the speculation led to terrible imaginings. Yet this made him even more determined to survive and carry on the fight, helping Danish patriots to manufacture machine guns right under the noses of the Nazis.

"That is all you need to know for now," said the girl. "Take your time, but don't dawdle too much. And for heaven's sake, don't get caught."

"I never get caught."

There was a long pause. Then she said, "I know."

He frowned. "Hey, have we met?"

"I..."

Two things happened at that point. A group of brownshirts appeared in the plaza, moving in a cluster of shiny boots and polished weapons. Their customary swagger and loud, joking voices commanded attention. Magnus hated their cheery confidence. He hated that they were young well-fed men with their polished boots and holstered Luger sidearms. He hated that they seemed utterly unafraid of anything.

The brownshirts had a special knack for ferreting out troublemakers. When he first joined the resistance, Magnus had learned to play up his schoolboy-innocent looks. Usually, the Nazis paid him no more mind than they would a stray cat.

The other thing that happened in that moment was that she ducked her head and hunched up her shoulders in a way that tweaked his memory. "It's uncanny," he said at last, speaking without looking at her. "I could swear we've met somewhere. Do we know each other?"

"It doesn't pay to know anyone these days." She pressed her lips together in a tight seam.

He couldn't believe how hardened she was for one so young. Yet her eyes looked as old and cold as rock itself. What had she endured, to armor herself like that?

We've all suffered.

The wind came up and ruffled her kerchief, snatching it from her head. The thing blew across the path of the Nazi soldiers and unleashed a curtain of pale gold hair that had been concealed beneath the soiled fabric. She grabbed for the scarf, but a soldier's bayonet stabbed into it and lifted it like a flag of surrender.

Magnus had an urge to grab the blonde girl and run. Instead, he gritted his teeth and forced himself to hold still. He had learned early on in his underground work that you don't challenge the brownshirts. The first summer of the occupation, his friend Ikey had seen some soldiers tormenting a dog in Golden Prince Park. Ikey had stepped in and objected, trying to save the dog. For his troubles, he'd had his face smashed in by the butt of a rifle, and would never look the same.

The soldier with the bayonet toyed with the blonde girl. "You want this?" He teased, holding the scarf just out of reach. "Ask nicely."

She held out her hand. "Please give me back my scarf." She spoke in Danish, not German. A common washerwoman wouldn't know German.

Even from ten paces, Magnus could feel the rage emanating from her. He could also see other people watching. Like him, they knew the dangers of interfering. The Nazis had been in occupation long enough to have trained the locals to keep their distance. People got smart—or they disappeared. Like Magnus's parents.

"Come closer, little maid," one of the brownshirts said.

It was dangerous to be beautiful in Denmark. Magnus was annoyed at the girl for being beautiful. Didn't she know any better?

"Never mind," she abruptly said to the soldier. "You can keep it as a souvenir. I must be going. I have work to do."

She turned away, but the soldier grabbed her arm.

Magnus regarded the hand on her arm and nearly exploded. With every cell in his body, he wanted to leap to her defense. But the soldier was surrounded by three others. They always traveled in packs, like wolves.

He couldn't simply stand by and do nothing.

"Greta," he called out. "Ah, there you are, Greta." Magnus approached the soldier, offering a subservient nod. "Thank you for finding my sister. She wandered off and forgot her appointment at the public clinic."

"Who the hell are you?" the soldier asked.

Magnus touched the brim of his cap. "Her brother, sir. I try to look after her, but she is..." He pointed a finger at his ear and twirled it around. "Simple, you know?"

"In fact, I do not know, boy," said the soldier.

"It gets her in trouble sometimes." As he spoke, Magnus plucked the scarf from the bayonet and handed it to the girl. "I must get her to the clinic for her dose of penicillin. She has an unfortunate condition." He dropped his voice. "The kind you can't wash off. You didn't get too close to her, did you?"

The soldier stepped back, a disgusted expression on his face, and shooed them both away. "Be gone, then. Take this filthy thing with you." He spat on the ground and turned away.

Magnus took the girl by the hand and towed her down a side alley in the direction of the Royal Free Hospital.

"Simple?" she hissed in outrage. "A condition that can't be washed off?"

"Or what about this?" Magnus retorted. "What about 'Thank you for saving me from those Nazi pigs?'"

"I didn't need saving."

"Oh, no? Those guys were moments from dragging you off and raping you."

Her spine and shoulders stiffened, indicating that she knew what *raping* meant. Unfortunately, so did Magnus. The Teacher had described it in painful detail. Sometimes boys were the victims, but most often it was an especially terrible act of violence against a woman. These days, it pained Magnus to think about the Teacher, the man who had set him on this path. Because the Teacher was gone now. He had been assassinated by a German sniper, right before Magnus's horrified eyes. The blood of the Teacher had spackled him for days afterward—under his cuticles, in his nostrils, in the whorls of his ears.

"Like I said," the girl snapped, "I know how to take care of myself. I've been doing it for a long time." Despite her words, she was visibly shaken, her face the color of ash, her hands and her voice unsteady.

"Well, you're not by yourself anymore," he muttered through gritted teeth. "You're with me."

They passed St. Stephen's church, where he used to worship with his family, lost to him now. He looked around and saw that they were alone in the alleyway. Abruptly, he pulled her into the sanctuary, which was deserted. The carved wooden pulpit resembled a spiny dragon rearing against the tall semicircle of colorful windows surrounding the apex of the altar. Their footsteps on the stone floor echoed off the buttressed walls.

He shoved her down onto a wooden prie-dieu, which resembled a narrow ladder-back chair. "Don't move," he commanded her. Then he dug into his pocket and took out his utility knife. It was outfitted with a razor-sharp blade, which often came in handy for acts of sabotage.

"What do you think you're doing?" she demanded, squirming and pulling back to stare at the knife. "I'll scream. I'll—"

"Be still." His heart was pounding, but he knew he was doing the right thing. He'd seen the way the soldiers had looked at her.

"But—"

"Shut up." With his free hand, he grabbed a handful of blond hair—silk, it felt like pure silk—and it smelled of sweet herbs and flowers. Placing the knife blade close to her head, he made a decisive cut, sawing through the locks. A half meter of honey-colored silk wafted to the floor.

"Stop it!" she said, scrambling off the prie-dieu and falling to her knees. "You're crazy. Leave me alone!"

"Hold still. Get back in the chair and quit your squawking. You have to let me finish."

"I will not! I'll scream bloody murder." In a mindless panic, she tried to gather up the long strands of fallen hair.

"And bring the soldiers in here to grab you again? Hold still, damn you." He pressed his cupped hands on her bony shoulders and put his face very close to hers. "Listen. The brownshirts take what they want. They are extremely fond of young girls with silky blond hair."

She dropped the strands of hair. "I know. That's why I wear the scarf—"

"And it was no help today. I know of one girl who slashed her own face with a razor to keep the soldiers away." He hoisted her back into the chair and held the blade in front of her nose.

She batted it away. "That's a lie."

He could tell from the wild look in her eyes that she knew he wasn't lying. "And something else," he said. "Some girls get taken away in secret, and they have to have babies with SS officers." Magnus didn't quite understand this, but at a recent meeting, one of the agents had read an article from *Land og Folk,* an underground newspaper, describing the program.

"You're just trying to scare me," said the girl.

"You're already scared." He covered her hand with his as she clutched the seat of the chair. Her fingers were ice-cold. "Hair will grow back. There are other things—like dignity and self-respect—that will not."

She glared at him in defiance, yet as she glared, a fat, tragic tear pooled in her eye and then spilled down her cheek. He was reminded then that she was just a kid. A frightened kid like all of them, with delft-blue eyes and porcelain skin, all but defenseless against the dangers of occupied Copenhagen.

Then it hit him. He finally remembered where he had seen

this girl. At the very start of the occupation, not long after his family had been taken and he'd joined the underground, he had rescued a girl with yellow hair and terrified eyes. He still remembered that shining April day, the gentrified neighborhood suddenly polluted by the presence of German transport trucks and military police.

Magnus's assignment had been to warn the Winther family of their impending arrest for acts of rebellion—acts that included saving people from being seized and transported. Magnus had failed to warn them in time. He'd arrived too late. Mrs. Winther had been hauled off right before her daughter's eyes while Mr. Winther had been arrested at the hospital where he worked. But they had left behind their blond-headed daughter, who broke away from the soldiers.

Magnus had caught up with her as she was running for her life.

Although she was a stranger, he understood her terror and her guilt. She was terrified of the brownshirts, yet consumed by guilt because her parents had been taken, while she had survived. The same thing had happened to him on the night of the fire. That night, he had learned that the need to flee and survive was more powerful than grief. Even when a part of him wanted to crumble to the ground and surrender to despair, an inner fire burned for justice.

Knowing this now, he had yearned to help the fleeing girl by sending her up to Helsingør to be with her grandmother.

"Annelise," he said. "You're Annelise Winther."

Her face turned marble hard. "I am not that girl anymore. She died the day her family was taken." With that, she slipped out of the church door, into the fading sunlight.

As they walked along together, Magnus learned that she had not stayed in Helsingør for long, because her grandmother had passed away. Like him, she had lost everyone and everything. And like him, she had found a purpose, a reason to survive, with the *Holger Danske*.

Over the next year, he ran into her a number of times. She was young and nimble and not the sort of threat the Nazis were looking for. She tended to take part in operations that required the agent to be out in the open.

But there were dangers at every turn. In the world of shadows Magnus inhabited, a leap of faith could quickly become a freefall. One small mistake—making eye contact with the wrong person, executing a maneuver too soon or too late—could sometimes lead to discovery and then disaster.

The German occupation was turning more vicious. The Danes kept up their labor strikes and acts of sabotage. When the Germans tried to force the courts to punish Danish saboteurs, the entire government resigned. Now they were under martial law, and arrests were rampant—Jews, non-Jews, Danish civilians and military personnel—everyone was fair game.

Tonight's instructions were simple. He was to don a waxed cotton fisherman's apron and a pair of rubber clogs, and head down to the wharves where the herring fleet was moored. This time of year, the daylight lingered to nearly midnight, spreading an eerie reddish glow across the water and sky. Wherries plied back and forth through the churning sea, longshoremen and fishermen stood around, drinking Whiskey Mac and smoking rough hand-rolled cigarettes.

The organization switched people around. They'd learned the hard way that agents were easily vulnerable to the Gestapo. By rotating personnel, no one learned too much about an operation. If you didn't know anything, then no amount of torture could extract information from you.

Unfortunately, that sometimes meant Magnus found himself working with new, inexperienced operatives. That was the case tonight, not because of the identifying flat seaman's cap, the one with the white tabs out the back, which matched the hat Magnus wore. No, he recognized his inexperienced comrade by the creases in his work pants and by the fact that he was smoking a machine made cigarette—a dead giveaway that the agent was an outsider. And if that wasn't damning enough, the guy was smoking way too fast, not in the relaxed, laconic way of a worker at the end of his shift, but as if he were a man about to face his own execution.

Wheeling a barrow of netting over to the guy, Magnus said, "Your pants are too clean."

"What?" The guy looked down at the blue canvas coveralls.

"They've still got the creases in the folds."

"I beg your pardon."

The guy even talked funny. Magnus couldn't quite place his accent. His Danish pronunciation was odd. He might be from some area of England.

"My point is, you look like a phony," Magnus said. "Get rid of that cigarette before they see you. And quit smoking it as though it's your last one."

The guy dropped the cigarette and ground it out with his heel. In the half light, Magnus could see that he was young, probably still a teenager like Magnus himself. He had olive-toned skin and dark hair—not your typical Dane.

"Do you have the instructions?"

The guy said nothing. He cleared his throat, shuffled his feet.

"Oh, for Christ's sake," said Magnus. "The moon is supposed to be full tonight."

The guy breathed a sigh of relief. "But how does one know when the summer light never fades?"

That was the phrase they were supposed to exchange. And with those words, they were comrades on the mission. The foreigner explained his orders and the two of them teamed up at the loading docks, moving baskets of herring presumably destined for the fish stalls in Market Square.

As they worked, Magnus kept sneaking glances at his partner. He wondered where the foreigner came from. He was Spanish or Italian in looks, though his accent sounded English. American? Magnus had never met an American, though he'd seen plenty at the picture show. Cowboy movies were his favorites. They were everyone's favorites. In school, he studied English, but it was at the movies that he truly learned to speak the language.

He decided to test his hunch. "The soldiers," he said in English, trying to sound like Roy Rogers, his favorite cowboy, "they're as alert as trained guard dogs, you know?"

The guy's head snapped up. "Sorry," he said, obviously flustered, "I don't understand."

"You have to watch for your chance," Magnus continued in English. "The bastards are slippery. They watch every move. They watch every person. If they see a guy who is supposed to be a workman, but the work pants are creased and brand-new-looking, they get suspicious, you know? If they see a guy smoking a machine-rolled cigarette, they figure you for either a spy or a thief. And if their ears are tuned into your conversation, they might wonder why you're speaking Danish with an English accent. They might conclude that you're from England."

The guy kept working. Magnus shrugged and hefted a load. It was probably just as well they didn't learn anything about one another. It was a hard way to live, though. Disconnected, close to no one. Sometimes he wondered if there was any purpose at all to living.

Then he would think about the promise he had made to little Eva before she disappeared. And sometimes he would think about the girl he'd encountered that afternoon in the plaza—the beauteous Annelise Winther, shorn of her pretty hair, thanks to him. And these thoughts made him more determined than ever to get through the hard times. It was awful, though, because nothing seemed to stop the Nazis. Likely one day they would prevail and dismantle what was left of Denmark.

Magnus already knew he would leave. He didn't know when the day would come, though. Or where he would go.

"America," the guy said, in a delayed reply to Magnus's question. "California, to be exact."

Hearing the words made his heart speed up. He was proud to have ferreted out the information, and intrigued to meet his first American.

Magnus was dying to know how a Yank had come to be helping with the underground resistance. Everybody knew the United States was staying out of the war, even though there were rumblings from some quarters that they would join the Allies to stop the Germans once and for all.

After the baskets of fish were stacked high enough, Magnus jerked his head toward the German supply ship. "Look sharp now. We need to go and pick up the marked crates."

They moved their barrows behind the concealing baskets and wended their way among stacked boxes. They were looking for a particular set of crates marked For Specialized Distribution.

"It's here," said the American, indicating a group of boxes with the phrase stenciled in German. "Do we load them up?"

"Yes. Don't hurry." The boxes were not terribly heavy; Magnus wasn't certain what they contained. It could be ordnance, supplies or even weapons. Or perhaps the boxes were filled with more of the stupid leaflets the Germans loved to distribute, promising the Danes a better life once they submitted entirely to German protection. The leaflets were nothing but noise and propaganda.

Magnus was overcome by curiosity. Using a utility knife, he pried up one corner of a crate.

"Should you be doing that?"

He shrugged and kept working. At the top of the crate was a layer of newsprint. Inside were squares of cloth. He pulled one out, angled it toward the light. Needles of ice spiked his blood. "Son of a bitch," he whispered.

"What is it?"

He showed the guy what he had found. "Badges."

"What do you mean, badges? What sort of badges?"

"I think you know." He showed him one of the palm-sized badges with a yellow six-point star and the word *Jude*.

"For the Jews, you mean," the American said. "The Star of David."

"Well, they could hardly be sheriff's badges, could they? This is not the Wild West." Magnus felt cold despite the warmth of the summer night. "Forcing the Jews to wear the badge is just a precursor to rounding them up and deporting them," he said. "It is only a matter of time."

"I have heard of these deportations. The Germans promised the Jews that they were being taken to work camps in Poland for their own safety. Now we know those are actually extermination camps where people die by the thousands."

"I heard the same thing," Magnus whispered. "Where did you get your information?"

"A group from Poland called the Bund sent an eyewitness report to England last year in the springtime. Since then, there have been many verifications, including photographs and eyewitness reports."

The horrifying truth about the camps was so sinister that some people still didn't believe the stories. Magnus himself hadn't believed the early reports. No one had. The notion of killing off an entire race of people—including women, babies, grandmothers, old men, innocent kids—was too far-fetched, too appalling. By now, however, word was out that the Germans had instituted a system of deportation of Jews in order to kill them off.

At first, Nazis had organized mobile killing squads—*Einsatzgruppen*—to round up and massacre the Jews of Eastern Europe by shooting them in cold blood or asphyxiating them in gassing vans. Then they became more systematic about exterminating the entire race. Now that word was out about the Nazis' "Final Solution," no one even bothered to pretend the camps were anything but factories of death.

"We're to load these crates onto that horse lorry." Magnus gestured at the waiting vehicle.

"Sounds simple enough."

"If you say so."

"Why must we keep them?" asked the American. "Why not sink the badges into the harbor?"

"That is not for us to know. Maybe we have to make certain they can't be recovered."

He and the American wheeled the cart to the flatbed cargo truck. They placed the badges in the middle and then surrounded them with the baskets of herring. The driver didn't speak, just stayed huddled at the front. Magnus and the American hoisted themselves onto the back deck of the cart and sat with their feet dangling. Magnus put two fingers to his lips and whistled, and the cart lurched forward.

"Remember what I told you," Magnus warned. "We do this every day. It's just another load of fish."

"Got it."

As they passed through the exit gate, Magnus swung his feet and offered a casual nod. The guards gave the cargo only a cursory glance, as the laden carts were a common sight. The dogs didn't alert to any strange smell, either; the reek of herring was overpowering. They drove right past the guards. Magnus and the American sat in silence until they were clear of the harbor.

"What can I call you?" asked the stranger.

Some agents were keen on code names, but that was a bit silly in Magnus's view. It only meant more to remember. "Magnus," he said, "and that's my given name. You?"

"Ramon. My given name."

"Doesn't sound very American."

"You'd be surprised. America is many things. Especially California." He paused. "It's always warm there. Sunny all the time."

A place where it was sunny all the time sounded as if it was made up, like a movie set or somebody's dream. "Why the devil did you leave? Are you here because you want to oppose the march of the Third Reich?"

"No. I'm here because I didn't want to marry Evelyn Skeedy."

"Who is Evelyn Skeedy?"

"A girl I know, back in California. She tried to trap me. I had to escape."

Magnus pondered the irony of it. For several years now, people had been trying to escape Copenhagen. "How is it that you ran away from California and ended up in occupied Denmark? Are you crazy?"

"There are many ways to escape. I had a girl after me—or rather, her father and brothers. I had to get away fast."

"What do you mean, after you? If a girl was after me, I would hardly run. I would welcome her."

"Not this girl. She was looking for a husband. She told her father some things—lies. She said I...compromised her, you know?"

"I think I do." He thought about girls almost all the time, but he was too bashful to actually do anything about it.

"I would never," Ramon said, balling his hands into fists. "But she was very convincing."

"And so you ran."

"To San Francisco. A big port city."

"I have heard of this place."

"I joined the merchant marine. Do you know it?"

"Yes, of course."

"They don't ask a lot of questions. If you look as if you have a strong back and know how to follow orders, you're in."

"And this is how you came to be in Copenhagen?"

"The skipper's brother is the vessel owner. Both are Danes. The Gundersen brothers."

"Ah, I know of them." Magnus braced himself as the truck bounced over an increasingly rutted road. The Gundersens were a local shipping family. From the very start, they had openly opposed the occupation. The family patriarch had appeared before King Christian's counsel to argue against surrender.

"How did you learn to speak Danish?"

"I'm not very good at it, but I have a knack for picking up languages. I already had Spanish, English and German, and so I get by."

"Are you still with the merchant marine?"

"No. I jumped ship here in Copenhagen. Now I'm working for an agency called the Red Cross. Do you know it?"

"Sure, everybody knows the Red Cross."

"I am better suited for this type of work, you understand?" Ramon regarded him pointedly.

Magnus realized that was just a cover for what he was really doing. The Red Cross was supposed to be entirely neutral, but when an agent in service of the Allied forces appeared, they tended to look the other way. People affiliated with the Red Cross were less likely to fall under scrutiny. They crossed borders at will, and they were granted access to prisoner of war camps for inspections.

As the international community grasped the real purpose of the Germans' work camps, the rescue efforts gathered force. Red Cross workers were often bound by red tape and regulations, but a number of workers went underground in the war effort.

Magnus regarded Ramon with new respect. "What is it that you do?" he asked.

"I've been involved in transport. Grew up running farm equipment so I can drive anything. Nobody pays much attention to me. It's an advantage."

The truck drew to a halt. "Coast is clear," Magnus said. He could tell because the driver climbed down—the all clear signal. He and Ramon jumped down and looked around. The truck was parked precariously close to a stone bulkhead on a deserted section of the harbor. A rotten smell filled the air.

"I thought we were taking these parcels to a warehouse somewhere," he said to the driver.

"We were," said the driver.

Magnus recognized Annelise Winther's voice. "Then what the hell are you doing here?" He hadn't seen her in a number of months, maybe more than a year. In the half light, he could see the strain on her face. She looked...old.

"Same thing you are."

"You nearly drove the thing into the harbor."

"I stopped in time, didn't I?" She jerked her head at Ramon. "Who's he?"

"A comrade. He's okay," said Magnus. He checked out the area, and realized she'd brought them to a dumping station where household garbage was barged to the mainland for burning. "We're supposed to be at the fish warehouse. Why did you bring us here?"

"Because I have a better idea," she said. "Let's row the crates out to the barge like the garbage they are."

"I still think we should dump them in the harbor," said Ramon.

"When the tide goes out, they could be spotted," Magnus explained. "That's why the barge is moored so far out."

"Good point. Is there a boat?"

"We'll take that fishing dory." Magnus gestured at a small wooden boat tied to a mooring cleat.

"It's pretty small. Can you take them all in one go?" asked Annelise.

"We can try. You go keep watch."

"I always have to keep watch," she said. "It's dull. Nothing ever happens."

"And you'd better hope it stays that way," he said. "Go on with you."

With a huff of resentment, she returned to the truck and stationed herself on the driver's side, facing the incoming alleyway. The night was eerie, lightless due to blackout restrictions. Sounds came from some of the taverns in nearby Harbor Street—raucous voices arguing, singing or laughing. The occasional rumble of an engine intruded, though vehicles were prohibited from using their headlamps.

Magnus began to unload the crates, one by one, carrying them from the truck to the dory. Ramon was in charge of loading them into the wooden boat, making use of the expertise he'd gained in the merchant marine.

"We might have to make more than one trip," Magnus said, eyeing the dory. The wind had picked up, wafting the scent of rotting garbage across the water.

"We'll be fine. Just a few more crates," Ramon muttered.

The engine sounds grew louder, followed by a gnashing

of brakes. "That's likely a Nazi patrol," Magnus said. "Let's hurry it up."

Annelise helped them carry the last of the crates to the dory. Ramon got into the boat and used a line to secure the load.

"Get in," Magnus told her, picking up the oars. "I don't want you waiting here by yourself."

"There's no room," she said, whipping a glance over her shoulder. "I'll wait here. If you're spotted, I can create a diversion."

"Out of the question. Quit being so stubborn, and get in." He heard something else, somewhere in the night shadows. Footsteps. Boots on cobblestones. "Get—"

"Hurry back," she said, and with that, she loosed the mooring line and gave the boat a shove. Within seconds, it was out in the tidal stream.

"Start rowing," said Ramon. "No point in arguing with a stubborn girl."

"I don't like leaving her there." Nonetheless, Magnus rowed swiftly toward the barge, about a hundred meters off shore. Craning his neck to look past the precarious load, he tried to keep an eye on Annelise, but the darkness swallowed her. He didn't know why he felt so protective of her. She was contrary and feisty and bossy. Deep down, he admired her for it.

He didn't like tonight's setup, though. The tavern sounds, the rumbling engines, the unknown threat of darkness.

He rowed as fast has he could, ignoring the blisters forming on the palms of his hands and in the crease between his thumb and index finger. The sweetish reek of garbage intensified as they approached the barge. As quickly as possible, they hoisted the crate aboard and used an iron shovel and rake to bury the cargo amid the mounds of smelly household trash. Ramon choked and gagged, but Magnus gritted his teeth, working fast to get the job done.

"There, finally," he said, replacing the rake on the side of the barge. "Let's get moving. I don't like this."

"I'll take a turn at the oars," said Ramon.

"Thanks. I've got blisters." He settled in the stern and wiped his face with his sleeve. "It'll take ten bars of soap to get the stink off."

Ramon rowed swiftly toward the shore. "In California, we have an outdoor shower that uses water from a hot spring."

"Sure," said Magnus. "You're making that up."

"Not even. My father rigged a cord you can pull to drench yourself in warm water, as much as you could ever want. Damn. I miss the sunshine."

Magnus pictured showering outdoors in the California sun, and the image brought a smile to his face.

Just then, a light flickered over the surface of the water. Seconds later came the sound of a gunning engine. Magnus swung around to look at the shore. "She's in trouble," he said, feeling an instant freezing sensation in his gut. "She wouldn't run the truck unless something was up." A sense of urgency pounded in his chest.

"Row faster."

"I am. Take it easy, it's probably—"

There was a popping sound. "I hope to God that's the truck backfiring," said Magnus. He knew better, though. By now, his senses were finely attuned to the sound of gunfire. He leaped to the bow of the dory and knocked Ramon out of the way.

"Hey—"

"I'm faster." He felt the blisters on his hands rip open, but he ignored the pain. "She turned on the lights to create a diversion," he said. "Stupid girl. Stupid, stupid…."

There was more gunfire and a metallic crash. The lights sank, and Magnus gasped in horror. "She drove the damned thing into the water."

CHAPTER FOURTEEN

"Magnus is correct," Annelise said, her gaze focused on the day's last sunlight falling across the floor. "I did drive into the water. It was a foolish mistake made in terror, because the night watch had arrived. As it happens, I ended up creating a diversion, and Magnus and Ramon were not caught."

"But you were," Tess said softly.

Annelise nodded. "That was the night I was captured and taken to the birthing house on the island. I was detained there for nearly a year before I escaped."

They all sat in silence for long, uncounted minutes. Isabel thought about that young girl and what had gone on in the house where she was imprisoned. A vein in Annelise's temple gently throbbed, but otherwise she sat motionless, her graceful hands calmly folded in her lap.

Finally, Magnus cleared his throat. "I wish I'd saved you that night," he said, his voice low and broken. "I'm sorry I failed you."

"Regrets won't change a thing, and we all survived," Annelise said.

His hands trembled, and he pressed them hard against his knees. "When we met again, you should have said something, if not to me, then to someone who could help you."

"I told no one." Then she looked around the room, her gaze steady, her eyes surprisingly calm. "Until now."

Isabel couldn't believe she'd kept such a secret inside her for so long. She found herself looking at Mac, who had not moved a muscle while the old woman spoke. His eyes were damp, though, and easy to read.

"When I escaped, I said nothing, because I was afraid not just for myself, but for the child. I feared what would happen to a baby with such a strange heritage. And of course, in one so young, the shame and confusion were a constant torment."

Magnus took her hand in both of his, and pressed a kiss on it, his shoulders trembling. *"Please,"* he said to her in Danish. *"Please tell me you found a way to…"*

Isabel didn't recognize the next word.

Annelise gently removed her hand from his and continued in English. "It was so very long ago, yet the occurrence is knit into my very soul. I can no more rid myself of it than I can rid myself of my eye color or memories of my mother." Her movements were efficient and decisive as she helped herself to more sherry. "Perhaps I should have unburdened myself sooner. Even the deepest secrets always seem to find their way to the surface," she said. "They slip out in sneaky ways. I believe now that what happened to me colored every choice I've made in my life. Perhaps that is why I became a children's art teacher—so I could see beauty once more, and to love again. Later I became a dance teacher so I could learn to touch people again without fear. Other decisions as well sprang from the secret I carried inside."

Isabel's chest ached in sympathy. She wondered if Annelise was referring to her choice to stay single, to have a baby with Magnus, to give the child to Eva to raise.

"I'm grateful that you told us," said Tess. "You're not alone, and you don't have to bear the burden of the past by yourself."

"It is a relief to speak up at last. Everything feels...lighter, somehow. You are all the family I have, you girls and Magnus. It seems appropriate that you would be the first to hear the truth."

The word *family* brought a lump to Isabel's throat. "I'm so sorry," she said. "I hate that it happened to you, and to girls like you."

"We're very grateful that you survived," Tess said. "Did you ever find out anything at all about the baby that was taken from you?"

A smile flickered in her eyes. "The 'baby' would be in his seventies, wouldn't he? Sadly, the only thing I know is that it was a boy, and I can't even be completely certain of that. I was quite groggy, and he was red and screaming the only time I got a glimpse of him, just before the nurses swaddled him up and took him away. I was told nothing of the family that took him. At the end of the war, records were hidden or destroyed. My real name could not have been put on the birth record, because when I was arrested on the night we destroyed the badges, I never disclosed my real name. Like most of us in the underground, I had already created a fictional story about myself, just in case I was caught." She glanced over at Magnus. "I went by the name Greta Herman."

Everyone sat quietly for a while, watching the evening gather in the big picture window at the front of the shop. The occasional farm truck rolled past, laden with crates full of early harvest plums or berries. In the grassy meadows that flanked the road, swallows swooped and dove, black arrows darting against the crimson sky.

After a while, Mac asked, "What became of the badges?"

"They were hauled away on the barge with the rest of the garbage," Magnus said, "and I assume they were burned and forever lost. No Jew in Denmark was ever forced to wear one."

"It was quite a coup," Annelise said. "Elsewhere throughout Europe, the Jews had to display the badge every time they went out."

"A small victory, but good for morale," Magnus said. "There's an apocryphal story that many Danes and even King Christian displayed the badge in order to confuse the Nazis and to show support for the Jews, but it's only a story."

"Because there were no badges to distribute," said Mac.

"Few people know how the Star of David badges in Denmark disappeared," said Annelise.

"They will know once my friend Cormac writes the story," said Magnus. "But had I known then what the maneuver would cost, I never would have done it." Devastation shone on his face, deepening the lines and brightening his eyes with tears.

"I would not change a thing," she said very quietly. "Who can say why life plays out the way it does? Had I not endured what I did, then later, saving Ramon and rescuing Eva would have been impossible."

"This is true," Magnus said.

Isabel was desperate to hear how her grandmother had been rescued from a concentration camp and why Ramon had needed saving. She wanted to know how they had all ended up on a Norwegian ship bound for America. She was filled with more questions, but she could tell Annelise was emotionally drained; it showed in the downward slope of her shoulders. "Let's stop, okay?" she gently suggested. "The rest of the story can be told another time."

There was gratitude in Annelise's tremulous smile. "I agree. The important thing is that we all made our way in the world. We carried on. What else is there to do?" Annelise got up from her chair and put out her hand to Magnus. "Walk with me," she said.

Mac, Tess and Isabel all stood as they left the shop. The elderly couple took the gravel road toward the house, arm in arm, their heads bowed together as they talked. Surrounded by the blooms and new leaves of springtime, they moved with dignity, their bond a tangible force that could be sensed even from a distance.

"Excuse me," Tess said quietly. "I need to go find Dominic. I need to collapse and make him hold me and drink wine with me for the next couple of hours."

Isabel gave her a brief hug. "I don't blame you. That was very intense."

"Do me a favor and set the alarm when you leave," Tess said. "You know the code. The door will lock behind you."

When Isabel and Mac were alone, she said, "I guess we didn't see *that* coming."

"Nope."

"It's fascinating and horrible all at once. Mostly, I just feel sad for her, to have her innocence taken at such a young age."

"Yes. But be glad she survived, came to the States, became a teacher," he said. "She taught art and dance classes."

"That's how I like to picture her, surrounded by kids or teaching a couple the tango. But like she told us, that insane ordeal will always be a part of her." She noticed that Mac had not made a single note while Magnus and Annelise had been talking. He probably didn't need to. Like her, the situation would be etched deeply in his mind. "You must hear a lot of grim things in your line of work. How do you stand it?"

"I remind myself that their stories are important, and they deserve the best work I can produce. But yeah, some of the stories are hard to hear."

She nodded and went to the window, gazing out as she tried to picture young Annelise, alone in the world and on the run, still bleeding from giving birth. "The sheer courage it must have taken to simply survive is staggering to me," she said. "And the fact that she went right back to helping the war effort is remarkable, too."

"I've read studies of trauma survivors. Some fall apart later, and others move on with their lives. One key element for the ones who make it seems to come up again and again—they take action for a cause bigger than themselves. The work helps pull them through."

Isabel could relate, all too easily. After leaving culinary school, she probably would have ended up in full-on melt-down, except that her grandmother had needed her so badly. Bubbie's illness had, in a way, saved Isabel. She felt a wave of shame, knowing that.

"I wonder if being a victim of the *Lebensborn* experiment had anything to do with her decision to give her son to Magnus and Eva," Isabel said. She made a last, lingering study of the collection Annelise had shown them. The objects seemed so benign, yet now they seemed to possess a sinister power. "I bet that's why she never married. It's unusual for someone from her generation to stay single all her life. Not that there's anything wrong with being single," she quickly added.

"I didn't say there was," he quietly replied.

She didn't hear him move, but suddenly he was behind her, his voice right next to her ear. Although he didn't touch her, he was close enough that she could feel the warmth of him, catch his faint scent of piney soap. When she turned, she found herself nose to chest with him. "What?" she asked.

"I've got an idea," he said. "Let's get out of here."

"All right." She went to Tess's big antique desk and armed the shop's alarm system. "We can leave the shop now."

"I mean, really out."

"I don't understand."

"You will."

They left Things Remembered and walked up the gravel roadway toward the house. The quiet of the gathering evening settled around them, disturbed only by the occasional hoot of an owl or the swish of a passing car on the road.

"That was overwhelming," she murmured, her chest still aching from Annelise's story. "I had no idea...none of us did."

Their hands brushed as they walked, and in a movement that felt completely natural, he laced his fingers with hers. "I'm sorry for what she went through. Sorry you had to hear it."

"I can't believe she endured all that and still moved ahead with her life. Where did she find the courage?" She shook her head. "She was so brave. Grandfather and Bubbie, too, and so many others we'll never hear about. These people were ripped from the safety of childhood without a moment's notice. They had to survive on their own for years before putting their lives together. They were powerless to change what happened to them. And yet they didn't allow the past to limit them. It's humbling to me."

"Humbling. In what way?"

She stopped walking and looked down at their clasped hands. "Hearing about how they survived reminds me that I've been timid about my life." Very carefully, she withdrew her hand from his, not because she didn't like holding hands with this guy, but because she *did*.

"What do you mean, timid?" he asked.

She started walking again. "Well, tentative, maybe. Overly cautious. I don't really advocate being reckless, but I tend to stay too much inside my comfort zone."

"And now you're wondering what you might find outside the zone."

"Yes. I wish I were more daring. More of a risk taker."

"Planning Tess's wedding isn't a risk? Every day, you take your life into your own hands."

She laughed. "It's not that bad."

"How about creating a cooking school? You don't think that's risky?"

"Of course it is, but that's not the kind of risk I'm talking about." To her, falling in love was the biggest risk of all, the ultimate loss of control. Life was much simpler when she kept her heart under constant guard.

Instead of heading toward the house, he went around to the gravel parking area and held open the passenger side door of his Jeep. "Get in," he said.

"Where are we going?"

"Taking a little detour."

"Where?"

"Out of your comfort zone."

"Hey—"

"Get in, for chrissake, it's not as though I'm kidnaping you."

There was a foolish flutter in her heart—apprehension. Yes, she liked him. Yes, she was inspired by Annelise and her grandfather's story to be braver about things. But...tonight? With him? She could feel her body tightening in response to the idea and thought, why not enjoy the guy's company? He'd be gone soon, anyway. He was just—as he'd said—a detour.

"Fine," she agreed, pushing past the apprehension. She climbed in and fastened her seat belt. The radio was tuned to a station blaring an old song by The Clash, and he drove down the farm-to-market road into town.

"See, no need to freak out," he stated, parking on a side street off the town plaza. "Just wanted to take you for a bite to eat."

"Good idea," she said.

"I'm full of good ideas." He pocketed his keys. "Where to? Assuming, I guess, that there's a restaurant that meets your standards."

"Archangel is full of great places. Let's take a walk around the plaza and you can tell me what you like."

"Everything," he said as they entered the plaza. There was a big park in the middle with gardens and walkways. "I like everything."

"Bees?"

"I don't mind bees, except when they sting."

"And they don't sting unless you threaten them."

A trendy-looking group of people came toward them, laughter and conversation filling the air. There was a guy with a portable light set and another with a shoulder-mounted video camera moving along with them.

Isabel nearly tripped over her own feet. In the middle of the well-groomed, perfectly made-up group was someone painfully familiar. He wore his trademark outfit—black jeans, black fitted Western-cut shirt, black cowboy boots with toes pointy enough to stomp a cockroach in the corner.

"Now what?" asked Mac, placing his hand at the small of her back to steady her. "You look as if you just saw a ghost."

"Calvin Sharpe," she said. "Not my favorite person." She prayed the guy wouldn't spot her.

He spotted her. His gaze focused like a laser aiming device. He still had some uncanny way of sensing her. Even as he re-galed his admirers while the camera recorded him, his stare honed in on her, taking in Mac's hand at her waist. Just for a moment, a fraction of a second, something hard and threatening flowed from him to her. She shivered and turned in the opposite direction.

"Isn't that the guy you ran into the morning of the bee stings?" asked Mac.

"The very same."

"He keeps turning up like a bad penny," he said.

She crossed to the other side of the plaza. "Hmm. I've never actually seen a bad penny. How can a penny be bad?"

He shrugged. "I can tell he bugs you. Who broke whose heart?"

She quickened her steps. "Why would you ask me that?"

"Because it's obvious you have a past with that guy. Come on, spill."

"It was a long time ago. And believe me, nobody's heart got broken."

"*Something* got broken. He's swanning around town with an entourage, and the sight of him makes you go green around the gills."

"So you say."

"I have ways of making you talk."

That drew a laugh from her. "Right."

"It's true. I'm a professional."

She glanced back over her shoulder at the group making the video. "All right, if you must know, Calvin Sharpe was a chef-instructor at the cooking school I attended in Napa. He was—and I guess, still is—supersuccessful, with an ego to match. I was—and maybe still am—supernaive and I followed him around like a lost puppy."

"Shit. Tell me this is not going where I think it's going."

"Sorry, whatever you're thinking is probably on the money. It was every cliché you're imagining—a promising, eager student enamored with her older, charismatic teacher." Her stomach still churned when she thought of those days, the way she'd let him become her whole world, at the expense of her dreams. "He wasn't—he's *not*—a good guy. He treated me like his unpaid help and I was stupid enough to be grateful for the privilege. He took credit for work that I did and..." She stopped herself before blurting out the rest—the pregnancy, the assault.

"And?" he prompted. "And what? It ended badly."

She shook her head. "The worst part isn't that it ended. The worst part is that it didn't end. I simply left the culinary program and never went back. Didn't finish school, didn't contact him ever again. There was no closure, no confrontation. As far as I know, he still assumes I'm a member of his fan club."

"You can close that chapter anytime you want," he said. "Up to you."

"Right. Do I just go up to him and...what? Simply tell him off about something he probably doesn't even remember? And then I'll magically be over him?"

"You need to get over *yourself*."

"Sure. Doing it now." She knew he was right, but she didn't like being pressured.

Mac looked back over his shoulder at Calvin and his entourage. "Have you ever told anyone the truth about that guy? Even yourself?"

She felt the color flare in her cheeks. "Can we please change the subject?"

"Change it to what?"

She gestured at a row of tasting rooms and colorful cafés. "Food and wine."

"My two staples. Take me to your favorite place." He surveyed the area, and a smile spread across his face. "I like it here. Great energy. Great smells. Live music." He indicated a guy on a three-legged stool, tuning up a guitar.

"You're right. I'm sorry, Mac. Seeing that guy and his crew put me in a mood. Let me finish showing you around, and we'll find a table somewhere."

"Much better."

It was a gorgeous evening, with a breeze shimmering through the trees, people strolling hand in hand through the quaint streets and the plaza. The shops, bistros and restaurants were abuzz with patrons. She showed him where the farmer's market took place every Saturday, and pointed out her favorite spots—the town library, a tasting room co-op run by the area vintners, the Brew Ha Ha café and the Rose, a vintage community theater. On a night like this, she took a special pride in Archangel, with its cheerful spirit and colorful sights. She refused to let the Calvin sighting drag her down. He had ruined many things for her, but he was not going to ruin the way she felt about her hometown.

After some deliberation, she chose Andaluz, her favorite spot for Spanish-style wines and tapas. The bar spilled out onto the sidewalk, brightened by twinkling lights strung under the big canvas umbrellas. The tables were small, encouraging quiet intimacy and insuring that their knees would bump as they scooted their chairs close. She ordered a carafe of local Mataró, a deep, strong red from some of the oldest vines in the county, and a *plancha* of tapas—deviled dates, warm, marinated olives, a spicy seared tuna with smoked paprika. Across the way in the plaza garden, the musician strummed a few chords on his guitar.

The food was delicious, the wine even better, as elemental and earthy as the wild hills where the grapes grew. They finished with sips of a chocolate-infused port and cinnamon churros. The guitar player was singing "The Keeper," his gentle voice seeming to float with the breeze. Isabel savored a bite of the churro, licking a sugary crumb from the corner of her mouth.

"Hang on," Mac said, staring at her. "Don't move."

"What's the matter?" She froze. Maybe he'd spotted a bee or mosquito on her.

"Nothing. I just want to freeze this moment."

"What?"

"Because it's kind of perfect."

She melted a little inside. "Kind of?"

"Yep."

"What would make it *really* perfect?"

"If I knew I was going to get lucky afterward."

"Get…" She blushed, suddenly catching on, and finished the last sip of her cordial. "You don't want to get lucky with me."

"Wrong. I'd like nothing more."

She shook her head. "We're better as friends." As soon as the words were out of her mouth, she knew she was lying. She was falling for him in the worst way, but it was the kind of falling that was guaranteed to have a rough landing.

"How the hell do you know that?"

"I just know. I'm not interested in casual sex."

"Who said anything about casual? To be honest, I don't do casual sex, either. Just warm, intimate, slow, amazing sex." He stared pointedly at her mouth. "It's my favorite."

She shifted uncomfortably in her chair. "I'll take your word for it."

"You shouldn't. You should make me prove myself."

She looked away so he wouldn't see the yearning in her eyes. "What I mean is, I don't… I'm not interested in just sex, or a fling or whatever you're calling it."

"You're a red-blooded American girl. How can you not

be interested? Don't tell me you're one of those women who doesn't like sex."

"I do," she said. *She did.* "But forgive me for having standards. When I get intimate with a guy, I like to know there's a possible future."

"And you don't see that with me."

"Not unless you're okay with hanging around in Archangel."

He scanned the area, filled with music and soft breezes and delightful aromas. "This doesn't suck."

"Tess says you're a rolling stone. You never stay in one place for long."

"I never had a reason to stay." He leaned forward, still studying her mouth, his knees under the table straddling hers. He was going to kiss her. She knew it in every cell of her body. She *wanted* it with every cell of her body.

"Let's not do this," she said in a rush, and scraped her chair back.

"Why the hell not?"

He was a complication she absolutely did not need. Not now. Not ever. "We're bad for each other."

"We might be made for each other. But if you have that attitude, we'll never know."

Better that way, she thought. *Better not to know. Safer and neater.* "Then I suppose you're right. We'll never know."

PART VI

The color, aroma and flavor of honey is a reflection of a specific region and time of year. Honey in its purest form isn't clear, but misty with pollen. While plain sugar and other sweeteners are merely sweet, honey can express floral, grassy, fruity or woody flavor notes, depending on the source of the nectar. Honey from summer wildflowers is considered the sweetest variety.

HUMMINGBIRD CAKE

3	cups flour	3	beaten eggs
2	cups sugar	1	cup chopped toasted pecans
1	teaspoon baking soda	1	cup vegetable oil
1	teaspoon table salt	2	tablespoons honey
1	teaspoon ground cinnamon	1	(8-oz.) can crushed pineapple, undrained
2	cups diced overripe bananas		

Preheat oven to 350°. Sift together first 5 ingredients in a large bowl; add the remainder of the ingredients, stirring just until dry ingredients are moistened. Pour batter into 4 greased and floured 9-inch square or round cake pans.

Bake for 20 to 25 minutes or until a toothpick inserted in center comes out clean. Cool in pans on wire racks for about 10 minutes; then remove from pans and place the cakes on wire racks, to cool completely.

BROWNED BUTTER FROSTING

1	cup butter	1	tablespoon honey
1	lb. powdered sugar	¼	cup chopped pecans
¼	cup milk		

Melt butter in a heavy saucepan over medium heat, stirring constantly for 8 to 10 minutes or until butter begins to turn golden-brown. Remove pan immediately from heat, and pour butter into a small bowl. Chill for an hour or until butter begins to solidify.

Beat butter with an electric mixer until fluffy, and add sugar alternately with milk. Stir in the honey.

Frost the cake and sprinkle with pecans. Chill for at least 1 hour before serving to make it easier to cut and serve.

[Source: Adapted from a traditional Southern recipe]

CHAPTER FIFTEEN

"Here, taste this." Isabel set a slice of cake in front of Tess. "If you like it, then we'll make it for your wedding cake."

Isabel had always been good at cakes. It was a special talent, making a cake that was both beautiful and delicious. Tess's green eyes danced as she regarded the creamy iced wedge of two-layer cake in front of her. "Am I drooling? Because if this tastes half as good as it looks—"

"Not half," Isabel said. "All the way. You have to trust."

"I trust." Tess leaned down and inhaled the fragrance. "Butter and pecans."

"It's a browned butter frosting, and the filling is a cream cheese custard sweetened with honey."

"Stop. You're making me have an orgasm."

"Tess."

"A cake-gasm, then." She dug in, savoring the first bite with closed eyes and a blissful expression on her face. "Incredible," she said. "Why would anyone eat anything else when there is hummingbird cake in the world?"

"Exactly. I'm glad you approve."

"Well, I hope you know CPR, because when the wedding guests taste this cake, they are going to keel over and die."

"So it's a go?"

"Are you kidding? Total go. Get the defibrillator paddles. This might be the best wedding cake ever made. Oh, and don't try to make it look like anything but a cake, you know? I'm not a fan of those silly cakes that look like the Liberty Bell or birdcages or something in a 3-D cartoon. A mile high cake on stilts, big enough to feed the world. That's all we need."

"Got it," said Isabel. "I'll have the caterer pretty it up with fresh flowers, but no sculpting. No sugar dough blossoms."

"Right. Oh, Isabel, thank you."

"Welcome." The loud grind and whir of an air hammer disturbed the quiet of the patio and pergola area. This was followed by a crash and some cursing in rapid-fire Spanish. Isabel cringed, then yanked off her apron and went outside. "What happened?" she asked the foreman.

He waved a hand, indicating a pile of coping stones that had apparently fallen from a forklift down a side slope. "It's okay, senorita," he said. "The walkway is steep, though. We might have to re-grade it."

"All right," she said, answering him in Spanish. *"Do what you have to do."*

"The surveyor is coming this evening about the excavation for the pool," he reminded her. "You can meet with us, yes?"

"Of course," she said.

"La piscina?" asked Tess. "Doesn't that mean swimming pool?"

"We're getting a pool. Crazy, right?"

"Crazy good. When did this genius idea come about?"

"It was an impulse, and it won't be ready in time for the

grand opening, but it's in the plans for Phase Two. Mac's suggestion, actually."

"So, a pool?" Tess shaded her eyes and studied the area, currently a terraced slope spiked with surveyor's stakes. "That's exciting. But you look stressed out."

"You think?" Isabel wiped her brow with the edge of her blouse. "It's the hottest day of the year so far, I've been working nonstop, the car service for Annelise was late, something's going on with the plumbing in the teaching kitchen, and oh, yeah, I added a pool to this insane project…. What was I thinking?"

"That everything is going to be fantastic," said Tess. "Deep breath."

"Got it."

"So, you and Mac…."

Isabel planted her hands on her hips, pretending she hadn't thought about him every waking moment since the night in the plaza. "Stop it. He's here for Grandfather. And we're becoming friends. End of story."

"It doesn't have to be the end. Honestly, Isabel, I'm desperate for you to have a little romance in your life. You haven't dated anyone since I've known you."

She brushed a sweaty strand of hair off her forehead. "If you must know, I had a date with Mac the other night."

"Seriously?"

"No, it wasn't serious at all. We went to town for tapas and wine. That counts as a date, right?"

"Totally. Why didn't you tell me? Was it wonderful?"

"It was nice, and the nicest part of all is that it wasn't serious."

"That's a good start. I'm glad you got out for a little bit. He's a catch, don't you think?"

"He doesn't want to be caught. And I'm not in the market for a boyfriend, anyway."

"But you're attracted to him."

"Hello, he looks like Thor's big brother. I'd be declared brain dead if I wasn't attracted to him. Doesn't mean I want him for my boyfriend, though."

Tess beamed at her. "I think I'll invite him to the wedding."

"Don't you dare."

"Watch me." She grabbed her phone and tapped out a text message.

"He'll be gone before the wedding," Isabel said. "We'll never see him again."

"Miss Johansen?" The plumber approached her with a clipboard. "I have a quote for the repair in the new kitchen."

"It's brand-new," she said, hyperventilating when she saw the estimate. "How can it need repairing?"

He launched into an explanation so technical that her eyes glazed over. Isabel approved the bid, then was pulled away to deal with a delivery of landscaping plants. As she stood in a jungle of potted honey locusts and Italian plum trees, checking inventory off a list, she had an urge to run away from home.

That was when Mac showed up. "You wanted to see me?" he asked.

"What? No. Why would you think that?"

"Tess said. I had a text message from her."

"That's right." Tess took the plant inventory list away from Isabel. "You need to take her away from here for a while. She's been working nonstop and has to decompress."

"Hey," Isabel said again. "I don't have time to—"

"Actually, you do," Tess said. "Trust me, I *know* how toxic stress is."

Isabel knew she was alluding to the state Tess was in when she'd first arrived at Bella Vista. "I'll be okay," she said.

"Yes, but only after you take the afternoon off." Tess grabbed Isabel's phone. "Unplugged."

Isabel scowled at her sister, then turned to Mac. "Thanks for the offer, but I can't go anywhere right now."

"Sure, you can," he said. "Let's go."

What part of *no* did this person not understand?

"Hey, Tess," he added, "thanks for the other message you sent. I'd be honored to come to your wedding. I've heard the food is going to be incredible."

"The guest list is closed," Isabel said.

"There's always room for one more," Tess assured her. She turned back to the landscape delivery, officiously checking the plants.

"What makes you think you'll still be here for the wedding?" Isabel asked.

"You," he said easily. "You make me think that." Just as he'd done the other night, Mac took her hand. "I have an idea. It's a great one. It's going to knock your socks off."

"What—"

"I'll show you. I was going to wait until we were further along, but today's as good as any other." Keeping hold of her hand, he started walking, but not toward the house. Instead, he took her down to the machine shop. It was dimly lit with slices of sunlight cutting through the rustic wood planks on the walls.

Her grandfather's tractor was parked there, with the flail and rotary mowers nearby. There were a couple of bin trailers and a forklift, and stacks of bushels, bins and ladders. The gooey smell of motor oil tinged the air, emanating from the repair bay.

"What are we doing in here?" she asked, wishing for a breeze.

"I spotted something when your grandfather was showing

me around. Major find. I think you're going to like it." He went over to the repair bay and pulled away a canvas shroud to reveal an old-fashioned motor scooter. "I don't suppose you recognize this."

She stood back and frowned. "Should I?"

He wheeled it out into the sunshine, and she followed, still mystified. The scooter was a neglected hulk of a thing, its seafoam-green paint furred with dusty grease. A headlamp rested atop the front fender, and what might have been chrome was pocked with black spots. Yet its homely, bulbous shape was curiously appealing. There was a triangular leather saddle with springs and a square one behind it, and both shone from a recent polishing. The tires looked new, incongruous next to the shabby state of the rest of the scooter.

"It belonged to your mother."

Her jaw dropped. "How's that?"

"She brought it over from Italy when she moved here."

"You're kidding me."

"Nope. Magnus told me that when she and your father met in Italy, this was her ride to and from classes every day."

She walked around the old bike, trying to picture a young woman riding around Italy on it. "My mother went to university in Salerno. I knew she and my father had met there, but I never heard a thing about a motorcycle." Whenever she spoke of her parents, Isabel felt curiously ambivalent. She was speaking of two strangers she'd never known, yet without them, she would never have been born. A part of her yearned to find out more, yet another part held back in fear. What if she learned something disturbing about her mother? It had been hard enough to hear Annelise's unbearable truth.

But a motor scooter? There couldn't be anything sad about that, could there?

"Magnus thinks Francesca's father gave it to her, so I guess she was keeping it for sentimental value. It's a 1952 model. It was put away when she found out she was pregnant with you. And then, I assume, forgotten."

That was understandable, considering the drama around the time of her birth. "So you're saying this thing just sat in a corner of the shop until now?"

"That's what your grandfather told me. There are some bicycles, too, including a tandem bike, but this is by far the most interesting thing we found."

"And you just happened to pull it out."

"Magnus and I were talking about his son, and the conversation got around to Francesca, and we found her old scooter stored under an old tarp in the machine shop. Said he never took the time to get rid of it, and even considered getting it restored, but then just forgot about it."

"He's always been a pack rat."

"We've been working on the sly."

"So this is where you've disappeared to every day."

"Yep. We replaced the tires and a lot of other parts," said Mac. "And there's good news." He dangled a key in front of her, then inserted it and turned the fuel tap lever. With one foot, he kick-started it. There was a backfire, and then a chugging sound. With a puff of exhaust, the thing started. "I got it working."

She took another step back. "You did not."

"Yep." He gunned the engine.

"Wow. I'm impressed. I can't believe you got it running after all this time."

"Living in developing countries has its perks. You learn to fix stuff on your own."

"Unbelievable." She gave a little laugh. "One of these days, I want to hear about these countries."

"Not today. It's all Italy today. There's a lot more work to be done, but this will do for now." He mounted the scooter, his feet resting on the flat floorboard. "*Vieni,* signorina."

"Is it safe?" she asked, raising her voice over the chugging of the engine.

"Why is that always your first question?"

"We don't have helmets," she said. "I'm wearing flip-flops."

"You're living on the edge," he said. "Come on, this thing is so underpowered, we won't go faster than thirty, tops."

"I'm sure it's not even street legal," she said.

"Not even," he shot back.

"It's filthy."

"Get dirty with me, Isabel."

"But—"

"Get *on.*"

Despite her apprehension, she bunched up her skirt and slung her leg over the bike. Gingerly, she groped for the edge of the saddle.

"Hang on," he said.

There was nothing to hold on to except him. She clung to his waist, grabbing a handful of his T-shirt with her fists. He smelled of sweat and exhaust, a combination she found wildly appealing. This was crazy, because she always assumed she was attracted to men who wore cologne, and long-sleeved dress shirts and knife-pleated trousers. Not—

"Here we go," he said, and accelerated. The scooter lurched forward, and they were off. He drove down to the main road, turning left, away from town, and opened up the accelerator. Isabel held his shirt in a death grip, certain the contraption was going to fly apart at any moment.

The landscape of Bella Vista flowed past, a sun-drenched smear of color—lush greens, the purple of wild iris, poppies the color of egg yolk, all under a sky of the deepest, most promising blue. The scooter chugged, and then hit its stride, humming along with a steady drone.

Suddenly Isabel found herself imagining her mother, in a way she never had before. She had always pictured Francesca as a two-dimensional image—a smiling young bride, carefully coiffed and posed in the yellowing wedding photos pressed in Bubbie's fat, musty-smelling album. Now she could see someone vibrant and alive, someone who rode a motor scooter. Rather than a smiling woman in a fading photograph, Isabel could now envision her mother as an adventurous soul—young and in love, bravely leaving everything she'd ever known in Italy, all for the sake of an American named Erik Johansen.

Perhaps that was why she'd had her scooter shipped to Archangel, to have something familiar, something from home. Isabel wondered if Francesca had ridden these byways as a new bride, maybe stopping at a farm stand here or there to bring something home for supper, her parcels nestled in the willow basket behind the seat.

They skimmed past the sprawling Maldonado estate, heading north. "Do you know where you're going?" she asked, shouting into the wind.

"Not a clue. Take me somewhere," he said.

Take me somewhere. No one had ever said that to her before. Suddenly she wanted to take him everywhere, to show him everything. The warm breeze eddied through her hair and caressed her skin. It felt wonderful. It felt like freedom.

"The vineyards on both sides of the road belong to the Maldonado family," she said.

"As in Ramon Maldonado?" As he spoke, he turned his head to the side, and she had the sensation of his words flowing past her on the wind.

"Grandfather's friend from the war years, yes. It was the Maldonado family who granted Bella Vista to Grandfather after the war," she said. "Did he tell you how it all came about?"

"Not yet."

"He will, I'm sure. They've been friends ever since." She thought about the recent trouble with Lourdes, who was Ramon's granddaughter, but that situation couldn't be blamed on Ramon. "I can take you to see some incredible views. Do you think this thing will make it up a hill?"

"Yes, but it'll be slow."

"I don't mind taking it slow," she said.

They crossed the single lane arched bridge that spanned Angel Creek, a winding, stony waterway of worn rocks, flanked on both sides by farms and vineyards. The landscape turned wilder as the road narrowed and wound its way gradually up Angel Peak, the highest hill of the Archangel valley. She tipped up her chin to look at the sky, fringed by the boughs of eucalyptus trees along the roadside. The air cooled, and a part of Isabel was amazed that she was actually riding on the back of a scooter, like a carefree teenager running off with some guy she barely knew.

She pointed out Elsinore Pond, where as a girl she used to play amid the reeds or crouch at the water's edge, collecting frogs' eggs and bringing them home to watch the tadpoles hatch. The pond had been named by her grandparents after they settled in at Bella Vista, and only now did Isabel understand the significance of the name. It had never occurred to her to wonder about it.

Through the stories Grandfather was telling Mac, the past was taking on a life of its own. It didn't just sit frozen like an old photograph. She was finally getting a true sense of the drama her grandparents had survived. It was one thing to run her finger gently across the numbers tattooed on her grandmother's inner forearm, as Isabel used to do, aching for the suffering Bubbie had endured; now she could picture little Eva, yelling out in pain and terror as the numbers were gouged into her tender flesh. Yet Isabel could also picture a girl who played in the garden and sang songs, and once had a friend named Annelise.

On the north slope of the peak was a redwood forest with branches arching over the roadway like the buttresses of a cathedral. The timeless sentinels added a curious hush to the coolness. The last thousand feet of the climb gave way to grassland and oak savannah, and the crest of the peak itself was covered in grass and wildflowers. There was a gravel parking area and then a final walk up a path to the highest point.

The scooter chugged along, emitting a backfire when Mac cut the engine.

She dismounted, stepping back while he set the kickstand. "Well. Honestly, I think it's amazing that you found the scooter and actually got it to run."

"Vespas are awesome," he told her. "The word *vespa* is Italian for *wasp*."

"I didn't know that."

"Yep. The body is built like an aircraft, made of a single piece of metal. These scooters can run forever if you take care of them. Your granddad and I have big plans for this one. I'll take it apart and polish up each little piece, and put it back together. It's going to be better than new."

Why? she wanted to ask. *Why would you do something like that?*

"Your grandfather and I will finish the restoration together," he said. "Guys talk better when they're busy doing something with their hands."

She nodded. "It's not just guys. I'm better talking in the kitchen, preparing food. That's why the cooking school is such a good project for me. Cooking and talking are my two favorite things. I love everything about preparing food."

"It's in your blood," he said. "Erik and his state fair pies. I found another folder of his recipes in his room."

She frowned. "Really? I thought I'd found them all myself, years ago."

"They were in an old travel book. I'll show you when we get back."

"All right. My grandmother said she used to cook with Erik when he was a boy. Could be that's why I loved cooking with her, too. She was incredible in the kitchen. The things she could do with apples could make a grown man weep."

"I have a feeling she'd approve of what you're doing with Bella Vista."

"She loved having people over, fixing food, laughing and talking. Knowing what I know about her now, what she survived and the life she made for herself afterward, I'm even more in awe of her. We're going to call the herb garden 'The Garden of Eva' in her honor. Too hokey?"

"Not at all. I like it. Would Eva have liked it?"

"Sure. She loved growing fresh herbs, tended them as though they were her children. Bubbie did her gardening in the morning, wearing a floppy sun hat, with a fresh flower stuck in the brim." Isabel smiled at the memory.

Mac inspected the gauges on the scooter, wiping the covering with a corner of his shirt. "Not bad for a test run."

"You haven't tested it before today?"

"Not with a passenger, and not uphill for…" He checked the odometer. "Five kilometers. She did great, eh?"

Isabel fluffed out the hem of her skirt. "I got a big grease stain on this."

"Buy a new one. Girls like shopping for clothes."

"Guilty as charged." Isabel did love shopping—when she

had the time. She was already planning a trip to Angelica Delica, her favorite boutique in town. She still hadn't figured out what to wear for Tess's wedding. Tess didn't want the bridesmaids to wear matching dresses. Instead, she asked them all to find a dress they loved and shoes that made them want to dance.

"What's that smile?" he asked her.

"What smile?"

"The one I don't see enough of."

"I smile all the time," she objected. Didn't she? Now she wasn't so sure. Mac O'Neill noticed things. She wasn't certain whether it was the journalist in him, or if he was simply observant. Or even if, for some reason, he was particularly interested in observing *her*.

"I was thinking about all the dress shopping I get to do. I have to find a maid of honor dress for Tess's wedding. And something to wear for the grand opening of the cooking school." Feeling slightly discomfited, she walked over to a sign that read Angel Peak, Elev. 2212 Feet. "Come check out the view from here. We came on a good day. No coastal mist."

"Wow," he said, coming up behind her. "Damn, that's awesome."

She breathed deeply of the crisp, clear air. To the west, the Pacific Ocean was rimmed by rocky arches and rugged sea cliffs. To the east, the green-clad Archangel valley stretched toward the distant, even more dramatic Sonoma valley. The alluvial plains were flanked by forested hills and abundant farmlands. "Jack London country," she said, gesturing to the north toward the state park that bore the writer's name. "One of my favorite wilderness areas."

"One of my favorite writers."

"Really?"

"Sure. I've probably read most of his work. He was an incredible stylist and storyteller. How about you?"

"I was born and raised right here in the valley, so of course I'm a fan. Every high school student around here spends a semester reading Jack London. I read *The Call of the Wild* at an impressionable age. After that, I never looked at a dog the same way. And then there was *Love of Life,* you know, the one about the guy whose partner abandoned him in the Yukon."

"I read that one in high school, too."

"I had to write an essay about the survival instinct, and I wrote about my grandmother. I asked her how she survived a concentration camp, and she had no answer. 'You go on,' she told me. 'You just go on.'" Isabel looked at Mac. "I think I understood her better after reading the story."

"There are lots of writers I like, but reading Jack London made me want to *be* a writer."

"Seriously?"

"When I was a kid, I knew I wanted to write, but I didn't want to *live* like a writer, buried in a library or chained to a computer. I wanted to be more like Jack London—traveling, having adventures, living and then writing, not the other way around."

"And is that what you do?"

"When I can. Writing hasn't always paid the bills. I've had a lot of other gigs."

"Like what?"

"Scooter mechanic, for one."

"Seriously?"

"Guiseppe's Piaggio Works in Little Italy, all through college. The training has come in handy more than once."

Isabel found herself wanting to hear about his college days at Columbia and all his other travels, as well. Why did he have to be so darned interesting? It was very distracting.

"Well," she said, "you should definitely go check out Jack London State Historic Park while you're here. Same goes for the beaches—they are not to be missed."

"I never met a beach I didn't like."

She nodded, shading her eyes. "From here, it looks as if the coast is all rough headlands, but there are a lot of secluded coves, as well."

"Do you have a favorite beach?"

"Definitely. It's called Shell Beach." That was where her favorite picture of Erik had been taken. Whenever she went there, she would stand in the same spot for a few minutes, thinking of him.

"You should take me there. And to the state park, too."

"You're a big boy. I'll give you a map."

"That's no fun. It wouldn't kill you to take a day off now and then and show me around."

"I *am* showing you around. How is this not showing you around? Between the wedding and the cooking school, I can't afford to take a whole day off. In fact, we should be getting back...."

"Not so fast. Trust me, the world won't come to an end because you're taking a couple of hours away from work."

He had a point. And the idea of showing him around this beautiful, beloved place had a powerful appeal. She found herself wanting to see his face as he walked along the lake created by Jack London. She wanted Mac to stand on the shore with her and watch the glassy turquoise waves shattering on the rocks at some out-of-the-way beach, the sea thundering like a small tempest into the gouged-out caves along the shore. She could easily picture the two of them walking together, wrapped against the wind....

She cleared her throat and bent to pick up a stray gum wrapper, carrying it to the lone trash barrel in the parking area. "When I was in high school, my friends and I used to come up here."

"And what did you do?" he asked.

"Kid stuff. We were always climbing trees, building forts, listening to music, drinking beer stolen from our parents' fridges, smoking weed, making out...."

"Who'd you make out with?"

She flushed from the memories. "I was too bashful."

"Even with the weed?"

"It wasn't my thing. I never saw much action in the making-out department. But I dreamed." She sighed, an old nostalgic feeling flowing through her. Those had been times of innocence, times when she put no limits on herself. "Sometimes I think that first storm you feel, that first real crush, is the greatest emotional rush there is. You spend the rest of your life trying to find that feeling again. And of course, you never do."

"You find something better. If you're lucky," he added.

She wondered if that was how he felt about his wife. "Have you ever been that lucky?" she asked, hoping he'd enlighten her.

"Nope. Still waiting."

The reply shocked her. He'd been *married*. Discomfited, she pivoted to face away from him.

"What about you?" he asked.

"Gosh, no. If I ever got that lucky, I wouldn't be single."

"So tell me about your first crush."

Even now, fifteen years after the fact, the memory brought a blush to her cheeks. "Homer Kelly, ninth grade," she admitted, turning back. "He had shaggy hair and soulful eyes of the lightest blue, and he played the drums with his shirt off. I was completely lost. I went to bed every night thinking of him and wishing he'd ask me out. I sat behind him in civics class, and I used to stare at his shoulders and write terrible poetry about him." Even now, she could picture his slender torso, the curl of sandy hair at the nape of his neck. "And he didn't know I was alive."

"You never told him?"

"Not in words. I baked for him. Sometimes I think I owe all my culinary skills to that boy. I perfected my butter croissants and blueberry turnovers in the hopes of getting his attention."

"Did it work? I know guys who would marry you for your croissants alone."

"Not Homer Kelly. He wolfed down my baked goods, but he never asked me out."

"What an idiot. He's probably a loser now, stuck in a dead-end job with a wife who never makes dinner, and kids who give him sass."

"He plays with Jam Session."

"Oh. But I bet he's an asshole. A fat one."

"He still plays with his shirt off." She shrugged. "It never would have worked out, anyway. He was way too cool for me. Almost as cool as you."

"You think I'm cool?" He gave a little laugh. "I'm flattered. But what makes you think I'm cool?"

"I can just picture you as *that guy* in high school. The heart-breaker, the one with all the girls after him." It was easy—and far too entertaining—to imagine a younger Cormac O'Neill, not as rough and muscular as he was now, but still with that boyish smile and those dancing eyes.

"Heartbreaker? Not in my wildest dreams," he said. "My parents had a different assignment every few years, so I was always the new kid. Never really fit in. I'd just be getting comfortable in the new school, and we'd up and move again."

"And your first crush?"

"Hell, yeah, I had crushes."

"And? Come on, I told you about mine."

"Okay, ninth grade. We had a summer in D.C., lived near Embassy Row in Georgetown. Her name was Linda Henselman, and she was the star player on the girls' lacrosse team. I thought I was dreaming when she said she'd go out with me. I'd never even kissed a girl yet. I sweated bullets through the whole date—*Groundhog Day*."

"I love that movie," she said. "It's one of my favorites."

"I wouldn't know. Can't remember a single thing about it, because I kept trying to figure out how to get my arm around her. She had the biggest...uh, damn, she was cute. When I went to kiss her good-night on her front porch, it was a disaster."

"Your first kiss was a disaster?" Isabel pictured entangled braces, bumping noses, the usual awkwardness.

"Yeah, I was so blown away that I stepped back...right off the porch into a hawthorn bush."

"Ouch."

"Ouch is right. Don't worry, though. I've been practicing."

"Practicing what?"

"Kissing. Wanna check it out?" He made a smooching sound.

"I'll take your word for it." Obnoxious, she thought. He really was the most obnoxious guy. She had no business wanting to check it out, as he so gracefully put it. Despite his long list of professional credentials, he had the maturity level of a seventh grader. "That's the most personal thing you've ever said about yourself."

"This from a woman who watched me whip off my pants the first time we met."

"Something else I've noticed about you is that you make a joke or sarcastic remark when things get too personal. I wonder why that is."

"Oh, so now you're psychoanalyzing me."

"No, just making an observation. You're free to tell me I'm wrong."

"Look, I'm just not that interesting. I'm no Jack London, that's for sure."

She had an urge to confess that everything about him was interesting to her, that she wanted to hear more about kissing Linda Henselman and being a scooter mechanic. That when she was with him, she didn't feel afraid—yes, she wanted to tell him that, but then he'd wonder why she didn't like being alone with guys, why she was so guarded. At Andaluz, she had come close to explaining herself to him. Perhaps she would one day.

"Why not let me be the judge of how interesting you are?" she asked.

"Fine. I'm an open book." He spread his arms wide.

"Very funny."

"Ask me anything."

"Tess told me you were married, and that your wife passed away." She got it all out in a rush, as if the words had been waiting to escape.

His expression was completely neutral. The mountain breeze lifted his dark blond hair. "That's not a question."

"I'm sorry for your loss." She watched his face. Square-jawed, impassive. He gave away nothing.

"Thanks."

"I'd like to hear more about her. That is, if it's not too painful to speak of it."

"No more painful than *not* speaking of it."

"All right, then…?" She waited.

"Why, Miss Johansen, are you taking a personal interest in me?"

"Yes," she admitted. "Yes, I am, so sue me." She softened her tone. "Seriously, I want to know."

His jaw tightened visibly. He kept silent, staring at the ground, holding his arms crossed.

"Would this have anything to do with your nightmares?"

He dropped his arms to his sides. "It *is* my nightmare. Her name was Yasmin Nejim. I met her on assignment in Turkmenistan—heard of it?"

"Barely," she admitted. "Something about the Gates of Hell?"

"That's all most westerners know about Turkmenistan. It's famous for having a crater of burning natural gas. The fire started when the Soviets caused a drilling accident fifty years ago, and it's been burning ever since." He rested his hands on his hips and looked at her. "I used to like telling people I met my wife at the Gates of Hell. After she was killed, it wasn't funny anymore."

"Mac, if you really don't want to talk about it—"

"I can talk, or I can keep silent—it won't change what happened."

Isabel nodded, hearing the echo of Annelise's wisdom in his words.

"Her father was a petroleum engineer and the subject of the article I was writing, and she was working for an NGO. There was a radical uprising, and we had to get the hell out. I, uh…okay, I married her because it was the only way I could think of to get both her and her father out. We had to be family. I figured there wouldn't be a problem with the evacuation since we were married, but she and her father were detained and I was deported. I never saw her again. So when you say my wife passed away, it sounds like she went on some gentle voyage. The truth is, she had her throat slit while trying to bribe her way out of detention."

Isabel felt a chill that had nothing to do with the mountain air. "I'm sorry, Mac. So sorry."

He stuck his thumbs in the back pockets of his shorts and

turned to look out at the long blue horizon. "It was a long time ago. But it still haunts me, every day."

"You must have really loved her."

"News flash. I *failed* her."

No wonder he suffered from night panics. No wonder he didn't seem eager to give his heart to anyone else. His heart was frozen in time, irrevocably bound to a person he could never be with again. Isabel wondered what he really wanted with *her,* why he kept coming on to her. Typical guy, she told herself, with a guy's urges. And a frozen heart.

"Things that happened long ago make their mark, don't they?" she said. When he didn't answer, she added, "Thank you for telling me."

"All you had to do was ask." He flashed an ironic smile. "And here I thought I was going to cheer you up with a scooter ride."

"You did," she said. "I mean, you *are.* Oh, my gosh, I don't mean that. It's horrible, what happened to your wife and it didn't cheer me up one bit. I would never think—"

"Shh." He pressed his thumb softly against her lips. "I get it, Isabel. I do."

His gentle touch both surprised and tantalized her. Flustered by her reaction, she moved away from him.

"Listen," he said, "I was living a different life back then. I was a different person. It's true that I'll carry that with me forever, but I moved ahead with my life."

"Did you? Honestly?"

"It wasn't as easy as I'm making it sound, but, yeah. Isabel, we're here now, and that's all we have, and just because these shitty things happened in the past… It's no reason to ignore what's right in front of us."

"And that is…?" She felt the color flare in her cheeks.

He grinned, his gaze touching her like a physical caress. "You know. We both know."

"Stop it."

"Why should we? We're single, we're attracted to each other—"

"And we'll end up making a mess of things, and what's the point of that?" she demanded.

He looked as if he wanted to say more, but then he simply turned away. He took a few pictures of the area, then slid the phone into his pocket. "We've still got half a tank in this thing. Show me something else."

"We should get back. We've both got work to do."

"This is work," he said. "It's research."

"That's all I am to you," she said. "Research."

"Yep, that's all. One thing's for sure, after finding this scooter, I want to know more about your mother."

"For my grandfather's story?"

"Maybe," he said. "Or maybe for you."

Something passed between them, a fleeting feeling, undeniably intense. For a crazy moment, she felt like touching him, perhaps giving him a hug. Then she smiled as an idea entered her mind. "There's something on the way back down the mountain. It's a little side trip off the main road. I think you'll like it."

"Great," he said. "Let's go."

She felt more natural with him now, and less self-conscious as she circled her arms around his waist. About halfway down the mountain, where the oak forest grew thick, she pointed out an unmarked turn-off that led to a rugged trail. "We'll have to hike in, but it'll only take about five minutes." As she led the way along the wooded path, she tried to remember the last time she'd come here. Or the last time she'd done anything but devote her day to the cooking school and to Tess's wedding. She couldn't remember.

The path intersected with a rushing stream and then connected with a rock-rimmed spring. "It's called Mystic Creek Springs. Not many people know about it," she said. "Only the locals."

"Pretty," he said. "I like the natural pool."

"You're going to like it even more when you try the water."

He bent and scooped his hand into the crystal clear water, and when he looked up at her, his grin was wreathed in wonder. "You've got to be kidding me."

"Not kidding you."

"It's *hot*."

"A hundred and two degrees year round, or so I've heard."

"It's a freaking natural hot springs."

"Right here in the wilderness."

"Damn. I *love* hot springs."

"There are a lot of them around here," she said.

He stood up and peeled off his shirt.

Her heart skipped a beat. "What are you doing?"

Then he kicked off his flip-flops, peeled off the knee brace and shucked down his shorts. "What does it look like I'm doing?"

She tried to tear her gaze away. "Mac—"

"You can't bring me to a natural hot springs and not expect me to get in," he explained, his tone utterly reasonable. He lowered himself into the pool. "Ahh, that's magic."

"I didn't think—"

He surged over to her through the waist-deep water and took her hand. "That's good. Don't think. Just get in."

"Absolutely not." Yet to her surprise, she didn't mind that he'd taken hold of her hand. She liked it. A lot. It had been a long time since a man had taken her hand and she'd liked it.

"Listen, Isabel, because I mean what I say. You can either peel your clothes off and get in the water with me, or I'll pull you in fully dressed, and you'll have to ride home soaked to the skin. Those are the only alternatives."

"Forget it." She pulled her hand away from his, even though the warm, clear water looked tempting. "I'll wait for you at the scooter."

"Chicken," he said. "What are you afraid of?"

Everything.

She sniffed. "I just don't think I'm prepared to get naked with you. Under any circumstances."

"Come on. What's the worst thing that can happen?" When she didn't answer, he said, "Tell you what. I'll turn my back. I'll stare straight at that tree behind me, and I won't look until you're up to your neck in the water. Scout's honor."

She knew she was being a baby, making an issue of this. And hadn't she just decided to challenge herself more, to be less afraid? Here was a perfect opportunity to do something way out of her comfort zone. She offered a curt nod. "Turn your back."

He affably complied, and she slipped off her skirt and panties, and then her camisole top, and quickly immersed herself in the warm, rushing water. He was right, the hot spring felt like heaven. She slid deeper and leaned against a flat rock. "Okay," she said.

He turned, churning up the water. "One of these days, we're going to do this again, and I'm not going to be a gentleman."

His words should have offended her, but instead, she felt a pulse of excitement. "You're already not a gentleman."

He touched his hand to his chest. His very muscular chest. "Hey. I'm wounded."

He didn't look wounded. As he leaned back into the warm current, he kept staring at her. She sank down even deeper, up to her chin, getting her hair waterlogged. "What?" she demanded, unable to read his expression.

"I've got a confession to make."

"What's that?"

"When you took off your skirt, I peeked."

"Of course you did. Why am I not surprised?" She scowled and scooted farther away from him. "You said 'Scout's honor.'"

"Yeah, but I never said I was a Scout." He clasped his hands together and squirted a stream of water at her. "I wanted to see for myself."

She wiped the water from her eyes. "See what?"

"How you're managing to get around with that stick up your ass."

She surged toward him, splashing a wave of water in his face. "Oh, my gosh, why did I think bringing you here was a good idea?"

He opened his arms, embracing the splashing against his chest. "It was a great idea. I love it here. I even like being with you. And just so you know, you have a really nice butt."

"Oh, I'm so flattered," she said, scowling at him. "It's always nice to hear that someone thinks I have a stick up my ass."

"I was just joking," he said, then mumbled, "kind of."

"What's that supposed to mean, 'kind of'?"

"You're not like anyone I've ever met," he said.

She could say the same about him, but she didn't.

"I mean that in a good way. Don't be so suspicious."

"It's just that you're extremely good at backhanded compli-ments." She fluttered her hand through the soft, clear water.

"Take it easy. All I'm saying is I'd like to get to know you better."

"You're here for a job," she pointed out. "And then you're gone."

"Which makes me the perfect guy for you."

★ ★ ★

As he brought the scooter back to the machine shop, Mac found himself liking this assignment more than ever.

Isabel was a surprise. There were depths to her he wanted to understand, and maybe, just maybe, she would let him. She was skittish, though, not exactly distrustful, but protective of herself. At the mountaintop, she'd given him a glimpse of the girl she'd been, growing up in a lush and sheltered place. At the hot springs, he'd had a glimpse of her that was going to haunt his dreams. Yes, he'd looked. Of course he'd looked. He was only human. Under that long, printed dress, which she seemed to wear as body armor, was a figure that nearly made him groan aloud, just remembering.

Oblivious of his thoughts, Isabel dismounted and shaded her eyes toward the slope where the beehives were. The girl she'd hired, Jamie, was up there working away.

"You look worried," he said, observing her frown. Even frowning, she was wildly attractive, with her dark eyebrows and full, bowed lips.

"I am," Isabel said softly. "Jamie's a remarkable girl—emphasis on *girl*. How is she going to cope with having a baby?"

"Have you asked her?"

"No, but I intend to. For example, I'm pretty sure she hasn't seen a doctor yet. So that's going to be my first step with her. It's incredibly important, but I don't want to scare her off by coming across as pushy. She seems, I don't know, keyed up, I guess. I feel as if I need to win her trust."

"You gave her a roof over her head. A job. I bet she already trusts you."

"When the time is right, I'm sure we'll have a big talk."

"In the kitchen, right? That's where you said you get all your talking done."

She flushed and looked away. "Not *all* my talking," she said.

"That was nice, today," he said.

"Yes. Thanks for taking me. And for getting this old Vespa running."

The thought of restoring Francesca's scooter for Isabel made him happy. *She* made him happy. At first, the feeling had been so unfamiliar that he scarcely recognized it. Here at Bella Vista, he woke up feeling something unexpected, something even more surprising than his attraction to Isabel. He felt attracted to her whole world. He started picturing life right here. A permanent home, something he'd never before even contemplated. Would he? Could he? And would he feel this way about Bella Vista if Isabel weren't part of the picture?

That was easy. No way.

Which meant he was falling for her. And that, of course, was the problem. Isabel had pointed it out herself. What was the point of falling for someone when, in just a few more weeks, he was going to have to walk away?

He had committed to his next assignment long ago. Yasmin's father had been given safe haven in Turkey. They planned to work together on telling the truth about how Yasmin had been murdered. It was something Mac was obligated to do, not for himself but for Ari Nejim.

After the Magnus project, Mac would shift gears and do what he always did—move on to the next project. But these days, when he thought about Isabel and Bella Vista, he didn't relish the idea of leaving.

He also didn't know how to stay. Didn't even know if he had the emotional hardware to do that. He'd married a woman in order to save her life and he'd failed.

Isabel inspired him, though. She made him wish he could be with her without messing her up. Maybe even forever.

CHAPTER SIXTEEN

"Why would you do that for me?" Jamie Westfall was in the commercial laundry, the facility recently installed in a long-neglected utility room in the house. Soon enough, they would be using it for guests. At the moment, Jamie was folding clothes with unhurried deliberation, making small stacks of her faded jeans and cotton tops, her towels and washcloths. She paused in her chores to regard Isabel from across the long work table.

"What, offer you health care benefits?" asked Isabel. She plucked a towel out of a basket fresh from the dryer. "All the employees of Bella Vista are entitled to that."

"Seriously?"

"Seriously." She lined up the edges of the towel and folded it into a neat square. "And I expect you to use it."

"I've never had health insurance before. I don't even know how it works."

"It's not simple but you need and deserve it. Everybody does." Isabel took a card and a slip of paper from her pocket and handed it to the girl. "Here's your temporary coverage card. If you like, I can help you with the online forms."

"Thank you. That would be great."

Isabel indicated the slip of paper. "There are two obstetricians in town. Both come highly recommended. I wrote down the numbers. It would be good for you and the baby if you were seen right away."

Jamie ducked her head as she shook out a denim work shirt that had seen better days. "Yeah. About that…"

"Have you seen anyone?"

"No. Well, I went to Planned Parenthood in Napa and got some information. They said the same thing. Regular doctor visits, but there was a waiting list a mile long for the free clinic. I've been doing a bunch of reading, taking vitamins."

"But you haven't seen a doctor." Isabel ached for the girl. The uncertainty must be so frightening. What if something was wrong?

"I wasn't able to afford a doctor," Jamie said quietly. "Big surprise, huh?"

"Now you can. No excuses, okay? I know I'm being pushy, but it's because I care. You're not the only one in this situation."

"Okay," Jamie mumbled, taking the slip of paper. "I'll get in touch with one of these doctors."

"You seem hesitant."

"I *am* hesitant." She folded a pair of jeans, smoothing her hand over a small, fraying hole at the knee. "Last time I went to the doctor, I was in junior high. Had to go to the emergency room with a broken arm."

"Nothing's broken now. Really, you shouldn't wait."

"Don't you think I know that?" she snapped.

"Then what's stopping you?" Isabel snapped back.

"Everything." She practically shouted the word. At the same

time, she swept the stack of perfectly folded clothes onto the floor and stared down at them, red-faced and panting. "Every stupid fricking thing in the whole world, that's what."

Isabel set her hands on her hips. "Are you finished?"

Jamie's shoulders slumped. "I don't know anything about having a baby. Or raising a kid. I'm scared. If I go to the doctor, I'm going to have to figure out what to do. About the baby. About everything."

"And if you don't go?"

She sighed. "I know, I know. I'll still have to decide."

"There's one decision that's a no-brainer. You need to take care of your health, for your sake and the baby's. That means you have to go to the doctor. The sooner, the better."

"Can I tell you something?"

"Anything."

"I've already decided. I'm going to—"

"Jamie." Isabel's irritation dissolved. She went around to the other side of the table and pulled the girl into a hug. At first Jamie felt tense, as if ready to bolt. Then she sighed and relaxed into the hug. When Isabel felt her go soft in her arms, she felt incredibly protective. "Time is on your side," Isabel said. "You have a good long while to figure out what you want to do, and you're safe and sound with people who care about you. We'll support any decision you make."

"I know," the girl whispered. "I know." Jamie had been on her own since she'd left home at sixteen, and she'd done an amazing job of making her way in the world. She'd educated herself and gained practical experience in beekeeping and honey production. She'd faced challenges Isabel could only imagine. But a pregnancy was something a girl shouldn't ever have to face without a support system.

"Aw, Jamie," she said softly, patting her back, "everyone's

scared when they're about to have a baby, that's what I've heard, anyway. But I've also heard it's wonderful."

"It is," the girl whispered. "I know it's going to be. Sometimes when I think about it, I think it's the best thing ever."

"Agreed. I can't wait until it's my turn," Isabel admitted, stepping back and watching Jamie collect herself. "In my case, I suppose I'd better work on finding a guy I want to be the father of my children."

That drew a brief smile from the girl. "That guy—Mac—he's still not your boyfriend?"

Isabel thought about the hot springs, and the way he'd looked at her, the things he'd said. The way she'd looked at him and the thoughts that had gone through her head. "*No. Why would you ask me that?*"

Jamie shrugged. "Because like I said before, I can tell he's into you. And lately the two of you just seem... I don't know."

Isabel *did* know. She hadn't realized it was something other people could see. "We're not," she insisted. *We can't be.* "I've been focused on things other than romance, like Tess's wedding and the cooking school." Bending down, she gathered up the spilled laundry and started refolding, piece by piece. "Men and dating—not my forte."

"Oh, right. What about other guys? Like, in the past."

Isabel most certainly did not want to discuss the past. "I've never been big on going out and meeting people, having a boyfriend. Never found anyone I connected with in a special way."

Jamie stared at her. "You say the word *never* a lot."

"Really? I never noticed—I mean, that's an interesting observation."

"You're really pretty, and cool. Hard to believe there hasn't been someone special for you."

There had been, but it had gone so wrong, it scarcely

counted as a relationship. More like a *mistake*. "I could say the same about you," Isabel pointed out.

"I'm a freak." She held up a tank top and shook it out before folding it.

"Why would you say that?"

"Hello. I heard it all through high school."

"Don't let other people tell you what to think of yourself," Isabel said.

"Fine, but guys don't like me. Not the right kind of guys, anyway."

Isabel could relate to that, all too well. "So, the doctor..."

Jamie picked up the last of the clothes. "I'll go. I know it's the right thing to do. Thank you. Honestly, there's no way to thank you. I've never had anyone look after me before. It's really nice of you."

"If you need anything, promise you'll let me know."

Jamie placed her clothes in a neat stack in a wicker basket. In a small, almost childlike voice, she asked, "Will you come with me?"

"Of course. Absolutely. Just say when."

"Maybe, I mean, if it's okay, we could call now."

Dr. Wiley had an opening later that week, and Isabel felt excited to be part of the process. The prospect of a new life coming into the world filled her with wonder. She was eons away from going through it herself, but she was glad Jamie had brought her into the loop. She liked the girl, despite Jamie's distrust and secretiveness. Jamie reminded her, in some oblique way, of herself, years ago, returning in a panic to Archangel to escape Calvin Sharpe. There was something in the girl's manner that Isabel recognized, an instinct to bolt and take cover. *He was the worst.*

She only hoped the girl would be able to move on. It was

far too easy to be trapped by the past. Isabel wanted to explain that things would get better, but Jamie would have to find that out for herself.

While she waited, Isabel browsed through the magazines, remembering her last stay in a waiting room, the day she'd met Cormac O'Neill.

The thought of him raised a flurry of emotion inside her, something she hadn't experienced in…well, maybe never. It felt like a schoolgirl crush, only worse. It felt *real*. Like something that could last forever—if she let it.

To distract herself, she paged through *MenuSonoma,* a local foodie magazine. This fall, there would be a special feature on the Bella Vista Cooking School. The photo shoot had already been scheduled for the week after Tess's wedding. The editor had promised to feature the place on the cover. As a place to learn farm-to-table home cooking techniques in the middle of a working orchard, Bella Vista was unique.

She scanned an article about a restaurateur on a quest through the Highlands for a barrel of the perfect Scotch, and compared a recipe for *agrodolce* sauce to her own, which of course made use of honey. Then she flipped the page, and her breath stopped. "CalSharpe's Latest Venture Slated to Open Labor Day Weekend." She forced herself to breathe, even though it made her chest hurt and her stomach churn as she read on.

Renowned chef Calvin Sharpe, formerly a master instructor at Napa's Culinary Institute, rose to fame with his series on the Cooking Network. *Cooking Sharpe* launched his name; now he is poised to open his newest signature restaurant—CalSharpe's—in Archangel, one of the prettiest small towns in Sonoma County…

She felt nauseated. Violated, even. She'd known it was coming; she'd braced herself, but it still sickened her. Calvin Sharpe was opening a place in Archangel. It was as if he had crafted some special torture just for her, moving in as she was poised to finally realize her dream.

She closed the magazine with a decisive snap and set it aside. The wedding was practically upon them. Annelise had returned to Bella Vista for the event, and Tess's mother, Shannon Delaney, had arrived this morning. At the same time, the cooking school website had to go live soon, and she needed more photos and videos. This was how she should be spending her time—getting ready to launch, not regretting events in the past. She had to keep herself from being distracted by Calvin's presence.

Have you ever told anyone the truth about that guy? Even yourself? Mac's question had been weighing on her mind.

A nurse came into the waiting room and approached her. "Jamie wanted me to see if you could join us," she said softly.

Isabel's heart skipped a beat. "Is everything all right?"

"Yes, absolutely. She'd just like to have you in on the conversation if you're willing."

"More than willing," Isabel said. "She's very special to me."

She followed the nurse into the exam room. Jamie sat on the edge of the paper-covered table, wearing her street clothes, the disposable gown wadded in her lap. She looked terribly young, but different, somehow, from the cautious, tightly-wound woman who had come into the clinic just a short time ago.

"The baby and I are healthy, and I've decided on adoption," she said softly. "Dr. Wiley is going to help me make it happen."

Isabel's heart lurched. "Oh, Jamie…." She looked over at the doctor, a woman who exuded quiet confidence.

"The decision is a process," the doctor said, her tone measured and kind. "A journey. And I've told Jamie it doesn't have to happen right away. There's plenty of time to go over the options."

"I already know what I want to do. It's everything I've been going over in my head for weeks. It just feels like the right choice. Right for the baby, and right for me."

"You have lots of time to live with your decision. You're entitled to change it at any time," the doctor explained. "The adoption counselor will help you with that."

"You're a wonderful person with lots of love to give to a child," Isabel said. "You'd be a great mother."

Jamie stared at the floor. "I can love a child. I can be a good mother. But there are things I can never give him or her—a father. A *chance*." She pressed her fists into the paper gown. "I got myself into a mess, but something good is going to come of it."

Isabel exchanged a glance with the doctor. "I'm here to help," she said. "Anything you need…."

"There's a lot to be done," the doctor said, rapidly typing on her keyboard. "The most important thing is to make sure Jamie gets the best possible prenatal care and counseling."

"How are you feeling?" Isabel asked Jamie.

"Honestly? Relieved. I finally know what's ahead for me. And I'm good with it." She slid off the table and placed the gown in a stainless steel can, letting the lid close with quiet finality. "I'm good," she said again.

Strains of mariachi music greeted Isabel and Jamie when they got home. Catching Jamie's quizzical look, Isabel said, "Friends of ours. Neighbors, actually. Oscar Navarro's been playing in their band since they were all teenagers."

"They sound good."

"They'll be playing at Tess's wedding." Isabel paused at the kitchen door. "How about you? Are you still good?"

"Better than I've been in a long time."

She did seem less anxious after the doctor visit. Perhaps it was calming to have a plan in place of the fear and uncertainty. Isabel hoped the feeling would last, but she knew—and likely Jamie did, too, that the moment would come when the baby was very real to her, living and breathing as she held it in her arms, and she would have to surrender it to the adoptive parents. The doctor clarified more than once that Jamie could change her decision at any time, but today, the girl seemed determined that adoption was her best choice.

After the doctor, they had visited with a social worker who specialized in adoption counseling, and they'd come out of the meeting laden with books and brochures about the process, as well as a schedule of support group meetings, online and in Santa Rosa. Jamie seemed determined that this would be her path, and Isabel was determined to help her.

Back at Bella Vista, they spied Tess in the barn, showing her mother and Annelise the ballroom where the wedding would take place—how the tables would be arranged, the chandeliers hung, where the band and the bar would be set up. "Let's go say hi," Isabel suggested. "That is, if you feel like it."

"Sure. One thing I don't want to happen is to let this pregnancy take over every minute of my life."

"I understand. Come on, I think you're going to like Shannon. She works in museum acquisitions, and she just got here from Indonesia." Isabel liked Shannon, too, although she'd never expected to encounter her father's secret mistress. It had all happened so long ago; it was hard to hold her at fault. Isabel knew all about making bad choices at a young age.

"Jamie's my beekeeping expert," she told Shannon, making the introductions. "We're kind of obsessed with honey around here these days."

"Among other things," said Shannon, giving Isabel a brief,

firm hug. "The place looks amazing, like something out of a dream. I'm so impressed." She turned to Jamie, beaming. "And I do love honey. I don't actually know anyone who doesn't love it."

"It's nearly time for dinner," said Isabel. "I'm doing a cheese and honey pairing for cocktail hour."

"Sounds heavenly," said Annelise. "Can we come and help?"

"No need," Isabel said. "Just show up on the patio in about half an hour." She turned to Shannon. "How was your trip? And is your room okay?"

"The trip from Denpasar is always a killer, but Bali is so worth it that I don't mind. And being here is an instant pick-me-up. The room decor is fabulous. Vintage California—I love it." Shannon gave her another quick hug. "I'm so glad you and Tess are together. You're a blessing, Isabel, I swear."

Isabel felt a surge of affection for both Shannon and Tess. "I've had way too much fun helping with this wedding. It's addictive."

"I hope you left some chores for the mother of the bride."

"And the grandmother," Annelise said.

"Don't worry, there's plenty to do," Tess assured them. "Like these centerpieces." She indicated a table draped in linen, and a basket of materials on the chair beside it.

"Yay, something to fight over," Shannon said.

"Oh, no, you don't. We are *not* going to fight over glassware and flowers." Tess picked up a mason jar and some raffia and went to work.

"All right," Shannon agreed. "And check out these woven fabrics I brought from Bali." She set a stack of colorful cloth on a table. "Ikat and songket. Aren't they beautiful?"

Isabel and Jamie left everyone exclaiming over the decorations, pausing in the doorway to look back as Shannon excitedly showed Tess and Annelise her collection of pretty things she'd brought from Indonesia for the tables.

Shannon looked young for her age, and Isabel suspected she and Tess were often mistaken for sisters, with their Irish red hair and fair coloring. There was a lively play of light and shadow in the space as the sun filtered through the plank siding and the high windows, limning all three women in a diffusing glow. They resembled an Old Masters painting, gathered around the table, arranging the fabric, flowers and candles. There was a beautiful sense of continuity in that moment— the bride, her mother and her grandmother, humming with anticipation over the impending wedding.

Isabel felt an unbidden pang of envy. What would it be like to be standing there with her mother, filled with excitement about her future, imagining children one day, family holidays, that special bond of security a mother and daughter seemed to share? Isabel would never be in that place, never know that feeling.

She put her envy aside, knowing Tess had grown up with challenges of her own. "I wish I had a camera right now," she said to Jamie. "The three of them look so pretty, gathered around the table in that light."

"They do," Jamie agreed. "I've never been to a wedding."

"Really? Ah, you're going to love this one," Isabel assured her. "Music and feasting—what's not to love? Let's go. I'm going to help Ernestina in the kitchen, and you probably need a rest."

"Oh, no, you don't," Jamie said as they walked together toward the main house. "The doctor said I should rest when I'm tired. And I'm not tired. Let me help, too."

Ernestina went to set the patio table while Isabel and Jamie worked side by side at the kitchen counter.

"Are you and your mother close?" Isabel asked as she

blended a bit of culinary lavender into some local goat cheese she'd picked up at the farmer's market. "Where does she live?"

"In Chico, and no, we're not close." Jamie carefully arranged some radishes and crackers on a tray. "I haven't even told her about the baby."

"Oh, Jamie. Really? You don't think she'd want to help you?"

"My Mom? She'd be all, 'I didn't raise you to be that stupid,' and I'd go, 'No, you didn't raise me at all, I did it on my own.'" She changed her voice to emulate the dialogue. "And she'd be like, 'I was on my own, I did the best I could,' and then I'd be like, 'Yeah, me, too.' That's pretty much how all our conversations turn out."

"I'm sorry."

"Having a mother isn't all it's cracked up to be." She shrugged her shoulders, then shifted her attention to the hand-labeled glass jars of honey. "Which one do you want to use?"

"Something mild to go with the cheese."

"The milkweed blossom?"

Isabel nodded. "We're probably the only ones who'll notice."

"The different flavors of honey have always been obvious to me," Jamie said.

"Not to me. I've had to train my palate. Same with wines. I'm not a natural, but I love the alchemy of pairing flavors. If you were twenty-one and not pregnant, I'd give you a taste of this nice new sauvignon blanc from Angel Creek. It's going to go perfectly with the appetizers." She turned off the heat under the fried marcona almonds and gave the pan a shake.

"One sip," Jamie insisted, nibbling a bit of the goat cheese and honey on a cracker.

"One, young lady." Isabel poured a bit of the chilled white wine in a goblet and held it out to her.

Jamie savored a tiny sip, and smiled blissfully. "You're right. It's delicious."

Isabel took back the goblet. "Look at me, corrupting a minor."

"When I was younger, I used to try to get under my mom's skin by stealing sips of her beer. She didn't care, though. She always said it might help me be less shy."

"You were shy in school?"

"Yeah. Didn't really feel like I fit in. I was good at guitar, and I liked the 4-H club a lot. That's how I got interested in beekeeping. But it was the trifecta for a total misfit—guitar, 4-H and bees. It drove my mom crazy, because she was this überpopular cheerleader, homecoming queen type who wanted me to be exactly like her. It was just something else for us to argue about."

"I was shy in school, too, and my grandmother and I used to argue sometimes, but about the opposite situation. I was totally overprotected. Given what happened to my father, it's understandable. But it didn't exactly prepare me for the world. That's probably why I'm such a homebody."

"Pretty nice home," Jamie said, looking around the kitchen.

"Thanks," Isabel replied. "I do love it here, although I'd also love to travel more, see the world. But the cooking school—"

"Is not even up and running yet," said Mac, barging into the kitchen. His hair was damp from the shower, and he was wearing clean cargo shorts and a fresh T-shirt. Isabel couldn't help but notice that he smelled wonderful, of soap and fresh air.

"You should run away while you have the chance," he told her.

"Suppose I don't want to run away?"

"You do. I just heard you say it."

"I did not—"

"Dude, where do you want her to run to?" Jamie asked,

gesturing at the view. The arched window framed the rolling hills, covered in every shade of green and peppered by bursts of floral color, basking in the deep golden afternoon light. "What's better than here?"

"Right now, nowhere," he admitted. "Oh, man, what is that incredible smell?" He made a beeline for the salted rosemary marcona almonds, still warm in the pan.

"Oh, no, you don't." Isabel whacked his arm with the back of a wooden spoon. "That's for drinks on the patio. Fifteen more minutes."

"I'll die," he said. "You don't want me dying on your kitchen floor." He looked over at Charlie, the German shepherd, who was lying with his chin flat on the saltillo tile and watching the food prep as if it was his sole mission in life.

"Here," she said, handing Mac a tray of glasses. "Take these outside and help Grandfather pour the wine. Take the dog with you. He knows he's not supposed to be in the kitchen."

Mac sent her a wounded look. "Come on, Charlie. We know when we're not wanted."

Jamie held the door for him as he carried the tray outside. "See, he likes you. It's so obvious."

Isabel ducked her head, concentrating mightily on the tray of appetizers. She flashed on the day of the hot springs, and how they had been doing this flirty dance, back and forth, ever since. He took up far more space in her thoughts than she would ever admit to. She liked it. She liked *him.* She just needed to figure out how to keep herself from liking him too much. "He's here for a job," she reminded Jamie. "Nothing more."

"No, he *came* here for a job, same as me. Maybe he'll end up staying, same as me."

"I'm not putting him on the payroll. And what's with this

romantic streak of yours? Why are you so keen on hooking me up with Mac O'Neill?"

"I'm not doing anything. Just making observations."

Ernestina came bustling in from the dining room. "The table is ready. Shall I take that tray to the patio?"

"Sure, thanks. We'll be out in a minute. I'm just finishing the sauce for the pork roast." She leaned over the fragrant concoction simmering in a pan and gave it a stir. "I hope you're hungry. We've created a feast."

"I'm starved. But listen, if you want this to be a family thing, I'll understand."

"Oh, no, you don't. You're part of the tribe now, whether you like it or not."

"You know I like it. I just don't want to intrude."

"Listen," Isabel said. "You're not intruding. I want you to know this is your home now. Got it?"

Jamie nodded. Then she grabbed a tea towel and wiped her eyes. The sight of this hardened, body-pierced, purple-haired girl, now soft with sentiment, made Isabel glad she'd taken a chance on the girl.

Jamie went to the sink and rinsed her face, then stared at Isabel with her heart in her eyes. "How do you do that?"

"Do what?"

"How do you just take somebody in? Treat me like I'm family?"

"It feels right," Isabel said. "You and I click. We have from the very first day you showed up here. That's what I felt, anyway."

"Really?"

"No one could have done what you've done with the hives in such a short time, but it's more than that. You've brought something special to Bella Vista—not just your skills. Your energy and your spirit, your creativity and your music. I feel lucky that you arrived when you did, and I hope you'll stay. I mean that. I know Grandfather feels the same."

The girl dried her hands. "I hope I can stay, too."

"Nothing's stopping you. We all love having you here."

"Thank you." She hesitated, then said, "I'd like to tell everyone what I've decided. The adoption."

"Tell everyone…"

"I mean, I wouldn't make a big deal of it, just want to get the news out there. Because if I don't, people might be all like, 'Congratulations,' and you don't really congratulate someone who's not going to be a parent, right?"

"I see your point. But this is such a brand-new decision. Remember what the doctor said. You might want to live with it for a while."

"Honestly, I've been living with it ever since I realized I was pregnant. I always knew this is what I'd end up doing." She took off her apron and hung it on a hook. "If I say it aloud, and make sure everyone knows, then it'll help me get used to the idea that someone else will raise this baby. Someone better than me."

"Whoa, hang on." Isabel held her by the shoulders and looked her in the eye. "There is no one better than you. No one. But if you do end up choosing adoption, your generosity is going to give the adoptive family more joy than we can possibly imagine."

"Yeah, that's what I meant." She offered a shy, fleeting smile.

"You're very amazing," said Isabel. "You know that, right?"

"It's nice of you to say so. Sometimes I have a hard time believing it."

"We're always hardest on ourselves, aren't we?" Isabel mused. "Except right this minute, I can tell you unequivocally that *I* am amazing because I just made the most insanely delicious *agrodolce* sauce you've ever tasted." She offered Jamie a sample on a piece of bread. "Figs, olives, balsamic and honey."

"Delicious," said Jamie. "I love your cooking. Your cooking school is going to be a huge success."

"That's the plan, anyway. Let's go hang out on the patio for a while before dinner."

"I heard the *D*-word," said Dominic as they joined everyone.

"What, *dinner?* Or *delicious?* I can assure you, both are happening," said Isabel, accepting a glass of sauvignon blanc from him. Tess handed Jamie a flute of bubbly water with fresh strawberries.

"What's on the menu tonight?" asked Shannon. "And will it cure my jet lag?"

"It will cure everything," Isabel said expansively. "We're trying out a couple of things for the wedding feast, so I'm going to need your unfiltered opinion."

"Last time I tried that, you whacked me with a spatula," Mac pointed out.

"We're going to have a honey theme," Tess told her mother. She tipped her glass in Jamie's direction.

"I'm glad I can help," Jamie said.

"There's something else," Tess said. "Feel free to say no, but I thought I would ask."

Jamie's brow quirked. "Sure."

"Dominic and I were wondering if you'd be willing to play a song at our wedding."

The girl's smile encompassed everyone gathered on the patio. "I'd love to. All you have to do is let me know what you have in mind."

"That's great," said Tess, then turned to Shannon. "Mom, wait 'til you hear her. She's fantastic."

"I think it's a lovely idea," Shannon said. "So tell us about the baby," she added. "When are you due?"

Jamie took a quick sip of her water. "Um, yeah, about that."

Isabel held her breath. The girl was really going to do it.

Shannon looked flustered. "Sorry, if it's too personal...."

"Not at all." Jamie brushed her hand down over her belly. "Everything's good, I mean, with my health and the baby and all. And I'm actually glad you asked, because there's something I want everyone to know. I'm not keeping it. The baby, I mean. It's going to be adopted." The words tumbled out in a rush, and she gulped the rest of the water as if it were a shot of grain alcohol. "That's my plan, anyway."

"Oh, Jamie." Tess got up and gave the girl a hug. "I don't know what to say."

"That's okay," she said with a shaky laugh. "I told Isabel I didn't want to have to explain every time somebody said congratulations or whatever. The doc and the social worker said I can change my mind anytime I want, but I'm not going to do that. I'm not going to change my mind." Her expression seemed resolute.

"We all want to help in any way we can," said Annelise. "Please, you mustn't hesitate to ask for what you need. Anything, truly."

Jamie held the old woman's gaze for a moment. "Thank you. That means a lot. Anyway, I don't want this to be a downer or anything. Just wanted to let everyone know."

"I'd like to make a toast," Magnus declared, lifting his glass. "To our newest member of the Bella Vista family, Miss Jamie Westfall. To your future, and to the future of the gift you will soon give to the world."

A lump formed in Isabel's throat. She was humbled by this girl's bravery, and by the way Jamie was facing this monumental challenge. At the same time, Isabel felt proud of everyone here for the way they instantly rallied to offer support. This was exactly what Isabel wanted for Bella Vista, this sense of community, pulling people together and folding them in. It was a kind of magic, she thought. She wished Bubbie were here to witness it.

After dinner, Tess, Dominic and Shannon volunteered for clean-up duty. Annelise invited Jamie to the lounge room, saying she wanted to hear more about Jamie's honey production. Knowing what she did now, Isabel suspected the old woman and the young girl might have other things to discuss, as well.

Isabel took Charlie out for his nightly run around the yard. The air had a pleasant, chilly edge to it, perfumed by the scent of night-blooming jasmine. The dog ran along a hedge and then doubled back, giving a *woof* of warning. Isabel swung around and spotted Mac, silhouetted by the light from the windows.

Charlie trotted over to Mac, gave him a sniff, and went back to racing around. "He likes to patrol," Isabel said. "And I like that he keeps the critters away. Between Charlie and the cats, we're practically critter-free around here."

"Everybody has a job," Mac said.

She smiled and pulled her light knitted shawl around her. "Everybody has a *purpose*."

They were quiet for a few minutes, taking in the scents and sounds of the night. After a while, he said, "You arranged everything."

She knew exactly what he was referring to. "I just… I feel lucky to be in a position to help Jamie. She seems so alone. What? Why are you looking at me like that?"

"You're a good person, Isabel," he said. "Always thinking of others. I like your big heart."

His words startled her. "Really?" She didn't know how to

respond, and she was sure she was going to fumble it. "That might be one of the nicest things anyone's ever said to me."

"You've been hanging around the wrong people, then. It's not such a stretch. You do have a big heart, and I *am* nice."

"You are, huh?" She couldn't keep from smiling. "Good to know."

"Well, not as nice as you, but I'm definitely nice."

"I'll take your word for it." She sighed and tilted her head back to look at the stars. "I worry about her. Is she going to stay? Will she go through with it?"

"Don't buy other people's worries. Jamie's going to do what she's going to do."

"I get that, I do. From what she's told me, she doesn't have much in the way of family."

"She does now," he said.

"You *are* nice," she said. "What's your family like?"

"What do you think it's like?"

"Well, with a sturdy Irish name like O'Neill, I'm picturing a big Irish American clan."

"Shoot," he said.

"What?"

"We're a family of clichés."

"What do you mean?"

"My life is littered with brothers. It's me, Shane, Dillon, Finn, Ian and Declan. I'm the eldest. Also the smartest and best-looking. Not to mention the nicest."

"All those boys. Your poor mother."

"Hey, we treat her like a queen. Always have."

He took out his phone and showed her a picture. "My mom. She's awesome."

The woman in the picture had her head thrown back in laughter, her arms spread wide as if to embrace the world.

"She does look awesome," Isabel agreed.

"And here are my brothers." He scrolled to another picture. It showed six men all in a row, each one as hulking and handsome as the next. They looked as if they had been packaged as a matched six pack.

"A family of six boys. Why am I hearing about this now?"

"You only just asked now."

"Do I have to ask for everything? Don't you ever simply offer something without being asked?"

"You mean like this?" He took hold of her bare arms, slid his hands up to her shoulders and gave her a firm, sexy kiss that nearly made her knees melt. This connection, this soft exploration, was something she had been wanting ever since she'd met him, but until this moment, she hadn't realized it. Her fists curled into the fabric of his shirt as she savored every little bit of him—his smell and the way he tasted, the brush of his hair against her cheek, the strength of his arms as he held her.

And then she stepped back, nearly dizzy with disorientation. "That's not what I meant."

"Ah, come on, Isabel—"

"Charlie," she called, and gave his special whistle, that one that always brought him running. "We're going in."

"Chicken."

"I'm not…yes, okay, I am. And pretty soon, you'll thank me for that."

He slid his arm around her waist and brought her in against him, and then he leaned down so close she could feel the warmth of his breath in her ear. "Believe me, I've never thanked a woman for refusing to make out with me."

She stood back, arms crossed in front of her. Ah, that kiss. He was very persuasive—enough to get her past her fears? Annelise had been brave, Jamie was brave; maybe it was time for Isabel to be brave. "You're not that into me," she said.

"What are you waiting for? A sign from the great beyond?"

She didn't see the point of getting tangled up with this guy. "You have a job here, Mac, same as everyone else. Your purpose is to get the story down. You're going to meet Ramon Maldonado tomorrow. You're supposed to find out how my grandfather ended up here, and Annelise in San Francisco. How did they go on after what happened to them during the war?"

"How does anyone go on?" he asked, his posture stiff with frustration. "Some days, you put one foot in front of the other. Other days—" he took a step toward her, ran one finger over her shoulder, down her bare arm "—it's like jumping off a cliff."

She stepped back. "I don't get what you want with me."

"A chance, Isabel. How about we take a chance on each other?"

PART VII

Organic flowering plants are the best source of raw nectar for bees. Honey in its raw form retains a healthful substance called propolis. This is tree sap mixed with bee secretions, which guards against bacteria, viruses and fungi. Propolis contains phytochemicals known to protect against germs and to prevent certain types of cancer.

Honey was considered a powerful element in the ancient world, cited in Vedic, Sumerian, Babylonian and biblical texts. A dream of honey was believed to portend an unanticipated triumph over adversity.

VINCOTTO

Vincotto (Italian for *cooked wine*) is a tradition dating back to Roman times as a way to preserve wine. Its complex, sweet properties have recently attracted culinary interest as a condiment with many uses.

4-5	cups red wine—Primitivo is a good choice
⅔	cup honey
3	cinnamon sticks
3	whole cloves

Combine everything in a heavy-bottomed saucepan and bring to a boil. Then simmer, stirring occasionally, for about 30 minutes, until the liquid is reduced to about a cup. Once it's cool, remove the cinnamon sticks and cloves, and pour into a jar or cruet. It's delicious drizzled over salads, cooked meats, grilled vegetables or ricotta cheese.

[Source: Traditional]

CHAPTER SEVENTEEN

Copenhagen, 1943

Over the years of the occupation, Magnus had become adept at melting into the scenery around the city, whether it be slipping like a shadow along the numerous wharves, docks and landings, through the marketplace, the university or business district. Now that he had shot up in height, he could no longer pass for a schoolboy, so he sought other guises. Some days, he rode a delivery bicycle, delivering draftsmen's plans to machine and repair shops around town. Other days, he followed in the footsteps of the late, great Teacher, and masqueraded as a simple street sweeper or mud lark. He had an aptitude for fixing small motors and engines, and by trading or bartering his skills, he was able to earn enough to keep from starving.

He had stopped letting himself miss his parents and grandfather. He didn't cry himself to sleep at night anymore. His heart was like a small, tight fist in his chest, fiercely guarding itself from sentiment.

Every breath he took was focused on advancing the cause of the resistance.

As the war progressed, performing acts of sabotage became more and more risky. The suspicion of the Germans intensified, and rewards for information increased. Resistance cells were infiltrated or Danish collaborators ratted them out. Those who were arrested faced torture from the Nazis bent on extracting information.

Magnus's existence was a lonely one. Whenever his mind wandered, he caught himself aching for human connection. But mindful of the risks in his line of work, he befriended no one in the organization. He didn't want to make a friend only to lose him…or her.

But he discovered one day in late September that he couldn't help himself. He showed up at a gathering in Golden Prince Park, the site of a traditionally fierce rivalry between two prominent football clubs. The game promised to be a ridiculously close match, and it attracted its usual big, boisterous crowd. While feigning interest in the game from the sidelines, agents could pass messages and make plans. Hiding in plain sight, out in the open, was often a good strategy for Magnus, who had perfected the art of looking ordinary and unremarkable.

He stood on the sidelines, watching the soccer ball as if it were his sole purpose in life. In reality, he was awaiting word about the Nazis' latest atrocity—the roundup and deportation of the Jews in Denmark.

Thus far, there had been no formal deportation order. It had long been the case that many Jewish citizens had to close their businesses and some, like Sweet and Eva, had already gone into hiding. However, the majority of Jews had stayed in their homes, even attending the city's one synagogue. Observing the tenacity of the worshipers, Magnus was coming to realize that, for some people, faith was a powerful force. And because it was so powerful, it was dangerous.

He himself spent little time pondering the vicissitudes of faith. He was too busy living by his wits from day to day. The air was filled with cheers and the aroma of roasting hazelnuts, dry fallen leaves and cheap beer.

From somewhere in the crowd came a trilling whistle, a sound any fan of the game might make, except that this one was repeated three times. Without seeming obvious, Magnus turned toward the source of the whistle. Spectators were waving scarves in the colors of their favored team—yellow for St. Alban's and green with an owl emblem for the Akademisk Boldklub. He spotted a scarf with a yellow stripe down the middle—his contact.

And when he saw who it was, he froze for a moment, nearly giving himself away by staring in shock. Then, recovering himself, he made his way through the crowd.

"It's been a while," he said.

The girl called Annelise, whom he'd last seen the night they had sabotaged the badges, merely kept her scarf waving in the air. She didn't look at him. "That's not the code," she said simply, her voice nearly drowned by the cheering crowd.

A year had passed since that night, and she looked very different.

We've all changed, thought Magnus. But the differences in Annelise seemed somehow more profound. The bones of her face were harsh and prominent, her eyes narrowed in an expression of suspicion. He wondered what had befallen her, where she had been—in hiding? In one of the coastal towns along the water between Denmark and Sweden? Or had she been detained by the Germans? He kept flashing on images of her that night, growing smaller and smaller as she created a distraction while he and Ramon escaped.

"To hell with the code. I need to know—"

"What you need to know is that there's an important message to be delivered. Do you recognize those two over there?"

He stole a look at a group of middle-aged men standing in a knot, their attention riveted on the game. They held flags in the green and gold of the Akademisk Boldklub. "No," said Magnus. "Should I?"

"The one with the green neckerchief is Niels Bohr, a physics professor, and the tall one next to him is his brother."

"That's Harald Bohr?" Magnus was impressed. "He was on the Danish Olympic football team."

She sniffed. "That's all well and good, but it is the other brother who has a Nobel Prize. Which is probably the main reason they're about to be arrested by the Nazis."

"What?"

"Why should anything the Nazis do surprise you?" She handed him a football program.

Magnus could see an envelope and the thin yellow paper of a telegram peeking out from the program. "I'm to give this to them?"

"Yes, but be smart about it. We can't be sure who the others are."

During a break in the game, Magnus approached Harald Bohr. "Sir, can I get your autograph, please?" he asked, digging a pencil stub from his pocket.

"Certainly." He took the program while Magnus watched him intently, hoping the silent communication would be enough.

Apparently it was, as Mr. Bohr scrawled his signature on the program and then handed it back, smoothly tucking the telegram and envelope into an inner pocket of his jacket. Magnus grinned and admired the signature. Next to it, he'd scribbled, "Understood. Good work."

"Thank you, sir," Magnus said. "It's an honor."

"You're welcome, young man. Best of luck to you."

Magnus rejoined Annelise. "That was simple enough."

"One hopes so," she said. "You've been advised about the

meeting on Thursday evening? It must not be missed. There's a drysalter shop in Bay Street, do you know it?"

"No, but I'll find it. What time?"

"The usual."

Twenty past eight in the evening—the time settled on in order to simplify communications.

"I'll be there," he said. "Will you?"

"Yes. Of course."

He couldn't keep himself from asking, "Are you all right?"

She stared at him. Her eyes were as hard as stone walls. "I'm here, aren't I?"

"It's just that... I was wondering."

"There's no need." She fell silent, and Magnus could detect a hardness in her manner that hadn't been there before. He wanted to ask her what was wrong, if the pressures of the occupation were wearing on her, if she feared being caught and arrested. He wanted to say something that might ease the lines of worry in her face, the way he might have done for anyone he was concerned about. But he didn't know how to be a friend to anyone these days. He was simply a machine, not even that; a cog in the wheel of the resistance. He had no business worrying about anyone but himself.

When the whistle blew to signal the halftime of the match, she dropped her scarf on the ground and walked away. Magnus picked up the scarf and let out a cheer, but he couldn't focus on the game. He watched her go, moving slowly as though carrying a great weight on her shoulders. But he didn't follow her. These days, he didn't follow anything but orders.

At the meeting on the following Thursday, Magnus was still burning with questions. He arrived at the appointed time, slipping down an alleyway beside the Hørkramforretning— the drysalter shop where medicines were prepared. The basement door was marked with a charcoal smear. "Delivery for Mr. Christiansen," he muttered, letting himself in. The code phrase was accepted, and he found himself ushered into a crowded room.

It was the biggest gathering he had ever attended, with at least three dozen people present. They were mostly men, but the group included a few women, including Annelise, who sat very still on a bench on the periphery of the room.

Magnus was shocked to recognize Mr. Knud Christiansen himself, a prominent citizen who hobnobbed with the Nazis. As handsome as any Aryan ideal, he was famous for his athletic prowess on the Danish Olympic rowing team. He lived in a fancy apartment in Havnegade alongside German officials, and as far as the Nazis knew, he was a loyal collaborator.

This, of course, made him a key asset for the resistance. He could move freely among the officials in charge, and he had cultivated their friendship so that they would speak freely in his presence. They would be shocked to see him tonight sitting shoulder to shoulder with Rabbi Melchior, head of the synagogue in Copenhagen.

"I can confirm the rumors," said Mr. Christiansen. He paused, pinching the bridge of his nose. Then his jaw ticked as he gritted his teeth. "The maritime attaché, Mr. Duckwitz, has let it be known that the SS plans to initiate a mass roundup of the Jews on October the first. They're to be deported, most probably to a camp called Theresienstadt in occupied Czechoslovakia."

A chill rippled through the room like an ill wind. Everyone present understood what a "camp" was—a center where Jews and other "undesirables" were worked to death or murdered outright.

"Duckwitz is a Nazi. Why would he warn us?" someone asked.

"Apparently the man has a conscience."

"I heard he went to Berlin to persuade the central authority to cancel the arrests," said a man in a white cloth coat. "And when he was ignored, he went to Sweden to get assurance from the Prime Minister there that they'd be willing to receive refugees, same as they have all along."

"But so many. There are thousands in the city and all up along the coast."

They looked to Rabbi Melchior. "I shall tell everyone at services to go into hiding immediately. They'll be instructed to spread the word to all their Jewish friends and relatives."

"We can all go door to door," said a man called Marius, whom Magnus recognized as one of the leaders of the resistance cell. "We can get on the telephone. We know who these people are, better than the Nazis do. They're our neighbors, people we do business with."

"It's a risk, but what else can we do?"

"Some might not agree to leave," one man pointed out. "They're Danes, after all, even the immigrants who came from Eastern Europe seeking safety. They have their places in the community, their homes and families. Will they agree to leave everything behind?"

Magnus thought of Uncle Sweet and Eva, disappearing in the night with only a satchel of the most basic belongings. He made a silent vow to travel up the coast to Helsingør and find them before the deportations began.

"Is that going to be enough, to simply spread the word?"

"Of course not," someone else said.

"He's right. The one thing we can't do is ignore the situation. People can only hide for so long. Eventually they'll be found and taken."

"Not if we can get them to Sweden."

"Yes, they must go to Sweden."

"They're in jeopardy of being turned away. The Swedish government won't accept them unless the Nazis approve the request."

"The Nazis are ignoring the request. We'll never hear from them."

Ramon Maldonado arrived, dropping his messenger bag with a clatter. He was breathless as he handed something to Marius. "It's a telegram. The one you've been waiting for."

"Let me see that." Mr. Christiansen looked at the ceiling. "Thank you, Professor Bohr."

"Who's that?" someone asked.

"Neils Bohr. A physicist at the university. He and his brother were nearly arrested, but they made it to Sweden with their families. According to this communique, he has the ear of the whole world, not just the Swedish authorities. He's convinced the government there to make a general announcement that the borders and ports are open to refugees. It says here there will be Swedish radio broadcasts announcing that Sweden is offering asylum."

"Just like a good Jewish boy." Marius gave a satisfied nod. "His mother was Jewish."

Ramon took a seat on a bench next to Magnus and nudged his elbow into Magnus's ribs. "Good work," he whispered. "You, too," he added, leaning forward to include Annelise, who sat on Magnus's other side.

"It's not good to simply know what's about to happen and to warn people," she whispered back. "We have to do more."

True to his word, Rabbi Melchior warned people attending early morning Rosh Hashanah services of the impending German action. He urged everyone to go into hiding, with an eye to making their way in secret to Sweden. No one knew how long the deportation order would stand or how long the war would last, so it was the safest course to take.

Other members of the Jewish community and of the resistance movement sent word through the underground telegraph system. Everyone tried to do their part, even little old ladies who stayed up all night going through the telephone directory, picking out the Jewish-sounding names and calling people to warn them of the roundup.

Magnus told Ramon and Annelise of his plan to find Sweet and Eva. "I need you to drive me," he said to Ramon. "You have access to a Red Cross vehicle, yes?"

"I do. How far is it?"

"About forty kilometers. The trick will be to find the house where they've been staying. I don't have the precise location."

"Eva and her father have been living above a bake shop along the strand, not far from Kronborg Castle," Annelise said quietly.

"You know them?" Magnus was amazed.

"Eva and I are friends. And I'm going with you," Annelise announced.

The lovely seaside town of Helsingør, with its fairy-tale castle, its farms and fishing fleet, was the last place many Jews would ever feel the soil of Denmark beneath their feet. A few thousand meters across the sound lay Sweden...and safety. Officials who bothered to question the fishermen and ferrymen were told various tales about the hundreds of families hastily boarding the local boats. Some were going by water to attend their sewing club. Others to visit sick friends. Still others were braving the foul weather to cast their nets for the abundant herring.

The only story no one told was the truth; that people were avoiding deportation by fleeing across the Oresund Strait to

Sweden. Magnus felt a fierce pride in his countrymen who risked themselves to save the lives of people who lived in Denmark, regardless of who they were, even if it meant defying the authorities.

They watched a trio of lopsided boats leaning into the wind, the waves striking hard against the small hulls as the small fleet departed. "How can we be sure Eva and her father made it to Sweden?" asked Annelise.

"Show us where they lived," Magnus said. The moment the words were out of his mouth, he felt a sting of apprehension.

The place above the bake shop was deserted. Everything seemed left as if they had just stepped out briefly. A boot tray with a pair of wooden garden clogs lay by the door. There was a pitcher of milk on the table, a skin forming on the top. An ashtray containing the remains of a hand-rolled cigarette sat on the painted enamel table. An armoire with its doors agape stood half empty.

There was a peculiar smell in the air. Metallic and strange.

"Word must have reached them already," Magnus said, standing at the front window and looking out at the town. He pictured Eva walking through the charming cobblestone streets, or passing by the beautiful castle, admiring its spires against a sunny sky, or perhaps playing on the sandy beach across from the strand, able to see Sweden on a clear day. He wondered if he would ever meet her again, and felt a twist of emotion in his gut.

"We should go," Ramon said. "There's more to be done in the city."

Magnus wondered if the smell came from Sweet's photographic chemicals. Maybe they'd been spilled during the hasty departure. He glanced down at the floor and noticed a trail of dark spots leading toward a windowless back room.

And that was when he knew.

They found Sweet's body, broken in too many places to count, lying in a heap. Annelise turned and buried her face in her hands. They made a thorough search for Eva, dreading what they might find. But to their relief, there was no sign of her. Magnus stood unmoving, wishing his last glimpse of the man he'd loved and admired had not been this. Then he remembered every detail of Eva, the way she liked to make a wish on dandelion puffs, the way her eyes lit up when he explained to her how Christmas worked, the sound of her laughter, the silence of her sadness. She would be nearly grown now.

Back in Copenhagen, the Waffen SS had formed teams of police battalions with a Danish collaborator on each team to lead them on their hunt for the Jews. It was the Jewish new year, and the Germans assumed families would make the process simple for them by being at home for the holiday. Yet as the teams moved through the city with their transport vehicles and list of addresses to check, they encountered empty homes, time and time again.

Someone in the underground told Magnus about a Jewish family called Friediger in the east harbor district whom no one had been able to contact. He was to find his way to an address near Langelinie to make certain the family had gone into hiding. To his horror, he looked into the window and saw that they were still at home, gathered around the dining table, eating apples dipped in honey and sharing a loaf of golden braided challah bread.

He pounded on the door but didn't bother to wait for an answer. The door wasn't locked, so he burst inside. "I've come to warn you that you must leave," he said without preamble. "Now. The Waffen SS has sent out teams to find all the Jews in the city. If they find you, they'll arrest you and take you away for deportation."

"We are aware of the order," said a man with a gray beard. He wore a white cap embroidered with blue on his bald head. "We have decided to stay together as a family. My wife's parents are too elderly to be moved, and my daughter has a new baby." He gestured at the people gathered around the table, indicating an old woman in a wheelchair seated next to an old man whose hands shook with palsy. Mr. Friediger's wife and daughter were on the opposite side of the table, a tiny swaddled bundle in the daughter's arms.

"You don't understand. If you don't get away now, you'll be taken," Magnus said.

"We have money for bribes," the man answered. "Listen, young man, your concern is well-founded, but the decision has been made. It is the birthday of the new year. We shall celebrate as we always have."

Magnus thought about the night his own family had been taken. There had been no warning, no offer from anyone to help get them into hiding. In one brutal intrusion, his parents had been taken. Dear God, if they'd had even a moment of advance warning, he might still have a family. This was a gift, and the man didn't seem to understand that. His temper snapped. "Don't be stupid," he yelled, looking around the table. "What good is it to stay together as a family if you're going to be shipped to a death camp?"

"Young man—"

"I can help you. I'll get you on a boat—"

"Papa, maybe we should listen to him," said the daughter.

There was a pounding at the door, and the tiny baby let out a wail.

"Police," called a voice from outside. "Open up."

Magnus's pulse surged. "Put out the lights. Is there a back door?"

The man stood up. "Look at them," he said with quiet

resignation, gesturing at his family. "Can you truly think we can sneak away in the night? Now, the back door is through there. I suggest you make use of it. I can deal with the police."

The baby's cries sounded like the mewing of a kitten. With unhurried deliberation, Mr. Friediger went to answer the door. Seething with frustration, Magnus headed for the back of the house, lingering behind the pantry door. Perhaps Friediger knew something Magnus did not, and they would be left alone.

There was a shuffle of heavy footsteps. "You are to come with us," said an officious voice in German-accented Danish. "You may each bring two blankets, food for three days' travel and one small suitcase per person. Be ready in fifteen minutes."

"I can offer you fifteen thousand kroner," Friediger said calmly. "It is all the cash we have."

"Why would you think for a moment we'd accept a bribe?" the German demanded, and Magnus heard the sound of coins, spilling across the floor.

On October second, Ramon, Magnus and Annelise saw about two hundred Jews forced to board the ship *Wartheland*. Magnus's gaze combed the crowd for a glimpse of Eva. Each time he saw a girl with thick dark braids, he stiffened, thinking he'd spotted her. But she didn't appear to be in the group being forced aboard the ship.

"I feel sick," Annelise murmured, "but I can't look away."

Magnus understood her horror. The victims were entirely innocent; they were mothers cradling infants in their arms, elderly citizens bent over their canes, sick people coughing into wadded up handkerchiefs, a rabbi carrying a book and a flimsy suitcase. The guards screamed at them, kicked and beat them as they drove them belowdecks, seizing their luggage with impunity.

A young couple stepped out of the shuffling line and approached a guard. "There's been a mistake," the man said. "We're not Jewish."

"Shit," said Magnus under his breath. "That's not going to work." He started walking toward them.

Ramon grabbed his arm. "What the hell are you doing? You're going to be taken if you—"

"Then so be it," Magnus snapped. He strode forward. "Sir, I can vouch for them," he stated. "These two don't belong here."

"Who are you?" the guard demanded.

Magnus thought fast. "I was with the search team covering Langelinie."

The guard glared at the couple and then at Magnus. "Wait here," he said. "I must go and check on something."

While he went over to consult with his superior, Magnus leaned forward and whispered, "What is your name?"

"Jan and Marte Sonne. I am a brick mason, born and raised right here in the city." The man's voice shook. "Please, can you help? My wife is expecting our first child."

The guard returned with the officer, who showed them a hardbound leather book. "Your name is here, on the census record," the officer said. "You are listed as a member of the synagogue. How can that be a mistake?"

"He's a mason," Magnus said. "He was teaching me the trade, doing repairs at the synagogue. You know, after last year's incident," he added, referring to the explosion at the synagogue. "That is why his name is on the list."

The officer snapped the book shut. "Step out of line. We will verify this later."

"I'll wait with them over there." Magnus made a vague gesture toward the street, having no intention of waiting, of course. As he escorted the couple away from the line of people, the guards were distracted and the couple ducked into a shop.

"Where the hell is she?" Magnus asked Ramon, still thinking of Eva. "I'm going to get on that ship."

"You can't. It's too dangerous. If they catch you, they'll kill you."

"You think I don't know that? You think she's not worth it?"

"You'll be useless to her if you're dead," Ramon stated.

"Distract them," Magnus said to Annelise.

"But I—"

"Just do it."

She set her mouth into a seam of fury, but strode forward and approached a guard who was loitering on the quay. He couldn't hear what she said to him, but when the guard looked away, he loaded a crate onto a hand truck and wheeled it toward the transport ship. He got as far as the loading plank when a sharp command hit him like a blow: *"Halt."*

Magnus froze, then slowly turned. "Yes?" he asked, feigning boredom.

"What are you doing?" a soldier asked.

"Bringing supplies aboard."

"Under whose orders?"

He shrugged. "Just doing what I'm told."

"I'm telling you to make yourself scarce," the guard said. "Be off with you, now."

Magnus set down the hand truck. He clenched his hands into fists. He thought about the dagger he always kept concealed in his ankle holster. His fingers twitched. Cries of distress from the prisoners filled the air. An explosion detonated inside him, made of fury and impotence and raw despair.

Leaning down, he reached for the knife. Annelise grabbed his hand. "Come," she said. "We must be going."

Magnus had been looking for Eva for a year, ever since the roundup of the Jews. After being shipped from Copenhagen, the captured Jews had been driven like cattle into cars and locked in for transport. With no water and little ventilation, they were sent to Danzig and ultimately to a work camp. The Danish people had done their best to persuade the Germans to accept packages of food and medicine for the prisoners. The Danish Red Cross monitored conditions at the camp and tried to minimize the casualties.

The Allies applauded the action, but Magnus feared Eva had been among those seized. She had disappeared along with dozens of others.

After the Normandy invasion, the atmosphere in Copenhagen changed. Everyone noticed; it was like an ill wind sweeping down the city's narrow alleyways and through its harbors and docks. The Germans seemed to be on edge and even more suspicious than usual. The least little thing could set them off, and ordinary citizens were liable to be detained and questioned.

The Danish government had long since resigned in protest. Some of the largest ships in the harbor were scuttled to keep the Germans from using them.

In retaliation, several buildings in Tivoli Gardens, the city's one hundred year old amusement park, were burned down. Many blamed the Nazis or Nazi sympathizers. Resolute citizens rebuilt the place and even erected a Ferris wheel, determined to carry on.

Magnus was staked out one September day, garbed in a shapeless gray workman's overall and swirling a twig broom lazily across the walkways around city hall square, listening to snippets of conversation from passing government officials. For the most part, their conversations were mundane and dull—the unseasonably hot weather, the difficulties of managing their department workers, the latest office gossip, the need to find more electric fans for government offices.

On that September day, Magnus got lucky. He was rolling his two-wheeled waste cart past the side of the massive, steepled city hall when voices drifted to him through an open window.

Magnus stopped the cart and took hold of the broom, busying himself near the window. *"…arrest or deportation,"* someone said in German. *"It makes no difference to me."*

"Now that the HIPO are in place, we have no further need to delay action."

Magnus felt a cold sting of suspicion. "HIPO" was code for *Hilfspolizei,* a corps of Danish collaborators who had thrown in their lot with the Germans. Rumor had it that they would take the place of the proper Danish police. Ordinary citizens held them in contempt. Members of the resistance were dedicated to defying them at every turn.

"The Danish police have been of no use at all," said the German. "Write the order, effective next Monday."

"That's too much time," the first speaker said. "You know these Danes. They take each other in, help each other to hide. They'll slip through our fingers."

"Just write the order and be done with it." The man sounded exasperated. "In the meantime, the HIPO will keep order around here."

Magnus brought this bit of intelligence to a meeting of his group. Another agent corroborated the story, saying he had seen correspondence from the German in charge of civilian affairs. The Danish police force was slated to be arrested en masse.

Most of them went into hiding or escaped to Sweden. Without a functioning police force, crime skyrocketed, but this was nothing new to Magnus. He had been living outside the law for years. He welcomed the lawlessness, because it distracted the Germans from their hunt for rebels.

Secret telegrams crackled through the city. Acts of resistance grew more fierce and audacious. Ramon and Magnus went out one night to place detonators along a railway track to derail a German transport train. It was an act of sabotage that had been done many times, and guards patrolled the rail lines at two hundred meter intervals.

The night was gloomy, the air heavy with fog. They waited in a wooded area near the tracks, straining to see through the dark mist. Running along with their heads low, they placed the first three detonators, affixing them under the lip of the rail so the guards wouldn't see. As they were installing the fourth one, Magnus heard the sound of boots on gravel. "Shit," he whispered, "someone's coming."

"I'm nearly done," said Ramon.

"We can't risk it." He raced back for cover, but Ramon didn't follow. Magnus didn't dare call out for him. He saw Ramon stand up and start running. A voice barked out a command, but Ramon kept going. Magnus saw their two silhouettes clash, heard their grunts as they struggled. The guard, wearing a helmet and wielding a bayoneted firearm, stood up and stabbed downward repeatedly.

Magnus didn't stop to think. Yanking out his dagger, he rushed forward and jumped on the Nazi's back. The burley soldier let out a roar and swung around. Magnus brought the dagger down in a wild stab. It felt strange and terrible, penetrating the man's clothing and then his flesh. The soldier let out a howl and reeled back. Magnus raised the dagger again and brought it down, sobbing with the motion. The soldier staggered, and swore and then he prayed, but his words dissolved into a gurgle.

As his opponent sank to the ground, Magnus grabbed Ramon. "Are you hurt?"

Ramon climbed to his feet. Blood poured down the front

of him in a ghastly river. Magnus went light in the head, but he tore off his shirt and pressed it against the wound. "Tell me it's a flesh wound," he said.

"Let's hope so. You don't want to have to carry me." His breath came in short, sharp bursts. "I think he broke my ribs with a kick. *Gracias al cielo,* you saved my life."

"Let's get out of here." Magnus made it as far as the woods before he had to lean over and vomit. He didn't know if he had killed the soldier or not. He'd never killed anyone before. It felt terrible, as if something vital had been sucked out of him.

In March of 1945, a glimmer of information came through the Red Cross. "They're bringing people back from the camps," Ramon informed Magnus and Annelise, rushing into the chilly abandoned apartment where they'd taken up residence in the city. A group of vagabonds and resistance workers lived together there, trying to stay out of the Germans' way. "A transfer has been negotiated. The buses of the Swedish Red Cross are bringing them home." Magnus grabbed the news sheet Ramon had brought.

"How can we help?" asked Annelise. These days, she looked haggard all the time, thin and exhausted, but her eyes burned with hope now.

"The evacuation is already underway," said Ramon. "The ferry from Malmo is bringing them back by the busload. Two thousand souls."

Ramon looked different since the night at the train tracks. Although he'd recovered from the broken rib, he had a scar from his jaw to his ear where the bayonet had sliced into him during the fight. He and Magnus never spoke of that night, except for once. He'd said, "There's no way I can ever repay you. Just know that you have a friend for life."

"How can we find out if Eva is among the people brought home?" Magnus asked now. His heart was beating fast.

"When the ferries land, then we'll know," said Ramon.

The three of them haunted the dock, watching and waiting. And finally, on a spring morning, when daffodils colored the roadside verges and all the trees were budding, the buses arrived. No one said a word as they watched the operation. The ambulance buses had been painted white to distinguish them from military vehicles, and they were accompanied by a platoon of supply trucks, personnel vehicles, motorcycles, even kitchen trailers.

"I heard the Allies strafed the roads and some of the transports were hit," Ramon whispered.

Magnus nudged his shoulder. "That's not helpful."

"Hush," Annelise said to both of them. "We must watch for Eva."

It was disconcerting to see SS and Gestapo officers supervising every move of the platoon, but it was necessary. No matter what was happening elsewhere, this was still a police state, and nothing could happen without the cooperation of the Germans.

"At least they're keeping things orderly, I'll say that for them," whispered Ramon.

The processing was a slow agony, but Magnus reminded himself that others had suffered far worse agonies. The survivors were like ghosts, bony and draped in drab prison garb and tattered blankets. Many of them had to be carried off the buses in litters and loaded onto gurneys, too weak to walk on their own.

They studied every survivor who bore even the vaguest resemblance to Eva. Magnus's heart skipped a beat every time he glimpsed a head of brown hair. But she was not among them. They inquired of everyone they could find—medical personnel, military volunteers, even the Germans. Her name was not on any roster, nor was she among the shuffling tide of humanity exiting the buses. It was all Magnus could do to keep from sinking to his knees in despair.

The afternoon sun made a mockery of his mood. He was determined to go through every vehicle in the platoon in search of her.

And then he spied Eva, and his breath stopped in his throat. It was Eva, but she was not the girl he'd once entertained in his mother's garden. This was a woman with Eva's face, her dark eyebrows and thick wavy hair. She was parading around on the arm of a decorated German official, her red-lipsticked mouth smiling at nothing.

"That's her mother," he said when the realization hit him. "That's Katya." Apparently she still lived in luxury with her German lover.

The sight of her made Magnus's blood boil. He watched the woman say something to the German. Then she grabbed her handbag and rushed over to a small group of litters headed to a flatbed truck labeled "morgue." She dropped to her knees beside one and let out terrible wail that sliced through the air like a knife, cleaving Magnus's heart in two.

He ran to her, Annelise at his heels. Up close, the woman did not look so fancy. Her face was puffy, her red mouth twisted in a wordless cry, her eyes blackened by the tears running through her makeup. "Stay away from her," Katya snarled at them. "Leave her in peace."

"She is already at peace," Annelise said, and she stroked the face of the girl on the litter, a face bruised almost beyond recognition. Then she looked up at Magnus. "Oh, my God. She's still warm."

Katya Solomon suddenly discovered a conscience. She had Eva brought to a clean, bright apartment that served as the maid's quarters to a Nazi official. Day by day, she sat beside her daughter, spooning soup and tea and plain water into the girl's mouth.

Magnus and Annelise visited her every day. He could tell this made Katya uncomfortable, but she didn't dare speak up. Because whenever he and Annelise were present, a light came on inside Eva and she ate better. Before long, she was walking in the gardens of Golden Prince Park, holding on to both of her friends. Magnus noticed that Eva was the only person Annelise allowed to touch her.

One day, Eva rolled up the frayed sleeve of her sweater and showed them a crude row of numbers inked on her forearm. "A group of us were sent to Auschwitz, even though all the Danish Jews were supposed to be detained at Theresienstadt. They marked us and we probably would have been herded to the gas chamber if not for a man named Knud Christiansen."

Magnus recalled Mr. Christiansen from meetings of the underground. "What did he do?"

"He made a terrible ruckus and convinced the Nazis that if we came to harm, it would create an international incident. After that, everyone from Denmark was moved to Theresienstadt. Conditions were not much better there, but at least I was among my own people."

Ramon and Eva had not met until recently, but he seemed devoted to her, the way one would be to a stray kitten. He spent hours describing California to her in vivid detail.

"I love the springtime," she said, admiring an apple tree that was bursting with pink and white blossoms. "I love the summer even more. I wish it could be summer all the time."

"It is where I come from," Ramon said.

"I should like to see that," Eva said.

"Then you should come to California with me," he told her. He smiled when he said it, but Magnus could tell he wasn't teasing.

The park was in sad shape, as the German administration spent no resources on things such as public gardens and playgrounds. But the springtime still managed to coax flowers from the beds, and children played on the seesaws and swings.

Annelise pointed out an area of the playground. "My mother and I used to come here together all the time," she said. "I loved the swings."

"I once set a pipe bomb there," Ramon said. "Don't worry, it was at night, and the only ones around were Nazis."

"It was the last place I saw her," Annelise said dreamily. "It hurts now to look at it."

"Come, let's go play away the hurt." Eva led the way to the swings. She sat on one, her feet brushing through the overgrown grass. As she pumped her legs and flew higher, her sleeves fluttered back.

Magnus could see the ugly dark numbers that had been gouged into her forearm, and his stomach churned. She didn't speak of what she'd suffered in the concentration camp, but he had watched her sleep. He had seen her in the throes of a nightmare. He wished he could take all those nightmares out of her and just erase them.

Annelise took the swing next to her. "This is what my mother and I did on the last day we were together."

"On my last day with my mother," Eva said, "she took my Red Cross money."

"What do you mean she took it?"

"Just helped herself when she thought I was asleep this morning. So I decided it's my last day with her."

Magnus caught her swing in midair and stopped it, leaning down to make sure she wasn't feverish. "What do you mean, your last day?"

She smiled softly, making eye contact with Ramon, who stood behind him. "We have a plan."

"We're all going to California together," said Ramon.

"What the devil are you talking about?" Magnus demanded. "We can't go to California."

"Can't? Or won't?"

Magnus turned to Annelise, who was twirling idly on the swing. "Are you in on this crazy plan?"

"I am now," she said quietly.

"I'll tell you what's crazy," Ramon said. "Staying here in this dying city, waiting for the Allies to swoop in and…do what? They're busy in Germany, in Poland. Rebuilding Denmark is not a priority for them."

Magnus strode away, seething. He didn't like the way they had sprung this idea on him, as if his opinion didn't matter. Standing next to the wrought iron fence, with its peeling paint and its view of the neglected boulevards of the city, he thought about his homeland. It was the only home he'd ever known. He had grown up here, in the long, dark, wet winters and the short, brilliant golden summers. The dreams he'd had as a boy were long forgotten.

He didn't let himself dream anymore, but when Ramon mentioned California, Magnus's imagination took flight. Over the years, he'd heard plenty from Ramon about California, where the sun never stopped shining, where vineyards and orchards abounded, where people were far from the fighting, and free of the past.

Ramon stepped up beside him. "I didn't mean to force this idea on you. It's your decision entirely, of course."

"What would I do? I have no education. I'm a good enough mechanic, though I have no certification in the trade. I doubt there is a dire need in America for guys who know how to set explosives and commit arson."

"You know how to grow things. I've heard you talk about your mother's garden, her orchards and beehives. You used to torture me with descriptions of it when we were starving. You can grow anything in California. And that's not an exaggeration."

"It sounds too good to be true."

"It sounds like a good plan. I'm not saying it's going to be easy for you, but I do know you'll thrive there. We all will. My father's holdings are bigger than some of the countries I've been to over here. He's a generous man. I know he'd be honored to meet you. Come to California, Magnus. Leave all this behind. Make a new life for yourself."

Magnus tipped back his head and watched a seabird soar against the clouds. The sunshine warmed his face, and the breeze stirred his hair. Behind him, he heard Eva and Annelise talking, and the sound of children laughing as they played in the park. It was a beautiful day.

PART VIII

The term honeymoon *was coined to refer to the sweetness of a new marriage. But according to Norse legend, a man abducted his bride from a neighboring village. He was then required to take her into hiding until the bride's family abandoned their search. His whereabouts were known only to his best man. While in seclusion, the couple drank mead, a honeyed wine.*

THE BELLA VISTA
SIGNATURE COCKTAIL

1½	oz. good quality bourbon	1	oz. apple cider
½	oz. calvados	½	oz. honey syrup★
A dash of bitters		1	wide slice of orange peel

★To make honey syrup, boil ½ cup of water together with a cup of honey until the honey dissolves. Store in a sealed jar.

Measure everything into a cocktail shaker and add a good handful of ice. Shake vigorously and then strain the drink into a clear lowball glass with one large piece of ice. Rub the orange peel around the rim of the glass.

Garnish with an apple slice.

[Source: Original]

CHAPTER EIGHTEEN

Ramon Maldonado was having a good day. His wife, Juanita, had called Magnus in the morning to invite him over, knowing the window of opportunity was narrow. When Ramon was lucid, his memories were as sharp and clear as the slides he showed on his old Kodak carousel.

In the elderly Ramon, Mac could see only subtle glimmers of the dark, strapping young man who had fled the wiles of Evelyn Skeedy by becoming a Red Cross volunteer—a brightness in his eyes, an impish upturn of his lips. Now Ramon was diminished, tiny and shrunken, confined to a wheelchair. The scar from a German's bayonet still scored his neck.

Four of them—Ramon, Magnus, Annelise and Mac—sat in a distinctly masculine den at the Maldonado estate. It smelled of old leather and cigar smoke, and there was a big carved desk and a Chesterfield sofa set in front of an old-fashioned screen. The shutters were closed against the daylight, and the fan of the projector blew gently into the room. Juanita operated the old carousel from her chair in the back of the room.

"There is a special bond that forms between men who shared what we have shared," Ramon said, pausing at an image of two young men standing together in front of a wharf. Magnus, tall and fair-haired, and Ramon, built like a fireplug—squat and strong, struck a pose in front of a ship's hull. "Despite the prohibition against forming close friendships within the resistance, we became more than comrades-in-arms. It is impossible to share what we shared without creating a tight bond."

Mac glanced away from the projection screen, forming a mental picture of young Magnus, stabbing a soldier in the neck in order to save the life of his friend. Some bonds were forged in darkness.

"God only knows what would have become of me if I'd stayed in Denmark," said Magnus. "It was a ruin of a place. I didn't even have my school certificate, just my wits and mechanical and masonry skills, and a few prized possessions."

"It wasn't until much later that we learned how difficult it was to get transport to America, and then to get permission to immigrate," said Annelise. "Ramon pulled strings, and I suspect his father greased some palms."

"It was not so hard," he said. "I took advantage of my position in the Red Cross and I'm not sorry."

"We are all grateful that you did what you did."

"And what is it that he did?"

"He managed to get berths for the four of us aboard the SS *Stavangerfjord* at a time when even the VIPs were clamoring for space. We made landfall in New York, and then traveled by train clear across the country," Annelise said.

"I cannot begin to describe to you how vast everything looked to us. Vast and empty and new," Magnus said. "It was exactly what we needed. To make a fresh start in our new home."

"A *tabula rasa*," Annelise added.

"The generosity of the Maldonado family cannot be underestimated," Magnus said. "They gave us the orchard and
the house. It was more than I ever dreamed of."

"That was only the beginning," Ramon said. "The rest was
up to you, and you created a wonderful life." He showed a
succession of slides of the orchard and house, of Magnus and
Eva in the sunshine they craved so much. Then there was a
shot of Annelise in a cap and gown.

"Ah," she said. "Graduation day."

"You went to Cal," said Mac. "Not too shabby for a girl
who didn't finish secondary school."

"I was very ambitious, and hungry to learn," Annelise said.
"I took such a liking to Berkeley that I never wanted to leave...
until I found San Francisco. That is where I found my heart's
home, with my teaching job and dancing students and my
cats."

She was stunningly beautiful, Mac couldn't help but notice.
It was no surprise, given the way her granddaughters looked.

"You shouldn't get involved in this, Erik," said Ramon,
suddenly glaring at Magnus. "It's an ugly business. Carlos
has made a terrible mistake, but there's no reason for you to
suffer for it."

Magnus frowned. "Ramon? It's me, Magnus."

"Yes, I know, but the boy made his own trouble. I've told
him I'm through settling his gambling debts for him. *El está
en su propia empresa.*"

Mac had enough Spanish to understand. *He is on his own
now.*

"Ramon is tired," said Juanita, getting up quickly and opening the shutters to let in the light. She gently touched his
shoulder. "You've had a lot of excitement with your guests
today. This is a good time to take a rest."

SUSAN WIGGS

"Who's Carlos?" Mac asked Magnus after Juanita wheeled her husband out of the room.

"Their eldest son. Carlos and Erik were best friends, like Ramon and me. But unlike us, the young men had a falling-out. Shortly after Erik's accident, Carlos was found drowned in an irrigation pond." As he spoke, Magnus reached for Annelise's hand. "A terrible tragedy for both families."

"Were the tragedies related?" Mac asked.

"No," Magnus quickly declared. "We've imposed on the Maldonados long enough today," he added. "We should be going."

Isabel was putting lunch together in the kitchen when her grandfather returned from his visit with Ramon Maldonado. "It was good to see my old friend for a bit," Grandfather said, stealing one of her homemade tortillas from the hot plate.

"You'll have to tell me all about it," said Isabel. "We can—"

She stopped, hearing the spit of gravel on the driveway outside. Looking out the window, she saw a little red sports car grind to a stop. "Oh, boy," she muttered under her breath.

A young woman exited the car, slamming the door with an angry thud. "I'll go," Isabel said, hanging up her apron. She went out the back door and came face-to-face with Lourdes Maldonado. She was the granddaughter of Ramon, and Isabel knew very well she had a bone to pick with the Johansens.

"Hello, Lourdes," she said pleasantly enough.

Lourdes didn't seem to be in any mood for pleasantries. "Listen, I don't want you coming around and asking my grandfather questions."

"For starters, I wasn't there this morning. But I'm sure Ramon didn't mind visiting with his best friend."

"Well, I mind. You've already cheated my family out of a fortune, and I won't have you taking advantage of a sick old man." Lourdes, of course, was referring the treasure Tess had found, which had belonged to Magnus. A canny lawyer, she had laid claim to it and had initiated a suit to share in the fortune. It was an annoyance suit, but it was very real, and had been dragging on for months.

"No one's taking advantage of your grandfather," Isabel assured her. "As I'm sure Juanita explained, we were reminiscing. Would you like to stay for lunch?"

Lourdes made an unpleasant face. "I think not. Just stay away from him."

Isabel glared at her. "Have a nice day, Lourdes."

She left in a huff, punching the accelerator to stir up more gravel. Isabel sighed and went back into the kitchen.

"She seemed pissed," Mac said, folding a tortilla around a wedge of cheese. "What's up with that?"

"We used to be friends," Isabel said. "It's complicated."

"Women's friendships are often more complicated than romance," Annelise said. Isabel instantly thought of Annelise and Eva, the birth mother and the adoptive mother.

"If I thought it would settle things, I would offer Lourdes a portion of Bella Vista," said Magnus.

"She'd never accept that," Isabel said. "It's not the land she wants."

Her grandfather nodded in agreement. "I always felt this place was too big. When we first settled here, the land, the house, everything seemed so vast, particularly in contrast to things in Denmark. Eva and I had dreams of a large family. We both wanted many children. It was, I suppose, a reaction to what we had seen in the war, all the death and deprivation. Babies are like the springtime, a renewal. An affirmation of life."

Isabel's heart ached for him, a man who had lost his family in the war, then his son and his wife. "I feel bad that you didn't get to have a bigger family."

He shook his head. "You mustn't feel bad. I know that in spite of my trials, I've been blessed in ways I cannot begin to count. I discovered that life does not always give us what we think we want. Life tends to give us what we need." He sipped from his glass of lemonade. "Erik came late into our lives long after we had given up the dream of having children of our own."

Isabel caught Mac's eye. Before he had shown up, she never would have waded into the morass of old secrets. He'd shown her, though, that secrets could lose their power once they were exposed. "How did you manage?" she asked both Grandfather and Annelise. "I want to understand."

Magnus looked at Annelise. "Your grandmother Eva wanted a child so much," he said. "We were on a list to adopt a baby, but we kept failing to qualify due to Eva's health."

"So that's why you...the two of you..."

Annelise turned to face Isabel. "Your grandmother was my dearest friend. From the time we were girls, we always said we'd do anything for each other. She pined for a child—you never saw such yearning. And so we... Eva and I...we talked about it a lot. Finally, it was determined that I would have the baby. It was an unorthodox decision, and perhaps it was reckless, but we did what we did, and I have no regrets."

Isabel stifled a gasp. It had been Eva's idea, then. She tried to imagine what that had been like for them, to make such a radical choice.

"And did you get a vote?" she asked her grandfather.

"I felt the same way Eva did. I wanted a family."

"After I..." Annelise cleared her throat. "When I was several months' pregnant, Eva came to stay with me in the city. She returned to Bella Vista with your father."

Isabel's heart went out to her. What had that been like, to give birth a second time, to hand the child over and to be left empty and alone?

"Eva and Magnus were my most beloved and trusted friends," Annelise said as if she'd read Isabel's mind. "I knew the child would have a wonderful life with them."

"Erik never knew," her grandfather said. "We raised him with all the love and support we could give. He was a beautiful boy, full of laughter. But he had a reckless, impulsive streak." He set down his glass. "When we heard about the accident, we were in shock for hours. Days. There is a fundamental injustice in losing one's child. Any parent will attest to that. Eva and I raged. We cursed everything—God, the fates, each other."

He paused, took off his spectacles and pinched the bridge of his nose. "She cursed herself, believing it a punishment for taking another woman's child. I told her it was insanity to think that way, but there was a moment when she believed we'd tempted fate by never telling Erik the truth."

He polished his glasses and put them back on, and looked directly at Isabel. "It was you who saved us. You came along in the middle of the worst of life's turmoil and there you were, helpless and utterly dependent on us for your every need. You were the sweetest baby imaginable. I remember you used to get the hiccups, and I would pat you on the back until they went away. And you loved it when your Bubbie sang you a song. Our love for you drove out the grief. I know that sounds far too simple, but it is exactly what happened. We took you home and you changed our lives forever."

CHAPTER NINETEEN

"I need to show you something," Mac said, his shadow filling the doorway to her study.

"I'm trying something new right now," she said, staying focused on the computer screen. The landscape designer had sent her some digital renderings for the swimming pool.

"How about trying something old?"

She could tell he wasn't going to go away. "What's that?"

"Come on. I'll show you. Way more fun than staring at a computer."

A chance. That's what he said he wanted. Isabel was starting to want that, too. She walked with him down to the machine shop. There, he opened the tall double doors, letting the sunlight flood into the old stone barn. "It's ready."

"Oh, my gosh. You fixed up the Vespa."

"We did. Your grandfather really got into the project with me. He's a damned good mechanic."

"Farmers have to be," she said. "I've always admired Grandfather's mechanical talent."

"We had to replace about ninety percent of her, but the job's done."

The smooth, curved lines of the metal body gleamed with a fresh coat of seafoam-green paint. The chrome sparkled in the sunlight, and a pair of brand-new helmets rested on the rear rack behind the reupholstered saddles. New mirrors, new handlebar grips, fresh hubs in the tires. She took a slow walk around the scooter, admiring it from every angle and trying to picture her mother as a young woman, riding it around the coast roads and hill towns of southern Italy.

She loved the pride and anticipation in Mac's expression. When was the last time a man had done something just to please her? "It's beautiful, Mac."

"Glad you like it."

"It looks very continental," she said. "Just like the one in *Roman Holiday*."

"Never saw that movie."

"It's about an overly sheltered princess who runs away from her duties with a brash American reporter."

"A brash, *awesome* American reporter."

"True, Gregory Peck is awesome."

"And I take it they ride a Vespa."

"All over Rome—the Spanish Steps, the Mouth of Truth, the Colosseum...." She sighed. "We should watch it."

"We should ride a scooter around Rome."

"Let's ride the scooter right now," she said.

The helmets fit perfectly. The fresh leather upholstery felt luxurious as she mounted behind him. "It's got that new scooter smell," she said.

"Grab on, and let's go show your granddad." The upgraded motor sounded and felt a lot stronger as the scooter leaped forward. He drove up past the main house to the shady yard where Magnus and Annelise were sitting together with their notebooks and pens, laboring over their wedding speeches.

Mac beeped the horn and they waved as they went past, heading down the main road to town. The sunshine and wind-cooled air gave her a giddy rush of pleasure. She leaned her head back and looked up at the sky, brilliant blue and cloudless, typical of a Sonoma summer. The ride was so smooth that she dared to stretch her arms out wide and let the wind stream through her fingers. Their shadow, racing along the roadway, resembled a strange bird.

"Where are we going?" she asked.

"I'm taking you shopping."

"Oh, please. For what?"

"You'll see."

She savored a sense of anticipation on the short ride into town. Even the sight of Calvin Sharpe's restaurant sign—CalSharpe's, Coming Soon!—couldn't dampen her spirits. She refused to let it.

Mac pulled up and parked in front of the White Rabbit Bookshop. It had always been one of her favorite places in town, an eclectic, friendly store with a beautifully curated selection of books. The slogan over the door read Feed Your Head.

"When I was a kid, I didn't get the reference," she said, indicating the sign. "Actually, it was Homer Kelly who turned me on to the song."

"Ah, Homer Kelly the drummer." He held the door for her. "'White Rabbit' by Jefferson Airplane."

"He did have good taste in music."

"Just not in girlfriends."

"Ha. Where were you when I was in ninth grade?"

"Probably living at some diplomatic outpost in a country

no one's ever heard of, fighting with my brothers over who gets the top bunk," he said.

Victoria, the bookseller, greeted them with a smile. "Hey, Isabel," she said. "Are you looking for anything special?" Then Victoria blinked and turned to Mac. "Sorry, I don't mean to stare. Aren't you..."

He approached the counter and shook hands with her. "Cormac O'Neill. Nice to meet you."

She flushed and introduced herself. "Welcome to the White Rabbit. We don't get many authors in our little place."

"Well, that's impressive," Isabel said. "She recognized you by sight. You're more famous than you let on."

"Right," he said with a laugh. "Not even close. It just means Victoria's good at what she does."

"He's famous," Victoria assured her. "Don't let him fool you. Mr. O'Neill—"

"Mac."

"Mac, what brings you to Archangel?"

"A book project," he said. "I'm not working on it at the moment. Today, I'm a customer."

"That's great. But... I wonder, could you sign a few books for us? We always keep your titles in stock. They're really popular with customers."

"Sure thing," he said. "I'd be honored."

"I'll go get the books." Flush with pleasure, she bustled over to the nonfiction section.

Isabel smacked his arm. "You're totally famous, and you never even told me."

"You never asked. And besides, I'm not. Booksellers know me because they're in the business."

"And because you've been on every major network," said Victoria, placing a stack of books on the counter. "The top one has been really popular ever since that CNN interview you did a couple of months ago." She bustled away to get more books.

"What CNN interview?" asked Isabel in a low hiss.

"That thing I told you about in Turkmenistan," he said.

"Oh...."

"Here's the thing. Yasmin's father has a permit to settle in Turkey. I plan to meet him there so we can work on an article about the murder."

She caught her breath. "And you were going to tell me about this...when?"

He said nothing.

"What was it like, to have a wife one moment, and then to be told she had died?" Isabel asked. "I mean, do I have to Google that interview in order to find out?"

"Jesus, don't Google me."

"Then try telling me things. Don't wait until I trip over something you haven't told me."

"Yeah, I know. It was... I need to explain something. I married Yasmin to save her, not because I loved her."

"But you said—"

"I said I failed. Twice. I failed at loving her and I failed to save her."

"You tried."

"And look how that worked out."

"Does that mean you shouldn't try at anything else, ever again?"

"I could ask you the same thing. Listen, Isabel. I like you. We can be good together. Can we be good forever? Who knows? Just because we don't know shouldn't hold us back."

"But what if—"

"Here you go," said the bookseller. "Just a few more copies. I always say a signed book is a sold book."

He scrawled his signature in each of the books. "Here you go. Thanks. Isabel and I are looking for travel books today."

She directed him to a shelf along one wall.

"I love travel books," Isabel said. "I'm a great armchair traveler."

He perused a collection on Italy and pulled a book from the shelf, an oversize tome with glossy colored photos.

"Ravishing Ravello?" she asked.

"Okay, so it's not the best title, but let's check out where your mother came from."

She paged through the volume, which showed stunning views from the Villa Cimbrone and Ruffalo overlooking the deep blue Mediterranean, glorious gardens hung with color, quaint plazas lined with restaurants and shops, trees heavy with lemons, and the grand Duomo silhouetted against a blue sky. "It's lovely, like a dream."

"Let's go find out."

She gave a short laugh. "You're crazy. I'm not going any-where. I've got the wedding, the cooking school...."

"After the wedding's over, you can take a couple of weeks."

"No, I can't."

He bought the book and they went outside. "What's stop-ping you?"

"A hundred things."

"Then we'll deal with those later." He took her to the next stop—a photo and copy shop. "She needs a passport photo," he said to the guy behind the counter.

"I can do that instantly. I've got the forms from the post office right here."

"I don't need—"

"For chrissake, Isabel, have a seat."

All right, a passport photo. It couldn't hurt to humor him. She took a seat and finger combed her hair.

"Look at the camera straight on, chin forward," said the photographer. "Neutral expression."

A few minutes later, she had a pair of regulation photos. Mac stood over her, making her fill out the form. There was something curiously intimate about having him watch her write down all that personal information.

"I don't carry my birth certificate around with me," she said when she got to that section.

"Your grandfather gave me a certified copy." He took an envelope from his pocket.

"He's in on this?"

"It's not a conspiracy, Isabel."

"I don't like being manipulated."

"You're doing this of your own free will."

"No, I'm doing this so you'll stop bugging me."

They dropped the forms at the post office, and then he said, "Time for lunch. Take me somewhere good. Somewhere Italian."

She chose Vine, one of the cafés on the main plaza, and ordered a *burrata* and squash blossom pizza. The fluffy soft cheese, drizzled with fruity olive oil, paired beautifully with the crisp blossoms and homemade crust. Eaten with chilled elderflower soda, it was exactly what she'd been craving.

Mac, too, apparently. He made a sound of gratification. "Pizza. Nature's perfect food. Are you going to teach pizza making at your cooking school?"

"Sure. That's what the wood-fire oven is for."

"All the more reason to make a trip to Italy. See where the technique was invented."

"I don't get you," she said. "Why are you being so pushy?"

He shrugged and helped himself to another slice of pizza. "Born that way, I guess."

"Makes me suspicious of your motives."

"Yeah? You shouldn't be. I'm completely transparent."

She frowned and sat back in her chair, arms crossed. "Not to me."

"Look, do I have to spell it out for you?"

"Yes, maybe you do."

He finished his soda and set the glass on the table with exaggerated care. Then he took off his sunglasses and regarded her intently. She noticed in that moment how beautiful his eyes were, that color and fringe of dark lashes. "I'm falling for you, Isabel," he stated.

She felt all the blood rush to her cheeks.

"I'm falling for you, and it feels good. Remember I told you about Linda Henselman?"

"Umm...you kissed her and fell off the porch into a bush."

"Well, yeah, that, but it's the same dizzy feeling now, only it's the adult version of that. A huge rush, something I haven't felt since I was a kid."

"Mac—"

"Hey, you asked. Let me finish. I'm not a kid anymore. I know what I'm feeling, and I know it's the kind of thing that doesn't come along every day."

She felt a pulse of attraction, and had to physically restrain herself from reaching across the table, touching him. For some reason, she couldn't stop staring at his mouth. She'd spent far too much time thinking about the night he'd kissed her, and the memory came rushing back now. "You're here for Grandfather," she reminded him.

"I *was*. This sure as hell wasn't in my plans when I came here for your grandfather, but I'm good with changing plans." He leaned back in his chair and put his sunglasses back on. "Anyway, that might not be the answer you wanted to hear, but you asked." Then he went back to eating his pizza as if nothing had happened.

As if he hadn't just blown her mind. She suddenly wished her glass contained something stronger than elderflower soda. "So...um...what's next?" she asked, then took a nervous sip and held her breath, wondering what his plan was.

He took out a couple bills to cover the tab, plus a generous tip, and laid them on the table. "Next, we go to...what's that shop you said you liked? Angelica Delica."

That wasn't exactly what she'd meant by the question. "I can't believe you remembered the name of that boutique."

"You'd be surprised what I remember about you." He stood and offered his hand, and when she took it, the world felt different.

"It's a women's boutique," she pointed out. "What are you shopping for?"

He shrugged. "Surprise me."

Five minutes later, they were in the superbly eclectic boutique, filled with romantic, whimsical dresses and accessories, mostly by local designers and artists. The decor was shabby chic, with funky candelabras and antique cabinets. Women were browsing through the racks, and Mac was the only guy in the place.

"She needs a dress for the wedding," he said to Angelica, the shop owner.

"My specialty. Let's try some things on you."

Isabel felt a little flustered, but they had a point. She still hadn't settled on her maid of honor dress. "Sounds good to me."

"Perfect," said Angelica. "Long or short?"

"Tea length," Isabel said.

"Short," Mac said.

She glared at him. "I'll keep an open mind."

A few minutes later, she was in the dressing room with Angelica bustling around her, offering a variety of options—

chic minimalist, flowing chiffon, strapless and fitted, dancing skirts. Isabel dutifully modeled each look for Mac, who waited on a vanity bench outside the curtained area. He turned out to be vocally opinionated.

"You're going to a wedding, not a church social," he said when she came out wearing a drop-waist silk sheath.

"I think it's very stylish," she said.

"Let's try something more fitted," Angelica suggested. She zipped Isabel into a strapless silk jersey sheath dress that outlined every curve. She felt exposed, not just by the revealing dresses but by Mac's scrutiny. Yet his attention didn't threaten her. Instead, it transformed her. She didn't have to be afraid anymore.

"That's more like it," Mac said, his gaze lingering appreciatively.

"I can't even breathe, let alone move," Isabel said. "I need to be able to dance."

She tried on a half dozen more, but nothing felt like the perfect dress. "These three are 'maybes,'" she told Angelica, setting aside her favorites. "Maybe I'll come in with Tess later in the week."

Mac was at the counter, where another clerk was wrapping a few things in tissue paper. He caught her eye and said, "I don't know much about dresses, but I like the stuff that goes *under* the dress." He held out a small shopping bag.

She blushed again. He kept making her blush. "That's very presumptuous of you."

"Yep," he said cheerfully, and led the way back to the scooter. He stowed the parcels and they rode home together. She felt like a different person as they returned to Bella Vista. He had changed everything with what he'd told her. It was a giddy, soaring sensation, the way she imagined she might feel if she'd stepped off a cliff into thin air.

CHAPTER TWENTY

Having a crush on a guy was very distracting. Tasks that used to consume Isabel—picking out finishes for the teaching kitchen, dreaming up fresh ways to prepare summer vegetables, pruning the herb garden, tending the bees—all of these things fell by the wayside. She would catch herself in the middle of something and discover that she'd completely forgotten what she was supposed to be doing, because she was picturing the way his eyes crinkled at the corners when he smiled, or reliving something he'd said to her, or the sweaty smell of him which she shouldn't find the least bit sexy, but she did.

"Snap out of it," she muttered under her breath, and tried to apply herself diligently to making a final review of the catering menu for the wedding feast. It was just a silly crush, she reminded herself. A flirtation. She should just have fun with it, and then forget about him once he was gone.

He'd be gone soon. He and Grandfather were discussing more recent history—the very delicate topic of Erik's birth, and the horrific tragedy of his death. Once Mac gathered the information he needed, he would head to New York City to finish the manuscript, and then he'd be off to his next assignment—the one about his late wife.

All the more reason not to let her heart get in a tangle over him. But, oh, it was hard when he looked at her the way he did, the way he laughed and tried to steal kisses when no one else was around.

"Focus," she muttered, reminding herself that the hallmark of a successful chef was self-discipline. She had a whole talk prepared on just this topic, intending to present it to the first guests of the Bella Vista Cooking School. She would tell them that self-discipline was not some magical trait possessed by a lucky few. It was a tool a chef needed to use, the same way she might use her favorite knife in the kitchen—a tool to help you accomplish a goal.

She had dreamed up that talk before Mac O'Neill had entered the picture. With a mighty effort of will, she returned her attention to the menu to make sure the caterer they'd hired to work the event had everything necessary for an unforgettable feast. She had one sister, and this was her chance to give Tess the wedding of her dreams.

She and Tess had designed the menu together. Every recipe was something they both loved. Isabel's task was to check her sources to make sure all the fresh ingredients would be available for the caterer on the day of the wedding.

Normally, she enjoyed this process, the way she enjoyed everything that had to do with preparing food, but at the moment, she found herself gazing out the window, watching the sun filtering through the trees and wondering what Mac was up to.

At dinner this evening, Annelise and Grandfather had regaled everyone with stories of their crossing from Denmark to America aboard a Norwegian ship. They had cut loose their moorings, severing ties to everything they knew, embarking for America. Isabel had felt their exhilaration. What would it be like to simply walk away from one world, into the unknown?

The breeze through the window ruffled the pages of the open book on her desk. *Ravishing Ravello,* her new constant companion. She felt transported by the images of the ancient town, with its secret stairways and grand villas, houses where families lived for generations, the place her mother had left, as deliberately as her grandfather had left his homeland.

A certain yearning tugged at Isabel's heart as she gazed at the pictures. If this book was even marginally accurate, Ravello was so beautiful it made her heart ache. Had Francesca believed that? Perhaps she had, but the promise of a new love had been more powerful.

"Knock, knock." Mac barged into her study.

Her heart skipped a beat, and she flipped the book shut as if he'd caught her doing something illicit.

"I'm glad you're reading the Ravello book. Are you feeling ravished?"

"Totally."

He shook his head. "You need to get out more. Being ravished by a book? Come on."

"Hey, you bought it for me."

"Do you have a minute?"

"No."

"Too bad. There's something I want you to see."

She frowned at her littered desk, but he was hard to resist. "What's up?"

"We found something up in the room that used to belong to your mother and father. Come check it out."

He turned on the lights of the honeymoon suite, which had been finished at last. The designer had used most of the original furniture, updating the finishes and fabrics to create a light-filled space that had the charm of a boutique inn. The bedding was over-the-top luxurious, a fantasy made of four posters and a carved headboard, covered in linens imported from Italy.

It was one of her favorite rooms, because it paid homage to the historic nature of Bella Vista, but had a cool modern edge in the crisp fabrics and an incredible Delia Snow original painting, an oversize and imaginative portrait of a dog rendered in luscious apple-green. Tess had acquired it at an auction, and Isabel had fallen in love with the image.

Now, though, her attention was drawn to a vintage steamer trunk in the middle of the room.

"What's this?" she asked.

"The electricians who've been working on the wiring found it in the attic, through that access panel there." Mac indicated a small half door in the wall.

Before the renovation of the room, a bookcase had stood in front of the access panel. Isabel hadn't realized it opened to the attic.

"Magnus said it's been stowed in there and forgotten for decades. He thinks it was put away after you were born, and probably forgotten."

Isabel could well understand the urge to stow things away after someone died. After Bubbie was gone, she had forced herself to go through the mournful process of sorting out clothing and accessories, keepsakes and jewelry. She recalled feeling overwhelmed, wishing everything would simply disappear. "What's in it?" she asked.

"Nothing earth-shattering. I don't think so, anyway. Just the ordinary things of an ordinary life. But since they belonged to your mother, I knew you'd want to see everything."

"Yes," she said softly. "Yes, of course." She stopped a few

feet away from the trunk, which stood on end. The top had a plaque with the initials *F.L.C.* engraved on it. "My mother's initials. Francesca Cioffi. I'm not sure what the *L* stands for." She turned to Mac. "Is it weird that I don't know my mother's middle name?"

"Not to me."

She went back to inspecting the trunk. The outside was scuffed and stickered with peeling customs and cargo labels. A tag from the San Francisco Transfer Company hung from one of the handles.

"Your grandfather said it was shipped along with the scooter. Check out the inside." He tipped back the trunk and opened it like a huge book. The inside was organized like a small wardrobe, with garments on hangers on one side and drawers on the other, covered in fading blue fabric. It smelled faintly of dry age and old perfume or powder. She pulled back a wispy drape on the hanging side to reveal a few dresses and blouses in ethereal fabrics with delicate stitching. In the drawers were the ordinary things Mac had mentioned—a tortoiseshell comb, a pair of gloves, an old customs form, a few pieces of vintage jewelry. But to Isabel, it was a trove of secrets, a time capsule that had belonged to the mother she'd never known.

Carefully she lifted out a very small white-bound volume marked with a gold dove and a flame—a missal or prayer book of some sort. On the inside cover, "Francesca" was written in painstaking childish script. There was also a tiny figure of some saint or other and a rosary made of alabaster beads.

Tucked in the back of the prayer book were a couple of old photos, the square kind with rounded corners. One showed a little girl with a lovely smile and eyes Isabel recognized from later photos of her mother—dressed like a tiny bride in a lace dress and veil. Her expression was one of pride and joy. She held the white leather missal in one hand, an ornate quill pen in the other, wielding it with an air of importance.

We all start out that way, Isabel reflected. The girl in the picture had no idea she would grow up and ride a scooter, and snare the attention of an American student. She didn't know her future held a tragic love affair and a painful death. Isabel realized then there was so much she had not asked her grandparents for fear of upsetting them. Had Francesca ever actually seen her, held her, spoken her name? Who had picked the name Isabel, anyway?

Blinking away tears, she turned the picture over. On the back were the words *prima comunione.*

"First communion," Mac translated. "She was probably about seven years old there. That's the traditional age for first communion."

"You speak Italian?"

"Solo un po'," he said.

"Show-off." She studied the other snapshot, this one showing the girl kneeling at a cushioned prie-dieu, her hands sweetly folded and braided with the rosary beads, a beatific smile on her face, her rosy cheeks shining. "Wow. I looked a lot like her when I was little. I would have killed for that communion get-up."

"I don't think they had to kill for it," he pointed out. "Just attend catechism."

"You know what I mean. Dressing like a bride is every little girl's dream."

"Is it every big girl's dream?"

She shook her head. "That would be dressing like Jennifer Lawrence."

Further inspection of the drawers yielded a collection of handwritten cards and notes in a small portfolio bound with string. "Recipes," she said with a rush of pleasure. "I'm going to draft you to help me translate these."

"Of course. Cool that your mother collected recipes."

There were a few postcards in Italian and English, which she set aside for later inspection. At the bottom was a crisp color photo taken with a good camera, perhaps a professional shot. The image took her breath away. It was a glossy eight-by-ten depicting a young woman in sunglasses, espadrille sandals and a skirt and top. She sat sidesaddle on the back of a scooter, her sun-browned arms looped around a handsome man wearing shorts and flip-flops, his head thrown back with laughter.

"It's my parents on the scooter," she said softly. "They look so young. So happy."

"I don't blame them. Riding around like that is a kick." In the background was a row of cypress trees and a stone railing against a misty blue sky.

She nodded. The caption on the back of the photo read "Ravello, 1981." She looked up at Mac, who was watching her intently. "This has been lost for decades."

"It never would have been found if you hadn't decided to create the cooking school," he said.

"That's true. I feel closer to them, somehow." She felt her heart stumble then, finally getting a glimpse into the spirit of the woman who had died giving birth to her, and the man who had fathered her. They were vibrant, carefree, filled with joy.

Isabel realized that she could finally *feel* her mother. She imagined the sound of Francesca's laughter on the breeze. The picture gave her a glimpse into the hearts of her parents, and the feelings overwhelmed her. She couldn't control the rush of tears then, though she gulped air to try to get a grip on herself.

A tide of long-suppressed emotion rose through her, poignant and bittersweet. Mac put his arms around her and she melted against him, grateful for his solid strength and for his silence. He simply held her while she let it all out, and then he offered her a box of tissues from the nightstand.

"Oh, my gosh," she said. "I'm a mess."

"You're fine," he said, then peered at her while she blotted her face. "Right?"

"Yes. I...it's hard to put into words. I've always wished I could know my mother better, what she was like in person. And of course this isn't the same, but it's just incredible, seeing this picture, knowing my parents were together and that they loved each other, at least in this moment, they did."

"It's easy to be in love when you're riding around on a scooter in Italy," he said.

"Do you mean it's hard, otherwise?"

He regarded her steadily, then smiled. "Not when you find the right person."

It suddenly felt too warm in the room, and she went and turned down the thermostat. The air-conditioning sighed through the vents. "Okay," she said, taking a deep breath. "Meltdown over. Sorry."

"Don't worry about it. My Irish grandmother used to say a woman's tears are the quenching of the soul."

She was surprised to hear such sentiment from him. "Really?"

"No, but it sounds like something an Irish granny would say, right? Do you feel quenched?"

"Smart aleck." She took a deep breath and went back to inspecting the contents of the trunk. "The clothes are beautiful," she said, holding up a chic sundress in a graphic print on textured cotton. "They look handmade, but very professional. I wonder if she was a seamstress. I should ask Grandfather if she sewed." She took out a sleeveless blouse in butter-yellow, its details highlighted with hand stitching. "This is really nice," she said, holding it up against her and turning to the old-fashioned cheval-glass dressing mirror in the corner. "I think this is the top she's wearing in the scooter photo."

He held it next to her. "You're right."

"And this skirt," she added, taking out an A-line skirt in a small plaid print. "Very cool."

The last dress in the wardrobe was loosely wrapped in thin tissue paper that tore away at the slightest touch. Isabel was intrigued by this one, a cocktail dress in peach-colored silk, embellished with a line of crystal bugle beads around the neckline, a fitted bodice and flaring skirt. In the glow of the bedside lamp, the dress was luminous and shimmering with a life of its own. "Wow," she said. "This is gorgeous. Seriously, *gorgeous*."

"I'm no expert, but yeah, it's real pretty."

She laid it on the upholstered bench at the foot of the bed and inspected the tag. "Valentino Garavani. Oh, my gosh. Mac, that's the designer Valentino."

"A big name in fashion?"

"The biggest," she said. "How on earth did my mother score a Valentino?" She held it up again, letting the luxurious silk slide through her fingers. The lining felt smooth and watery, the back zipper nearly invisible. "It's amazing. A real couture dress. I should show this to Tess. She's so smart about figuring out the value of treasures."

"I've got a better idea," said Mac.

"What's that?"

"Wear it to her wedding."

"What? Oh, come on. I can't—"

"Why not?"

"It would look funny on me. Or ridiculous."

"You said yourself it's gorgeous."

"It probably wouldn't fit." She laid it on the bed and stepped back. The style was timeless, and in spite of herself, she felt drawn to the beautiful dress.

"I bet it'd fit. You look just like your mother. You're probably the same size."

"It would need to be cleaned and restored, not to mention alterations."

"How about this?" Mac suggested. "How about you quit trying to think up all the reasons it won't work, and focus on why it will?"

"You're such a boy scout."

"Nope. I think that day at the hot springs, we established that I definitely am not." Mac gestured at the garments. "All this stuff would look great on you."

"It's not really my style. She seemed to like things that were more fitted, you know?"

"What I know is that you have an amazing body and it shouldn't be covered up."

Ouch. He was knew her too well. After she'd fled from culinary school, she'd wanted to hide herself away, and that included cloaking herself in a wardrobe of long, drapey clothes designed to cover everything. Mac was the first person who'd ever pointed that out to her. He seemed to know what she'd been avoiding for so long—that she needed to face her reasons for wanting to cover up.

"You're very observant," she said quietly.

"Yeah. I've made a lot of observations about you." With that, he took her gently by the shoulders. Then he slid his hands behind her and lifted her hair away from the nape of her neck. Leaning down, he whispered in her ear, "For instance, I've observed that you're wearing too many clothes." His breath was warm, his lips nearly touching her.

She told herself to put a stop to this right now, to pull away and make a dignified exit, but she was riveted to the spot. Her breathing was shallow, her arms useless at her sides.

"You wear them like armor," he said. "You don't need armor around me, Isabel. I'm not going to hurt you." And with that, he unbuttoned her dress at the back and let it drop to the floor.

Her skin tingled as she stood there in her camisole and panties, but to her amazement, she didn't feel apprehensive or even awkward. She was too full of feelings far more elemental— she wanted his touch; she yearned for him to put his hands on her, to caress her. There was a wild sense of urgency she'd never felt before.

But he didn't touch her. Instead, he picked up the peach silk dress and unzipped it. "You're going to try this on."

She practically groaned aloud in frustration. He'd been flirting with her for weeks, and finally she was ready to do something about it, but he was focused on the stupid couture dress. She instantly tried to think of an objection to trying it on, but discovered she was all out of ammunition. Truth be told, she wanted to know if it fit, and to see how it would feel to wear something that had once clothed her mother. It also occurred to her that she'd never worn an actual couture dress, had never even put one on.

She smiled at him and lifted her arms over her head, and he carefully helped her put the dress on. The luxurious fabric felt substantial and expensive on her frame. It felt as if it might fit.

She held her hair up out of the way as he closed the zipper, then he turned her in his arms, stepping back to admire his handiwork. "There. You're Aubrey Hepburn."

"Audrey. Really?"

"Go look in the mirror."

She walked over to the tall oval cheval glass. The chiffon lining of the cocktail dress whispered with each subtle movement. The dress looked incredible, and she felt as if she were a different person in it. The bodice hugged her every curve, and the crystal beads flashed in the lamplight. "Whoa," she said. "This *is* a special dress. My mother had good taste. I wonder how she ended up with a Valentino."

"I'm just glad she kept it, because it looks fantastic on you." He came up behind her and put his arms around her waist, then skimmed his lips along the line of her bare shoulder. "I'm really turned on right now."

She leaned back against him, even though she knew she should move away. "Don't."

"Why not?" His hand came up and traced the line of her collarbone.

"Because I don't want to start something with you."

"Damn, you smell good," he said, inhaling. "Why not?" he asked again.

"Because...." It was hard to think when he was doing that with his hands, his mouth.... "Because I might take this— *us*—too seriously."

"Is that possible, taking love too seriously?"

She pulled away then, turning to face him. "Who said anything about love?"

"I did. You got a problem with that?"

"Yes," she said immediately.

"With love in general, or with me in particular?"

"I'm not having this conversation." She knew his next question would be, "Why not?" She decided to preempt him. "Because I have a theory about love, and you're probably not going to like it."

"Why wouldn't I like it?"

"Always with the questions. Because I can never give you what you want."

"How do you know what I want?"

She couldn't think straight when he looked at her like that. She turned her attention to the things they'd pulled out of the trunk. She gazed down at the print of the beautiful couple on the Vespa. "I've never felt the way they look in this picture," she said. "I don't expect I ever will."

"Not with an attitude like that, you won't."

She sighed, brushed her hand over the fine silk of the dress. "I always thought, growing up, that a person had one great love in her life. Sure, there would be boyfriends and broken hearts, missed connections and mistakes. But ultimately, I believed there would be one great love. The one that would save me and keep me safe forever and show me the joy in life."

"And now?"

"Now I'm older. Wiser. I survived a terrible love, and it turned out not to be love at all. So I quit believing what that naive girl believed."

"Isabel—"

"No, let me finish. It was like being a kid and figuring out that Santa Claus doesn't exist. You're not surprised, but disappointed, because you really want it to be true. But then you move on from there. I found other kinds of love to fill my life—family and friends. People I work with. The occasional date or social occasion."

"Jeez," he said. "You definitely need to get out more."

"That's exactly what I don't need. Because the surprising thing that happened is that after I let go of all those romantic notions, my life filled right up. I discovered I didn't need that one great romance in order to be happy, the same way I don't need Santa Claus or the tooth fairy. Life is just fine without all that."

"Okay, but there's something I need to tell you," said Mac. He walked over to her, put his arms around her, stirring up a shimmer of emotion.

"What's that?" she whispered.

"I still believe in Santa Claus." He pulled her against him and put his lips very close to hers. "And the tooth fairy, too. And the Easter bunny."

The shimmer became a warm explosion of feeling. "Oh, boy."

"And I also believe in…" He whispered a suggestion into her ear that made her bones melt.

Despite the warmth of the evening, she got goose bumps. "Yeah?"

He slid down the zipper of the dress and skimmed it to the floor, taking her hand so she could step out of the pool of fabric. Without taking his eyes off her, he peeled his shirt off one-handed over his head. Then he unfastened her bra and swept it aside, laid her back on the bed and pressed her down into the luxurious mattress. "Yeah," he said.

CHAPTER TWENTY-ONE

On the day of Tess and Dominic's wedding, Bella Vista was surrounded by a coastal fog. The impenetrable white mist gathered like undulating wraiths in the valley carved by Angel Creek, and hid in the low spots between the rising hills.

"It is a sign of good luck," Ernestina insisted, pouring coffee at the kitchen counter. "The fog means you will spend your life enclosed in pure love."

Tess paced to the window, looked out and turned back to face Ernestina, who was flanked by Isabel and Shannon. "I've never heard that before," she said.

"I just made it up." Ernestina looked at her, then poured a mug of herbal tea from another pot. "No coffee for you. You're already nervous."

"I'm getting married today. I'm supposed to be nervous."

"But in a good way," said Isabel. "As in, excited. And the last thing you should be nervous about is the weather."

"She's right," Shannon said. "This is Sonoma, land of perfect weather."

"It will be sunny and clear by three o'clock," Ernestina promised, sounding unaccountably authoritative. "By five o'clock, when the ceremony starts, the whole world will be perfect. You'll see."

"Fine, I'm not nervous," Tess said. "I'm excited. I'm so excited, I could throw up."

"Drink your tea," said Isabel. "It's got chamomile and elderflower in it, to soothe your nerves."

"Did I ever tell you the first thing Dominic ever bought me was a cup of herbal tea?" asked Tess.

"I didn't know that," Isabel said.

She nodded. "He said the same thing—I needed to calm my nerves." She sniffed the tea and wrinkled her nose. "I told him it smelled like yard clippings."

"And here you are about to marry him. He must have done something right."

"Try some honey in it," said Jamie, coming into the kitchen with a stack of frames filled with cured and capped honey. She had been harvesting daily, cutting the combs from the frames, straining and sieving the honey and putting it in jars.

"More honey?" Isabel asked.

"Every day."

"That's so cool," she said. "Your yield is ten times what I got last summer."

"It'll get better every year," Jamie promised. She carried the frames to the stationary tub in the adjacent utility room, which had a rack of sterilized jars and equipment. Ever since choosing what she wanted to do about her pregnancy, she seemed more relaxed. She was even talking about getting a part-time job in town in the off-season, expressing interest in the local restaurant scene. She loved performing and knew she was good. Several local establishments featured live music, and she was planning to set up some auditions.

"It's going to take more than honey to calm my nerves," said Tess. "I'm getting married. *Married*."

Her mother went over and gave her a hug. "You're getting married. Ah, baby. I'm so happy for you." They touched foreheads, and Shannon brushed a wisp of hair from Tess's cheek. "But don't get me started crying so early in the day."

Annelise came in next, followed by Lilac and Chips, who had seemingly adopted her. Every time she came to stay at Bella Vista, the cats took to sleeping in her room and shadowing her every move. "There mustn't be crying on such a joyous day," she said.

"That's easier said than done," Tess told her, raising her tea mug. "But they're good tears. I want to make a toast right here and now, to all the good women in my life—my mother, my grandmother, my sister—you became my family at the very moment I needed you most. And to Ernestina and Jamie—you inspire me in ways you can't imagine. I feel so blessed that you're all here today."

Shannon lifted her coffee cup. "May the men in your life end up being as good to you as the women."

"Hear, hear," said Isabel. "To Tess…and her one true love." She heard the echo of her conversation with Mac, and of course that evoked memories of the night they'd spent together in Francesca's room. She still couldn't believe it had happened, that she had been so open and vulnerable. His lovemaking had been a revelation. Never had she been treated with such tenderness and respect. Never had she found a man's touch so arousing.

She would have loved to linger over thoughts of Mac, but the caterer and florist arrived. After that, the day kicked into high gear. The wedding planner orchestrated things like a practiced maestro, directing everyone to their tasks. Isabel was more than happy to take orders. She had already created the menu, perfected the recipes. Together, she and Tess had designed the venue. She and the others happily submitted to manicures, pedicures, hair and makeup. There was nothing left to be done except to dress for the occasion.

Two hours before the guests started to arrive, the women gathered to prepare themselves and the bride for the pre-ceremony photos. A handmade cream lace veil had been imported from Shannon's native Ireland. Tess had chosen an ivory couture dress from a boutique in San Francisco, and a pair of glittery dancing shoes for performing the surprise wedding tango they'd learned from Annelise. The Irish veil was held on with a crown of fresh flowers. Around her neck, Tess wore the pink alabaster lavaliere from Annelise, and it was hard for Isabel to look at her without getting teary-eyed.

Life had come full circle for these two, and Isabel's heart was full of gratitude for them both. This was exactly what she had pictured for Bella Vista—that it would be a gathering place for friends and family, for reunions and celebrations.

"You're so beautiful," she said. "You look like a dream."

"I feel as if I'm *in* a dream," she said, her eyes sparkling like emeralds. "Come on. The photographer wants us for pictures." Then she stepped back and stared at Isabel. "And look at *you*. My God, where did you get that dress?"

Isabel twirled in a rustle of silk and chiffon. "You like?"

"It's amazing."

"Mac and Grandfather found it in a trunk of my mother's things. It's a Valentino."

"Seriously? Wow, what a find."

"I had the cleaners in town do some restoration work."

"Lovely," Shannon said, "but you need shoes to do it justice. Bare feet aren't going to cut it, even with that pedicure."

"Oh… I hadn't thought about shoes."

"Someone did." Ernestina came forward with a black-and-white box with a suspiciously familiar signature logo. She removed the lid to reveal a pair of perfect champagne-colored peep-toe pumps inside.

"Hey Lady dancing shoes," Tess exclaimed. "Where did you get those?"

Isabel's face drained of color, which must have clued in Tess immediately.

"Oh, no, he didn't," Tess said.

"I mentioned the shoes once, I swear. I can't believe he remembered...." Unable to suppress a grin, she slipped her foot into the pump. A perfect fit.

"You look incredible," Tess said. "You should do 'fitted and revealing' more often. You're going to outshine the bride."

"Ha. Not a chance."

The ceremony was everything they had envisioned, only better, because there were unexpected surprises, like the way the deep amber light of sunset sneaked through the gaps in the barn walls and illuminated the podium, decked with stargazer lilies. And the solemn joy with which the groom's little daughter and son accompanied him down the aisle. And the fact that both Dominic's younger sister, Gina, and Magnus, had both decided to wear a top hat and tails.

Tess had never been more beautiful. She wore her red hair swept up and adorned with a single lily. Her perfectly fitted ivory gown had a sweetheart neckline that framed the rose-pink pendant. The skirt was a long fall of silk chiffon that seemed to dance with every movement. The most beautiful thing about her, of course, was the expression on her face when she looked up at Dominic.

Isabel loved every music-filled, emotional moment of the ceremony. She loved the fact that her family was expanding, that she would have a brother-in-law and a niece and a nephew.

While Jamie performed a delicate rendition of "Come to Me," Isabel stood by the podium, proudly holding her lilies and sneaking peeks at the gathering. It wasn't hard to spot Mac, thanks to his height and broad shoulders. That wasn't what made her go weak in the knees, though. No, that would be the fact that he was looking straight at her with an intensity she could feel clear across the room. And she couldn't help but notice that he wore a flawlessly tailored tuxedo, and was perfectly groomed from head to toe.

Neelie, the bridesmaid to her right, leaned over and whispered, "Your boyfriend cleans up nicely."

"He's not—" She stopped herself. When they'd made love, the bond between them had changed from friendship and flirtation to something deeper, much deeper. Emotions she'd never felt before filled her up in places she hadn't even known were empty. At some point, long before Mac had arrived, she had stopped expecting love to come along, and she thought she was okay with that, but he had revived a dream long since buried. The thoughtful words and beautiful music of the ceremony sharpened her yearning.

At the conclusion of the service, the mariachis burst into a zany version of "Don't You Want Me Baby." Dominic and Tess turned to face everyone with their arms raised like a pair of victorious prizefighters; then they practically danced down the aisle, followed by Dominic's kids, his sister, Gina, and Isabel and the rest of the party.

The reception began with a blessing from Father Tom, the priest of the local Catholic church and a close family friend. His words evoked both laughter and tears, and as always, his appearance evoked stunned looks from the women present, as he had the kind of Hollywood handsomeness that stopped traffic. Then the band started up with some surprising covers of '80s dance tunes to get everyone in the mood. Servers moved among the guests with trays of hors d'oeuvres and the signature cocktail, champagne with a honey infused liqueur and a delicate spiral twist of lemon.

The banquet was bursting with color and flavor—flower-sprinkled salads, savory chili roasted salmon, honey glazed ribs, just-harvested sweet corn, lush tomatoes and berries, artisan cheeses. Everything had been harvested within a fifty-mile radius of Bella Vista.

The cake was exactly what Tess had requested, a gorgeous tower of sweetness. Tess offered a gracious speech as she and Dominic cut the first slices. "I've come a long way from the city girl who subsisted on Red Bull and microwave burritos," she said. "There's quite a list of people to thank for that—my wonderful mother, my grandfather and my beautiful sister who created this place of celebration. Most of all, I'm grateful to Dominic." She turned to him, offering the first piece on a yellow china plate. "You're my heart, and there is no sweeter feeling than the love we share. Not even this cake. Wait, that might be overstating it. Everyone, be sure you taste this cake. It's one of Isabel's best recipes."

In addition to emotional toasts from friends and family members, there were special songs. Playing the acoustic guitar, Jamie sang "Reign of Love" with heartfelt tenderness, offering the melody like a gift floating on the breeze. Then the mariachis did a rendition of "Crazy Train" that was oddly evocative, with the blare of trumpets and unexpected vocals.

The bridal couple's first dance took everyone's breath away, because no one was expecting Tess and Dominic to perform a well-executed and stylish tango to *"Por Una Cabeza."* But it was a later dance that brought a sigh to everyone's lips. Magnus and Annelise danced a beautiful waltz to "Rose of

My Heart." Their old-fashioned dignity gave new meaning to the Johnny Cash lyrics. Isabel grew teary-eyed, thinking about the history the two of them shared, reaching all the way back to their childhood years in Copenhagen. The dangers and tragedies they had survived seemed to fade away as they slowly turned through the steps of the waltz, totally absorbed in one another.

Standing at the edge of the dance floor, Isabel felt Mac's presence behind her. She was so finely tuned to him that she recognized the quality of warmth he exuded and the unique scent of him. "It's never too late to fall in love," he said, watching her grandfather.

"Are they in love?" she asked.

"Looks that way to me. We'll have to see how fast she dives for the bouquet when the bride tosses it."

She laughed at the mental image. "Right."

"Would it bother you if the two of them...."

She turned and smiled up at him. "No. Of course not. Bubbie's been gone a long time. I want Grandfather to be happy."

"He's looking happy now."

She nodded. "I didn't know he was such a good dancer."

"I bet you didn't know *I'm* a good dancer," he said, cupping his hands around her waist.

"Really?"

The band started up with "The Way You Look Tonight."

"What about your knee?" she asked.

"The knee's fine. The knee can handle dancing with you." He offered a formal bow and held out his hand, palm up. "Try me."

She happily complied, and yes, he did surprise her. "You're showing me up," she said.

"Just let me lead, and you'll be fine."

"Where did you learn to dance like this?"

"With all those brothers, I'm an old hand at weddings," he said. "Toasting, roasting and dancing are the primary duties of the groom's brothers."

"Good to know. And by the way, thank you for the shoes."

"You needed dancing shoes."

"I can't believe you did that."

"Me, neither. Your friends in the boutique helped."

"Well, thank you again. Now, be quiet. I need to concentrate." She loved the way the silk dress moved, and she loved the idea that it had once belonged to her mother. She loved the twinkling lights strung from the rafters, and the purple twilight visible through the tall open doors. She loved the couture shoes, especially the fact that Mac had gone to the trouble to get them. She loved the way she felt in his arms.

"I have to ask," she said. "I can't help myself. Did you dance at your own wedding?"

He stiffened; she could feel the tenseness in the muscles of his arm. "It wasn't like that," he said.

"Oh. Maybe someday you'll tell me what it was like."

"Not tonight," he said. "I've got other plans for you tonight."

She ducked her head, feeling the heat of a blush.

"You have the nicest smile," he said softly into her ear.

"Shh. Let's just get through this number." But his comment only made her smile more. As promised, he was a good dancer, his lead easy to follow. She relaxed into the dance, and she even liked the attention she was getting from the other wedding guests. Most people around Archangel knew her to be a homebody, particularly cautious when it came to men, dating infrequently, selectively, and never letting anyone get too close. Certainly no one had seen her hanging out with someone like Cormac O'Neill. Or wearing a dress like the one she had on.

After more than one acquaintance gave her a not-so-secret A-okay sign, Mac asked, "Do you think they know we slept together?"

"Stop it. That's not—"

"I bet it is. And by the way, I didn't get a chance to tell you—that was one fantastic night." He let his hand slip down briefly to her hips.

"Yes." She couldn't lie or pretend to be outraged. "I feel the same way."

"So, tonight…"

"Mac, I don't know." She wasn't sure she could go down that road, not knowing where it was leading. It was hard to trust her own judgment when it came to men. She was already falling hard. But what was the point of falling for a guy who wouldn't be around to pick her up?

"I *do* know, and for the record, it was the best sex I've ever had."

That startled her. He was so worldly, so…adept. Not to mention blunt as a spoon. "Let me ask you something," she said.

"Shoot."

"Are you extremely good in bed, or is it that we're good together?"

"What do you think?" he countered.

Ah, that reporter's trick. She was getting used to it. "I'm asking what *you* think."

He twirled her out, then reeled her back in. "I think we're magic together."

CHAPTER TWENTY-TWO

I think we're magic together. He had an uncanny way of saying everything while saying nothing. She couldn't be sure whether he meant what he said, or if he was simply telling her what he thought she wanted to hear. Either way, it worked. They stayed up dancing and drinking until the bride tossed her bouquet. It landed in Annelise's lap, and the ensuing toasts were rowdy and full of laughter.

After a final round of drinks and farewells, Tess and her groom departed through a gauntlet of sparklers. Then Mac brought Isabel to his room and made love to her again, and it was even better than the first time, because they were getting to know each other in ways more intimate than she'd ever thought possible. She learned the ebb and flow of his pleasure and the rhythm of his breathing, the texture of his skin and the exquisite comfort of cradling her head against his chest and listening to the steady beat of his heart.

Despite the emotional upheaval of her love affair with Mac, life did go on. In the aftermath of the wedding, a quiet lull settled over Bella Vista. The preparations for the cooking school were nearing completion. Tess and Dominic were off to Iceland for their honeymoon. Isabel had to force herself to focus on the project that had consumed her for the past year, the project she'd dreamed about for the past decade. Carrying on with Mac O'Neill was no excuse for neglecting things.

The cooking school was wholly her own, something no one could ever take from her. It would last as long as she wanted it to. Romance was ephemeral; she already knew Mac planned to leave soon. The dream she'd created for herself would last. It wouldn't betray her or leave her or break her heart.

She liked being in charge. She was good at it. Like a battle commander before a major campaign, she organized a photo shoot and publicity coverage for the cooking school. *MenuSonoma Magazine* was due to arrive within the hour to do a cover story, and Isabel was determined to make certain Bella Vista looked and sounded as incredible as she knew it was going to be.

Filled with nervous excitement, she made her way to the teaching kitchen to get ready for the reporter and photographer. She had even hired a stylist to help her with her clothes, hair and makeup, knowing she needed plenty of help in this area.

Her phone rang, an incoming call from the magazine editor. "Hi, Leo," she said, sounding slightly breathless. "Are Jared and Jan on their way? Do they need directions, or—"

"Um, yeah, about that..." Leo's voice sounded hesitant. Apologetic.

Her hopes were already shriveling. "What's the matter?"

"The photographer and reporter aren't going to make it today. They're stuck on assignment with Calvin Sharpe."

Her heart shriveled a little. Of course Cal would be the one to disrupt her plans. Even now, she thought. Even now.

"So what's your plan B?" she asked.

"We can reschedule the shoot, but the first available date I have for them isn't for another five weeks."

"How will that affect your cover story about the cooking school?"

"I'm sorry to say, we'll miss the deadline, and the cover is spoken for until next spring."

"So what's going to be on the fall cover? Oh, wait, let me guess—Calvin Sharpe's new restaurant."

"He bought a lot of ad space," Leo admitted. "We can still feature the cooking school—"

"Question," she interrupted, acting on a sudden inspiration. "Have you ever heard of Cormac O'Neill?"

"Sure, everyone has. His book on Thai street food is a classic."

She didn't know anything about that book, but assumed that meant Leo was a fan. "Suppose Cormac O'Neill wrote the piece on the cooking school, *and* did the photography."

"I'd think you were biting the heads off those little pot-infused gummi bears he mentions in that book."

"Wow." Summoned by an urgent text message, Mac stepped into the teaching kitchen and stared at Isabel. He felt a flush come over his body, his attraction to her an inner fire that only increased as the days passed. This feeling was new, an exhilarating ride, and he was enjoying the heck out of it.

She was wearing a new outfit, not the usual flowy stuff that hid all her assets. The fitted skirt and blouse showed off her figure in a way he found extremely distracting. "Wow in a good way. Isn't that one of your mother's outfits?"

"Yes, restored to its former glory. It doesn't look too dated?"

"The kitchen looks great, and you look great."

"Thanks. Two hours of hair and makeup, and I'm a natural beauty." She struck a pose, wielding a spatula.

"You don't need that much help."

"I do for the photo shoot. That's actually what I wanted to see you about."

"The photo shoot? Oh, yeah, that magazine you mentioned."

"Yes. There was a conflict, and the photographer and writer aren't coming. If they reschedule, I'll miss the opportunity for Bella Vista to be on the cover of the magazine. So I was wondering... I know it's not your usual thing, but could you take the pictures and write the article?"

"What?" He wasn't sure he'd heard right.

"I'm asking you to do the piece on the cooking school. Right now. Today. It's the only way to make sure Bella Vista is featured on the cover." Her cheeks flushed. "I sound desperate, don't I? Sorry. I hate that I sound desperate."

He felt a wave of affection for her. "This is important to you."

"It's everything to me." She fluttered her hands nervously. "I'm sorry, it's probably a bad idea."

"Are you kidding me?"

Her shoulders slumped and she stared at the floor. "Okay, I get it, this is not your thing."

"No, Isabel, you *don't* get it." He touched her beneath the chin and tipped her face up. "You've never asked me for a single thing, and now you are. I'm just wondering what the hell took you so long."

The relief in her eyes nearly broke his heart. "You mean you'll do it?"

"I'll have my literary agent call the editor and make sure it's the featured piece."

"Oh, that would be fantastic. But you have to understand,

the magazine's budget is really small. I thought maybe we could work something out."

"I don't expect a fee. I don't need to work anything out. I just need for you to trust me."

"I trust."

"Remember you said that."

Jodi, the stylist who had helped at the wedding, proved to be an able assistant, patiently holding up reflectors and diffusers to correct the lighting. Isabel was surprisingly comfortable in front of the camera. Mac hadn't been expecting that. Then he realized she was a woman in her element, in a place she loved, surrounded by the world she had created for herself. No wonder she never wanted to leave this place.

They set up shot after shot, in the kitchen, the patio, the orchard and the field with the beehives. He took pictures of the landscape and the wood-fire pizza oven and the newly completed outdoor shower with its smooth river stone surface and rustic wood privacy screen. But mostly, he took pictures of Isabel herself. The golden light of sunset infused each scene with a honeyed glow, lending a dreamlike quality to every frame. She was so damned beautiful it made his eyes hurt, and she didn't even know it. He could look at her all day. He could look at her his whole life, and it wouldn't be long enough.

He gave her props, not just the expected kitchen utensils, but a flower, a beehive smoker, the Vespa, anything to bring out her personality. He had her lift a dipper of honey to the light and captured the dripping sweetness in the foreground. Finally, when the sunset sank into twilight, Mac called it a day. "You're going to love these pictures," he assured her. "The magazine's going to love them. Now we need to come up with an article to do them justice."

He put his gear away while she paid Jodi and walked her out.

"Thank you, Mac," she said, coming back inside. "An article by a national journalist like you—it will be quite a coup. The editor was so impressed. I don't know how I'll ever thank you."

"Come to Ravello with me. Let's go on an adventure."

She smiled softly. "You're already too much of an adventure for me."

"No such thing. We need to get started on the article."

"It's funny, I've watched you work all this time with my grandfather, but I have no idea how you do what you do."

"Here's how it works. You're going to talk to me. Really talk."

"All right. Brace yourself. I think I'm kind of boring."

"Believe me, you're not boring."

"Okay, then. But first I need to shower off all this hairspray and makeup. Not to mention this sticky honey. Why'd you have to use so much honey?"

"So I can lick it off you."

"Hey—"

He grabbed her hand and gently slid each of her fingers into his mouth, one by one. The sweet honey taste of her nearly killed him. Judging by the look on her face, she was pretty turned on, too. "Let's try the outdoor shower," he said.

"But—"

"No buts. I bet you haven't even tried it out."

She stared at him, her eyes saying no already.

"Come on." Keeping hold of her hand, he led the way. Landscaping lights illuminated the path through the darkness, down through the garden to the outdoor shower, a fantasy of lush plantings surrounded by rough stone in a rustic wood enclosure. There were fluffy white robes hanging on wrought iron hooks, and an array of homemade soaps and lotions, all perfectly arranged for the photo shoot.

He brought her into the enclosure, knelt down and took off her sandals. Then he put his arms around her and unzipped her skirt. She was quiet and sweetly compliant. Her skin felt warm beneath his hands as he undressed her and turned on the water. Then he peeled off his clothes and they stood together under the warm stream of water, exploring each other with soap-slick hands, kissing and tasting until he was about to explode. He took her there on the shower bench, gratified by the small, involuntary sounds of ecstasy she made. It was fast, and when she came, he felt the shudders rippling all through her body, and he couldn't hold back. He turned her in his arms and kissed her long and deeply while the water rinsed them clean.

"Best shower ever," he whispered, turning off the water and wrapping her in a robe.

"Yes," she said. "I feel…it's hard to explain. As if we go away somewhere, kind of like in a dream."

"That explains it, then."

She leaned her damp forehead against his shoulder. "What does it mean?"

"I think you know. But you don't want to say."

"Hey."

"It's okay. Tonight we're doing the interview. Don't worry, I'll get more personal after we're done."

Isabel floated back to the house with him. She *did* know why they were so good together, and he was right; she didn't want to say. Because it worried her.

The television was on in the lounge room, so they sneaked into the kitchen for a bottle of wine and two glasses, a dish of walnuts toasted with rosemary and salt and a wedge of cheese drizzled with honey. They tiptoed up the stairs to her room. He set down the bottle, backed her up against the bed, dipped his finger in the honey and said, "I might have to have you again."

Her response was ridiculous. She wanted his hands all over her. He'd created a monster. A nymphomaniac. "That sounds like an excellent idea," she said, drawing him down over her.

They didn't get around to the interview until much later. He was leaning back against a bank of pillows while she leaned her cheek against his bare chest, her hands gently stroking his belly. "You've lulled me into submission," she whispered. "Ask me anything."

"Oh, baby, you don't want to give me that kind of license." He leaned over and picked up his phone, putting it in record mode. "Let's stick to the interview. I want people to be blown away by the article."

"All right." She felt relaxed and replete. Floating. Filled with a kind of joy she'd never felt before. "Where do we start?"

"With cooking. Why do you love it?"

The question startled her. No one had ever asked her something like that. And no one had ever listened to her the way he did—with his eyes. With his whole body. "Well, it's elemental. Creating a meal for someone is incredibly personal. There's a kind of intimacy in the process. Feeding someone is…for me, it's a way of showing love, by providing nourishment that comes from my own creativity and craft." She flushed, because it sounded strange, putting that feeling into words. "How am I doing? Is this what you had in mind?"

"Just keep going. Don't worry about how it sounds."

"All right. I love knowing that I'm good at it. Cooking connects me with my family—the mother and father I never knew, the grandmother who raised me, the place where I grew up amid all this abundance, right here at Bella Vista.

"The kitchen is the place where I feel closest to my grandmother, especially. She was my mother, my grandmother, my lodestone. I lost her at a crucial time in my life. I was just twenty, and it felt much too soon. I hadn't learned everything I needed from her. Fate doesn't give you a choice, does it? Yet when I cook, I feel her flowing through me, guiding my spirit and my hands."

"What's your earliest memory of your grandmother?"

She thought for a moment. It was just a flash, but then it gave way to a gilded memory, misted like a dream. "Grandfather made me a step stool, so I could reach the counter in the kitchen. He stenciled a picture of a dog on it and a saying, 'Use this stool to reach for the stars.' I would set it next to the counter so I could be tall enough to help. I remember the flour dusting Bubbie's hands. She would roll up her sleeves and I could see the tattoo. One time, I took a magic marker and wrote some numbers on my arm, and she fussed at me and made me scrub it off. She said no one should have a mark like that, and if she could scrub off the one on her own arm, she would."

Isabel sighed, still able to hear her grandmother's soft accent. "I remember the smell of her wild blackberry jam, the steam rising up from the pots and utensils when she sterilized them. She used to trade her jam for jars of honey from the Krokowers down the road. More than once, she said she wanted to produce her own honey one day, right here at Bella Vista, but this was a working orchard and she didn't have a lot of spare time."

Isabel swirled her finger in the fine hairs on his chest, taking comfort in his calm, quiet presence. "Bubbie was just getting started on the honey project when she got sick. I guess that's why I'm so determined to keep bees. I want to do something she never had the chance to do."

"She'd love everything you've done," Mac said.

"I hope so. We had a long time to say goodbye to my grandmother," said Isabel. "Sometimes we thought that was a blessing, and other times, a curse, because it's just so horribly sad. When someone is ill and you know you're losing her, you want to make sure you've said everything that needs saying. It's a very long conversation. My grandmother and I didn't leave much unsaid between us—or so I thought. We were both keeping secrets, though. We were both trying to protect each other from the truth. I never told her about Calvin Sharpe, and she never talked about losing Erik." She paused, instantly wishing she hadn't mentioned Calvin. "And that, by the way, is strictly off the record."

"Whatever you say. But did you ever stop to consider that if the guy was a dick to you, he was a dick to others? I'm guessing you're not the only one."

Mac was right, of course. "I'm just glad I don't have to deal with him anymore."

"Not even when he finds out you poached the magazine cover he was counting on?"

She felt unapologetic as she leaned over to the bedside table for her glass of wine, holding it up to the light and then taking a sip. "She mentioned Erik the day before she died. She was drifting, then. Peaceful, in and out of consciousness. I recall that her final words to me were something mundane. I think she asked me to turn out the light or something. But our last conversation, that last big talk, was a good one. She made me write it down, because she wanted to make sure I'd never forget." Isabel opened the drawer of her nightstand and found her journal. She had never been consistent about keeping it, but she did write down the things that were important to her, things she wanted to remember. And a few things she didn't. In the back pocket of the journal was a newspaper clipping about her father's accident. Bubbie's obituary. And a small purple data card containing raw video from the teaching kitchen webcam that had recorded her final encounter with Calvin Sharpe.

She flipped to a page near the front of the journal, where she'd written down her grandmother's words. "Here it is. It's dated the day she passed away. 'In this life, I had all I ever wanted. Losing Erik was a sadness that knit itself into my soul, but that sadness was balanced out by all that came after. The years with you, my little girl, and with your grandfather and all the people of Bella Vista. It has been a life of abundance and I will always be grateful for that.'" She set the book aside and drew her knees up to her chest, her eyes misting. "And I have no idea what that has to do with the article about the cooking school."

"It has to do with you. I'm glad you told me," he said. "I wish I'd known your grandmother."

"She would have liked you."

"Everyone likes me."

I know.

"Tell me more about cooking. Why a cooking school? Why not a restaurant or catering service?"

"The idea hit me last year when Dominic's kids went on strike. They couldn't stand his cooking, and Tess's skills in the kitchen were nonexistent, so I started giving them lessons. When I was teaching, something, I don't know how to describe it... Something came alive in me, and I realized I'd found what I was supposed to be doing."

She offered him the small dish of walnuts. "Eating is one of those things we all have in common," she said. "We all do it, no matter who we are or where we come from. When we sit down together for a meal, we slow down, relax and talk with each other. It's also nice to be quiet while we eat and just enjoy the comfort and companionship of a shared meal." She smiled. "I bet your mom would describe it differently, with all those boys she raised."

"God, yes. Mealtimes were loud and messy at our house. I don't think relaxing applied in my family."

The image of a table crowded with boys wolfing down their dinner made her smile. She found herself wanting to know more about them, more about Mac's parents. More about his life. She wanted to know everything about him. "I knew when I dreamed up the cooking school that it wouldn't be for everyone," she said. "Personally, I feel a sense of abundance when I prepare a home cooked meal. I love the feeling that I've placed everything we need on the table. It's different from a restaurant enterprise—that's an act of commerce, a transaction. At home, no one worries about what to order from the menu or what the tab's going to be, what wine to pair with the food."

He lay back and folded his arms behind his head. She tried not to stare at his biceps. He grinned at her. "You make it sound very relaxing."

"For me, it is. And I love to see the way people taste and enjoy what I've prepared. It's a way of showing my care and regard for someone. When I create something delicious in my kitchen, it sends a clear message."

"Like to Homer Kelly?"

She laughed. "I tried sending that message to him, but he didn't get it. Homer Kelly was an idiot."

"Agreed. If you made your butter croissants for me, you'd have to get a restraining order to keep me away from you."

Getting involved with Mac was a bad idea for so many reasons. Even so, she didn't want to keep him away from her. She wanted to keep him close.

CHAPTER TWENTY-THREE

Magnus pushed the old accident report across the desk to Mac. They were finishing their final talk together, and Mac knew this might be the most difficult conversation so far. Of all the ordeals that had befallen Magnus Johansen, this was the one wound that would never heal.

"It is a straightforward story," Magnus said. "The tragedy occurred the way accidents befall people every day. My son had a quarrel with his hot-headed wife, who happened to be pregnant and more than a week past her due date. That, I imagine, would put any woman in a temper. At the time, I didn't know what they quarreled about, though I do now, of course. He got into his car and drove to the city."

Magnus took off his glasses and used a cloth to polish the lenses. Despite his age, his hands were steady and strong, brown from his years in the sun. Here in the office where he'd conducted the business of Bella Vista for decades, he still looked like a man in charge.

"Erik owned a red Mustang convertible, and he had a bad

habit of driving too fast. That day is still vivid in my memory. I was up on a ladder, doing some spring pruning, and several of the workers scattered, all of a sudden, like startled birds. It happened. As a grower, I tried to use documented workers, but sometimes their family members were undocumented. So when I saw two lawmen arriving, my first thought was of a raid. Then I realized the visitors were with the highway department. Somehow I came down the rungs of the ladder without falling, because I knew before they said a word. You see, if he had been injured and taken to hospital, there would have been a phone call urging us to rush to the emergency room. But the fact that they came in person..."

Mac had scanned the report. "He was declared dead at the scene."

"The longest walk I've ever taken was from the orchard back to the house that day, to tell his mother and his wife. Francesca became hysterical, her labor started, and so Eva and I had to take her directly to the hospital. There was no time for the horror to sink in. I was a man ripped in two that day, grieving the loss of my son, but at the same time, holding this beautiful new baby in my arms. Eva and I made a pact with one another for the sake of the baby. We would not allow ourselves to be broken by what happened. Instead, we would create a wonderful world for Isabel, and dedicate ourselves to her safety and happiness."

They sat together in silence. Mac made a few notes. In his mind's eye, he could clearly see the shape of the narrative he would write about this man. "It's been my job to learn your story," Mac said. "But it's been my privilege to get to know you. Thank you for bringing me into your world."

"I've enjoyed it as well, more than you know. Isabel has enjoyed it, too." He gave Mac a measured look. "I can tell. She's not an easy one to know. Like her grandmother, she holds her secrets close, but when she gives them up, she gives herself completely."

Had she done that? Mac wondered. Had she given herself completely? He thought not. And then he thought, not *yet*.

"She's very inspired by you," Mac said. "We all are. And when this is published, it will be a gift to anyone who reads it."

"Thank you. I know you will do your job very well." He offered a small smile, indicating the bookcase behind him. "I believe I've read all your books and some of the articles, as well. You started out in the area of true crime."

He nodded. "Right out of journalism school, I lucked into an assignment about an unsolved murder in a small town called Avalon in the Catskills, and the book got a lot of attention, because of what happened afterward."

"The crime was solved?"

He nodded. "Turns out the victim wasn't murdered after all. She died by accident. Finding out the truth didn't change what happened, but the family seemed to appreciate knowing."

"And your next project is about a crime," Magnus said.

Mac nodded. "I promised Ari Nejim that I would work with him to expose what happened to his daughter, Yasmin."

"It's going to put you in danger. You'll have a target on your back," Magnus pointed out. It wasn't a question. Mac had leveled with him about the incident, the terrible loss and the guilt he felt over it.

"Maybe. I worry more about Ari."

Magnus put his glasses back on and stood up with an air of finality. They walked out together into the brilliant sunshine. The boughs of the apple trees in their stately rows were heavy with fruit, and bees floated lazily through the lavender and milkweed. As the summer waned toward autumn, the light was deeper, the air heavy and rich with abundance.

"You've led an amazing life," Mac said, "and it's fantastic, this world you've built, this community."

Magnus scanned the vast, rolling landscape. "I never wanted to write a book, nor did I want someone else to write it. Then I realized I have one story in me, and it's a good story."

"Yes," said Mac. "And you can always add to it. There's a certain lady who made it her business to catch the bouquet at the wedding, remember?"

"I would never forget that." His eyes twinkled with a smile. "So the story is not over yet. Let it end when it ends."

"I have a proposal for you," Mac said, coming into the workshop where Isabel and Jamie were harvesting honey from racks that were capped and cured, bulging with ripe nectar.

Isabel's heart skipped a beat as she looked up from the big stainless steel centrifuge. "A proposal."

"Say yes," Jamie advised her. "You know you want to."

"I haven't heard the proposal yet," Isabel pointed out. Nevertheless, she felt an utterly silly thrill of false hope.

"A proposal's a proposal," Jamie stated.

"Out," said Mac, holding the door for the girl.

"Hello. I'm in the middle of something here." She gestured at the racks of sterilized jars, the scraping tools, the basins.

"Later," he said.

"Okay, fine. I'm meeting someone in town, anyway. I've got a line on a singing gig at a restaurant."

"Really? Jamie, that's great," said Isabel.

Jamie sent her a look, then hung up her apron and left the workroom.

"What is it?" Isabel asked.

He grabbed her and kissed her, long and slowly. "First of all, you look incredible in that apron."

"That apron just got you all sticky."

"Not a problem. I know where we can find an outdoor shower."

He was so much fun. She'd had no idea falling in love could

be this much fun. Before Mac, she'd regarded it as an angst-filled process fraught with uncertainty and stress. He'd shown her a different way. He'd shown her the joy. "So what's your proposal?"

"Besides drizzling honey on you and licking it off?"

"Mac."

"Okay, we can save that for later." He took a printout from his pocket and handed it to her. "My itinerary."

Her heart sank. She'd known this day was coming. "You're leaving."

"I have a weeklong meeting in Istanbul about my next project."

The Yasmin project, Isabel recalled. *It still haunts me every day,* he'd told her, speaking of his wife and the way he'd lost her. She didn't know what to say, so she folded the itinerary and set it aside.

"When I'm finished there, I want you to meet me in Italy," he said. "Ravello. Week after next."

The idea *whooshed* past her with the speed of sound. The speed of impossibility. "Mac, it sounds tempting, but you know I can't leave."

"Sure, you can. Take some time for yourself, Isabel. The wedding's over, you did a great job. You've got a window of opportunity to get away."

"The cooking school opens in a month. I don't have a minute to spare." She wished he would propose a compromise— a weekend away in Mendocino or San Francisco. But Mac wasn't the kind of guy to compromise.

"Make time. Everything will be waiting for you when you get back."

"I can't."

"You could."

"But I won't."

"Seriously? Jesus, Isabel, you frustrate the hell out of me."

She felt apologetic, but she refused to apologize. "Let's say I agree to go. Then what?"

"Then we have a fantastic time. We ride around on a scooter, we go to the market and the gardens, we drink local wine and make love...."

Every word he spoke was a small seduction. She held up her hand. "You know what I'm asking. Then what?"

"Then...we'll see," he said simply.

Now Isabel was the one feeling frustrated. What she really wanted him to say was that love would be enough. That if you start with love, the rest will sort itself out. But it wouldn't, would it? Real life didn't work that way.

She knew her heart was in her eyes when she looked up at him. "Saying goodbye to you is going to be hard enough. Running off to Italy is only going to make it harder."

"I get it," Mac said. "Finally, I think I get *you*. Watching you creating your dream is beautiful, Isabel."

She heard the "but," although he didn't say it.

And then he did. "I can't ask you to leave all this," said Mac. "And I can't stay."

She stared at the floor. "I know." She wanted to keep him close, but she simply couldn't see a way to do that without getting hurt, or without hurting him. She wondered if it was possible to give just a little of herself to someone instead of flinging herself into an impossible love. The scent of honey was ripe and sweet in the air.

He waited. Didn't touch her. She could almost hear him thinking.

"What is it?" she asked softly.

"There's one other thing..."

She felt a leap of hope. "Yes?"

"Before I go, we should talk about your father's accident. Your grandfather showed me the police report."

Her heart sank. She hadn't been expecting the conversation to lead to *this*. But that was Mac; he never did the expected thing. "You never stop working," she observed.

"I had some questions."

Of course he did.

"Were you aware that no one checked the dental records?"

"No. Why would that matter?"

"There's no proof that the accident victim was Erik Johansen."

"There's no *question* that it was Erik. Who else could it have been? It was him—his car, his wreck."

"But maybe... It was sloppy police work. It should be looked into."

"No," she said decisively. "Stop it, Mac. There's no point in stirring things up and upsetting Grandfather. I can't believe you'd suggest such a thing."

He took a step back, holding his hands palms out. "If it were me, I'd want to know."

"It's my grandfather. My family. We don't need to relive that pain," she said. "My father died before I was born. Dredging up a tragedy is never going to change that." Isabel saw clearly what was between them. Mac was on a mission to explore and examine everything, no matter how uncomfortable it made people. She believed in protecting herself and those she loved.

"I think you should go," she whispered past the ache in her throat.

Mac nodded. "I'm going to miss you, more than you know," he said, cupping her cheek in his hand. "I've never felt regret about leaving a place, but I do now. I'll probably regret leaving you all my life."

Then don't, she wanted to say, echoing his own words. But she understood all too well that geography was not the issue. She covered his hand with hers and then removed it from her cheek.

CHAPTER TWENTY-FOUR

Isabel took Charlie for a walk down to the main road to check the mail. As she and the dog walked past the sun-gold meadow, she could see the hives up on the slope in the distance, and it made her think of that first day Mac had arrived in the banana-yellow Jeep, almost instantly turning her world upside down.

His absence felt like a big gaping hole in her life. Now that he was gone, her bed felt like a vast wasteland. Even in sleep she would turn toward the empty space he used to fill with his warm presence. Half awake, she would breathe in, seeking his scent. Then the stark reality of his absence would slap her awake.

Give it time, she told herself. It'll get better.

Instead, it got worse. Nothing had a point anymore. Because what she'd had with Mac—that was the point of everything.

At last she understood the passions that had driven Magnus and Annelise, and even her doomed parents, Erik and Francesca. The heart wants what it wants, she realized. And sometimes you had to give it all without holding back...because it could be gone in the blink of an eye. She knew she had to learn to be okay with losing Mac, but she couldn't help wishing he had let her take care of him, and that she had let him in. She would have to fill the emptiness with the busy times ahead—launching the cooking school, getting Annelise settled at Bella Vista, helping Jamie with her appointments and counseling meetings. Isabel wouldn't have a moment to spare for regrets. Or so she hoped.

She pulled the day's delivery from the big rural mailbox. A thick, official-looking envelope dropped to the ground, and she stooped to pick it up. The return address read *U.S. Department of State.*

"My passport," she said to Charlie. He tilted his head quizzically one way, then the other. She opened the parcel, took out the small blue booklet and ran her thumb over the embossed seal. Then she opened it to the information page. She wasn't smiling in the photo, but her eyes were bright with excitement. She *had* been excited that day, swept into adventure with Mac O'Neill.

It hadn't been real, though. In theory, it had all seemed so exciting and romantic. In actuality, it was simply one more impossibility that could never fit into the life she'd created for herself.

She put the passport back in the envelope, then leaned against the mailbox and shut her eyes, her chest aching with regrets. There was no sensation worse than heartbreak. And there really wasn't any remedy, either. Only time. She had no choice but to endure the hurt and move on.

The sound of a car on the road brought her back to the moment. Charlie took up his guard dog stance next to her and gave a *woof* of warning. She looked over to see a red car stopped at the roadside, not far from Things Remembered. Calvin Sharpe's car.

Charlie's throat rumbled with a growl. Isabel dropped the stack of mail into the weeds. The car window rolled down, and Calvin offered a grin and a wave. She was about to send Charlie on the attack when the passenger side door opened and Jamie got out.

"Thanks," she called to Calvin. "I'll see you Friday."

Keeping the cocky grin on his face, Calvin offered a wave in Isabel's direction.

Charlie wagged and leaped as he greeted Jamie.

"What were you doing with Calvin Sharpe?" Isabel asked.

"That job in town I mentioned before," said Jamie. "I'm going to be singing at his new restaurant a couple of nights per week."

Isabel's heart turned to stone. She could too easily picture Calvin preying on Jamie, taking advantage of her youth and talent. "Take Charlie up to the house," she said. "I'll meet you there." With icy deliberation, she approached his car.

"Hey, there," he said, offering his Chiclet smile. "That's quite a girl. She can really sing."

"Just so you know, she won't be singing for you."

"That's none of your business. Back off, Isabel."

She remembered his icy, barely restrained rage all too well. But this time, it didn't scare her. "I don't think so," she said. "I'll explain to Jamie. She'll understand."

He killed the engine and got out of the car. "She's a grown girl. She can make her own choices." He narrowed his eyes, flicking his gaze over her. "Leo tells me you got some big-name writer to do a feature article on you."

Now Isabel realized exactly what this was about. He didn't need Jamie to sing at his restaurant. He simply wanted to get back at Isabel for stealing his limelight. "So what if I did? It's none of your business." She threw his words back at him.

"The hell you say. CalSharpe's is the biggest thing to happen to this town. It's not going to take a backseat to your amateur cooking class."

She offered a tight smile. God, that ego. "Actually, it is."

"I guess you fucked him to get your way," Calvin said. "Just like you did me."

Isabel stopped breathing for a moment, as if she'd been punched in the stomach. But she refused to move, to flee and hide as she'd done in the past. She finally realized what was behind Calvin's bullying.

It was hard to believe that there had ever been a time when she had gazed into that face, seeking approval and love. When she had craved the sensation of those hands touching her, when she would have done anything for him.

Have you ever told anyone the truth about that guy? Even yourself? Mac's words echoed through her mind once more, and at last, she knew what she had to do.

For once in her life, her spine felt like a column of steel. "I've got news for you, Cal. You don't need the magazine cover, because you're going to be leaving the area. Your restaurant's never going to open."

"Spare me the dramatics, Isabel."

"Not this time," she said. Adrenaline surged through her.

"You can't force me to do anything, you crazy bitch."

"I have the webcam footage."

He scowled, and then the scowl turned into a snarl of contempt. "From ten years ago. Big deal. It's going to be the word of a failed cooking student against me. You don't have a legal leg to stand on."

"Then let's see if your reputation can handle it. Bigger names than you have been brought down by less. You can join Paula Deen and the *Duck Dynasty* guy in obscurity."

Something wild flashed in his eyes. Fear. Yes, he was afraid. Of her.

"We'll see about that," he said, all bluster. Then he got back into his car, made a U-turn in the road and sped away with a roar of acceleration.

Isabel didn't bother to watch him go. She walked over to the mailbox where she'd dropped her things, then bent down and picked up the passport.

Leo, the editor of *MenuSonoma Magazine,* greeted Isabel when she arrived at his office in Santa Rosa. "Check it out," he said, motioning her over to his computer screen. "I can show you the layout of the article and photos for the cover story. It's a major coup," he said, all smiles. "Best article we've ever had. I can't believe you got Cormac O'Neill to do it."

"It looks good," she said, feeling a wave of emotion as she studied the gorgeous, lush photos of the cooking school. And of her. She looked good, better than she'd hoped. She looked like a woman filled with enthusiasm. One particular shot of her in the grape arbor grabbed her attention. She was gazing directly at the camera, her expression utterly transparent. She looked like a woman in love.

Mac had been good to her. Good *for* her. Good for the whole family, when it came to that. But she'd let him go. She'd let him go because she could not see a way to get him to stay.

"I'm excited for you, Isabel," Leo said. "I'm excited for Archangel. The town has Bella Vista, and the new Calvin Sharpe place... It's all good."

She had no comment on that.

"So I was thinking we could do something with the two of you together—the new cooking school, the new restaurant. Calvin said the two of you go way back, and he's game."

"I'm sure he is." A cold determination formed in her core. "That's actually why I'm here, Leo. I have something for you." She gave him a copy of the data card. Her hand shook, but her spirit didn't waver. "Everything you need to know about Calvin Sharpe is right here. I'm sending a copy to his network producer, too. You can do what you want with it."

Leo frowned. "What is it?"

"It's self-explanatory. I'll let you decide whether or not you want to do anything about it at all. Suffice it to say, there won't be any glad-handing between Cal and me."

She left the office, drained and breathing fast as if she'd run a great distance. Her heart was pounding, but she felt liberated, strong and sure of herself. Finally.

It was Mac, bringing out the truth in Magnus's story, who had given her the courage to tell her own truth. For years, she'd been too afraid, too ashamed to come forward.

Since Mac had left, she'd spent a lot of time thinking about the stories he'd drawn from her, and from her grandfather and Annelise. She'd learned so much from them. Knowing the trials they'd endured and the lives they'd built for themselves, put it all into perspective. The human spirit could brave anything so long as there was some better future to believe in.

At long last, she got it. As much as she loved Bella Vista, it had been her hiding place, walling her off from the rest of the world. Now Isabel wanted it to be a place to grow. The only thing holding her back was herself.

Mac would be proud of her. But he was gone; her doubts and fears had kept her from stopping him. She still ached for him every day, but knew now for certain that she would survive, although she'd never be the same. He had left his mark upon her heart, as indelible as a battle scar.

CHAPTER TWENTY-FIVE

Ravello was everything Mac had expected, only better. Autumn was a golden time in the rocky Italian hill town, with its ancient streets and alleyways, the markets and little shops and plazas tucked around the magnificent duomo and the beautiful ruins and gardens of the Villa Cimbrone. He'd come here on what might have been a fool's errand, but as it turned out, the hunch he'd been following was correct.

He'd been essentially fired from the previous assignment. He'd never before been glad to be taken off a story, but this time, it was a blessing. In Istanbul, Ari Nejim had set him free. It was the last thing Mac had expected from Yasmin's father. The man's daughter had been murdered. After the incident, the kind of rage that had burned in Ari's eyes had seemed as eternal as the endlessly burning fire in the Gates of Hell. Back then, Mac had been certain Ari would not rest until his daughter's murderers were exposed.

Yet in Turkey, he'd found Ari in a different place, emotionally as well as geographically. At a Bosphorus-side breakfast spot, over cups of thick native coffee, Ari had seemed diminished, resigned. But he was also focused.

"I do not want to do this," he'd said, referring to the project. "I'm sorry you had to come all this way, but I must make certain you understand I'm not being coerced. The murder of my daughter is for the authorities to deal with. Perhaps they will find the truth about Yasmin, perhaps not. Either way, I must step back from this, because it is killing me. After she died, I found myself with two choices. I can live in hell, or I can live my life."

"What do you want to do?" Mac had asked.

"I must let this go. I need to. I cannot bring my daughter back. My energy needs to go elsewhere, to a positive place. I've taken a position with the World Engineering Society. I'll be in charge of their charitable initiatives."

"That's good, Ari," said Mac. "I'm glad for you. So…what do you want me to do?"

"Let it go, as I have. Don't allow it to poison your future. Move ahead with your life. It's all we can do, yes?"

Mac had thought long and hard about that advice. He'd married a woman in order to save her life, and she'd died. The fact that he hadn't had a serious relationship since then was pretty telling. But Ari was right. It was time to move on.

Mac thought he might have discovered a way to do that here in Ravello, where Francesca Cioffi had grown up among the lemon gardens overlooking the sea far below. He'd found out some remarkable things about her and her family. He wanted Isabel to know what he'd learned.

But maybe some things should be left to rest. She claimed she wasn't interested in finding out more about her father's accident. Maybe she didn't want to know anything more about her mother's family, either.

It was late afternoon, and the vendors at the farmer's market were packing up their tubs of olives and racks of produce for the day. He passed by a booth where they were serving samples of honey from carnelian bees. The taste of honey reminded him of Isabel. Hell, everything reminded him of Isabel.

He looked around the old buildings with their stone archways and flaking plaster. The town had long been a mecca for artists and writers. This morning he'd passed by the house where D. H. Lawrence had lived and worked, writing his mournful, sensual books about people who destroyed themselves in search of a perfect love that didn't exist.

Don't look back, that had always been Mac's motto. But it was damned hard, considering what he'd left behind. Ah, well, he thought. Something new would come up. Some new project. Maybe he'd pursue the bridge wreck on his own and dig deeper into the accident that had taken Erik Johansen's life. Yeah, it would be cool to have an excuse to go back to California.

He licked the honey from his fingers and starting walking toward the *penzione* where he was staying. As he approached the old house, with its painted shutters and blooming window boxes, he heard the buzz of a scooter motor and looked up, spying a beautiful girl with bare legs and sandals on a Vespa.

His heart tumbled over in his chest. "No way," he breathed. "My God."

"I got my first passport stamp," Isabel said, taking off the helmet and shaking loose her long, glorious hair.

"Jet lag is fun," Isabel murmured, draping her naked self over Mac's body. It was three in the morning, and they had just spent the past hour making love in the *penzione,* a cozy little room with sturdy whitewashed furniture and a view of a patio garden. Cool air blew against the lace curtain on the window, scented with lemons and the smell of the sea.

"*You're* fun," Mac said, kissing her temple. "I still can't believe you're here."

"I can't, either. I can't believe I found your *penzione*. The address on your itinerary wasn't very specific. But the locals are really helpful. Did I surprise you?"

"Hell, yes. You're incredible, Isabel. Thanks for coming."

"I need to tell you something." She rolled over and propped her chin on his bare chest. "A lot has happened since you left. I didn't exactly level with you about Calvin Sharpe."

"That douche bag? What about him?"

"He's history." Isabel took a deep breath and told Mac the truth. She told him about handing over the evidence of the assault. She could say it now. She could say it without shame or guilt. The statute of limitations had run out for her to take action against him, but he'd been disgraced in that irrevocable way the mass media had of piling on. Regardless of the legal outcome, he was destroyed professionally. His network had fired him after his cooking show's sponsors had dropped him like the proverbial hot potato. His cookbook deal was toast. The backers of his restaurant empire had pulled out and his entourage had disappeared. He would be nothing but an asterisk on Wikipedia, a failed pseudo celebrity, a mistake. Obscurity was the worst punishment imaginable for a man with Calvin's ego.

"A guy like that deserves worse than getting dropped by his network," said Mac, fury vibrating in his voice.

"Believe me, losing his spot in the limelight will kill him. His restaurant franchise is dead in the water. Just like his career is going to be. I feel bad that I didn't speak up, that I was scared for so long."

Mac kissed her gently. "I'm sorry," he said. "I'm sorry about what happened to you. But I'm glad you're done with him."

"And I'm sorry I let what happened in the past affect my

feelings for you," she said. "You're a good man, Mac. You've been really patient with me."

"First time I've ever been accused of patience," he said. "But there came a point—probably the day of the hot springs—when I realized I was willing to wait for you to come around."

He held her tenderly for a long time. She yawned, feeling a wave of exhaustion. "I'm sleepy again."

"Then you should sleep."

"Jet lag's weird. I have no idea what day it is or what time it is."

"Shh," he said, stroking her temple. "It's *our* time."

Breakfast was a revelation of perfectly prepared cappuccino and a basket of *sfogliatelle,* flaky pastry filled with sweet cheese. The weather was gorgeous, a day of picture-perfect blue skies and a cooling breeze. "What are we going to do today?" she asked.

He looked at her for a moment. Then he said, "I have a surprise for you."

Suspicion darkened her mood. "I don't like surprises."

"Hey, you bowled me over yesterday. I get to surprise you. Finish your coffee. There's someone I want you to meet."

"Here?" She narrowed her eyes. "Who?"

"You have to trust," he said.

"I trust."

They strolled through the pretty streets with their cascading gardens, and Isabel felt as if she was in a dream, holding hands with him and watching the shopkeepers rolling out their awnings. There was a *profumi* where *limoncello* was made from local lemons, tiny ceramics shops and tourist kiosks. He brought her down an uneven, winding staircase of a street to a row of small, interconnected houses and stopped at a painted green door with potted geraniums on either side.

A woman opened the door. Isabel's legs turned to water, and she fell back against Mac. She stared, because she was looking at her mother. Her living mother. She recognized Francesca's beautiful face, her full mouth, tremulous with an uncertain smile. The woman was older now of course, and still lovely, with dark wavy hair and large dark eyes, the same eyes in the photos Isabel had studied all her life, yearning to know the mother who had given her life.

The woman at the door stared, too, her eyes brimming with tears. She said something in rapid Italian, and the only word Isabel understood was *Francesca*.

Mac replied to her briefly, and she motioned them inside. In the foyer, she paused and turned, pulling Isabel into her arms and speaking nonstop.

Mac said something calming, then took Isabel's hand. "This is your aunt Lucia," he said. "She's your mother's sister."

Somehow, Isabel found her voice. "It's good to meet you," she said.

Lucia spoke again.

"She's Francesca's sister. Her twin sister," Mac said.

Twins. Shock and wonder reverberated through her. "Could we...sit down?"

Mac translated. Lucia bustled them into a small sitting room filled with old-fashioned furniture. She sat on a love seat next to Isabel and held both her hands. She spoke some more, and Isabel realized she was comparing their hands, their faces. *We look alike.*

"How did you know to come looking for her?" she asked Mac.

"The photo," he said. "The one we found in the trunk. I knew it wasn't Francesca."

"You did? How?"

"The birthmark. The girl in the photo didn't have one, but

your mother did. And the girl in the photo was holding a pen in her right-hand. Remember? Your mother was left-handed, like you." He related this to Lucia in Italian.

"Wow," said Isabel. "I'm overwhelmed. I don't know what to say." She wept, then, and Lucia gathered her close, and the two of them held each other for a moment. Isabel felt enclosed by the warmth of this woman, this stranger who was identical to the mother she'd never known.

Then Isabel pulled back. "I have questions."

"I'll do my best," said Mac.

"You never tried to contact my mother?" she asked, and he posed the question to Lucia.

Lucia spoke for a moment; then Mac translated. "It was a terrible falling-out. She says their parents were already on a pension and there was nothing to spare to go traveling in search of someone who did not want to be found. They assumed Francesca had simply moved on without them. And it seems, in a way, that she did. Your grandmother sent a letter when Francesca died, and there was an exchange of cards at Christmas, but eventually that tapered off."

"I'm sorry," Isabel said. "I'm sorry for your loss. You lost her twice—once when she went away, and again because she died."

"Sì. Grazie."

"I wish I'd known what she was like. Maybe you can tell me one day."

"She says she can tell you right now," Mac explained.

Isabel leaned forward, waiting. "Yes?"

Lucia stood and brought Isabel to the hearth in the sitting room, turning her to face the framed oval mirror on the mantel, and she said something in a quiet voice.

"She was like that," Mac said. "Almost exactly like that."

Isabel's heart filled with warmth. "Really?"

"That is why she nearly fell apart when she saw you. Francesca was young and fresh and beautiful. Her voice was low and sweet, and she sounded just like you," Mac translated. Then he said, "Now you know."

They spent the day with Lucia, who promised that the following day she would take them up to Scala, an even tinier, loftier town where her parents now lived. That evening, Mac took her to a restaurant called *Il Flauto di Pan*—Pan's Flute—perched at the Villa Cimbrone among the gardens and crumbling walls. It was probably the most beautiful restaurant she'd ever seen. The centuries-old villa was embellished with incredible gardens of fuchsia bougainvillea, lemon and cypress trees and flowering herbs that scented the air. Their veranda table had an impossibly gorgeous view of the sea.

They shared a bottle of wine with the tasting menu, but despite the delicious food, she could scarcely eat. "I'm too excited," she confessed, and lifted her glass to him. "Thank you, Mac. Thank you for making this happen."

"You're the one who got on that plane," he said. "You got your passport stamped."

"I did. It was fun. I wish I could stay longer, but you know I need to get back." She gazed at the color of the sunset through her wineglass. There was a part of her—a very big part—that wanted to stay here forever. To stay with *him* forever, traveling the world with him, leaving Bella Vista behind. Could she...would she give that up for the love of this man? Or was the sacrifice too great? Could she give up a dream for the one she loved?

"What's that face?" he asked.

"Daydreaming. I just thought..." She stopped herself from trying to explain, and instead took a sip of wine. "I'll be a different person when I go back. I feel...complete."

"You've always been complete, Isabel."

He had a talent for saying the sweetest things. He said everything she needed to hear…almost. "So," she dared to ask. "What's next for you?"

"I have a book to write. It's very portable."

"Then where are you taking it?"

"I want to be with you, Isabel. I figured you would get that by now."

"But for how long?"

"How about forever? Would forever work for you?"

She felt the blood rush to her face. "You are never serious."

"How do you know I'm not serious?"

"Because you never are."

"Listen," he said, drilling her with a look. "I tried marrying once, and I did a lousy job, okay? I didn't love her and she died. What's worse than that?"

"It's terrible, Mac, but you did what you thought was best at the time. You couldn't have known what would happen."

"Exactly. And I don't know what's going to happen now. All I know is that this is completely different. You're not like anyone I've ever met. You took care of me, Isabel, and no one's ever done that before. You take care of the people in your life, but I think you're still waiting for somebody to take care of *you*. I want to be with you so bad I can't sleep at night. I can't think of anything except how much I love you."

"Oh.…"

"That's it? Just *oh?*"

"I don't know what you want me to say."

"I want you to say what's true."

She got up from the table, blinking back tears. She walked over to the stone veranda, away from the other tables, leaned on the rail and looked out at the amber sky. Under the palms of her hands, the ancient pale stone was still warm from the sun.

He came up behind her, his hands circling her waist. Turning, she wound her arms around his neck. Yet she'd never felt more vulnerable.

Isabel shut her eyes—and leaped. "What's true is that I love you. It started the first time you took me riding on the scooter, and this feeling keeps getting bigger every day and I never want it to end." She let the tears come then, because she was happy and nervous and filled with hope. "I've learned so much about love from you, Mac. I never even knew a feeling like this was possible."

He held her gently. He was always so gentle with her. "So," he said. "I guess you're cool with me coming back to Bella Vista."

She gave a shaky laugh. "I'm cool with it."

"Forever."

"That sounds good to me."

The quartet eased into a smooth melody, like a song without words. They held each other and watched the sun go down, and Isabel knew in that precise moment, everything was perfect. It wouldn't always be, but she didn't need for it to be. Here in Mac's arms, she had everything she needed. She would always go back to Bella Vista, the one true place where she was most at home in the world. But everything was different now. She wasn't afraid anymore. Mac had opened her eyes to possibilities she hadn't let herself see before. Nothing had changed. And yet everything had changed.

Ahead of her was all she wanted—the cooking school. Jamie, Grandfather and Annelise. The sun-drenched acres of Bella Vista, which had sustained her all her life. And Mac, who said he wanted forever. The whole world was there for her, just waiting for her to begin.

EPILOGUE

The swarm of honeybees clung to a low-hanging branch, making that distinctive flying-monkey hum Isabel always found unsettling.

She still found it unsettling in a visceral way, but she'd learned a lot about beekeeping in the past year, and she knew this time she wouldn't fail.

"Are you getting this?" she called over her shoulder to Mac.

He was a safe distance away with a video camera, its telephoto lens aimed in her direction. "Yep," he said, "we're rolling."

"Okay," she said, eyeing the swarm through the veil of her bonnet. "Here goes."

"Looks like a nightmare," he called. "Be careful."

"Bees gorge on honey before they swarm," she reminded him. "Makes them docile."

"Oh, yeah, docile like the bees that sent me into shock last year?"

She'd been so annoyed at him that day, so certain he was

bringing disaster into her world. How could she have known he was bringing love and joy, and a future she never could have envisioned for herself?

He never failed to surprise her, and she loved that about him. After Ravello, they had returned to Archangel together for the launch of the cooking school. Mac's article had been picked up by the international press, and the place was booked solid for the next year.

There were other surprises and unanticipated blessings. Last autumn, her grandfather and Annelise had married in a quiet, family only ceremony. At Christmas, Tess and Dominic announced they were expecting a baby.

And on New Year's Eve, braving the cold to be the first to jump into the newly finished swimming pool, Mac had surprised her once again. Taking a ring from the pocket of his trunks, he had slipped it on her finger, saying, "When I said I wanted forever, I meant it."

The memory of that day nearly made her forget where she was, but the throaty hum of the bees intruded.

Don't think about flying monkeys, she reminded herself, carefully positioning the collection box under the swarm. Before she lost her nerve, she lopped off the branch, and the swarm dropped into the box. Working quickly, she carefully scooped up a few stray bees and covered the top with mesh. Then she loaded the box into the back of the pickup and took a bow for the camera.

"That's a wrap," Mac said. "Is the coast clear?"

"It's fine. I want to wait until sunset to introduce them to the hive. They'll be okay here in the shade until then."

With a feeling of triumph, she took off the bonnet and veil and unzipped the white suit, throwing it into the back of the truck. Mac gave a wolf whistle, eyeing her shorts and tank top. "What do you say we go for a swim, and then I'll take you to bed and make long, sweet love to you?"

She laughed.

"Is that funny?"

"What's funny is that before you came along, I couldn't even imagine someone saying that to me."

"I'm serious," he said, pulling her into his arms. "I seriously love you."

"I know, Mac. I love you, too."

"So listen, before we go, I've got something to show you."

Another surprise? "I love it when you say that," she said, remembering their scooter rides and the trunk of her mother's dresses. "It's always worked out really well for me."

"I can't promise you're going to love this." He grabbed something from a stack of mail on the dashboard of the truck.

She frowned. "Try me."

Unsmiling, he took out a plain legal-size envelope with a metal clasp. "I've been doing some research into Erik's disappearance. I've got a lot of friends in the business, and I traded a few favors to dig into this."

"Mac. I told you before—"

"Just take a look at this. You get to decide what to do about it, but you need to see what I found." He opened the envelope and took out an enlarged photoprint.

Isabel stared at the image. It showed a man on a beach, wearing shorts and a red baseball cap turned backward. It was strangely similar to the photo she had of young Erik at Shell Beach, the picture she'd always liked so well. This wasn't young Erik.

"It was taken last week," said Mac.

"That's impossible," said Isabel.

The man in the photo looked the same, yet not the same. There was no mistaking Erik's features and the way he held himself. But the person in the photo was decades older. Just looking at it gave her a chill.

"Where did you get this?" she asked.

"It was taken by a guy I know from journalism school. The date, time and GPS coordinates are on the back. That beach is near Tangier."

"What? Tangier? As in Tangier, Morocco?"

"That's right."

"How did he get there? What's he doing?"

"That'll take more digging. Or not. You just need to tell me what you want to do."

She set the picture aside, feeling a mixture of excitement and confusion. "I don't know...." She melted against him, grateful for the solid feel of his chest beneath her cheek. "Maybe we should leave this alone," she said, feeling a curl of the old fear inside her. Then she stepped away and gazed up at Mac—her world, her love, her future. "Or maybe it'll be our next adventure."

★ ★ ★ ★ ★

ACKNOWLEDGMENTS

Thanks to Meg Ruley and Annelise Robey of the Jane Rotrosen Agency, and to my editor, Margaret O'Neill Marbury, along with Lauren Smulski, Tara Parsons and the amazing team at MIRA books. Kudos to Cindy Peters for keeping the social network humming.

Many thanks to the very talented Kerrie Sanson, whose insights into cooking and recipes inspired some of the culinary art in this book.

The United States Holocaust Museum, the Virtual Jewish Library, The Museum of Danish Resistance and the National Archives in Copenhagen provided a wealth of historical facts. Beekeeping information was generously offered by Little Milkweed Farm.

Special thanks goes to Suzanne Kelly, Lilac and Chips for their generous support of PAWS.

And finally, I owe a huge thank-you to Lindsey Bonfiglio for all the promotion efforts. Lindsey, you've helped me in more ways than words can say.

Keep reading for a sneak peak of The Apple Orchard
A Bella Vista Chronicles Novel
By New York Times *bestselling author Susan Wiggs*

ONE

San Francisco

Tess Delaney's to-do list was stacked invisibly over her head like the air traffic over O'Hare. She had clients waiting to hear from her, associates hounding her for reports and a make-or-break meeting with the owner of the firm. She pushed back at the pressing anxiety and focused on the task at hand—restoring a treasure to its rightful owner.

The current mission brought her to an overfurnished apartment in Alamo Square. Miss Annelise Winther, still spry at eighty, ushered her into a cozy place with thready lace curtains, dust-ruffled chairs and a glorious scent of something baking. Tess wasted no time in presenting the treasure.

Miss Winther's hands, freckled by age, the joints knotted with arthritis, shook as she held the antique lavaliere. Beneath a pink knitted shawl, her bony shoulders trembled.

"This necklace belonged to my mother," she said, her voice breaking over the word. "I haven't seen it since the spring of

1941." She lifted her gaze to Tess, who sat across the scrubbed pine kitchen table from her. There were stories in the woman's eyes, winking like the facets of a jewel. "I have no words to thank you for bringing this to me."

"It's my pleasure," said Tess. "Moments like this—they're the best part of my job." The sense of pride and accomplishment helped her ignore the insistent buzz of her phone, signaling yet another incoming message.

Annelise Winther was Tess's favorite kind of client. She was unassuming, a woman of modest means, judging by the decrepit condition of her apartment, in one of the city's rambling Victorians that had seen better days. Two cats, whom the woman had introduced as Golden and Prince, lazed in the late-afternoon autumn sunshine spilling through a bumped-out bay window. A homey-looking needlepoint piece hung on the wall, bearing the slogan Live This Day.

Miss Winther took off her glasses, polished them and put them back on. Glancing again at Tess's business card, she said, "Tess Delaney, Provenance Specialist, Sheffield Auction House. Well, Ms. Delaney. I'm extremely glad you found me, too. You've done well for yourself."

Her voice had a subtle tinge of an accent. "I saw that History Channel special about the Kraków Museum. You won an award last month in Poland."

"You saw that?" Tess asked, startled to know the woman had recognized her.

"Indeed I did. You were given a citation for restoring the rosary of Queen Maria Leszczynska. It had been stolen by Nazi looters and was missing for decades."

"It was...a moment." Tess had felt so proud that night. The only trouble was, she'd been in a room full of strangers. No one was present to witness her triumph. Her mother had promised to come but had to cancel at the last minute, so Tess had accepted the accolades in front of a small camera crew and a cultural minister with sweaty hands.

"The very second I saw your face, I knew you would be the one to find my treasure." Miss Winther's words were slightly startling. "And I'm so pleased that it's you. I specifically requested you."

"Why?"

A pause. Miss Winther's face softened. Perhaps she'd lost her train of thought. Then she said, "Because you're the best. Aren't you?"

"I try my best," Tess assured her. She thought the conversation odd, but in this business, she was accustomed to quirky clients. "This piece was with a group of recovered objects from World War II." Tess fell quiet as she thought of the other pieces—jewelry and art and collectibles. The majority of objects remained in limbo, their original owners long gone. She tried not to imagine the terrible sense of violation so many families had suffered, with Nazis invading their homes, plundering their treasures and probably sending many of the family members off to die. Restoring lost treasures seemed a small thing, but the look on Miss Winther's face was its own reward.

"You've made a miracle happen," she declared. "I was just telling a friend on the phone that we're never too old to appreciate a true miracle."

For a miracle, Tess reflected, the task had entailed a lot of hard work. But the expression on the woman's face made all the research, travel and red tape worthwhile. At her own expense, Tess had paid an expert to meticulously clean every link, baguette and facet of the lavaliere. "This is a copy of the provenance report." She slid the document across the table. "It's basically a history of the piece from its creation to the present, as near as I could trace it to its origins in Russia."

"It's amazing that you were able to find this. When I first

contacted your firm, I thought…" Her voice trailed off. "How on earth did you do it?"

Working backward through the provenance report, Tess explained the progress of her research. "This piece was found with a collection of treasures seized in Copenhagen. The lavaliere is pink topaz, with gold filigree embellishments. The chain and clasp are original. It was made by a Finnish designer by the name of August Holmstrom. He was the principal jeweler for the house of Fabergé."

Miss Winther's eyebrows lifted. "*The* Fabergé?"

"The very one." Taking out her loupe, Tess pointed out a tiny spot on the piece. "This is Holmstrom's hallmark, right here, his initials between a double-headed Imperial eagle. He designed it specifically to foil counterfeiters. This particular piece was first mentioned in his design catalog of 1916 and produced for a fashionable shop in St. Petersburg. It was bought by a member of the Danish diplomatic corps."

"My father. He brought the necklace home from a business trip to Russia, and my mother was seldom without it. Besides her wedding ring, it was her favorite piece of jewelry. He gave it to her to celebrate my birth. Though she never said so, I suspect she couldn't have more children after me." Her eyes took on a faraway look, and Tess wondered what she was seeing—her handsome father? Her mother, wearing the jewel against her heart?

The stories behind the treasures were always so intriguing, though often bittersweet. The sad ones were particularly hard to bear. There were some cruelties that were simply inconceivable to normal people, some injustices too big to grasp. Miss Winther must have been tiny when her world was ripped apart. How scared she must have been, how confused.

"I wish I could do more than simply restore this object," said Tess. "It wound up with a number of other pieces in a repository in the basement of an abandoned government building. I spent the past year researching the archives. The Gestapo claimed they kept objects for safekeeping. It was a common ploy. The one helpful thing they did was to keep meticulous records of the things they seized."

Here was where things got dicey. How much information did Miss Winther really need? Did she have to know what had likely happened to her parents?

There were facts Tess had no intention of sharing, such as the evidence that Hilde Winther had been seized without authority by a corrupt officer, and probably treated like a sex slave for months before she was put to death. This was the trouble with uncovering the mysteries of the past. Sometimes you ended up discovering things better left buried. Was it preferable to expose the truth at any cost or to protect someone from troubling matters they had no power to change?

"This piece was taken from your mother after she was arrested on suspicion of hiding spies, saboteurs and resistance fighters at Bispebjerg Hospital. According to the arrest report, she was accused of pretending her patients were extremely ill, and she would tend to them until they conveniently disappeared."

Miss Winther caught her breath, then nodded. "That sounds like Mama. She was so very brave. She told me she was a hospital volunteer, but I always knew she was doing something important." Behind her spectacles, the old lady's eyes took on a cold glaze of anger. "My mother was dragged away on a beautiful spring afternoon while I watched."

Tess felt an unbidden shudder of sympathy for the little girl Miss Winther had once been. "I'm so sorry. No child should have to witness that."

Miss Winther held out the necklace, the facets of the large

pink topaz catching the light. "Could you...put it on me?" she asked.

"Of course." Tess came around behind her and fastened the clasp of the necklace, feeling the old woman's delicate bone structure. Her hair smelled of lavender, and her dress under the pink shawl was threadbare and faded. Tess felt a surge of emotion. This find was going to change Miss Winther's life. In a single transaction, the old woman could find herself living in the lap of luxury.

Miss Winther reached up, cradling the jewel between her palms. "She was wearing it that day. Even as they were taking her away, she ordered me to run for my life, and that is just what I did. I was very lucky in that moment, or perhaps there had been a tip-off. A boy who was with the Holger Danske—the Danish resistance—spirited me to safety. Such a hero he was, like the Scarlet Pimpernel in the French Revolution, only he was quite real. I wouldn't be here today if not for him. None of us would."

None of us...? Tess wondered who she was referring to. Ghosts from the woman's sad past, probably. She didn't ask, though; she had other appointments on her schedule and couldn't spare the time. And knowing the human cost of the tragedy made Tess feel vulnerable. Still, she was taken by the old lady's sweetness and the air of nostalgia that softened her features when she touched the reclaimed treasure around her neck.

We're both all alone, we two, thought Tess. Had Miss Winther always been alone? *Will I always be?*

"Well, I'm certainly glad you're here." The old lady's smile was soft and strangely intimate.

"This is the appraisal on the piece. I think you'll be very pleased."

The old lady stared at the document. "It says my mother's lavaliere is worth $800,000."

"It's an estimate. Depending on how the bidding goes, it could vary by about ten percent up or down."

Miss Winther fanned herself. "That's a fortune," she said. "It's more money than I ever dreamed of having."

"And not nearly enough to replace your loss, but it's quite a find. I'm really happy for you." Tess felt a glow of accomplishment and pleasure for Miss Winther. In her frayed shawl, surrounded by old things, she didn't look like a wealthy woman, but soon, she would be.

All the painstaking work of restitution had led to this moment. Tess spread a multipage contract on the table. "Here's the agreement with Sheffield Auction House, my firm. It's standard, but you'll want to go over it with a contracts expert."

A timer dinged, and Miss Winther got up from the table. "The scones are ready. My favorites—I make them with lavender sugar. It's an old Danish recipe for autumn. You sit tight, dear, and I'll fix the tea."

Tess pressed her teeth together and tried not to seem impatient, though she had more appointments and work to do at the office. Honestly, she didn't want a scone, with or without lavender sugar. She didn't want tea. Coffee and a cigarette were more to her taste and definitely more suited to the pace of her life. She'd been running since she'd rocketed out of grad school five years before, and she was in a hurry now. The quicker she brought the signed agreement to her firm, the quicker she earned her bonus and could move on to the next transaction.

However, the nature of her profession often called for forbearance. People became attached to their things, and sometimes letting go took time. Miss Winther had gone to a lot of trouble to make scones. Knowing what she knew about the

Winther family, Tess wondered what the woman felt when she reminisced about the old days—fear and privation? Or happier times, when her family had been intact?

As she bustled around her old-fashioned kitchen, Miss Winther would pause every so often in front of a little framed mirror by the door, gazing at the necklace with a faraway look in her eyes. Tess wondered what she saw there—her pretty, adored mother? An innocent girl who had no idea her entire world was about to be snatched away?

"Tell me about what you do," Miss Winther urged her, pouring tea into a pair of china cups. "I would love to hear about your life."

"I guess you could say finding treasure is in my blood."

Miss Winther gave a soft gasp, as though Tess's statement surprised her. "Really?"

"My mother is a museum acquisitions expert. My grandmother had an antiques salon in Dublin."

"So you come from a line of independent women."

Nicely put, thought Tess. Her gaze skated away. She wasn't one to chat up a client for the sake of making a deal, but she genuinely liked Miss Winther, perhaps because the woman seemed truly interested in her. "Neither my mother nor my grandmother ever married," she explained. "I'll probably carry on that tradition, as well. My life is too busy for a serious relationship." *Gah, Tess, listen to yourself,* she thought. *Say it often enough and you'll believe it.*

"Well. I suspect that's only because the right person hasn't come along…yet. Pretty girl like you, with all that gorgeous red hair. I'm surprised some man hasn't swept you off your feet."

Tess shook her head. "My feet are planted firmly on the ground."

"I never married, either." A wistful expression misted her

eyes. "I was in love with a man right after the war, but he married someone else." She paused to admire the stone once again. "It must be so exciting, the work of a treasure hunter."

"It takes a lot of research, which most people would find tedious. So many dead ends and disappointments," said Tess. "Most of my time is spent combing archives and old records and catalogs. It can be frustrating. But so worthwhile when I get to make a restitution like this. And every once in a great while, I might find myself peeling away a worthless canvas to find a Vermeer beneath. Or unearthing a fortune under a shepherd's hut in a field somewhere. Sometimes it's a bit macabre. The plunder might be stashed in a casket."

Miss Winther shuddered. "That's ghoulish."

"When people have something to hide, they tend to put it where no one would want to look. Your piece wasn't stored in a dramatic hiding place. It was tagged and neatly cataloged, along with dozens of other illegally seized pieces."

Miss Winther arranged the scones just so with a crisp linen napkin in a basket, and brought them to the table.

Tess took a warm scone, just to be polite.

"It sounds as though you like your work," Miss Winther said.

"Very much. It's everything to me." As she said the words aloud, Tess felt a wave of excitement. The business was fast-paced and unpredictable, and each day might bring an adrenaline rush—or crushing disappointment. Tess was having a banner year; her accomplishments were bringing her closer to the things she craved like air and water—recognition and security.

"That sounds just wonderful. I'm certain you'll get exactly what you're looking for."

"In this business, I'm not always sure what that is." Tess sneaked another glance at the clock on the stove.

Miss Winther noticed. "You have time to finish your tea."

Tess smiled, liking this woman almost in spite of herself. "All right. Would you like me to leave the contract with you or—"

"That's not necessary," the old lady said, touching the faceted pink topaz. "I won't be selling this."

Tess blinked, shook her head a little. "I'm sorry, what?"

"My mother's lavaliere." She pressed the piece against her bosom. "It's not for sale."

Tess's heart plummeted. "With this piece, you could have total security for the rest of your life."

"Every last shred of security was stripped from me forever by the Nazis," Miss Winther pointed out. "And yet I survived. You've given me back my mother's favorite thing."

"As you say, it's a thing. An object you could turn into comfort and peace of mind for the rest of your days."

"I'm comfortable and secure now. And if you don't believe memories are worth more than money, then perhaps you've not made the right kind of memories." She regarded Tess with knowing sympathy.

Tess tried not to dwell on all the hours she'd spent combing through records and poring over research in order to make the restitution. If she thought about it too much, she'd probably tear out her hair in frustration. She tended to protect herself from memories, because memories made a person vulnerable.

"You must think I'm being a sentimental old fool." Miss Winther nodded. "I am. It's a privilege of old age. I have no debt, no responsibilities. Just me and the cats. We like our life exactly as it is."

Tess took a sip of strong tea, nearly wincing at its bitterness.

"Oh! The sugar bowl. I forgot," said Miss Winther. "It's in the pantry, dear. Would you mind getting it?"

The pantry contained a collection of dusty cans and jars,

its walls and shelves cluttered with collectibles, many of them still bearing handwritten garage sale stickers.

"It's just to the right there," said Miss Winther. "On the spice shelf."

Tess picked up the small, footed bowl. Almost instantly, a tingle of awareness passed through her. One of the first things she'd learned in her profession was to tune into something known as the "heft" or "feel" of the piece. Something that was real and authentic simply had more substance than a fake or knockoff.

She set the tarnished bowl on the table and tried to keep a poker face as she studied the object. The sweep of the handles and the effortless swell of the bowl were unmistakable. Even the smoky streaks of age couldn't conceal the fact that the piece was sterling, not plate.

"Tell me about this sugar bowl," she said, using the small tongs to pick up a cube. Sugar tongs. They were even more rare than the bowl.

"It's handsome, isn't it?" Miss Winther said. "But the very devil to keep clean. I was not in a terribly practical frame of mind when I picked it up at a church rummage sale long ago. It's been decades. Rummage sales have always been a weakness of mine. I'm afraid I've brought home any number of bright, pretty things that just happened to catch my eye. Once I get something home, though, it's anyone's guess whether or not I'll actually use it."

"This is quite a find," Tess said, holding it up to check the bottom, and seeing the expected hallmark there.

"In what way?"

Could she really not know? "Miss Winther, this bowl is a Tiffany, and it appears to be genuine."

"Goodness, you don't say."

"There's a style known as the Empire set, very rare, produced in a limited edition. I'd have to do more research, but my sense is, this could be extremely valuable." Not that it would matter to the old lady, who preferred her artifacts to cash. "It's a lovely piece, regardless," Tess conceded.

"What a surprising aspect of your job," Miss Winther said, clasping her hands in delight. "Sometimes you stumble across a treasure when you're looking for something else entirely."

Tess watched the sugar cube dissolve in her cup. "It keeps my job interesting."

"Tell me, is this something your firm would sell?" asked Miss Winther.

"It's possible, though even with the sugar tongs, a single piece—"

"I didn't mean just the bowl. I meant the entire set."

Tess dropped her spoon on the table with a clatter. "There's a *set?*"

The Apple Orchard
by New York Times *bestselling author Susan Wiggs,*
available now wherever MIRA Books are sold!